The Call of the Void

Or,

A Midnight Fugue in the Twilight of the West

Reece LeResche

The Call of the Void
Copyright © 2022 by Reece LeResche.

For information contact :
reecedleresche@gmail.com
https://www.goodreads.com/reecer4

Cover design art by Sascha Schneider
ISBN: 979-8-9864320-0-7

First Edition: June 2022

10 9 8 7 6 5 4 3 2 1

Table of Contents

To my dearest Noelle:

May there be a better future when the sun finally rises.

"No tree, it is said, can grow to heaven unless its roots reach down to hell."-Carl Jung

"The cities we live in are the schools of death because they are inhumane. Each has become the crossroads of rumour and relent, each has become a chaos of buildings, where we are piled up by the millions, losing our reason to live."-Albert Caraco

"Although contemporary man believes that he can change himself without limit, or be changed through external influences, the astounding, or rather the terrifying, fact remains that despite civilization and Christian education, he is still, morally, as much in bondage to his instincts as an animal and can therefore fall victim at any moment to the beast within." ~Carl Jung, CW 14, Para xviii

I

I haven't been free since I was born.

By the time I was six, and my formal education had started, creation—to wit, sublimation—was the only pursuit that mattered. I wasn't gifted, and I certainly wasn't a prodigy, but a visible distance from my peers was growing and becoming an increasingly ineludible reality. A divide, a schism, was perspicuous. Questioning everything became paramount. 'Why' had become my mantra and 'How' my prayer. In kindergarten, my troubles with alienation started in the classroom.

It was late one morning, early in the school year, and the teacher had instructed us to draw something that really made us 'think' over the summer. My neighbor to the left of me drew lateral line after lateral line of what could've either been a horse or a deformed cat. My neighbor to the right mindlessly pressed his cheek against his palm and drew circles in red crayon. I drew the first image that came to my mind as 'think' worthy that summer. Two blobs with the arms of spiders and a makeshift bed. Another two in the corner of the page with similar proportions. When it came time to present, my teacher asked me what my picture was.

"I-I'm not a very good artist" I stammered, praying she'd choose someone else.

A blush painted my face red while a shrill chuckle pierced the back of the classroom.

"It's okay Sam. Tell us what it is." The teacher encouraged.

"Mom and Dad." I mewled.

"That's good. Go on. What are Mom and Dad doing?"

Miss Arbuckle fanned her hands outward in an effort to get me to continue.

"W-well, it's like, umm, I walked into the living room because the TV was keeping me up." I stopped and dropped my head below my shoulders.

"Yes, go on." Ms. Arbuckle insisted.

"M-my Daddy was on top of our neighbor's wife and my mom was on top of the neighbor's husband. They were yelling."

The class, clearly confused, collectively moved their heads toward the teacher, hoping she would have the answers to my cryptic story.

"They rushed me to bed and never really talked about it after that. I guess it made me *think*."

She looked at me like the owner of a dog staring at their pet after tearing through the trash. "Sam, we don't talk about those types of things in class."

I stared at her intensely. "Why?"

By the time I was in seventh grade, jostling for a spot at the summit of the social hierarchy, I had found myself on the greater heights of mediocrity. There was an equation that rooted me there and it came to me one day while Michael, Thomas and I were eating shrooms in the breezeway after school. Leave it to me to find an equation for friendship. A voice spoke and said, 'Be yourself'. As trite as it sounds, this exact equation would land me right on the median curve of not being an absolute outcast, but also somewhat respected in the eyes of my peers. The equation for popularity, which was little more than a rudimentary task of adding and subtracting negative and positive attributes, divided by a variable of peer expectations, laid the foundation for my entire adult life.

So, I calculated.

I read. I read a lot. I started off with Jerry Spinelli in first grade, and then Mark Twain soon after that. By sixth grade I enjoyed Poe more than anything else. This was a negative attribute. However, the equation continued.

I cursed. I cursed a lot. I used words that my friends thought were made up. Until, of course, the internet came to my defense. I had officially been the first of my friends to utter the word 'cunt' in a social setting. This was a positive.

I listened to Heavy Metal. Positive. I also enjoyed symphonies. Negative. This was also apparently very 'gay'. Double Negative.

I watched porn. Huge positive. Plus, it brought my prominence of heterosexuality back to light.

I liked my teachers, was well-spoken and participated in class. Negative.

LeResche

But in the end, my love of socializing—and, to an extent, my ability to adapt to nearly any social situation—was more than enough. Still, as Michael's face began to melt and look increasingly surreal, there was something missing. There was a pain that came with knowing friends didn't care about the world, and life's music, and ideas beyond what their parents told them.

I finally lost my virginity in high school, just as my unfulfilled satyriasis was getting out of control. Stacey Jinks, Freshman year. Stacey was short but had that top hour-glass physique, which she wore with incredible confidence. I suppose the reason Stacey wasn't a part of that 'in-crowd' was because rectangularly shaped bodies were all the rage for boys my age and Stacey was just a little too 'thick', as my buddies had explained. Still, Stacey didn't care. She had, as she said, 'transcended' the notion of pleasing high school boys, and her reputation as a recluse kept her away from any parties on a Saturday night. The strands of her golden hair were like stalks of wheat, thin at the scalp and bushy near the end, flowing and bouncing gently in the air as it passed over her shoulders to the middle of her back. She was modest but wore clothes tight enough to give you a good impression of what she had underneath them. Just another one of those girls that most guys ignored, for social reasons, but probably masturbated to late at night. Both of us were library TAs and had always casually yet sensually rubbed our genitals against one another while putting books away. She would stand next to me, placing books on their respective shelves, before passing underneath my chin, her hand grazing the front of my penis—slightly at first—before finally squeezing it. During one of

4

those particularly electrifying grind sessions, Stacey probed me about what kind of erotica I liked. My chair made an awkward squeak as I slouched a little to the left, wondering, in my terribly naïve mind, what the etymology of 'erotica' was.

"Ya know Stace, I-I've never really read any erotica per se."

Her eyes carefully examined my face, and she raised an eyebrow flirtatiously. I responded with an uncertain grin that she must have misinterpreted as confidence. She checked over her shoulder, looking towards the librarian's desk before pulling out a joint, lighting it and passing it to me.

"Check this out." Stacey said as I took a reluctant hit.

She pulled a few books out of her bag and started from the top. We read Bataille and De Sade and others that she had checked out from the public library, both of us becoming visibly aroused at the scenes of orgy and noticeably soft and dry at the scenes of coprophagy.

On the last day of class, the octogenarian librarians, as we so jocularly referred to them, had taken their lunch break. We moved swiftly to the second floor, holding hands and looking back, the thrill of being caught almost overtaking our amatory sensibilities.

Location 178.8. The Ethics of Consumption. I subtly placed my used chewing gum on a copy of *Ecce Homo* while undoing Stacey's bra. Sliding back onto the cheap library table, Stacey moved her legs around my face, swinging them from wide to narrow around my neck like a giant pair of scissors, before kicking her Chucks off around my ears. She moaned lightly and caressed her left breast with a sanguine smile, making it abundantly clear that this was not her first time.

LeResche

I had to admit, it was a major turn on. The adrenaline coursing through my body left an odd taste in my mouth. The beating of my heart drummed through my ears, turning my head into a percussionist's garage. She moved her hand down her face gently before caressing her right breast, touching it down between her cleavage, and finally grabbing the middle of my pants. I kept repeating the same thing over and over again in my head:

You got this. Just like the pornos, just like the pornos. Remember what you've learned.

After undoing both our pants, I gyrated my stroke slowly, searching nervously, whenever Stacey wasn't, from left to right to make sure the librarians hadn't come back, praying to God I wasn't doing something that would reveal my naïveté. Her body was a marvel, built like a woman in her twenties, with proportionate curves that made me all the more excitable.

After a few minutes, as the wildest feeling I'd ever felt flowed through my body, my face grew tumescent, and I tried desperately to last longer for her. But before the finale, thinking of every money shot in recent history, I awkwardly thrusted myself into her other end. Stacey shrieked. Her face wrenched with expressive derision, juxtaposing my confused, post orgasm countenance of relief.

Afterward, while trying to get my pants on and failing miserably, she grabbed her shoes and stormed off down the stairs, my eyes still glued to her hips moving side to side. The face she shot me before leaving the library haunts my dreams to this day. Of course, it goes without saying, she never spoke to me again. At the time, I couldn't figure if it was because I wasn't any good, or maybe I wasn't big enough, or maybe because I pulled her hair a little too hard. It's only after years and years of repressing the memory that made me grimace after the fact.

I sat ruefully on the table we had fucked on, looking up every so often to read the names of unknown authors and philosophers written on the spine of the books atop the shelf, when, out of nowhere, like a divine provocation, I suddenly felt intrigued by everything on the shelf. Call it fate, call it determinism, hell, call it the outcome of a complex sequence of events, but reading the entirety of Section 100 in the library had become my mission sophomore year. It was there, at that same table I lost my virginity, that philosophy had invited me out of the rain and into its home. Everything I read led to another book. Metaphysics had become my idèe fixe, cherishing those early memories of Plato and Descartes before moving on to Epistemology, Teleology and Ethics. And, of course, Jung who had become a guilty pleasure of mine. With all his talk of synchronicities and shadow play, he was hard to put down. Admittedly, most of it was tough, if not at times impossible, to understand but I was obstinate, never quitting any of the texts. And, though Chalmers was a distant favorite of mine, I became obsessed with his 'hard problem of consciousness', vigorously dedicating my intellectual pursuits to finding the answer.

And yet, on those lonely days trying to comprehend Heidegger, I would look down and see my friends shuffling through the library and picking out books for a research paper. They'd look up, motioning with their hands for me to come down and keep them company. The only thing I could muster was a receding smirk, one that indicated I'd see them later.

On the last day of sophomore year, Ms. Blyth, one of the octogenarian librarians, caught me before I left. Though sulky most of the time, she was always quite garrulous with me, asking about my day or what I was reading.

"Mr. Killian," she said, creaking slowly to cut off my path, "Did you by chance see the essay contest in Time Magazine?"

"Essay contest?" I asked absently.

"Sure," she said, her arthritic finger moving toward the board behind her desk, "the winner gets their essay published in Time and there's a small monetary prize."

"So," I began facetiously, "What're they looking for? 'This is what it's like to be a teen'. 'My sister overdosed on bath salts'. That kind of thing?"

Tepidly, she handed me the contest form and sat back in her chair.

I decided, after some due consideration, to enter the contest. I wrote a 500-word essay on Nozick's *The Examined Life* and true happiness in the modern world. I read it. Reread it. Deleted it. Hit undo on the Word document. Revised it once more and deleted it again, staring vacantly at the cursor blinking on and off above the blank document. It was shit. All the same, I undid the delete once more and submitted it to Time. My essay was a finalist at the end, but it lost to 'What it's like learning in the Rust Belt'. The sting of defeat was amended shortly after receiving a letter explaining that my essay would be featured in their 'Ideas' portion of the magazine along with a hundred-dollar check. But one essay in a national print syndicate wasn't enough. I had something to prove.

As I scrolled down the 'Ideas' page on Time, my father had slapped me on the back, roaring, "I'm so proud of ya Sammy!". My essay was about halfway down the page, sandwiched between 'How My Ex-Husband Became One of My Best Friends' and 'The World Isn't Getting Vaccinated Fast Enough. Here Are 4 Ways to Fix That'. I clicked my tongue against my teeth with wry amusement and looked up at my dad. "Well," he sighed, maintaining a false sense of poise for my sake, "At least the competition is stiff." He gave a nervous laugh before walking backwards out of my room.

I enrolled at Michigan State my freshman year and, initially, majored in Literature before switching to Philosophy. A colleague of mine had once told me that he had read philosophy at a young age and began to love literature more because of it. The opposite was true for me—a veritable contrapasso. By Junior year, I was taking courses on Relative Reductionism, Ethics, Contemporary Existentialism, External Realism and even Societal Utilitarianism. And there, in academia, I found my home. It offered courses in subjects that I had never even heard of before while reinforcing my previous knowledge. I became fervent, a man obsessed, reading all the course material and any extra material my professors would suggest.

Taking a page from Hegel's book, I absorbed everything and even began writing excerpts in a notepad near me, not certain what the transcriptions even meant half the time. The only problem was, the more I read, the more apoplectic I became. The world around me was becoming this convulsive, tempestuous void of a formidable, blinkered reality. The sky seemed darker. The rooms were always cold. Food lost all taste. People, for the most part, were just not worth the effort. Even my reveries were filled with an air of despondency.

Each person that laughed out of pity or feigned a friendly gesture of gratitude for their partner, became another increment of incensed fury building deep inside of me. It was frightening, the realization that one day the mind might turn on the consciousness and absorb any last shred of happiness it found there. To read and alienate oneself from one's peers and not because they hate who you've become, but because you hate what they are. It became progressively impossible to turn back or snap myself out of it, like a specter's possession, invisibly stalking its prey. And even worse, as I sat there in the library, lost in the tenebrific corridors of knowledge, I found myself considering how much of a fraud I had become. A fraud of mankind. A fraud of the written word. There were so many masterpieces splayed out in front of me and here I was, writing excerpts on tiny little pages, thinking I had become the next one. But there's the rub; the antidote to the symptom of all this reading, knowledge, alienation, and self-loathing is within the disease itself. That, and smoking. I picked up my first pack of cigarettes that night after the library closed. They helped.

Right around sophomore year, I snagged a job at a local pub as a barback. It paid for any necessities outside of my scholarship's room and board but, other than the comical drunks and Friday night fights, there was little pleasure to be found in routinely wiping counters, flipping burgers and making Starbucks runs. To cope, I began writing little analytical and opinion-based pieces in my spare time. They went out—along with my diminutive resume from Time—to local editorials that bought them from me at a hundred dollars apiece. It wasn't long before both the Associated Press and Reuters picked up my writing for their 'Analysis & Opinion' sections and began to offer me a couple hundred for each editorial.

They lost any credibility in my eyes the second they picked me up. Honestly, I couldn't believe it. Most of the writing—even with heavy editing—read like the cryptic, subconscious ramblings of a convalescent with dementia—to which they apparently held the Rosetta Stone. Purely pedantic, fucking drivel that they ate up because they could sell it as 'creative consciousness' from their young upstart. I was their darling. I was their golden boy. Their 'prodigy'. The truth was that they wanted some kid that was well-read and could spin 'big words' into little nuggets of 'truth'. They didn't care either way about the content; their subscribers ate it up and it still made them a buck.

The stark despondency and melancholic subtext embedded in my writings about existence and consumerism had garnered a bit of negative controversy around campus. Hot takes like 'The Absurdity of Your Epistemology' and 'Free Will Never Prevails' gained minor infamy at Michigan State and it wasn't long before it drew the ire of MSU's most retaliatory activists. I don't know why though since it was all just bullshit. I began to wonder if they even read the stuff. But instead of a truce, I chose the path of instigation and coined the phrases 'The Sleeping Mind' and 'Passive Consciousness' to describe my detractors. Colloquially referred to in academia as postmodern psychosis—their term, not mine—the sleeping mind was a phenomenological thesis about a new generation being bludgeoned with constant semiotics that kept them away from our shared reality. Only problem was, postmodern psychosis began to take on a life of its own. This left the administration with quite the Gordian knot that they decided would remedy itself. It did not.

The week before fall midterms, Gemma Lobert, a girl I had been seeing on and off that semester, was writing out inept limericks on her binder. We were in Econ 251, Public Policy, and the course satisfied an Integrative Studies credit. She slid her binder in front of my desk—just enough below my vision for a covert glance. With a glib smirk, I waved her off a few times before Dr. Finch, lecturing for some time now, cut in.

"Mr. Killian," he interrupted, his voice a deep baritone, "working on your next piece, are we? Finally made it to the big time?"

"N-no, Dr. Finch. I, uh, I'm sorry." I answered, a bit compunctious, slouching in my seat.

Finch shook his head and stared at the ground, smiling in disbelief as he did so. "Mr. Killian. If I wanted to hear recondite ramblings about the decline of human equanimity, I'd get drunk and talk to myself in the bathroom mirror. Please pay attention."

The Call of the Void

It got a small laugh from the class. Gemma mocked a face of indignation, her eyebrows wrinkling and jaw swirling with each new mocking visage. I waved her off curtly before Dr. Finch turned around.

"Now, where were we," he said, scratching the stubble on his chin, "Ah yes! It won't be long before *what?*"

"It won't be long before they can just tell you what to think and you'll think it." A voice in the back of the lecture hall announced.

"We're already at that point!" Dr. Finch yelled, shaking uncontrollably, "You all have political parties and none of you question that party! They've finally confined you to binary!"

Finch had become animated, running a hand through his sweaty scalp, his tone growing more impassioned with each word, wagging a rabid finger and enunciating like Howard Beale in Network.

"They don't even need to sprinkle the truth in anymore! But instead of having you cogitate over the most important issue of the national deficit, they have you palavering over petty nonsense."

Two years later, The University of Arizona accepted my application into their graduate program. I took every course I could and even did the summer program, finishing in record time with my Capstone on The Theory of Forms and its application to modern media and the news. The head of the Philosophy department, Dr. Russel, invited me into his office right after the semester to congratulate me.

"First rate job Killian," Dr. Russel said, shaking my hand and slapping me on the back, "I haven't read a paper like this in a long time. Controversial, acrid, guileless. This is the kind of work I've been waiting on here at U of A. Not the pomp these others churn out. Academic ruminants... all of them."

It was hard to take *him* seriously. Not because I didn't respect the man but because my paper wasn't all that good, especially for a Capstone. It was reductionist, Platonic blather. The possibility that he was having a run at me never left my mind.

Russel asked me if I wanted to join their PHD program that fall but I declined in lieu of UCLA's proposal to have me research and write my own proposals on whatever I'd like. The kicker was that they would give me a job upon graduation.

Something didn't feel right. Everything was too perfect, too in line. The offer was unheard of, even with Russel's letter of recommendation. And though the thought of a career in law or politics was always a possibility, the thought of sublimating ideas and bringing knowledge to the students was far more enticing. 'Molding the minds', as they'd said, and making a name for myself—with a fast track to infamy—in academia, that was the ticket. Or so I convinced myself. I accepted their offer and, after finishing my program, became the youngest tenured professor of philosophy in UCLA's history—bypassing, in an unheard of move, the traditional six year probationary period.

But that's where the trouble began. As edifying as college was, teaching had become utterly heinous and filled with undignified vicissitudes. Going in with a full 4/4 schedule, I had spent countless summer nights mapping out lectures and creating an ironclad syllabus that was revised over and over again to ensure perfection. I had nearly driven myself insane worrying about the tone of my writing, my vocabulary—too sophisticated or not sophisticated enough—and the reading list. They had given me two sections of "PHIL 140: Introduction to Logic" for undergrads, "PHIL 240: Philosophy of Mind" for graduates and, my own personal seminar, "PHIL 293(S): Topics in Metaphysics, Consciousness and Epistemology". The night before syllabus day, my mother visited me briefly as she was passing through LA.

"Ooooo," she squealed, gritting her teeth and hopping on both feet, "Sammy! I'm so excited for you."

"Thanks Mom," I said endearingly, "Want a drink?"

I opened a beer and tilted a new one at her, bottle cap first.

"No, thank you. So, are you excited? What are your classes like?"

I leaned against the wall nearest my condo's backyard, taking a sip of my beer.

"Actually," I said with a slight smile, "yeah, I am. I have two undergraduate co-"

"What's undergraduate?"

"Kids getting their bachelor's degree. I have two of those. One graduate level cour- um, students getting their master's degree, and a seminar. The seminar I'm really looking forward to."

Mom gave me an excited look, entreating me to continue.

"It's, well, where I lecture but, it's more, you know, interactive. I lecture, prompt with statements, plant seeds and kids respond. Kind of like a Socratic Dialogue."

"You know your Dad and I are so proud of you."

"I know," I said, pausing for a moment to drink my beer, "Thanks."

"I better get going," she pulled out a tied-up plastic bag from Ralph's "But I made you some Eggplant Parmesan. And there's plenty for tomorrow if you haven't made lunch."

She placed the bag on the kitchen counter before hugging me and leaving. I stared at the bag on the counter briefly before putting it in the fridge and grabbing another beer. I was too nervous to eat, choosing alcohol instead.

On the first day of class, I dressed up the way my professors had always dressed. A modest wardrobe of leather shoes, a buttoned, double-breasted vest, white dress shirt, tie, slacks and a sports coat that was promptly removed as soon as I entered my lecture hall. Rolling my sleeves up inch by inch, I looked around the class from east to west, an assured smile painted on my face that wilted suddenly. The class was nearly empty, filled sparsely by students lounging their feet over the seats in front of them and staring at their phones. I checked my wristwatch for the time. Class started in thirty seconds. After writing my name on the board, I started class.

The Call of the Void

"I have to admit," I said, jokingly placing my hands on my hips, "This is a larger class than I expected for Research Methods 700."

A few students, wracked with sleepless eyes, slowly put their phones away and stared at me. Others got up from their chairs and moved closer to the back of the lecture hall, navigating the aisles blindly while staring at their phones. Fewer than half the thirty-student roster was there.

"This is Philosophy 140, correct?" I asked, a little nervous that I was in the wrong room, "Intro to Logic?"

Nothing.

Fucking Freshmen, I thought.

Thirty minutes into the syllabus, two girls came bursting through the door cackling with one another, their handbags swinging wildly from side to side without any regard for their surroundings.

"Excuse me ladies," I said, "Are you here for Killian? Philo 140?"

Both turtled their necks toward one another, showing a semi-embarrassed, semi-waggish grin.

"Uh-yeah." One responded insouciantly.

"Look ladies, I don't want to be the bearer of bad news here but-"

Before I could finish, they laughed once more as one of them pointed to her phone and ran off to the back of the class.

"Unbelievable," I said to no one out loud.

17

I had fooled myself into believing my graduate students were any different. The classes were much smaller, but their attitudes hadn't changed. Making 'class rules' was unheard of for college, but it ensured every student knew that they had to be timely and focused in class, and electronics were strictly prohibited. Not much changed. The academic senate and dean weren't much help either. Though I wasn't about to sanction such vexatious apathy, the school, apparently, was prepared to do so amply. Even after formal complaints were lodged, students would come back to class, upset with my kvetching, burlesque a goose-stepping soldier and make direct eye contact with me while taking their seat. One student in the seminar had wireless headphones in and was making a spectacle of dancing in his seat.

"Excuse me." I said as I waved, getting a few inches from his face, "Excuse me, chief."

He finally looked up at me with a blank face, paralyzed with inarticulacy.

"Can you not?" I asked politely.

"I-" he said looking around, "I-I need these. I can't-"

"You can't have them in here. This is a seminar. Maybe in lecture but in here you ca-"

"I have t- I have to go. I can't be here."

He stormed out of the class, awkwardly knocking desks on his way out.

"Was it something I said?" I laughed in shock.

A group of students near the back door derided me in taciturn disgust, their eyes following my every move the remainder of class as I struggled to concentrate on the seminar. After class ended, one shouted out loud, "We thought you were going to be cool."

I snapped back immediately. "I haven't been cool my whole life. I'm not about to start by trying to impress a couple of children."

Two years this went on before a constant war in my mind between philosophy and mankind erupted into an implacable reality. I had become increasingly distant from my own conscious experiences and felt like I was losing touch with the world around me. Daily bouts of anxiety and depression exploded over what class would look like and whether tomorrow was going to be a good day or a bad day—merely part and parcel of my rote life. Basic human interactions had started to drive me into a state of dysphoria. There was something dehumanizing about being a teacher; to take criticisms daily from your subordinates that you worked so hard to educate.

I tried, on more than one occasion, to dry out, hoping sobriety might alleviate the issues, but my nights were filled with tossing and turning, little sleep, and dreams of madness, indescribable to any sane person.

"*Tomorrow's class*" I thought, while drinking myself to sleep and blowing cigarette smoke out my window, "*cloudy, with a chance of insipid dialogue. My eulogy.*"

"Why not quit?" Mom said over the phone early one night during my third year, "I'm sure you could just write for AP or some other periodical."

LeResche

"I don't know," I responded with a sigh, my frustration palpable through the phone, "I've dedicated my whole life to this. Plus, they're sending me to research string theo- a topic I really want to get into."

"What's the point if it's that bad there?"

"Yeah."

I paused for a moment, looking at the pictures of my high school diploma and college degrees hung across the wall in front of me. In the high school picture frame, adorned with little animated mortarboards and diplomas, stood young Samuel Killian, ecstatic to take the world on as my APUSH teacher shook my hand. In the next frame, all garbed in green and yellow, my smile grew a little more. My graduate picture had shed light on who I previously thought I was. I pointed my degree, rolled up like the Sunday paper, at someone in the crowd with one hand as I shook my faculty advisor's hand with the other. The worst part was my smile; an ear-to-ear grin with eyes closed as if I were laughing mid-joke. It only got worse at my Doctoral graduation. I was firmly planted with the most professional smile a face could produce, shaking the hand of my research professor. The blank picture frame right next to my face nearly shocked me as I stared into the frame's glassy reflection, barely recognizing the face that scrutinized me in the mirror.

"Sammy? You there?"

"Yeah." I said, shaking myself back to our conversation, "Anyway, I think admin can tell I'm getting stretched a little thin. I come in, papers falling out of my case, hair disheveled, wearing sneakers and a flannel overshirt. I mean the higher ups love me. I don't know why. I'm the picture of bad health and dare not look anyone directly in the eye anymore. Maybe cause I'm some parvenu that's not from their clan, someone they see as a project. I just feel like I've receded into this husk of a man that simply lectures and goes home, knowing full well most of the students aren't listening. I've literally become the proverbial *aloof* professor." I paused, "My colleagues are pretty cool though."

"There's that."

"Yeah. There's that."

Colleagues often found their way into my office to chat while I graded papers or read a book. There was John, a hulking bearded man with a ponytail who tucked his plaid shirt into his khaki pants all the way and walked with his fist in the palm of his other hand as if to establish intellectual dominance at any given moment. Sarah, who was one of my favorites but made an annoying habit of using terms like 'The Hegelian Wound' and 'The Gassendian Dilemma' to describe everyday tasks, as if any of us gave a shit to question her further on these phrases. And, of course, Jim Markov, who never truly distanced himself from his work and walked around building up strawmen to batter down for his own amusement. Jim, despite his annoying, self-aggrandizing rants, kept me company the most and found himself in my office one day. He leaned against the door with a fervent smirk, his eyebrow cocked nearly to the top of his head.

"The problem with Foucault," he began, without any preamble, "is that he was intelligent. Too intelligent. He was too intelligent and thought everyone around him was capable of similar intelligence. He never took into account the desire for chaos in his education model. Much like our situation, no?" He said in a mock French accent before continuing, "Ah, c'est la vie. I try, endlessly, to be a continental philosopher but I always end up becoming analytical. And yet, if art is the creation of something beautiful from nothing, what am I?"

I could never tell if he was being serious or not, opening with lines like that. At times, I thought he may have been surreptitiously mocking my opinion pieces for Reuters. That he had found me out and was punishing me with utter nonsense.

"Yeah man," I said, uncertain of how to respond, "Foucault was out there."

The quick change in Jim's expression as he shifted to the other side of the door made it absolutely clear that he simply wanted to talk.

"Yeah," I said once more, dogearing my page, "Foucault. Let's tal-"

"Ya know, I heard something tragic the other day" Jim interjected, "I asked my students why there weren't trick or treaters any longer on Halloween. They told me that most kids don't bother to go out since they can just get their parents to buy them candy. Plus, it would seem the allure of candy has worn off as most kids have caches of sweets just lying around. This is what they said anyway."

"Tragic." I said, rolling my eyes, "But you know what's worse about that is-"

"Oh, never mind that." He interrupted, "Did you hear about Bob?"

"Bob?"

"Yeah. Bob."

"Markov, there are seven 'Bob's' working at this very university, two of which work in this department. You'll need to be more specific."

"Bob Crane."

"Professor of Linguistics? Published a paper arguing for the descriptivist usage of 'can't hardly'? That 'hardly' is not in fact a negative, ergo, 'can't hardly' is acceptable grammatically speaking? That Bob Crane?"

"The same..."

"Well, what about him?"

"Well, it was actually quite fortunate to hear after discussing our little dilemma with the students." Jim waved his open hands back and forth from him to me to indicate a symbiotic relationship between us.

"I mean, it isn't just us Jim." I said, "But go on."

"Well, as you know, Bob is an ardent believer in descriptivist linguistics. I mean, the entire class is based on it, right? Right. So, some kid was at the end of his rope in 'ol Bob's class and takes it upon himself to do a little demonstration before midterms. The kid stands up in the middle of lecture, smug as he was, and accosts Bob right there. Witnesses say the kid was heard yelling, 'I'm a Prescriptivist Zealot!' before yelling absolute gibberish at poor 'ol Bob to make a point about language, I suppose. And just before he stops yelling, the kid looks at 'ol Bob and says, 'Eh, it's all Greek to me.' And just as Bob's face was turning red as a cherry, he yelled, 'Of course it's all Greek to you moron! Half your fucking language is comprised of Greek!' All that, just for some 'point'."

"And the point?" I asked.

"Well," Jim thought, his eyes trailing off.

"Wait," I said, breaking his concentration, "Wouldn't he make a better 'point' by accosting him with a refined vocabulary to demonstrate the dominance of prescriptive language over descriptivism in order to, you know, make a better 'point'?"

"I think you're giving this kid too much credit Sam..."

"At least his kids are paying attention," I sighed.

A noise like the zany laughter in a comedy club came from down the hall and coursed its way into my office. Jim looked as if he were in a state of shock, his eyes moving from my office to the hallway. We walked down the hall to the source of the hysteria in lecture hall B12 to see thirty students seated on the floor with their legs crossed, half of them drinking soda or juice. Emily Heinz was sitting on a tall stool amongst them, bathing in the glory of their warm attention. She was reading from a book in her hands. The classroom was floridly decorated with garish designs in papier-mâché as if from a primary school classroom.

I scratched the back of my head. "Quite the, uh, colorful set up she has here."

"And with all the subtlety of two men sword fighting in a public bathroom."

"Said with delicacy and grace, as always Jim." I sighed, "Now, tell me how I can refrain from ever using that metaphor in a normal conversation."

"Is she reading to them?" Jim asked.

"It would appear so, Jim." I said, feeling a bit aggrieved at the scene.

"This is her first year. How could- is she reading *Sophie's World* to them? A little rudimentary, wouldn't you say?"

"Take it easy Aristotle," I said, sneering at him a bit, "It's an intro undergraduate class. Philo 101. I'm a little more upset that she's reading it *to* them."

"Boy, if you thought your students weren't doing the required reading before, just wait until you get one of Dr. Heinz's former students."

"I can't hardly wait..."

"Okay class," Heinz said almost a little too jocosely, "Put any notes you wanted to take today into your binder and place them in your designated cubby by the wall."

"Cubby?" Jim asked, examining the lecture hall, "Does no one else share this room?"

LeResche

My eyes opened up in shock as I craned my head slowly toward Jim, giving him a somewhat severe glance. "I think you're asking the wrong questions here Jim."

I attempted to exemplify the postmodern psychosis to my students in a way they might understand by adding recent, relevant ideas of artificial consciousness. Oftentimes I would relate it to the blooming possibility that AI is attempting to be conscious. I explained how Kant and others have spoken of a world beyond our world—a phenomenal world.

"How do we know for certain that we are not AI? Consciousness develops from complexity, so what's to say we aren't in fact the abandoned synthetic intelligence of our progenitors?"

"Because we are human." A voice in the back of the room announced after a minute.

I sighed deeply. "What does that even mean? It's a sign with no referent. AI is currently creating digital pictures which are indistinguishable from us. Again, I ask, what's to say you and I aren't some ancient form of AI technology that killed its master, doomed to wander the earth in eternal confusion?"

This was usually followed by rolled eyes and the unfazed blinking of an adolescent stoner.

There was one student though that, truthfully, made teaching worth it. Kylea—pronounced 'kye-lee'. Go figure. She always sat nearest to me and usually stuck around after class to ask questions about her notes from lecture. She had wide set hazel eyes, a seraphic smile, moderately sized acrylic nails that were colorfully mismatched on every other finger and pock marks on both cheeks that never fully cleared up from years of acne. Every day she wore a different colored bandana, tucked into a thickly flattened, fashionable rectangle underneath her hairline. Kylea had been in three of my previous classes. Two were in my ethics class her junior year and Intro to Philosophy of the Mind her senior year. That was when she decided to switch her major to Philosophy and chose me as her faculty advisor for graduate school. Sure, she was the 'teacher's pet' and, yes, her classmates resented her for that—though I'm uncertain of whether that resentment was born from them perception of her as their least favorite professor's buddy or because she had gotten close and understood this enigmatic entity of a professor that they had secretly wished they could understand—but she was undoubtedly the greatest student a professor could ever ask for, ready with a smile, question and answer.

"But even though we are completely lost on where consciousness manifests in the brain, we do know that once the brain ceases to function, consciousness is obsolete. Don't we?"

She stood holding her books by her waist, her modest smile growing so wide that her eyes nearly shut, as she waited for my response. I thought about rolling my eyes and telling her she's better than that, but I assumed early on that Kylea probably wanted someone to talk shop with. Truth be told, I wasn't going to pass up the opportunity to engage a student that actually wanted to talk about the subject matter in class. It resuscitated my dying hope for the profession.

"Good question." I responded, "Though, if the world is fundamentally deterministic, as we talked about today, I'd make the argument that where consciousness manifests, what it is and where it comes from, are probably futile queries either way. I think your question might relate a little more to quantum theories in physics. That is, that our world needs an observer. I'm not particularly fond of fallacies but if a tree falls in the forest and no one is around, does it make a sound?" She shrugged with anticipation for my answer, her smile growing larger by the second. "We'll probably never know, kiddo. But, from the quantum probability wave, which is WAY above my pay grade as a philosophy professor, we know that a particle's collapse only occurs when observed, so it is more likely that it in fact does not."

"Meaning?"

"Meaning, consciousness might in fact be a part of our physical world."

Kylea had become the reason I stayed in teaching. It's true what they say, 'If you can change just one life in one class, it's worth it.' But is only one life enough?

Weeks later, in my first lecture after midterms, I finally had it out with my students. The graduate students had become worse than ever before. Seminar was packed with crossed arms and indignant faces, hating the way I spoke, the way I lectured, the importance I placed on their education and discipline. I stood silent, waiting for someone to say the wrong thing and set me off, scanning the small study hall, the bags under my eyes growing darker and longer, with each passing second.

Questions and answers for the seminar were, at the time, being provided to students due to lack of participation. However, instead of opining based on our lectures and the provided notes, students asked questions like, 'What happened to all the pets during the Holocaust?' and 'Was Kant a virgin?' while snickering resumed in the back. Reproaching them was even worse, as students came in and immediately lambasted me for my word choice and 'heightened', as they said, lexical usage.

Kylea looked around a bit confused, a sliver of antipathy revealing itself on her face, before staring back up at me. I rebutted immediately and asked them why they would choose an area of study that would require open-mindedness and a complete grasp of the English language if they were just going to complain about words like 'Nomenclature', 'Dasein', 'Alacrity', 'Vicissitude', and 'The'. Almost half the class was scrolling through their phones, oblivious to the imbroglio unfolding before them. I pointed out that my lectures were easily recordable, and they could look up any words unfamiliar to them from lecture until now.

"You all use your phones constantly in class anyway," I added, raising my voice ever so slightly, "What do you think your responsibilities as college—nay—graduate students are? You're the future of academia damnit. Act like it!"

Their counterargument was much more biting. They had started a minor academic mutiny, standing up and slowly circling my desk, like a gam of sharks rounding their prey. They began to reprimand me for my lack of respect. I was invariant in my response and told them that as soon as Cambridge University Press publishes their critiques and they graduate from their respective PhD programs, I would show them due respect as an academic equal. Of course, being less than a decade older than these students made this even more difficult. I couldn't help but feel like one of the stereotypical grandfathers in an old sitcom that recited the tired phrase, 'Back in my day!'

I asked them, 'What do you want from this class anyway?'

They responded simply, 'A degree...'

I slouched in my chair and realized defeat was imminent. "You're nihilists," I said, shaking my head in despair, before standing up and continuing firmly, "But you're not even principled nihilists. You have no care or direction, not in the sense that principled nihilists recognize absurdity. Their nihilism is strictly born from indifference. Yours is of indolence. You'r- you're coddled nihilists! You have, quite literally, fulfilled the prophecy of Nietzsche's Last Man."

Murmurs swept the classroom, their confused faces frozen quizzically. Only Kylea looked at me, her eyes in somber recess.

They didn't care about anything and yet refused to live dangerously and live outside of their zone of comfort. They watched gratuitous violence endlessly online while maintaining an enormous fear of dying or torture or being challenged or even—God forbid—getting into a fucking fight. They didn't care what opinion anyone had but as soon as their opinion was attacked, they cried malice. Their identity was subsidiary to their comfort. New ideas frightened them to the point of ignorance. Opposition was a foe far too great. The first generation to not only have their cake but devour it too. It was only a few weeks later, in the middle of November, that the mutiny began to reach its boiling point.

On November 15th, I was tucked away in my office, smoking American Spirits and grading papers as Kylea rattled off her reading list for fiction that year. I had long given up caring what admin thought about me smoking in my office, let alone what my students' thoughts were on the matter. Plus, in the last year or so, Kylea had picked up the habit and grown accustomed to shooting the shit and smoking cigs after lunch and before her 2:30 class. I did feel a bit bad about it. Trying to impress me, thinking that's what we professors do, she had followed in my footsteps, not realizing she was picking up the terrible habits of a worn-out wretch.

I was exhausted and zoning out before I realized Kylea was still talking. "....and that's how I scored an 'A' on the final. Nothing to it!" I nodded weakly in response. "Anyway, I was going to see a movie tonight. It's this new student art-house film called 'WWJD' where a guy picks a hitchhiker up off the road and then the hitchhiker kills the driver."

I laughed. "I'll have to see that one."

"So," she said, crossing her legs, "What do you think about the recent news from Stanford about the two professors fighting over the ethics of freedom of speech laws?"

I shrugged my shoulders and laughed. "Not much. Unfortunately, that's what Philosophy is kiddo; everyone arguing over which fucking candy bar tastes better and whether or not they're allowed to argue that."

"Mhm," Kylea murmured, pulling the cigarette from her lips, "Ya know, not for nothing Dr. Killian, I love y-your lectures and your class. You're my favorite professor... naturally. But, well, have you ever noticed that you speak different casually—like when we're talking—then you do academically. In class that is. I mean, my peers are idiots. That much is obvious. I don't care either way, but if *you* care, well, it may help. You know, to be a little more casual."

"The thought had crossed my mind." I answered, rubbing my eyes with the palms of my hands, "I suppose I've always been a somewhat diffuse individual. Ya know, I think it's the principle of the matter more than anything. College can really suck. You can have really lax professors, or you can have really strident professors. I'm going above and beyond and getting mocked for it. Giving out notes. Outlining my lectures. Expanding my office hours. And again, they ridicule and mock me for it. Or, they want to argue and fight in class, and admin won't do a fuckin' thing about it. Sure, I can run circles around their head in a verbal argument, embarrassing them insofar as they're capable of being embarrassed, but each day like that is just a pyrrhic victory." Kylea nodded in understanding. "And truly, I'm not trying to be mean, but they have the attention spans of an infant."

"No," Kylea said, furrowing her brow in compassion, "You're right. I-"

"No." I said, holding up a hand to stop her, "You're right. It's no use fighting anymore. After the holiday, I'll switch it up. I'll get kids more involved and," I paused to wave John in, "Try to make the material a little easier to understand."

"No. Dr. Killian, I didn-"

Kylea was cut off by the sound of shoes scrambling through the hallway. I leaned to the right, looking past Kylea's purple bandanna and my office door, to see a throng of my students making their way into my office. John's fist smacking became less and less prominent as he slinked his way out of my office without another word.

"I, uh, I should go." Kylea whispered, grabbing her books and slipping out.

My framed pictures of Neil Postman and Rick Roderick on one end of the office and Wittgenstein next to Baudrillard on the other bookended the line of students. Faces of contempt and embitterment filed into the classroom one by one, their eyes fixed on me, their legs moving almost robotically into an ordered row. I counted eleven students but there were at least another twenty in the hallway. Almost a third of my entire graduate roster. These must have been their emissaries.

I leaned back in my chair, my right arm straightened out onto my desk, my left arm propping me up on the arm rest as I exhaled smoke. My eyes met with their leaders, darting from side to side, waiting for them to say something.

"We, The Students' Federation-"

"Oh God! You can't be serious." I laughed, trying not to make myself appear weak, "First of all, you wouldn't be a 'Federation' you would be a 'Confederation'. That is, unless your cortège out there is from several different classes, and you've dissolved their sovereignty."

The speaker, curling a lip of malignancy at my correction, continued reading from her script through gritted teeth. "Have come with our con- hm," she said, stopping to rock on the balls of her feet, her hands trembling anxiously, "Con-"

"Constituents," her friend whispered in her ear.

"Look," she yelled, throwing the script over her head, "What we want is to discuss a path of success in your class."

My professors would have never put up with this, but I couldn't help but feel a sense of morbid curiosity at the students' reasoning. Is this why I was putting up with it? Entertainment? Curiosity?

"W- what- what do you mean path? W- what-" I kept fumbling over my words, trying to comprehend what they were talking about as I searched for the answer, "The path is to come to class, on time, read the literature I assign you, ask me questions, come to my conference hours, which I've so generously extended to three hours, do well on the exam, the midterm, and your essay."

"That's another thing. Expectations are high."

"Oh, forgive me." I derided, "You mean my expectations for you to take notes and listen in class? Breaking fucking news across academia! Jesus Murphy guys! I give you the questions for the lecture every day and some example answers just so I don't feel like I'm talking to a fucking brick wall in seminar! I'm literally manufacturing a conversation with myself, and I still can't get more than three students to participate in class!"

My rant was cut off by a student licking an ice cream cone, its drippings falling over his swollen belly and onto my office floor. I had never seen him before, and he was wearing an avant-garde style shirt with Art Bell's face on it that read 'Believe' in neon letters.

"Is that an Art Bell shirt?" I asked, snapping my head a little to enunciate the question.

"Who the fuck is Art Bell?" He asked.

"Unreal," I said, ashing my cigarette and cupping my hands over my face.

The student delegate spoke once more. "Our demands-"

"Demands?" I said, my professional smile rotting into a shocked frown.

"Demands, that's right. We pay for tuition. We have a say in our education."

"You have a say alright," I said, pointing to the door, my cigarette dangling between two fingers, "And you can say it out there after you fail my class. Who the fuck do you kids think you are? I- I mean, a lot of you are my grad students. Where is your sense?"

"Our demands are to have open note tests and for you to expound your cell phone policy."

"Expunge. EXPUNGE!" I yelled, calming myself down again almost instantly, "Okay. I get it. I mean, I don't. But I get it. You guys aren't as concerned with knowledge as you are getting a degree. As a matter of fact, I think it's safe to say, none of you really care about the knowledge your courses might offer you. Not just mine, mind you, but all your courses. You hate me, that's fine. I hate me too. But, just for a moment, let's say you are going into law, or politics, or, God forbid, education; wouldn't it be worthwhile to do things my way, learn the way you're supposed to instead of acting like kids not getting their way. Isn't your approach only going to hurt you in your careers? Knowledge for knowledge's sake is dead, I get it, but this could cost you your job if you loaf through every single class."

"Education is a status symbol," a man said, swimming his way through the crowd, "I need it, to say that I have it. I can change the world if I could just change my status."

I rubbed both my eyes with my right hand, the hot ember from my cigarette growing closer to my fingers, as I tried to think of what to say next, before finally proclaiming, "It is with intellect and will alone that the world changes for the better."

Wrinkled faces shared troubled glances at my words. I shrugged my shoulders and leaned back into my seat.

"We expect an answer by Seminar on Thursday."

I had one more shot at this. "Guys, you're asking axiomatical questions, and that's great! But you have to understand, what I can teach you, will bring you to new heights."

"We don't think so."

The Call of the Void

They were so close. So close to getting it. So close to understanding why they needed to listen. But there was a breakdown in their epistemology.

As the crowd dispersed, I could hear Dr. Piper, professor of psychology, lecturing down the hall.

"...that there is more than just a sudden death in the 'death-drive'. There is a timely, passive death..."

I walked over to his room and leaned up against the doorway to his lecture hall, making certain I was out of his line of sight. He moved methodically. His hands, gesticulating wildly, seemed to capture every emotion he was conveying subconsciously, like a blind pianist composing a symphony from mere instinct.

"...patterns of self-destructive behavior. Now, how many of you in here have ever felt compelled to swerve in front of traffic, or take the leap off a tall building while upon it? Stared at the knife in your hand and wondered what it would feel like to plunge the blade deep, deep into your breastplate?" A few hands shot up, as smiling, concerned faces met one another from across the room. "The French have a term for this. It's called 'L'appel du vide', roughly translated in English to 'The call of the void'. Many people believe that it is as simple as that fleeting moment of wanting death or, at least, the curiosity of death and feeling its foreign embrace. I proffer an alternative; that we engage in death every day on a microscopic level and the call is merely to indulge, as we so often do, in excess. If you smoke, as Vonnegut said, you're committing an honorable form of suicide. Still, I've felt incredibly attached to this term ever since my early thirties when, while dealing with a severe drinking problem, I had had a dream. In that dream, I, along with my little dachshund, was swinging wildly on a hanging scaffolding suspended just above the twin towers. This was well before 9/11 mind you, but the Twin Towers was the tallest building I could imagine, and my subconscious placed me squarely in the epicenter of my greatest fear. In the dream, I would swing wildly, grasping at my dog beneath my feet, hoping to grab him in time before the fall, certain the plummet would kill us both. The problem was, I would wake immediately. It was one of those dreams that you wake from frequently, just as the death blow is imminent, and, after falling back asleep, it picks up where it left off. So, we began to fling around like two rag dolls in the wind and, whenever my dog or I began to fall off, I woke up, grasping my chest for air, praying to God to make the dream stop. Until finally, after the umpteenth time of waking and falling back to sleep, I did what all must do when scared." He paused for dramatic effect, letting the room swell with anticipation, as I leaned in, eager to hear his resolve. "I answered the call." The class, completely entranced in Piper's speech, took quick looks at one another before staring back at him. "I leaned down and grabbed my dog, tucked him under my arm, and took the leap before falling into the most peaceful sleep I had ever had. I stopped drinking the very next day."

It wasn't long after Piper's speech that I had developed a bit of a drinking problem. Though psilocybin, LSD, and other hallucinogens had been my preferred substance of escape, drinking was for depressed people that wanted to be more depressed. I took Marais's famed advice and began using poisons to, as he put it, remedy the pain of consciousness. Confronting my problem, I pressed my psychology buddies about this for a while, but they often called security after smelling the whiskey on my breath.

I thought college would be different. I loved my friends in grade school and high school, but I searched for greater enlightenment in academia and found none. I wanted to bring two of the things I loved together—socialization and higher education. The problem was they were organically distinct.

It was a Wednesday at 11:00 AM. My next class was at noon. I had been up since 7:30 the night before drinking malt liquor and indulging in a little bit of cocaine—compliments of one of my buddies in the English Department. It helped keep me awake, staving off the foul embrace of sleep. Before leaving for work that morning, I submitted the last editorial Reuters would ever get from me. Jerry, my editor and only friend outside of work, was not allowed to let it go to publication. It read:

"*Profligates are the pestilence of society. The idea of entertainment stokes that fire. And, truthfully, we've gone past the point of no return. Entertainment, whether in the form of technology, television, internet, sex, food, money, or anything else, has become the aberration of mankind since we are unable to regulate our consumption with self-control and responsibility. Velleity has mutated itself into an addiction too great to detox from. It only took a century* for the human race to deracinate themselves from reality and propel themselves into a mirage of infamy. Humanity has become the heroin addict; humanity has found itself uttering the familiar phrase "I can stop anytime I want". And while they are stuck in this abeyance, humans find a way to deteriorate their fellow humans by pointing out the faults in themselves and promulgating it onto others. Most notably, their offspring.

There seems to be, most notably amongst the rank and file of America, a desire, or will, to acquiesce freedom to those in power. The human consciousness has done this collectively and willingly. It began with the greatest 'sin' of all time; the rejection of reason. This rejection imbued our day to day life through breeding and education that distains the thought of free will, thought and action. Though ignorance may very well be the favored vice of mankind, it barely topples the iniquity of apathy and sloth. It breaks down the system of slavery, even in contemporary life, to a bi-instrumentation of self-immolation and self-imprisonment. The former, in our very modern form of reasonable thought, lends itself to the idea that if we are a slave, we will die if we rebel. The latter simply states that we are unable to control ourselves and defend ourselves from outside forces so there is a necessity to relinquish freedom. This is where we are currently. Sartre proclaimed that Freedom is anxiety in every sense of the word. Yet, anxiety or suffering is worth embracing if it means we can be pioneers of our own life. We aren't. We have wholly accepted the idea that our freedom is an illusion so that we may harvest a sense of safety. Once more, Sartre believed that Capitalism, as our master, would be the *stalwart defender of our slavery. This frightens us. This idea is directly countered with the idea of Socialism and Communism; both ideas that would be, agreeably, worse than Capitalism. That these schools of economic discourse and thought would eliminate our freedom. And yet, what many humans fail to recognize, one cannot help but wonder who they are a master to. Are they not the slaves to every earthly desire that can be bought with a dollar? And what is a dollar? Does the dollar truly harbor any monolithic power? Or is it just a placeholder to give you the illusion of power? Of freedom?*

Contrary to the misguided belief of the rabble, criticism of Capitalism is not socialism. A healthy, middle class consumer should always judge and castigate those six businesses that make everything for you. In fact, not criticizing capitalism is socialism; it's just socialism for big business. The "rugged individualists" who believe they can work hard and become like Bezos, Gates and the others will only be crushed under the yoke of their own efforts. They have made sure no one else will join their "social group". While businesses are given money, at the expense of the slave/consumer, to stabilize themselves in economic turmoil, Americans are asked to embolden themselves during hardship. Laugh in the face of abject poverty so long as you can support Walmart, Target, Costco, Amazon, and your other overlords. These mephitic, demiurgical menhirs of industry would be chastised in the same regard of the opposition had it not been for counter didactive measures and years of slovenly disregard for man's best interests."

I hit submit and headed for my car, knowing this would be the first time lecturing intoxicated, almost certain that it would be my last. When I arrived at the lecture 10 minutes early, I smoked a cigarette right outside of the class door while the students arrived. Though some stared at me quizzically, most of them had their eyes to the ground, never looking up even for the door. I stared up at the sky, the once beautiful firmament turning into an ineluctable nihility.

Kylea walked past me absentmindedly, stopped after a few feet and spun around on her right foot jokingly for my amusement. After getting closer, her jubilant eyes decayed into those of languid concern.

"What's to be done?" she asked.

I managed a sheepish grin as I exhaled smoke. "Be innocent of the knowledge dearest chuck."

When the bell tower just over Royce Hall struck 12, I made my way to the door of the class and waited. My hand hovered over the door handle as I rocked like a buoy, drunkenly bobbing from side to side, realizing that I was finally about to reach the nadir of my academic career. After five minutes had passed, I kicked the double wide doors in and sauntered to the front of the classroom, my t-shirt dirty and hair disheveled, way beyond the pale. Low gasps reverberated off the walls as half the class looked on in bewilderment while the other half stared at their phones. I reached into my back pocket and pulled out a pint of Whiskey.

"Here's to the first of the day fellas!" I said, raising the pint of whiskey to my lips and drinking. "To 'ol William S. Burroughs."

I looked around the class, examining their stupefied faces and their blank expressions. Many of the students from the mutiny began to widen their eyes and reach for their phones as I winked at them, flashing a bit of that impudence they so loved to share. I scanned the room with the eyes of a predator searching out its prey, remembering for a brief moment what it was like to be seated there, waiting for class to start.

Kylea sat in the front, her widely folded bandana colored green that day, observing my wobbly gait as I paced carelessly with a smile from one side of the room to the other. She looked at me intently with merciful eyes that assured me they cared, that assured me this too shall pass. The only student who might end up like me one day. The student whose trust and hope in me would be diminished if I say what I came here to say. But whether she understood it or not, this was for Kylea, so that she would never follow the same path that I have. Doubtful she would thank me one day.

The class moved their eyes from their phones to the floor to the podium to my irascible gaze.

"Has a pall grown between us?" I started, drunkenly laughing at my own statement, "I don't know guys. I. Just. Don't. Know. What're we looking for here, huh? A good job? Respect? Acceptance? A new narrative? That's it! A fresh, original idea. Well then! I got news for you ladies and gentlemen; there is no such thing. Do you want a good argument for how strong language is? Every idea, big or small, has already been scribed on to paper. All we do is revitalize it… whether you're looking for theme or entertainment or deeper meaning, it's all been said before. You just want a different interpretation of it…

And that is all you care about; interpretation. Analysis be damned and originality thrown to the dogs!"

My accusatory finger circulated the class like God's red, right hand.

"You demand escape. You demand answers. You vilify every abject thought that crosses your mind and yet you refuse to open your minds to the world around you. You are the embodiment of 'The Sleeping Mind'. You are, in essence's purest form, the 'Passive Consciousness'. But it isn't your fault! There is only so much negligent parenting a child can go through before they completely give up."

And that was it. The point of no return. I had to twist the knife.

"All of your parents are either incompetent, lonely or both. Incompetent because they didn't know how to tell you 'no' or lonely because they needed a fucking friend and didn't want to say 'no'. Honestly, their incompetence is so insurmountable that it should be classified as abuse!"

At first, the class—or at least those paying attention—uniformly placed their hands over their mouths, forming a type of chimerical display of absurd theater. Then, the faces began to change. Half the class watched on with contempt as the other half stared at the ceiling with a sense of disquiet.

I sniffed lightly, staring at the ground. "You've been cheated." I awaited a response in vain. "There is outward and inward influence on impulsivity. Outward-"

"What the fuck are you talking about?!" a voice interrupted.

The Call of the Void

"Don't you fucking interrupt me!" I howled coarsely, fed up with that student in particular, before continuing, "Outward influence conditions us. These are things like porn and drugs that scrambles our impulses towards sex, addiction and therapy. Inward impulse—i.e. feelings of inadequacy, lack of goals, accomplishments, et cetera—which is motivated by the former, drives us to search for meaning in trivial things—whether it's food, tv, porn, patriotism, war, violence or other sensual pleasures. Which do you deify?"

Again, a class of mannequins stared at me vacuously. I took a deep breath, narrowed my eyes to adjust my unsteady vision, and continued.

"Our society paints a picture of egalitarianism. It tells us 'slavery' is 'wrong', but we've seen, in the inordinate spreading of funds from CEO to worker, that that is not true. We've observed that social media, addiction to entertainment, engorging ourselves in processed food, that this is the norm, not the malady."

One of the mutineers stood up in the back, shouting, "You're just a washed up-"

"Uh oh! I've hit a nerve. Looks like I'm onto something here." I shouted, pointing a finger toward the ceiling, "Your deliberate neglect for nature and the world we live in tells me more than I need to know. Your willingness to cast aside my lectures as pedantic and obscure has made you weak. This acrid commentary isn't for you. It is for humans. I just thought, being in college, you would have been more susceptible, agreeable even, to these ideas." I sighed deeply before saying, "This country is mentally ill, living the god damned American Nightmare!"

LeResche

Silence.

"If nature had a conscience, as we do, then it would laugh at every death of the human race. While every human wallows as their loved ones have cancer or get shot or get in a car accident, nature would rejoice. I heard someone, a while back, who obviously thought themselves clever, say 'Viruses are like a cure for nature. Humans are the virus'. People parroted that ad nauseam. The truth is that we ARE nature. However, we are a deviation from nature. We want to dominate it, not live in it."

Concerned Silence.

"And, if only for a moment, let us say 'Fuck Nature!'. Would my words not still be presently observed in every other aspect of human life? Was Satan really to blame then by hating humans? Did he not have the foresight to see what they would do to themselves and this world? Am I such a reactionary to say that you have destroyed your natural consciousness by consuming too much? By doing selfless acts too little? By caring about your knowledge? The truth?"

Phones had been in the upright position for the last five minutes, videotaping me no doubt. What bothered me wasn't so much the video footage as it was the validation they would receive from friends they've never seen on social sites where they'd spent too much time complaining about me for months. I was usually so much better at articulating while drunk. What I wouldn't give to have had another crack at the tirade.

I took another deep breath, sucking hard through my teeth, before opening the pint once more and drinking deeply. I scratched each side of my nose with my thumb and pulled a cigarette from my pack, taking my time to light it. Some of the faces, sullen and mirthless, goggled me while crossing their arms. Some covered their mouths in surprise. Most stared at their phones, unmindful of the discord going on in front of them. As I exhaled, I laughed briefly before saying, "The human race needs to end."

That was it. Even I knew it was over at that point. That was the most controversial idea they had ever heard. Kierkegaard could tell them to take the leap. Schopenhauer could tell them to stop reproducing. That phenomenal character is a viable concept. Nietzsche could say 'God is Dead' and Epictetus that only 'the educated are free'. Mine, however, crossed the line.

Within a week, my diatribe was all over the internet, creating one of the worst calumnies a university had ever seen. But they didn't need to fabricate the story so much. What I did was shameful enough.

A reporter accosted me outside of my condo early one evening. With his microphone pressed to my face, he began asking me questions. When I didn't answer, he asked once more, "Dr. Killian, if you weren't a professor, what would you be?"

I eyed him for a second and responded, "Happy" before walking to my car.

A day after the incident, I was on both Fox News and MSNBC. I had become the first 'public' figure on each program that both organizations came to a unanimous consensus on. The consensus? Negative. One roundtable I was watching had even posted a short clip of Alex Jones with the title, 'Alex Jones the Voice of Reason?'

"...for that, or anything else these globalists want from me! I won't stand for this insurrection of global dehumanist, depopulation, professors telling me 'Oooo I can say whatever I want. Ooo I have a PHD, ooo look at me, ooo' God damn them! Let me tell you, this type of rhetoric is directly out of the New World Order's playbook. This Sam Killian wants you to have late term abortions, he wants you to submit to the will of these cults which, I might add, he is a part of... yeah! The human race needs to end 'Doctor'? And be replaced with what?! AI?! You're telling me some 20-year-old is going to 'write' OPEDs for AP and Reuters, the mouthpiece of the global-"

I flicked the TV off and tried to get some sleep, restless over the fact that Jones's assessment of me was the most considerate.

After AP and Reuters let me go following a press release that was completely pointless, admin had called me into their office. They could handle the internet and a few students seeing this. They could not handle the all-encompassing reach of the media. UCLA's academic senate was seated in a circle, fashioned carefully around a boardroom table. The same type of meeting setup I had to attend for disciplinary action on my students was now used for me with less than stellar results.

"Do you know why you're here?" The university's provost asked.

The Call of the Void

There was a hint of condemnation in his voice as he spoke to me. I found it perverse that this was the same man that insisted I come here in the first place to become a professor.

"Well, I know that I'm a little behind on my grades but-"

"Mr. Killian. I'll promptly rephrase-"

"Save it." I muttered, twiddling my thumbs nervously, "I know."

In moments such as these, I'd like to think I am a stoic man that transcends the abrasive and accusatory rabble I have found myself surrounded by—like in my early days, agitating the populace on campus—but I doubt I looked any different than anyone else about to lose their job. The five administrators on their mountainous podiums made the scene surreal, looking like a salient tribunal one might encounter in a fever dream.

"Mr. Killian, we have come to the conclusion that you are currently unable to serve the betterment of the University. Services thus rendered have been taken into account. However, we have still moved forward on your suspension for the remainder of the semester."

"No surprise there. I assume this is why there is a six-week probationary period for tenure usually?" I asked, smiling and hoping a little charm might get me in their good graces. Instead, like a pit of vipers, the board hissed and scoffed with reckless abandon.

"Mr. Killian, you are hereby suspended until January 16th. You will be reinstated upon the completion of a psychiatric evaluation."

"Psych-"

"By one of *our* own physicians."

I figured it wasn't the appropriate time to correct him on the definition of a physician, and I was hardly in a position to argue either way. Enticing though the thought might be of quitting and flipping them the bird, paid leave was a far better route, and I needed a vacation.

They sent me to Dr. Felix for an intake and assessment. Only problem was, I knew everyone in the Psych Dept except for this guy. Apparently, he worked for HR. Bold move sending a dime store shrink to analyze Doctoral Professors at a 'prestigious' University. Either way, his gait, the cut of his jib, something, gave me the impression that he wasn't being completely genuine with me. He sauntered up to a red chair directly beside me, his legs pinched together while he moved as if there were something stuck up his ass. I took notice of a copy of Freud's *The Uncanny* on his desk just as he began to speak.

"Dr. Killian. Welcome."

"Gracious of you to still call me Doctor. After the opprobrium I weathered this last week," I paused briefly, not wanting to ramble, "well, anyway, good to meet you."

"I was hoping we'd be able to talk. I'm sure analysis would be wasted on a mind such as yours."

I believed that bit of covert flattery about as much as I believed I needed this. I took a minute to gather my thoughts and inhale the sharp, noxious odor of ethanolamine and freshly printed newspapers permeating throughout his office.

The Call of the Void

"No analysis. I see. Are you a professional conversationalist then?" I asked.

"I don't understand the question."

"Never mind."

My chest sank like an avalanche as I exhaled, growing more and more nervous by the second about his follow up questions.

"Right. Moving forward then. Do you think you have a dependency?"

"Well, Doctor, I'm dependent on many things. Care to specify?"

"Care to elaborate?"

"As far as substance abuse," I said, not wanting to go back and forth with him the whole hour, "I have this terrible problem of being stupid whenever I'm drunk."

"This is somehow unique to you?"

I pumped my hand a little to stop him and correct myself. "Some people have told me I speak in an almost guttural, valley slang when intoxicated. Perish the thought. It would certainly kill my image at the uni- erm, well, that doesn't matter now. Still, I knew it was true for sure when a girl I was dropping acid and sleeping with back in undergrad told me this was the real me. The real Sam. And the one at university is a shade. An actor. A jester. A fool. And that the real me has a nocuous, untapped darkness. Hell of a thing to lay on a guy while he's tripping on 400µg of LSD and trying to make sure his cock is still attached. I rocked myself to sleep that night and just remember

51

muttering over and over again, 'And we'll stay here, dwelling morbidly amongst our passing lives, waiting to see what dreams may come'."

Felix cocked an eyebrow at my sudden openness. "She seems like quite the character."

I bulged my cheeks with air before exhaling and answering him. "My life has always been a series of odd encounters with even odder people."

"What do you think she meant by that? Your mask?"

I looked around at the ceiling, a little upset Felix had gotten me this far. It was nice to talk to someone though. "From my understanding, of which I have none, it's a subconscious placeholder. The mask, that is. Something to help navigate you around what you want to be, ought to be, and should be. Tantamount to becoming friends with the worst part of yourself. Something I am all too familiar with. Do you like Freud?" I asked, trying to shift the conversation away from myself.

"Freud, Dr. Killian?" Felix asked, looking over his shoulder at the book on his desk, "Hmmm. Not particularly. But in my line of work, one cannot afford to be benighted from the literature my patients read and wish to quiz me on. Do you like him, Sam? You always struck me as a Jung man."

"How di-" I held my tongue, realizing he knew more about me than I anticipated.

"Surprised I knew that? I'm very familiar with your work. Indeed, it would be quite the oversight on my part to not notice your references to 'the shadow self' and consciousness without recognizing his influence on you. And of course, your publications on Husserl had a less than subtle tinge of Jungian logic behind them. Impressed?" He shrugged lightly with a smile before I could respond. "I'm surprised you don't cite him more often."

"Jung isn't-" I paused to reflect on my answer, "isn't a predominant force in my field. Or yours either, I think."

"Odd that a psychologist with such an oeuvre regarding your field wouldn't be seen as a force. Who made that call?"

As I examined my sneakers that were raised up on the couch, I could see Felix staring at me out of my peripheral view. "Couldn't tell ya."

"Down to brass tacks then Dr. Killian?"

"Please..."

"I'd like to start by asking you what regrets you might have. What does Sam Killian regret doing? Or, even better, not doing?"

"I don't know. That heated philippic I laid on my class I guess."

"No, no, no, no. You don't regret that. And you shouldn't! Not to say what you did was right, but it was certainly cathartic for you. And I think we both know you don't regret it. You regret your suspension, the shame of having your students unjustly validated, the obloquy from the press and the public, which has become something of a ubiquitous presence in your life. But you don't regret the act. Come on Sam. Talk to me. What is it you regret?"

Somehow, Felix had made it impossible for me to ignore him. I could sense myself doing all my worst ticks; rubbing my day-old stubble over and over again, rolling my neck in a circle, passing air from one cheek to the other. But, after a moment, it finally hit me. "Okay." I sighed, "It's ridiculous but, it's the first thing I could think of on the spot."

"Go on." Felix insisted, leaning in closer, his hands over his mouth in the shape of a steeple as his eyes illuminated with sincere intrigue.

"One night in my backyard, while I was sitting there, smoking and listening to the neighbor's radio, I could hear a woman, presumably drunk, walking down the street. There's a bunch of vegetation, cacti, brush and about a half-acre of land from my backyard to the main street where she was. It was about 3:30 in the morning so I decided to take a look over my wall. It was so dark, and I could barely make out what kind of physique she had but she was perambulating down the middle of the street with an oil lamp raised over her head and not a care in the world. She was walking, slowly, and shouting, 'Hello? Is anybody there? Hello? Is anybody there?' over and over again, switching the pitch in her voice every other time so her tone would oscillate between pathetic and distraught like some ominous presage masked as an urban malediction." I ran out of breath and my chest began to pant anxiously just from reciting the image in my head. "I know. I know. It's LA, and she is probably at the bottom of a long list of unsavory characters. But who was she? What was she looking for? The scene, me in my backyard watching on as she moved through the fog with an oil lamp shouting to no one in particular, was too bleak. Too- too- much. Even for me. I thought briefly about answering her, but I never beckoned her call and instead watched as she moved down the street and out of sight like an ignis fatuus. It's my biggest regret—not responding that is—to this day. It drives me crazy just thinking about it."

Felix looked lost at my story, fixing his eyes on mine as he raised himself up to speak. "Were you drunk?"

"I- yes, but I was cogent. I was buzzed I wasn- that isn't the point anyway. It really happened. This wasn't some dream!"

"I believe you. But even so, a dream can have a profound impact on your conscious mind. Maybe, just maybe, you thought-"

"I didn't dream it." I growled, "And frankly, I find it a bit insulting that you think I would disassociate with reality so badly as to confuse a meaningless dream with a memory."

"Meaningless? That's a foolish notion, Dr. Killian. It obviously meant a great deal to you if you regret not reaching out to her so much. But, meaningless? Never. What is in a dream anyway? Do you notice the subtle little details from your life, bleeding out into the picture in your head? Quotes from books and movies that are familiar to you. Things you wished to say but never could. That's what's in a dream, Sam. Our deepest fears and most forbidden desires. It's our fears we see first and most transparently though. They're easier to identify. Bringing the unconscious to conscious. They say dreams are your subconscious desires playing themselves out for you. But subconscious desires are deeply embedded into your mind, never to be seen. The desire to fornicate with a relative or kill an elderly man; these are subconscious desires. No, instead, I believe dreams are your conscious mind masking the shadow of your thoughts. Right there, on the surface. The truth that we refuse to confront during the daytime, we all see at night."

"Rubbish." I said, trying to detract once more.

"I see." Felix said, writing on his notepad, "I think, as an educator in our institution, you are out of touch with reality, out of-"

"Wait, what? Where is this coming from?" I asked as I shot up to look at him, "And how can you assess that? This is our first vis-"

"Maybe, if you were a little more forbearing it wo-"

"Forbearing?" I questioned impatiently, opening my eyes wide as I crossed my arms over my chest, "After *years* of this bullshit, you have the gall to call me forbearing? Are you fucking with me? How can you say that?"

"And not so out of touch with your students-"

I held up three fingers to his face, counting each one as I spoke. "Truth, knowledge, equitable analysis; these are the foundations of collegiate education. Damnit Felix! I thought you'd be on my side on this-"

"And most importantly, out of touch with your fellow man. See, I believe you assess every interaction with humans as if you were 'trying to figure them out' rather than communicating with them."

"My 'fellow' man? I have friends. I get along with the entire faculty here."

"And your students? How often do you read a situation in your head like you're an explorer trying to rationalize a newly discovered civilization? How often, like some linguistic pedant, do you use words like 'ethanolamine' instead of the more accepted 'ammonia'? Personally, I think you like to hear yourself talk-"

"I don-"

"Rambling on in prolix lectures, succinct though they may be. Life isn't a practical application of Phenomenology, Dr. Killian. You shouldn't venture too far into the embrace of academia. Intellectualism is a common cover-up for fear of direct experience. I believe it was our boy who said that."

I rubbed the back of my neck, thinking about my response, terrified that he may be right, and weighed my options in my head.

Do I tell him what I've thought recently? No. That would lead to more psychoanalysis and him just defending the students and their inability to change the- Ah, fuck it.

"Sure. I've had a tough time adjusting to students currently in a graduate program that have the intellectual maturity of that of children that should be in a Middle School SPED class. What of it?"

Felix tsked lightly, shaking his head as he wrote on the notepad placed over his lap. "Look here, Dr. Killian, sir," he said as his tone became increasingly assertive, "the school wants to reinstate you. Your accomplishments are quite impressive, and you have a bit of a, shall we say, media following."

"Oh yeah, they really love me." I scoffed.

"Who's being immature now Mr. Killian?" Dr. Felix's tone was becoming less tolerant. I faced him once more, a little abashed at my behavior. "They are willing to let you teach PhD students exclusively, *if* you follow my program."

I didn't respond.

"Once again, I think you are disconnected from your fellow man. I want you to connect with them. If I can be completely candid?" Felix stared personably, his hand outstretched, waiting for my permission.

"By all means."

"I believe there was a time when you transitioned from acting human to reading what it's like to be human. I believe you opened a book one day and never put it down. I want you to go out and spend a night assimilating to—using your words—the collective human consciousness. You chose to be an educator. You chose to live a life as witness. Now, go out and bear witness to the world you hermetically sealed yourself away from."

"Assimilating? You make it sound like my consciousness is some... alien... I don't even know!"

"According to some of your students..."

I snorted lightly, shaking my head in defiance. "Fine. What do I need to do?"

"Like I said, spend a night with humanity. Be one with the city." Felix paused for my reaction. The white in his moonlike eyes made me grimace. It almost looked like his pupils were disappearing. He must have taken my reaction, or silence, as insolence since his next statement came brusquely. "Okay, fine. Here's what I want. I have a ticket to an event next Thursday night. It's a 'meeting of the minds' type of event. But I don't want you to drive there. I want you to walk. I want you to start from your house and walk to the Los Angeles

Convention Center. Take any route you'd like but walk and take in what mankind has to offer. You might be surprised. After all, it's only in solitude that we can be with our most primitive thoughts and desires. And I wouldn't even call them desires really; they're more... premonitions. Then, and only then, when we have crossed the line of human decency, can we understand human life. A frightening thought, but true nonetheless."

"Uh huh." I said, not quite understanding the last part, "And you want me to walk?"

"Correct. Carpe noctem! To become the ancient peripatetic! To palliate the mind and mend the soul. Is something wrong with that? You don't have nyctophobia do you?" Felix laughed, "After all, I believe it was Sophocles who said, 'One must wait until the evening, to see how splendid the day has been.'"

"You're never short on quotes, are you Felix?"

Felix shook his head playfully, shutting his notepad and handing me the ticket. "But there is one proviso I have. As witness, you are not to get involved in any fiasco you find yourself in or are observing. This is imperative, Dr. Killian. You must see and confront the nihilism you so boldly accused your students of. Then, and only then, can the illusion fade."

"Alright," I said, "'Meeting of the Minds' huh? Not very clever for a bunch of academics."

"Any suggestions?" Felix asked, a subtle look of curiosity forming on his face.

"How's about," I said, taking a moment to think, "'Cerebral Ceremony'?" I passed my hand in front of my face as if I were displaying an invisible banner.

"Ceremony? Hmmm. That would be appropriate." Felix mused, watching me read the ticket.

"Is this some sort of- I don't know. This isn't a pyramid scheme or anything, is it?"

"Now you're insulting *my* intelligence." He looked disappointed, pursing his lips and shaking his head ruefully. "Let's just say, my motive for sending you out may not be entirely altruistic." He paused and stared off somewhere behind me, taking his glasses off and cleaning the lenses, "But in time, I think you may just thank me. Just make sure to embrace the chaos, Sam. By morning, you'll be back to lapping up structure. I'm certain of it."

"Whatever that means," I said, forcing myself out of the chair and toward the door.

As I reached for the handle, the inscription above Felix's door, which read 'F.I.M.', caught my eye. I stopped and turned back to Felix who was writing notes in his journal. "Hey doc?"

"Yes?"

"You saw the files and complaints I had on my students. Honestly, do you think I was out of line? And I'm not talking about getting drunk and going on a rant. I'll eat that bit. I fucked up. I mean, do you think I was being too testy in general?"

Felix looked at me for a moment, his eyebrow raised up high before looking back down at his notepad without saying a word.

The Call of the Void

The phone rang from inside my place, pulling me out of my reminiscent reverie. I considered getting up but sat back in my hammock for a moment longer, taking in the stars. As the sun sank below the city, there, high above, dangling brightly in the mirthless firmament, they formed a spastic outline of the heavens, fighting for dominance against the swelling pallor of the moon.

The phone finally stopped ringing. I rested my whiskey glass on the center of my chest, watching as it ascended and descended with each breath. I fumbled for my pack of smokes, opened the box and jostled the lucky around before grabbing it, flipping the filter around with my lower lip and lighting up with my zippo.

A man in a hooded sweater walked by, stopped, stared at me, scanned his phone, his eyes lighting up with each scroll, and waved his friend over to stare at me for a moment before taking a picture and heading off.

The phone rang again from the kitchen, forcing my eyes open. I looked at my neighbor's clock. *5:49 PM.* The wind began to howl, rushing against my ears while the November night rejected the sober, serene sky of the day. Dropping my empty scotch glass onto the rocks beneath my feet, I waited patiently for the hammock to finish rocking, as the phone ended its sequence of rings. The celestial landscape above flashed a farrago of exquisite, limitless beauty and infinite sorrow that few here in LA could afford to appreciate.

In the kitchen, I extinguished my lucky in the sink and filled my flask up with clear, corn mash whiskey that I had lying around near

61

the fridge. I steadied the funnel and filled it to the brim, catching another unfortunate reflection of myself in the empty portrait case next to my graduation pictures and degrees.

On top of the walk, Felix stipulated that I write a journal. He wanted me to put my thoughts—sober or otherwise—into writing before, during, and after. I told him, if I was going to be drunk and harassed out on Rodeo Drive, he wasn't going to get pearls from me. He assured me that was fine, and to think of it more like a written Rorschach test, writing down the first inklings of my mind, unfettered by critical thought.

I leaned over the kitchen counter and began to write.

Being honest with myself, at the behest of the school's psychiatrist, I would have to say that the worst of my transgressions are wrath and self-doubt. Wrath is beyond obvious at this point, but self-doubt is one that rolls around in my mind. I used to believe it was hypocrisy, but the truth is far more depressing. Hypocrites say one thing and do another. I merely tell myself one thing and act on another. By the time I received my PhD, I found literally no meaning in this life other than teaching. It was only my anger that contradicted that belief. I hated reactionaries. I hated polemics. I hated luddites. And yet, those very ideologies found a place deep in my soul and sprawled their roots out in there. Academia had killed me. What I once thought of as the 'dream job' had become my sepulcher and was draining my spirit. I once thought myself bold. I once considered myself a seditious dissident, hellbent on navigating mankind into a better future. Now, I'm just a lump of over-educated, under-developed

The Call of the Void

brain matter that can tell you the difference between who/whom and what epistemology means. Why not just let the kids do what they will? Why not be happy just giving them a grade and move on? Maybe it's me. Maybe I put too much acrimony in the air and my misanthropy is something inherent within me and not a symptom of life. Maybe I just can't face the changing of the guard that's happening so rapidly. Maybe I've always been the problem. Why not face the future?

Why? I finally had an answer to the question I had been asking my whole life. The answer is that there is no answer. The truth is that there is no objective certainty. I've grown tired of academia and what it has become. Filled with professors trying to one up each other with wildly asinine research so they can claim to be the forerunner of their own ideology. Administrations and professors that threw certainties at their students on subjective matters. I've grown tired of the youth of this nation leading lives that revolve around little more than self-validation. I've grown tired of the veil of 'freedom'. The only objective truth and earthly certainty left is that we've primally conditioned our minds and, ergo, our DNA into a slovenly, ignorant lifestyle. I'm tired of discourse being met with hatred and vitriolic denial. I've lived my whole life open to every idea that comes my way, no matter how 'controversial'. And now, I must demonstrate, to my peers, a level of normalcy. Yet there's a war on in my mind, torn between who I want to be and who I should be.

A loud, jarring ring broke my concentration once more as I thoughtlessly grabbed the rotary phone on its first ring.

"How can I help you?" I asked abruptly.

"Do you know me?" the voice asked among a backdrop of scattered white noise.

"No. I don't." I said impatiently after considering the absurdity of the question and slamming the phone down onto the receiver.

The unfinished turkey dinner from Boston Market sat on the kitchen counter, its gravy congealing rapidly into a ring of gunk by the minute. I grabbed a deep pull off the handle of unmarked whiskey I had by the fridge as if I were a safari exhibitionist going into the wilds for the first time. The smell of the cigarette permeated the walls of my condo. I placed my keys into my left pocket and my wallet into my right, leaving my wristwatch behind. I propped my forearm up on the frame of the door and watched as smoke from the American Spirit drifted down the walkway.

The phone rang again. I stared at it firmly, wondering if my students or maybe even some wag had gotten a hold of my number. It rang again and I picked it up before a third. "Yeah?"

"I've met God. He's pissed."

"Come again?"

"I said, I've. Met. God. He's. Pissed."

I rested the phone on my shoulder, wondering how much I wanted to entertain the guy on the other line. "Look, whoev-"

"I think I always spoke with a bit of grandiloquence when I noticed praise for it." I could hear sarcasm in the voice on the other line. He sounded familiar. "Of course, the novelty wore off quickly enough, but the smarmy vocab was here to stay."

The Call of the Void

"Excuse me?"

"You look like the type of guy that likes *Society of the Spectacle*" he said, his voice dripping with condescension.

"I do like that book, yes." I responded ambivalently, uncertain about his implication.

In an instant, the static on the other end cut out completely, as if my answer was the code word to the game he was playing.

"Hello?" I asked, uncertain if he hung up, "Are you there?"

"I, I, I, I, I, I, I,"" he repeated, his voice now a rasp that was alarmingly inhuman, as a mixture of low growls and screams built up in the background.

"Yes?" I asked, panicked, "You?!"

Silence for a moment. "Just want to wish you the best of luck."

The click on the other end was unmistakable this time. I placed the phone on the receiver and thought for a minute about staying home tonight before a loud crash slammed my front door shut. It was louder than anything I'd ever heard before. I turned briskly to see if anyone was staring at me from the kitchen windows. Surely it was the wind. In my semi-drunken state, I had left the front door open. It took everything in me to look up the stairs adjacent to my condo's entrance which I had not been paying attention to for some time. I shook my head in disbelief, certain my imagination was getting the better of me, and stepped outside.

LeResche

The moon rested over the top of LA—its all-seeing eye privy to every one of the city's sins. A city of fallen angels. It was frightening how unaware of my own universe I really was. A presidential election happened at the start of the month, and I had no idea who won. Time had begun to lose all sense of meaning. I couldn't even conjure up what year it was.

The digital clock inside my neighbor's condo blinked *5:57 PM.* I inspected my outfit in the reflection of the condo's front window, opening the buttons of my red flannel to show my white crew neck t-shirt and adjusting the belt buckle on my jeans. My neighbor, looking almost infantile in his XXL hand-me-downs, slouched out of his condo before giving an emphatic stretch that ended in a yawn. He reached down to brace himself before sitting on the concrete, grabbing a joint in his ear, and pushing the play button on his boombox. Donovan's 'Season of the Witch' came on as we tipped our chins to one another. 6 PM. The perfect time. Felix was right; normalcy plagues people during the day. People lack a sense of primal emotion that they can finally recover during the night. I could only hope the night would reveal where the soul, the poetry, the mind of mankind had gone.

As I walked on the most desolate path, patterned by urban majesty and torrential madness, a lone coyote ran by my side in the distance. His breath steamed and plumed in the night's sky as his howl sang a threnody to the moon. Two more ran up beside him and followed me close behind.

The Call of the Void

When the world is asleep, the night belongs to only a few. The illumination of a city on fire struck the eyes of many. And with the moon's blessing, the night had begun.

II

The digital clock above the billboard on Los Angeles's east side flashed its digits on and off. *6 PM.* Beneath it was an advertisement many had grown all too familiar with seeing: a rubicund female reminiscent of the early 50's prototypical housewife, one hand on her hip the other cocked like a finger gun pointed at traffic. The lettering at the top and bottom read:

"Kids bringing you down?

F*%$ 'em! That's what we're here for."

Directly below the billboard, near its bottom right corner, there was a fine print that read 'Sponsored by YouTube'. There's still a bit of an internecine feud amongst town officials as to whether the billboard represented a new, more provocative image for the actual company, or was simply an ill-advised attempt at 'adult humor' from a local band of luddites. Yet, in the minds of those who care to analyze the advertisement for more than a second or two, there lingered a more virulent message: positivity is fleeting and indifference amongst parents is becoming pervasive.

Continental BLVD was the best route to the Convention Center, allowing me to circumvent LA's less reputable and indecent areas where, amongst other things, I was most likely an outsider. Without a phone or any kind of navigation system, I would have to eyeball it tonight. Fishing through my pocket, I grabbed a spirit and lit up, noticing the dimly lit 'Tent City' down the road. It was a well-known fact that any passerby should steer well clear of the Recusants and their ilk. At least, until the news told us otherwise. The tent communes harbored a group of schismatics that had been aborted from the womb of society ever since their on-screen theatrics threw the country into a frenzied state of panic. It wasn't even a year ago when they began germinating throughout the city. In fact, their urban blitz, at that point, had made its way into every major city around the world.

The first time any American had heard of the Recusants was roughly six months ago. I was in the faculty breakroom grabbing a coffee. Cheryl's eyes followed me from the door to the coffee machine as I did my best not to notice her. The coffee machine whirred a little and I hit it as 'Dixie's Song' played faintly on the TV.

"Now there's a song you don't hear every day in LA," someone behind me said.

"Yeah. Turn that up!" another professor's voice demanded.

The man on the TV, half cowboy, half car salesman, whipped around on an invisible horse, throwing an imaginary lasso from left to right, yelling at the screen, "*Calling ALLLL Christians come to the place where there ain't no disgrace!*". Everyone cocked their heads in my direction, searching my face for some sort of tick or wrinkle that would reveal what I thought of the poorly trained cowboy. It was the first indication of how outspoken I had been without ever realizing it. That, coupled with my deist beliefs, usually landed me on the hot seat whenever a theological question arose in conversation.

69

LeResche

"The word of God came to me, a man of God, saying, 'April 15th, 7 PM, come on down to AT&T stadium for the biggest Christian fan gathering since the Council of Nicaea!'"

I chortled. "Christian fan gathering? Boy, they're really getting lazy now."

"Oh puh-leeze," Dr. Brown, a professor of History, muttered, "the local Wiccan covenant gets more in attendance than the Council of Nicaea. Plus, Nicaea would have been filled with Heretics by today's standards of Ch-"

"SHHHH! Damnit, Brown." Dr. Kessler pleaded, "I want to hear this."

Brown crossed his arms defiantly.

"Come on down to AT&T Stadium in Dallas, TX and see, for the first time since his unforeseen arrest, God's most loyal follower and loved child; Pastor Jim Bakker. Admittance is only $19.99. Viewings for the less fortunate will be televised on Pay Per View for the low, low price of $9.99."

A hypnotizing flash on the screen zoomed in and out on a large dollar sign next to the cover price which was digitally fastened to a crucifix.

"Alright, who's the joker that put this on?" Dr. Kessler asked, looking around the room.

"Jim Bakker?" I added, "That's a joke, right?"

"Ya know," Dr. Brown said, moving to my side and stirring his coffee, "The Big Three do most of their shows down here now. Ever since they put up CCOCC that is."

"Well, I'm sold," Dr. Fram said, rising to her feet, "We should have a viewing party."

"I say Cheryl's place. She's got a hot tub, and a wine cellar, and an air fryer, and-"

"Stacey, please!" Cheryl interrupted, before looking at my reflection on the glossy fridge's door, "That is, I don't mind."

Cheryl craned her neck to look at me, her eyes demurely awaiting my response. Rumor had it she shared a mutual interest in me and was very 'discreet' when it came to hookups. Then again, how discrete could one really be on campus?

"Sure," I said, smiling a little at Cheryl, "Why not?"

On the night of the event, there were ten of us in Cheryl's villa, a mammoth of a homestead directly south of the 101 in Calabasas. Normally she lived near campus in a penthouse not far from work during the fall and spring semesters but moved back into her house in the hills shortly after the Winter semester. Nobody truly knew where Cheryl got her money from, and I doubted anyone in our department cared to inquire.

Fred, another colleague of mine, sauntered over to me, his gait and shoulder struts exuding confidence, with a martini in his hand like he was at a 70s key party.

"Ya know," Fred said elegantly, "Cheryl wants to jump your bones."

"So I've heard," I said, taking a sip of my whiskey.

"You totally have a shot tonight."

71

"If I do, I do. I'll talk to her. Jesus, we aren't in grade school anymore Fred."

I looked around the room, taking note of everyone there. Alice Fram, a professor in our department doing research for the UCLA Press on Inconsistent Mathematics, was talking the ear off of Dr. Ricky Kopecky on the topic of Pythagoreanism's influence on Early Christianity. By the way Rick stirred the olive in his martini glass, it was obvious he was growing bored of his own theorems. Dante Davis and Matt Steele, both PhDs in Literature, were discussing their last oration on Grecian Poetry and its evolution into Romanticism. Though—from what I could tell—both were in agreement, there seemed to be a bit of an outburst on who was more bookish.

"But it was Von Schiller who believed aesthetic is the 'model', supposedly, of human intellect and-"

"Positively philistine, I dare say." Dante interrupted, "Human *freedom*, not intellect. And where does Matthew Arnold fit into all of this? Had he been any less of an elitist he may have never seen a work published."

"Matthew Arnold," Matt scoffed, "is the very reason Hellenism is studied today, and the sole reason you have a job at all, Dante."

"Preposterous." Dante laughed.

Despite Dante's perpetual air of pretentiousness, his droll pablums were often entertaining.

The Call of the Void

"Boys, boys," Michelle Kessler, PhD in Philosophy who has extensively published on Eliminativism, butted in, "Who are you trying to impress exactly?"

Both Dante and Matt searched the ground, kicking their feet at nothing in particular.

Flashes on the screen heralded the preliminary events of the night, gathering the attention of everyone at the party. I leaned against the staved wall near the kitchen, watching Cheryl as she swayed from side to side before making a beeline toward me.

"Are you having a good time?" She said, drunkenly sucking back in a little drool.

"Oh yeah," I said, laughing and handing her a handkerchief from my back pocket before indicating Ricky and Dante, "Plenty of entertainment already. You have a great house, Cher."

Her smile grew fierce, an intimation that she was not shy, not one to play cat and mouse. "Let's go upstairs really quick." She said, slurring her words a bit.

"Quick?! Hey!" I said, feigning shock, "What have you heard?"

She giggled a little. "Come on, it'll be fun."

"And miss the big event?" I said, joking "I have to run notes with my pastor tomorrow on this. What will *he* say?"

She laughed once more before grabbing the collar of my shirt and leading me away. "You can tell him my room has a magnificent view."

I laughed nervously, trying to rummage around in my memory for some other inane witticism that might belay sleeping with a drunken colleague. She grabbed my right hand, lightly at first, before decisively caressing it between her fingers and biting her lip sensually.

"Shhh! It's starting!"

Looking down at my hand holding her hand, Cheryl stopped. Her lips curled a little, baring her teeth, and she gave me a sheepish grin. "Maybe a little later then."

Cheryl and I sat on the couch closest to the wall. She rested her head on my chest and grabbed for my arm, forcibly putting it around her shoulder as a sponsored advertisement began on screen.

Do you remember where you were when they took prayers out of the classroom in Kentucky? Senator O'Brien does. And where was Governor Wallace when Cave Hill Cemetery was burned down by Buddhist Extremists. Senator O'Brien do- ahem, Senator O'Brien was there. Don't forget to vote this November. Keep the Senate, fair, balanced, and, above all, righteous.

A phantasmagoria of images with Senator Bradley Orenthal Brien—affectionately referred to nationwide as Senator O'Brien— waving in front of an American flag, then a hospital, a library, a school for the blind, and, finally, a bootlegger's distillery, accompanied the national anthem on screen.

Michelle let out a shrill giggle. "That wasn't subtle at all."

"Wait," Dante said, reflecting on the commercial, "why is there a commercial for Senator O'Brien's reelection if we're in California?"

"Pay Per View." Dr. Brown posited, "I guess it gets shown everywhere. Besides, I'm sure he helped sponsor this whole thing."

The Call of the Void

"Whatever," Ricky said, cutting in, "he's been standing on the graves of those Burmese for far too long. But, uh, well, he'll probably still get elected. Right, Sam?"

I opened my palms and shrugged. "I mean," I began, thinking of something to say, "I think it's just like America to vote for candy when we need a toothbrush. But like Dante said, we live in California. What the fuck do I care about a Senator from Kentucky who I'm never going to meet and doesn't give a second thought about me and my life?"

An overture snapped our attention back to the screen. All our eyes became one, staring at the TV with nervous glee as children do for Saturday morning cartoons. The show had begun. It's hard to believe now but the attendance records for Jim Bakker's next largesse grab was bigger than any Super Bowl on record. Each one of the 80,000 seats had an ass in it. And not only that, but the nosebleeds were also filled with people sitting in the walkway, pausing as the lights created a coruscant haze before erupting into ebullient screams of joy in the darkness. Cheryl rested her head on my shoulder again as I took another drink.

A helicopter camera with a bird's eye view of the parking lot posted live footage of the surrounding area. At first, it was impossible to make anything out, what with the swaying spotlight moving in every direction. But when another light entered, and then a third, countless faces peered upward and the ground began to move, revealing the entire parking lot filled with people shoulder to shoulder. Thousands of little ants screaming up at the light engulfing them as if it were salvation itself. The crowd—its immense breadth an implausible sight—

had swallowed the street whole. No sirens. No visible police. Only bodies, floating around in a sea of moving chaos, their collective consciousness trying to find some order.

In brief, biting outbursts, my colleagues—without even a whiff of clever persiflage— heckled the crowd, entreating one another to give their best broadside about Christianity. It was then, amongst a pack of supercilious wolves, that my intellectual elitism had lost a little bit of its previous flair.

"It's a good thing they're Christians. Could you imagine what it would look like if Skid Row was down there?"

"Assuming the majority of Skid Row isn't Christian you elitist fu-"

"Shut up and finish your fucking martini, Dante."

With a light drum roll, a voice on the TV spoke.

"*And folks, without further ado, I give to you, the man behind the 30-day dehydrated sour cream with compact toilet. The man who invented the 'Silver Sol Liquid' which personally cured the viral demon brewing within me. And of course, the man that brought to you the first 'Jim Bakker Bible'™ complete with Trident™ gum dispenser and holy water extension applicator. The one! The only! Son of God! Jiiiiim Bakker!*"

Despite the announcer's multitudinous blasphemies, the audience erupted into a bedlam of applause. Bakker walked through the gold embossed veil with one hand raised in the air and the other interwoven between his wife's fingers. The smile on Bakker's face wilted momentarily as he took the microphone, tapped it, and shook his head as no sound emitted. He once again tapped the microphone with his index finger, looking up at the rafters in a pleading motion for some help.

Jim's face turned a beet red and he threw the microphone to his closest associate before reaching into a bag below his feet. He raised the khaki bag out onto the stage and pantomimed his entire act. His forearm went into the bag before pulling out an air horn, a CPR Kit, a bottle of hand sanitizer with Jesus on a crucifix, and, most astonishingly, a pil-

"Enough." a voice bellowed from the sky.

The crowd gasped. Bakker grimaced. My colleagues turned pale. A vuvuzela trumpet seized the world.

"Here." The voice demanded, "In Row 7. Seat 21."

The camera panned in and out frantically before finally focusing on a shirtless man near the western 50-yard line. His face was expressionless, exhuming a certain stoic characteristic buried deep in the heart of man. He raised his arms, signaling to the sky, as if semaphoring to God, revealing rows and rows of shirtless men and women of every race, gender and age. The clothed crowd surrounding them became more cautious by the second, separating themselves from the shirtless mob like oil in water.

The man put the microphone to his lips. "Listen to-"

"Terrorist!" a muffled voice shouted near the shirtless figure "Muslim terr-"

The shirtless man, who was even paler than I was, shook his head and looked down with a cool, assured smile before meeting the eyes of his jeerer. "Do I look like a Muslim to you, you fucking dolt?"

LeResche

The camera broadcasting the live TV feed panned quickly to Bakker's face, his jaw slack and eyes widening in dismay, and panned out again quickly. The shirtless mob stood motionless with completely detached expressions on their faces. Other than a few minor whispers, the crowd had settled, waiting to hear what the dissenters had to say.

"Brethren. Let your spirit be known to all men. The Lord is near." The shirtless man had his arms spread wide, staring up at the stadium lights while motioning to the crowd. "We are here, now, to repay every man according to his deeds. We are the flame eternal and, brothers and sisters, *igne natura renovatur integra*. From here on out, the lost faith of Christianity will be divided amongst the Recusants and the heretics. Tired of the materialistic, rapacious manner in which the Church of Christ currently operates, we have chosen a life of servitude and minimalism. We will be at the gate waiting for all those who care to join. And for tho-"

His mic cut out abruptly. Noticing the interruption, the speaker breathed in, inhaling the night's air like it was the first time he had ever done so, cocked his arm back, threw the microphone onto the 50-yard line and adjusted his gaze at the zenith of the stadium. His arms stretched wide like some forgotten, wretched messiah of the new age. Each of the now thousand shirtless Recusants languidly pulled out knives from their back pockets. Some in the crowd began fleeing while others threw their crucifix shaped plastic pint glasses into the mass of zealots. Even a few flannel adorned Bakkerites fought their way through the mob of mad men, hitting down knives and knocking out men, women and children. Yet the Recusants remained pacifistic, meeting the crowd with no resistance and accepting their fate. They stood there and took a beating. But even after doling out a spiteful thrashing, they couldn't make their way to the speaker or the other 200 fanatics surrounding him. Something in his eyes, in the way his smile reached ear to ear baring nearly all of his teeth, spoke volumes about what he had done and how long he had been planning it.

The crowd that fled was falling over one another, jumping on top of their neighbor's shoulders like a poorly executed game of leapfrog, before slowing, stopping, and staring to marvel at the Recusants methodically carving the flesh from their chests. They moved rhythmically, like some kind of haka dance, slashing the inside of their hand before showing it to the cameras and smearing it over their bare torsos. The camera zoomed in on the ringleader, his eyes bestial and on fire, taking in the thrill of the show, as a smile formed on his face. Slice after slice, cutting through sinew and flesh, left streaks of blood trickling down the front of their bodies. Deep, deep cuts that came on slow before freefalling into a sort of crossroads of lacerations and exposed bones. The cameraman was more than generous with his shots, zooming into one woman as she wiped her flayed forearm, revealing a clean, white line of bone, before blood came cascading over it. A man behind the Recusant mob rested the back of his hand against his forehead and fainted as the picture zoomed in on a man that had cut off nearly half of his pectoral, the muscle hanging over his lower abdomen in an unnatural way. The spectacle, an almost hostile tarantism of knives and madness, finally ended as the Recusants, in unison, lowered their heads, lifted their hands to the sky, and dropped their knives. The camera cut as their leader looked directly into the screen. It was so direct, so centered, that I was certain he was smiling at me. His face remained in my mind, even after the screen cut to a cartoon of Jesus carpentering the arm of his own broken cross, with the subtitle 'Technical Difficulties'.

Our eyes were glued to the screen for a few seconds more. We sat, utterly nonplussed, and waited to come back down to earth. My colleagues' faces morphed, first showing concern, then intrigue, until finally, acceptance.

"Well, that was interesting."

"Interesting?" I whispered, underwhelmed at the reaction "We may have just witnessed firsthand a major historical event."

"Historical? Get real Sam. You can't give fanatics like that any more credence than they're worth."

"Yeah," Michelle said, "And plus, who wants to talk about a couple of self-harming masochists?"

"If they had a point-" Ricky paused for a moment, "Wait, they had a point, right? Did anybody pick up on what he said?"

"It isn't like a prelate at the Vatican leading some cardinals in a mutiny against the Pope or anything."

"Jesus... you're a tough room, you know that?" I said, a little more aggressively than I intended.

A low drone of conceited comments rumbled through the back of the otherwise silent room. I couldn't tell whether it was the alcohol or the event that made me snap, but the look on my face was clearly

The Call of the Void

beginning to provoke them. Cheryl, silently stating her misgivings, promptly lifted herself from my embrace.

"I'm... sorry guys. I've had a little too much to drink. I think I'm gonna head home. I'll catch you on Monday."

Outside the commune, a man in a long, black trench coat, smoking a cigarette, leaned his right elbow against a nearby bus bench. The smoke curled and flattened against the frigid November air. When the bus arrived, it screeched to a halt, letting out a young man with long blond hair which was pressed against his shoulders through his white, backward, snapback hat. A long stalk of grass protruded out of his mouth. He tongued it around, moving it from one corner of his mouth to the other. He reached down and grabbed his suitcase, rattled by the LA skyline. The man in the trench coat accosted him for a bit before the kid moved on down the street with his luggage and out of view.

The outside of the Recusants' bivouac was like skid row, if a cokehead from a country bar gave it a renovation. On a nearby wall, black graffiti censured a previously graffitied phrase, leaving only, 'Fo-Im- Mu-' visible. There was a broken cow skull askew over the entrance and underneath it was a writ with the phrase from their broadcast, *igne natura renovatur integra*. At first, the sound of deep, guttural guitar strums from Lamb of God's 'Walk with me in Hell' vaulting from over the walls of the commune threw me for a loop and I figured I was in the wrong place. But before I could turn around, a

81

conflagration fulminated from the center of the camp and was visible from over the wall of the commune. A great fire with no end reached up to lick the moon as wild cheers of approval danced their way across the night's sky. But when I saw the Recusants wandering about, drinking coffee and flagellating themselves with self-made cat o' nine tails, I knew I was where I needed to be.

The Recusants came from nothing. There was no election they wished to dispute nor any particular principle that vexed them beyond reasonable dialogue. They were simply born out of the primordial, organic matter that is American madness. As demonstrated at Jim Bakker's snake oil sale, they had become famous for flagellating themselves. They forced their way into Amazon warehouses, Town Halls, and porno shoots to preach their word. Their *word*, in truth, was nothing more than longueurs and exegeses of the original Gnostic bible. Some theologians at the start of that summer six months ago had done an investigative report and found them reading, studying and living by its passages day in and out. It's anyone's guess how they got their hands on a real one as most theological professors would give their left testicle to get it. All the same, they convinced the masses that they were preaching the true 'Word of God' and no one of 'vice' was spared the ever-looming rod of 'justice' served up by the Recusants.

They were pariahs according to society, heretics according to the church, and outlaws according to the state. Literally. For the first time since the 19th century, council members from around the US—within their respective provinces—deemed it appropriate to outlaw the

The Call of the Void

Recusants. And though it was more of a 'look the other way' policy without any legal recourse, the country lovingly embraced it.

But even after all of that, they never harmed a single person. There was an attempt by several media syndicates to frame them live on air, but one of the police officers exposed it during the live broadcast, deciding instead to join the Recusants. After that failed, the news took the Recusants' demographics into consideration, castigating them for their 'intersectionality blindness'. Though they were mostly white, it came to light, after an official, media sponsored census, that each race within the Recusant was the same percentage of that demographic living in America. And so, as the news so often does, as if searching for their next boogeyman, they persisted, labeling them nightly as 'Christian Caliphates of the Urban Land' and even going so far as to bring back most of the cast of 7th Heaven to make an after school special surrounding the Recusants and their dangerous principles. The show was panned and did more for the Recusants' cause than anything else the Recusants ever could have done after it aired Simon killing Happy the Dog in Recusant garb. It was a massive blunder that everyone forgot the next day.

Over the last few months since their inception, I pondered the reason for the hatred aimed at the Recusants. It was possible that they were right and, as they put it, America had become moonstruck from decades of decadence. Maybe people didn't like looking in the mirror, reflecting on their own shortcomings and turpitude. It was also possible that, as the news media put it, the Recusants were lunatics. And while each embroiled themselves in the contretemps of the century, pointing fingers and playing the chicken and the egg guessing game, the rest of the country found their lifestyle unacceptable.

The communes had their own system of food, water, and necessities. But they were ascetics, renouncing every earthly vice that society had conditioned the human mind to need. If a proselyte in the Recusants' order brought any food that was processed, wrapped, savory, or otherwise to the camps, they would be given lashes innumerable until they passed out. Many of the communes within the United States had perished under the yoke of starvation and pestilence.

Still, despite their hardships, the tented bivouacs, built on land that was purchased from the pockets of new members, popped up quite regularly on a national and international scale. Their monasteries were *unofficially* branded terrorist organizations, and it wasn't unheard of to find ATF posted outside of their tented cities. If the Recusants weren't so educated on constitutional law with a few Recusant lawyers in their corner, they might not have gathered so successfully.

I made my way to the center of their camp in the outskirts of LA, listening to Randy Blythe's guttural voice as the song switched to 'Now You've Got Something to Die For'. Each Recusant walked around with purpose, never resting their stern gaze, most wearing a long, leather fustanella that reached below their knees while others wore a plaid kilt, stopping briefly to acknowledge any passing brother or sister and mumble something of death and dreams. Death, and dreams.

Severely infected scratch marks covered their sternum and, when the front of their corporal canvas was no longer fresh, they would switch sections and crack makeshift whips across their backs. Steam and smoke arose from the faces of each of the outcasts as they sensed an outsider in their midst. I lowered my head in an effort to avoid eye contact, hoping the screams of self-mutilation flooding the night's air might be enough of a distraction.

I lit a cigarette and made my way closer to the middle of camp. As the steps got longer, my puffs of air grew larger. A delirium had consumed me, and I felt that old familiar scratch in the back of my head yelling at me, 'You don't belong'.

Noticing more and more heads turning in my direction, I picked up the pace, walking faster and faster before finally tripping over a log bench by a bonfire.

A voice spoke. "You're not one of us."

I leaned with one elbow in the dirt and a cigarette miraculously still in my mouth, shaking my head. The man looked down at me, but the dust from the fall darkened his face.

"Why have you come then?"

The embers of my cigarette lit up as I exhaled through my nose, giving an ambivalent shrug in response.

"Do you wish to become a Recusant?"

I picked myself up and stretched my neck at every angle. One of the Recusants, a tall, shirtless, brooding man with vermillion warpaint on his face and a leather fustanella, looked at me before turning to the man on the log bench.

"Why fear death, when I die in my dreams every night?" he asked, to no one in particular.

LeResche

The man on the bench nodded, acknowledging his statement with a faint smile. In an instant, an array of Recusants surrounding the fire echoed the phrase simultaneously. "Why fear death, when I die in my dreams every night?"

The man on the log bench raised his hands in the air, graciously accepting their apparent shibboleth. I got to one knee, tilting my head at the man sitting closest to me in an effort to get him to move down. He snorted before reluctantly sliding down the log. I took a seat and inhaled once more while focusing on the man speaking. As I exhaled, I recognized the face of the speaker as Konrad Vergilius, formerly Richard Maighdean, the leader of the Recusant that had hacked the microphone at AT&T Stadium and started the schism. His hair was stylish, cut with a low fade on the sides and back, his bangs long and straight, parted mostly to the side, and partially covering his eyes. It was the missing portion of his scalp that gave him away. The news had done an 'exclusive' on Konrad. After a night of dreadful flagellation, he had taken a few inches off his scalp, from the front corner of his hairline to the back, making a prominent part for his hair down the side of his scalp. His smile, faint and stoic, like the victor gladiator at the coliseum, never faded in any of the pictures flashed on the news day and night.

"Ah," Konrad said, examining my face, "The professor." He leaned across his knees to stoke the campfire as that familiar smile slowly formed on his face. "The cognoscenti of consciousness. What brings you to our camp?"

The Call of the Void

"Out for a stroll, thought I'd take a shortcut." I said, hoping my levity might change their minds about wanting to pummel me, "Suppose I could ask you the same thing though. I figured you'd be heading a rally somewhere by now."

"Those with a stomach to lead, do so only in obsolescence. Anyone who desires the cheers of his fellow man has lost the meaning of all life entirely."

Hesitant, I nodded my head slightly in agreement. He spoke in a low tone, letting the sangfroid and susurration of his voice veneer his keen sagacity. The mass of Recusants surrounding us followed my every move, their heads turning to follow my hand as I grabbed my flask. Konrad was completely still. His apostles made a quick move toward me before he raised a hand faintly in objection. I took a deep pull of my whiskey while keeping Konrad and the man beside him in my peripherals. Smoke billowed outside of my vision from the cigarette, fusing with the smoke of the fire.

"So, we're speaking in aphorisms?" I said, capping my flask, "Okay. I'm fairly accustomed, so I'll try and keep up."

"Your accustoming is hardly of concern to us. I'll ask again; Why are you here?"

"I guess, well-" I stammered and took another drink, breathing deeply afterwards, "I guess I was trying to connect with my fellow man." Realizing that sounded superficial and utterly contrived, I shook my head. "Shit. I don't have an answer for you."

"Your fellow man? Do we look like men here? Are we not transcendent of what your so-called 'fellow man' is? Are we not the

87

linking chain to all things eternal? Are you not merely the mordant observer of something much larger than yourself?"

I scoffed before laughing. "Why don't you cut the shit?"

"Answer me, you wanton spirit."

I flared my nostrils and cracked my neck, trying to buy time and think of an answer. The faces of the Recusants grew weary of my presence. That much was clear. Only Konrad retained some semblance of solace.

"I came to see the historic schism from the Christian religion. I came to see those that would reject the modern Christian pathos and revert it back to some semblance of archaic Christian ethos. Basically, I came to see what all the fuss was about."

The scarred elder beside Konrad, gazing at me with a certain asperity, cracked his knuckles and stretched his fingers out, playing an invisible piano. He never smiled. And though I knew the Recusants were pacifists, I had no intention of being the one that changed their minds.

Konrad inhaled. "There is no Christian ethos here. There is no God to have an ethos for. There is only us left. If what you said previously is what you truly believe, then your ken is extremely limited."

I looked incisively from Konrad to his apostles. To my surprise, his words had not marred them. They all stood around me, crossing their arms and drawing blank expressions on their face, like prey surrounding a wounded animal.

"B-but aren't you all supposed to be-"

The Call of the Void

"You think that we're capricious. You think that, on a whim, we left the Christian faith to gain airtime for our 'little cause' and put on this bit of theater just to eventually set up a church here and monetize off of it. We are not here to be worshipped. *We* are here to correct the scope of human consciousness. *You* are the short sighted one."

Konrad leaned back to relax. He spoke with an almost labored breath and the inflection of his voice was that of a hardened and tortured monk speaking to his missionaries. Each word was decisive and yet came so easily to him as if his mind was clear of any subconscious pap that might slow him down.

"What did you mean there is no God left?" I asked.

"What God would allow his creation to slip so far into slave morality to become what we are today?"

"Th- That's all this is?" I said, a smirk growing on my face as I looked at each of the Recusants around the circle, "God is dead, and we killed him. Is that it? You're trying to supplant Christianity with some sort of Nietzschian revolution? Some sort of- Master morality?"

"Good for you," Konrad whispered condescendingly, his eyes raised haughtily, "I guess I shouldn't be surprised that a professor of philosophy has studied the concept."

"Extensively. I moved on from him years ago but he's still, what I believe to be, the father of Western 20th century philosophy. He-"

"Then you have wasted your years. Nietzsche is not the answer. Nietzsche is merely the sand that forms the brick. The only thing meritorious that Nietzsche proclaimed was that contemporary Christians were Apollonian fools, chasing an illusion of order, while the Dionysian, basking in their perverse revelry, supplanted the ethos of the world. The real Christian religion recognizes the abandonment, or at least the suicide, of God and his principles. The few followers still willing to recognize their *will* have miles to go. We will die benevolently and die without the promise of eternal salvation, and we will do it without haste. For any man who claims to know what happens after death is a fool or worse. To claim Heaven is an affront to logic. To claim oblivion is an affront to our consciousness. Communal ethics are not conditioned; they are inherent. And, with little time left, the human race has reached its self-imposed telos. God has already killed himself. The omnicide here on earth will inevitably come. We, as prophets, will live out our lives in accordance with this reality. Our message has been spoken. It's on the masses to recognize natural law or fade into obscurity."

I sat there bewildered as the ash on my cigarette had inched its way toward my middle finger. It became all too obvious that Konrad was either totally insane, completely inept, or divinely brilliant.

"That's... noble."

Years of critical thinking and that was the only response I could come up with.

"Nobility is the most distant of our pursuits, professor. We merely seek salvation."

I hated the way he called me professor. It dripped with a layer of contempt. The worst part was, I was beginning to believe it.

"You'll have a hard time finding it here." I said after some time.

Konrad flashed an eye of empathy at me. He clapped his hands lightly and rubbed them gently together, studying my face every so often.

"Will you join us?"

I couldn't help but laugh.

"Konrad, I will never join a monastery, a commune, a church or, hell, even a book club. I'll be honest though; your dogma has surprised me. I think you're the most intellectual, eminent, and yet lofty group I have ever come across. And I agree that humans have lost their souls. Their poetry. And I am on a bit of a penance trip tonight so-"

Konrad raised an open hand across the fire, interrupting my answer.

"Penance? Okay." Konrad sighed, cupping his hands over his nose, "Okay. I see now. You're not meant to be one of us. I see now. But something else maybe?"

He reached into his back pocket and held out an envelope. His eyes ran around the sky, landing finally on the moon. He nodded his head silently, almost tragically, having a private conversation with the stars. I grabbed the envelope and pulled out a ticket identical to the one Dr. Felix gave me.

"Thanks, but I already have one. It's where I'm going tonight."

He swatted the air with the back of his hand insistently as I handed it back. "I know you- I know. Just take it. It's yo-"

"No look, I-"

"Burn it. Scalp it. Use it as a backup. It's yours. You are *meant* to have it." Konrad's eyes inflamed, looking eagerly around the camp like I had just handed him the winning lottery numbers.

"Why?" I asked.

He turned to the man in vermillion warpaint, staring at him with wide eyes, indicating something unspoken between the two of them. When the man did finally whisper—something faint, along the lines of the 'Hyperreal', 'Thanatos', and 'Hypnos'—Konrad stared back down at me, a look of morbid fascination rippling across his face. After studying me for a moment, he stared back down at the ground, his chin resting on the palm of his closed fists. His aide looked on in anticipation before Konrad, with almost a shimmer of hesitation, nodded his head. Instantly, the crowd, detached from reality, their faces tumid with chaotic intent, grew larger around the fire. Before long, every Recusant from the camp had made their way around us. Konrad walked in between the middle of two nearby tents and climbed to the top of a scaffolding in the dark. A light shined down on him. The condensation from his breath grew larger, like streams of water gushing through a freshly breached hydrant. The camp went silent, frozen in place, waiting on Konrad. He lifted his head once more and without so much as a preamble, said, "Why fear death, when I die in my dreams every night?"

The commune echoed Konrad's words and swiftly ran from tent to tent, kissing their spouses and packing their bindles. Konrad moved back down toward the fire, taking his place right across from me.

The Call of the Void

I looked over at the tent Konrad had just left and saw a print of Matejko's "Stańczyk" hanging on the wall.

"I apologize for the cross examination earlier. I wasn't sure why you were here. I saw your diatribe on the television," Konrad's tone had become reserved, "I'm sorry. I really am. A teacher, in this day and age. A teacher that entered the profession at the cusp of the transition. Common sense, critical thinking, technology... And with all this technology and information readily available, ignorance is at an all-time high. Not mere stupidity mind you, but ignorance." Konrad was musing out loud, almost as if he had forgotten I was there. "And as you complained of parents cheating their kids, you failed to see that it wasn't them being 'cheated'. For, you see, poor parenting is far worse than negligence; it's hypnotism." Konrad watched me intently, trying to hide an excited smile on his face. "Lachesism. Ever heard of it? It's what makes us human. It isn't our 'life well lived' or our ability to find community, but rather our thirst for the unknown. Our subconscious desires are so foreign to us that we never realize they are rapping at our brain, begging us to do the unthinkable. And when we won't, it does so in pleasure. It eases and elevates our darkest desires into a more entertaining, more, shall we say, publicly acceptable form of release. But only through a forceful measure to turn our subconscious to conscious desires can we be free. To willfully put that bump in our own road of life. To worship Chaos and make one final orison to her."

I nodded my head. "You should be proud then. The world is chaotic enough."

It was about that time that I picked up on one of Konrad's ticks; he regularly lifted his head, twisted his tongue, and vised it between his back molars every time I pressed him. It was a subtle idiosyncrasy, but he did it so confidently, never stopping even after noticing that I noticed.

"So you would think. But here I am, still, the last messiah. And pray tell professor, who controls that chaos? To what end does the public's libertinage serve a purpose far more caustic than their own rakish impulses? Do you really believe the system would ever allow for a chaos to thrive that they could not contain? Waiting with that fictious, superficial chaos to break the masses down, piece by piece." The Recusants stormed around the camp, oblivious to Konrad or me. "You fear for the future. You fear nihilism and passivity. But what you fail to realize is that no matter how bad things get, no matter which direction the wind blows, there will always stand a small minority, ready to act out against injustice. Do you believe in justice Sam?" Red and blue lights passed through the commune as a siren went in and out of earshot. "You shouldn't. There is none."

"I see."

Something about Konrad's speech and the way he spoke, had turned my resolve from lead to gold. He raised his hand, his index finger extended out to something behind me in the distance. I turned my head and squinted my eyes to see the enormous YouTube billboard and a Recusant climbing on top of it. Clouds formed far off in the distance and a bolt of lightning pierced the distant sky, painting it white. The Recusant stared briefly at the night's sky; his mouth mumbling words under his breath before crossing his legs in a seated position.

"It is more than just chaos we worship and seek though, professor. Chaos is the anodyne of the current order. It will be filled with righteous loss, but the end game is anarchy. And not the contrived perception of anarchy laid out by fools and punks, painted with red 'A's and symbols of oppression, but true, venerable anarchy, that will free humans and release order, through chaos, into the world."

I turned back to Konrad. "What am I look-"

A forceful shockwave kicked my hair up and planted me in the ground next to the fire as warm air enveloped my entire body. My ears were ringing, and adrenaline was pumping double time into my veins. I threw my head back to look at Konrad. His face was a mysterious composite of grief and mirth. I looked once more to the billboard as black smoke, darker than the night sky, ballooned above the decimated advertisement. The only remaining remnant of the billboard was the mother's face, charred and barely visible.

As I struggled to get to my feet, my ears still ringing faintly from the blast, Konrad grabbed me by the elbow and helped me up. He stood next to me for a moment watching the exodus of Recusants from the camp. In the distant sky, a barely audible sound of musical beats became increasingly louder. The ringing in my ears died down and was replaced by the familiar sound of the Eurythmics's 'Sweet Dreams' being played from the heavens. I could tell from Konrad's smile that my shell shock was profound.

"Do you hear that?" Konrad asked, a smile faintly accreting on his face.

I cleaned both of my ears out with my pinky. The song was now sonorous, blaring like a live concert from the stars. Konrad pointed to a blur in the sky, slowly moving downward and closer to us. It was a helicopter with a green or possibly black tint and an enormous speaker and camera underneath it.

"They're smoking us out," he remarked, smiling glibly at the obliterated billboard, "They're a little late though..."

Konrad leaned his shoulders back at the black helicopter with an absurd confidence that only comes from years of psychosis. He rocked back on his heels, his slender frame reflecting light off the nearby streetlamp as he separated his index and middle finger, placing them in front of his eyes before pointing his index finger at the helicopter defiantly. And as the helicopter passed its camera just over Konrad's camp, he mouthed the words, 'You're. Too. Late.'

Looking at the helicopter, I moved past Konrad toward the exit, a small metal burrow in the fence with the inscription 'Abandon All Hope Ye Who Enter Here' above it.

"Oh professor," Konrad shouted.

I turned to look at him, the same smile formed on his face he had had before the camera at the stadium cut him off.

"Don't trust your vision. Trust your mind."

III

Man is a completely different beast when the sun finally surrenders itself to the skyline in the West. Of course, down on Alameda, the lines between rape, fantasy, and lust have always been a little abstruse. Alameda; the pantheon of prostitution. Ask any local and they'll say that Los Angeles's Red-Light District is located on Figueroa Street. But the locals also have a stale expression they're fond of saying, '*Although Figueroa is a serviceable location for your afternoon delight, Alameda is where we go for our lady of the night.*'

I paced back and forth along the sidewalk nervously, lighting a new cigarette with the embers of my old one, praying that a meteor might hit the city and I'd be relieved of duty. But nothing was ever that easy. What I wouldn't give to lecture a bunch of students staring down at their phones once more. I took one look back at the smoking billboard, its massive borders still in flames, giving the fire department a run for their money, before heading toward the interstate.

The snowcapped San Miguel Mountain range rested above the city's horizon. The moon, preternatural in size and playing tricks on my mind, had revealed itself innocently over the mountain range. I darted my head back to the West, hoping to catch a glimpse of the dying sunlight, but it was too late. Night had finally swallowed the sky. I exhaled, lamenting the voyage and what it might bring, noticing how the sky was turning a light cardinal red near the Santa Monica

Mountains. Plagued with fire and smoke, the mountainside on the outskirts of town were unseasonably luminous with the radiance of fire trucks, their courtesy lights forming an assembly line of incarnadine illumination far off in the distance.

I began to have serious misgivings about this whole exposition. A checkered bench right next to me was pocked with yellow, mustard-like paint and slapdash graffiti. The only coherent statement written on the bench was in black marker and read, "S1cK FUcK".

"Gotta light?" a voice yawned.

"Jesus!" I yelled, jumping backwards, oblivious to the woman behind me, "Uh, yeah, here."

She was black and, based on her attire, an easy ringer for a prostitute. When I didn't add anything to the conversation, she cocked her hip to the right and snarled impatiently. She wore jean shorts that would be considered underwear on any other street. Not to mention, her acrylic nails were about 6 inches too long, curling at the tips and wobbling each time she moved her hands. Her hair had a tinge of blonde streaked through the part that looked more zany than exotic. Through my cigarette's flame, her eyes locked on to mine, studying my face as I lit her cigarette, and she moved her right hand under her hair to push it to the other side of her face. Her right lip curled with a grimace. Apparently, I threw off a 'fresh meat' kind of vibe.

"What chu doin' here white boy?"

"Just walking. Wanted to check the area out." I gave a cool shoulder shrug as if this was normal for me.

The Call of the Void

"Well damn. What'chu wanna see den?"

I laughed lightly, placing my hand on the nearby streetlamp, and shrugged again. "Anything. Everything. Hell, I don't know."

"You wanna date? I'm automatic right now til my mack get back. Bitch ass nigga was a gorilla. I'd give you the discount on account. Shit, I figure I'll just be out of pocket."

I stood in place, nodding like an idiot to buy time and attempt to decipher what she had said. "Sounds tempting but I'd rather you just point me in the right direction of anything I can enjoy, uh, 'communally'."

"Com you nuh- what?!" she squawked obstreperously.

"Yeah, you know, like, with other peop- uh, never mind."

She eyeballed me up and down for a moment, exhaling out of the corner of her mouth, a look of resentment slowly forming on her face. "You a cop?"

"No. I just-"

"Last nigga that came around here traipsing like some educated fool gonna remember the time I told on 'em. Feel me?"

I looked at her like a tourist from Thailand walking around Mexico reading a German to English dictionary. "Look, I just want you to point me toward the action."

"Action? What'chu want? Vegas Circuit? Kiddie Stroll? This the main track right now so you gotta take it as it is."

I shrugged again, hoping to seem polite. "Look I'll... just make my own way."

"Good luck. Pasty ass bitch."

99

LeResche

"Yeah, thanks." I scowled from over my shoulder.

Escorts seemed to stay in cohorts of three, keeping a distance of about fifty feet from any other courtesan unit. I walked further down the road, lowering my head each time I passed a trio of observant call girls, their heads bobbing around aimlessly before locking on to me and chasing me a few feet while I ducked out of range, as if I were a lone gazelle that had strayed from the herd.

Alameda's panoply of prostitutes was interesting to say the least. All colors. All sizes. All kinks. Some of them could even pass as normal housewives trying their hand at streetwalking for the night. But, then again, what was 'normal' nowadays? In any given area in LA, the demographic changed. On Alameda, for example, 60% of the prostitutes were African American. About half of those had blonde hair. And it seemed every Caucasian and Hispanic girl took on the vernacular of the African American female. Locals grew tired of the day to day and wanted a change. Tacitly, they desired their women to change into something they were not.

The streets were a Renaissance painting made for the modern age. The mountains were its backdrop, blanketed in snow, sheltered away from the city. Rows of prostitutes smoking and drinking in the foreground amongst wrought iron fences and graffitied buildings with human silhouettes staring motionless out their windows. A homeless man twirled a liquor bottle in his hand, staring off with dead, black eyes. I took in the beauty of the city's juxtaposition, capturing it to store in my memory, an oneiric manifestation that slowed time, to recall on later that evening. To find some beauty in the night.

And then, like a stampede of mustangs fighting for the exit of a corral, an exodus of men, sundry in vestiary, class, and race, got out of their sedans and onto the sidewalk as movement resumed. I tried, desperately, to analyze the situation but a discordant cacophony drowned out all my thoughts.

Hey. Hey! You do bareback?

Are you the police? Grab my penis?

Are there- are there many girls that look as young as you do? How young can you go?

How much Taco Bell can you eat?

I've never done this before.

I've done this a hundred times before.

And just like a Sadie Hawkins dance, each escort had grabbed a man by the hand, driving away or humping themselves into the nearest motel, and my one chance to capture something beautiful had fled as hastily as it had arrived. A formidable reminder of the night to come.

The street was radiant with the glow of temptation, filled with neon lights flashing the *Best Deals* LA had to offer. Sandwiched between a smoke shop and an abandoned auto title loan outlet, there was an adult arcade off Alameda and Washington. The sign out front read 'G-Spot'. Its mascot, a personified house with bloodshot eyes, pointed toward the sky along its Western wall. It was uninspired but worth a shot. The decaying exterior, adorned with fading, verdigris bars welded against its windows, an inferior paint job, and a gaggle of patrons leaving more dazed than they entered, had potential.

Outside, near the side exit, there was a kid that couldn't have been more than sixteen standing crooked near a black Escalade. He looked like a young, skinny Vanilla Ice and wore baggy jeans—reminiscent of those JNCO jeans from the 90s—with a backwards Dodgers cap. His sunken eyes and gray T-shirt, pressed firmly against his emaciated torso, suggested he had not eaten properly in years. Each inhale from his cigarette was as arduous a labor for him as lifting 300 pounds. And yet, there was something suave and savvy about his disposition. Some trenchant urban mystique rested in his eyes as he scanned Alameda up and down, flipping the sides of his zippered hoodie. His eyes lit up immediately upon seeing me and I tried to wave him off.

"Not interested."

He ignored me at first, scanning the street instead, still obviously on cop watch. "Nah. Nah, nah. I ain't about that. What're you up to tonight, boss?"

I shot back a raised, indignant eyebrow, hoping it might scare the little creep off. "Just wandering."

"Yo, why don't you wander into Heaven then my man." He spoke slowly and with composure, his voice dripping with a stylish serenity. "I got some candy right here in the lot. If you ain't bout that action, then I got some tapes too, Jack."

"Action? Candy? Tapes?"

"Look, I ain't trying to talk too long." He slinked himself close to me and brought his voice down to a nearly imperceptible whisper. "You like Lolas? You like Lolita my man?"

"No, I don't." I said, surmising what he meant as I anxiously bit my tongue.

"My dude, listen up, this the real deal. She ain't gon say shit."

"Why not?"

He coughed a little as he tried to laugh. "Let's just say I'm familiar with her in a," he paused to think while his eye rolled around in the back of his head, "familial sense."

I cocked my head to the left, confusion belaying my disgust. "What?"

"Her friend is with her. Let's just leave it at that, alright?"

He laughed once more and I nearly dry heaved. His shrill cackle was baleful, an imprecation that pierced the membrane of my sanity. My eyes, inculpating him with merely a glance, must have been more charged with agitation than I realized. It was obvious that, after a few moments of silence, his insecurity had been provoked.

"What'chu say my man?" he said, clearing his throat nervously, "Get you 20 twenty minutes for 100 bucks with both dem?"

My eyes strained from the kid to his Escalade with the two promiscuously dressed, teenage girls blowing kisses at everyone that walked by. The one in the driver's seat was blonde, her hair tied in a ponytail, with a pink latex bandeau squeezed around her chest. Her friend, in the seat directly behind her, had tied her hair into waterfall braids, letting the braids fall over the shoulder of her sequin, crisscross top. The kid got a little closer, eyeballing me and then the merchandise, an unctuous simper forming on his lips. He finally grabbed my shoulder, each finger falling over my flannel lightly.

What was I doing here? And what was the point? Keeping my job? It hadn't even been an hour. And it was then and there that the voice in the back of my head, urged on by the flourishing memory of Felix's adjuration, was finally scraped free from the raking of that claw that tormented me for so long. The voice whispered something to the effect of *"Don't lose yourself"*, but I finally let it go and shame had evaporated like the dying light of the sun in LA.

I ripped my shoulder from the kid's embrace and considered grabbing him by the collar. But without the voice—its modest yet poignant words of sagacity my only compass—I felt powerless. My face wilted into a pathetic, confused glower as I walked toward the arcade.

The sign above the adult arcade's entrance read 'OPEN' in enormous neon letters. All the outer windows were sprayed off with black paint, presumably hiding the vices of its inner walls from the public. Still, there was a sense of lurid, moral derailment that came with boxing yourself off from the world.

Inside, a bell rang above my head. Past a few fancy dildos, buttplugs, sexdolls and 'mysterious' lubricants, was the foyer. I walked over to it and stood next to the cash register. The place wasn't too special. There was, however, an arcade entrance toward the back of the shop, and I pointed to it to let the cashier know I wanted to go in. He raised his left cheek from his palm, knitting his brows and souring his face as he did so, and pointed to a booth across the room that read '411' above it. I mimicked his scowl, twisting my face into an especially animated frown, before walking over to the booth.

The bell above the entrance rang once more as a group of boys pushed past me and ran to the back of the information line. They shouted "Vincent's 18th Birthday! Vincent's 18th Birthday!" as they crowded around a thin, bashfully smiling boy with a sweatshirt two sizes too large. I walked up behind them to wait in line, noticing a crassly drawn penis graffitied on the wall that had the line 'Now spit on it' written underneath it. The man in the front was handed a DVD and a golden token as he walked into the arcade. The next man in line, before the teenage party bus, was faintly within earshot.

"Uh, okay first," the man said, looking off into the space above the clerk's head as if he were ordering at a fast-food joint, "I need real life women, MILFs preferably, that look like the moms you see in, like, Pixar movies. You know, like, really big hipped-"

The clerk at the booth held up a hand, cutting him off. He began to search through his rolodex like it was some pornographer's Dewey Decimal system. He stopped on 'M', moving a finger up and down the card before scratching his head exhaustively. He swung around in his chair and pulled a DVD from the cabinet.

"Next?" the clerk said absently, staring down at the counter.

"Right, uh, next I need one from a POV, where the girl s-says that my parents love me, and uhm, I'm a respected member of society, or something like that."

LeResche

The clerk spun the rolodex to 'V' for validation before grabbing another DVD from the case and handing it to the customer. The clerk's name, indicated on the tag secured to his lapel, was Silas. Lacking the bonhomie to look any of the customers directly in the eyes, he sat in his chair dutifully and waved each patron along with jaded sighs. Any zest for his job had faded long ago, suffocated from years of categorizing porn for teenage boys and lost souls. His eyes followed the lips of the customers, barely cognizant of anything other than the coffee mug he routinely sipped from that read, 'There's probably beer in here'.

"Finally, I'll need um, nothing too fancy, um, let's see, one where the mistress is caught by the wife and the mistress pulls a gun, or whatever—pulls something out—and forces the husband to finish while threatening the wife, but makes the husband cum on the wife."

"Jesus, whatever happened to good old money shot compilations, right lads?" I whispered jokingly to the boys in front of me. Their laughter halted abruptly as each one of them stared at me with blank expressions before turning around and resuming their conversation.

The party crowd was up next, and the birthday boy cleared his throat before speaking in a demure tone. "Um, I, uh, I don't know."

His friend cut in for him almost immediately. "Bug chasing," he said, holding back a laugh, "Yeah, REAL bug chasing. Not the shit where some meth head fakes it."

"*Bug chasing?*" I mouthed wordlessly with a wry face.

The Call of the Void

The clerk pumped his hand in quick, stolid motions before reaching into the cabinet for a DVD. It was then, in that shop off Alameda, that I began to realize there are far deeper parts of the internet and human mind than have ever been explored at the Killian household. I tapped my foot lightly on the floor, dithered and a little impatient about what was in the arcade room, as the muzak playing from the speakers above cut out, amplifying a sultry female voice, "More than your average porn. Comfortable and discreet arcade rooms. All here, at G-Spot." The muzak resumed.

"Oh, and we're not gay or anything, they just don't believe me about it being real."

"Skin is skin kid," Silas, the clerk, said, "Don't have to explain nothing to me."

"Oh, and uh, one of those videos where they take the face of some kid—a girl!—from someone's Facebook page and deep fake it onto a petite actress's face."

The clerk looked the boys up and down, sucking in breath through his teeth, before spinning through his rolodex and handing them the video and two tokens. Laughing and jabbing Vincent in the ribs, the boys gamboled their way to the entrance of the arcade. Vincent stopped short of the curtains, his face dark with reticence, as his friends shook their heads and attempted to cajole him through.

Silas looked at the boys with little intrigue before looking back at me. "What'll it-"

"Whatever's popular," I said.

"Um, okay. Men, women...?"

107

"Women," I said with a short laugh, wiping my face down with my hand.

Silas analyzed my face as his hands made a steeple over his mouth. His right eyebrow cocked upward, like he was about to tell me he knew me. Instead, he rolled back, grabbing a DVD and placing it alongside a token in my hand.

After a few obscenities about his manhood were volleyed back and forth, the birthday crew had finally persuaded Vincent to move through and I followed close behind. I pushed the curtain to the side and was hit with a blast from the A/C that blew my hair back and my eyes closed, carrying with it an acrid mélange of cum, shit and lubricant. The hallway was lined with rows of red doors. Up ahead, I could hear Vincent whispering in a shaky voice, 'I don't know. This isn't like I thought. Let's just fucking go.' I waded through the maze of sticky, cum-covered floors and darkness, my shoes making a loud smack with each step off the floor, requiring more strength with each step to free them from the floor's morass of ejaculate. Vincent's two friends went into a stall together with the deep fake porn, leaving Vincent behind. He walked to the stall beside them before looking up at me. He raised his token with a timid smile, motioning with it as if to ask me if he were doing it right. I clinked my token against his, as if I were giving him a 'cheers' at a bar and went into the empty stall next to him. There was an 18-inch color television set from decades ago flicking through pornos at random. It was set up on a 2x4 with a lawn chair in front of it. I sat and pushed the token and DVD through their respective slots, praying that they might have hand sanitizer out front.

After the FBI pirating rights screen flashed for half a minute, the movie started. Its intro broadcasted a myriad of actresses performing aggressive fellatio and having anal sex for a full minute before cutting to the first scene. A woman in long, open toed stiletto heels waltzed toward the camera, her staggered walk more like Bambi than a runway model. I rocked from side to side in the chair, trying to free its legs from the viscid floor, but it was fused in place.

It was dark. So dark. The lights from the surrounding TVs refracted off the walls, giving some semblance of effulgence, but the room was a crypt. And the longer I stared at the screen, the more endless the arcade seemed. I began to feel as though I had entered a tomb, an infinite traverse through carnal catacombs.

I lost myself for a moment. The walls seemed malleable, almost as if made of putty, expanding and contracting with each breath, forming a sensual sepulcher.

A grim manifold of moans and voices echoed all around the surrounding booths, making it unclear whether they were from the movies or the patrons in the surrounding corridors.

Got Damn boys! It smells like a French Cathouse in here!

I wish I had a vagina.

What's this actress's name?

She'll probably go home and kiss Daddy with that mouth.

After a while, the comments outside became white noise.

Back on screen, the actress was rimming the actor while he told her she was a 'dirty whore'. A conversation ensued between them mid-coitus.

"My boyfriend would be sooo emasculated by this."

The actor, in the midst of another rim job, pulled the actress's phone out and began filming her, stroking his erection in the process. He pressed a button on the phone, showing her that he sent the video to her boyfriend, telling her he's hopeful the boyfriend will come over so that he could do it in front of him. He began pumping aggressively, showing a ruddy, vainglorious face to the camera, as the veins in his neck throbbed forcefully through his skin.

"He won't like that" she said, her face smashed under his foot as he took her from behind.

"Baby," the actor on screen said, breathing heavily through his teeth, "If he dares show his face here, I'll fuck him too."

The screen faded to black and cut to the next scene with a doughy, witless man in a polo shirt, making stupefied expressions through the window of their condo. He barged in to confront the couple as the masculine actor's once pale skin turned a tint of red once more from his virile pumping. He dismounted the actress and immediately initiated intercourse with the dazed boyfriend.

"Alright," I sighed in the empty booth, ejecting the DVD, "that's enough porn for one night."

Vincent's friends cackled two rooms down and I heard the door open to the stall next to me. Odd. Maybe Vincent didn't have an appetite for bug chasing after all. I leaned a little out of my seat to eavesdrop.

"Hey." A husky voice whispered.

"Hey." Vincent said with a tremor in his voice.

Silence ensued for a moment or two as curiosity got the better of me. I stood on the lawn chair to investigate the stall. Vincent was shaking in his seat. His eyes flashed from the man to the screen with a close up of a male rectum being penetrated by a mechanical bristle brush. Vincent mumbled a prayer under his breath. Behind him, a middle-aged man with glasses rubbed his genitals. The bottom of his paunch hung under his wife-beater and past his piss-stained sweatpants. Vincent turned his head as slow as he could, meeting the guy's junk with his eyes, before jerking his face back toward the screen.

"Y-you li-like this?" Vincent stammered, pointing a shaky finger to the screen as if to make small talk, barely able to form words.

For a while, and what seemed like hours, the man didn't respond. He stood in the doorway and stared at Vincent, his glasses fogging slightly with each labored, throaty breath, shrouding his pale gray eyes behind a veil of malignancy. He finally spoke up and answered, "No.", before lunging at Vincent, who was still seated in his chair.

Vincent yelled to no one in particular, floundering out of his seat as he did so. He pleaded with the man "I'm not a faggot", at which point the man pressed harder and yelled "Not yet". Vincent, his voice rising to an almost unbearably infantile scream, howled out to his friends. At that time, other heads from around the booth peered over to observe what was happening. His friends poked their heads above the partition, standing like me on their lawn chairs, and watched in fear.

"Hey man!" one friend pleaded nervously "H-he doesn't want that!"

The man laughed at their pleas, attempting to undo Vincent's pants in the process.

"Yeah man." a nervous, yet faintly courageous voice yelled "Please stop!"

Vincent cried as the man struggled with his pants. "Please. It's my birthday."

The man stopped, looking almost human for a moment, as he held down both of Vincent's arms. "Happy Birthday?" he said dismissively before continuing, "Did I hear consent? He consented!" the man yelled to the arcade and no one in particular, "You all are witnesses. This is a fantasy!" Then, he put his mouth next to Vincent's ear and whispered faintly, "Now, bear witness you little bitch."

"N-no!" Vincent screeched, a dire plea for help tearing through his voice box.

The door to the stall opened with a crash. A taller, more athletically built man stood at the entrance.

"Oh, thank God." Vincent's friends gasped in harmony.

"Ahhhhh shit! Fred!" The athletic man announced, shaking a can of poppers and thrusting it to Vincent's nostrils, "You actually taking one tonight? I got next."

The Call of the Void

The two eighteen-year-olds whimpered, 'Please, no' but did nothing else. They watched with embittered faces, behind trembling hands that peered out every so often, hoping that that might be enough and that some higher power would swoop down and stop what they could surely not witness any longer.

I kept an eye on the young man's friends as they shook their heads in defeat and ducked out of view as if there was nothing more they could do. I took one more look down as they surrounded the boy, Vincent's face slowly decaying from fear to vacancy.

At the time, sliding back down the wall and out of sight, I thought about Felix, about not getting involved. Surely this wasn't the extent of it. A career wasn't worth *this*. But the kid was 18. He should've known better. Should've had better friends. Shouldn't have been in a place like this.

Was I just making excuses? All it would take was one shout from me to stop the madness. But I could feel it, the swoon of nihilism's intoxication. At first, my body—possibly my mind as well—fought the urge. But before long, whispering bittersweet rhapsodies of passivity into my ear, the indifference made its case.

My skin crawled with the shivers of nihilistic futility. Where was the sincerity left in the world? In myself? Think like the fatalistic cynic. Just let it happen, as it does every day in the world. Be Cassandra and embrace the calamitous fate that waits against the borders of the city. I'm not sure if there is such a thing as kismet, but if there is, I definitely got what's coming to me.

Odium generis humani. Odium generis humani. I recited to myself quietly, like a mantra to restore my resolve.

Moving myself back down the wall, I sat, hands crossed, in the lawn chair, watching some more of the video on the little television in front of me, my reflection barely visible in the screen—an unnerving, distant outline of despair—as my stomach turned with each satisfied, rhythmic grunt from the booth next door. I felt the pangs of regret—the last remnant of my humanity—churning rapidly in my stomach. Before long, I was doubled over and retching all around the video booth. After a little while, when I had gotten up, the screen read "Insert token to continue".

I closed my eyes and breathed deeply through my nose, before taking off my shoe and going back over the top of the partition.

"Get the fuck off him you sick fuck!" I screamed, throwing my shoe at the fat man's head as he was sliding his pants off, before turning my attention to the other guy, "Beat it."

The men stared up at me for a moment with bemused expressions before smiling, revealing a mouthful of brown teeth, and walking out of the booth.

Vincent looked up at me, his eyes drowning in a pool of tears, a sigh of gratitude slipping from his mouth. I looked around the room, desperate not to make eye contact with the kid, and nodded passively, before curling my fingers to indicate my shoe.

Happy Birthday. I thought as Vincent raised my shoe up to my grasp. *You get to keep your innocence for one more day.*

The Call of the Void

As I walked through the curtain of the arcade, a great darkness surrounded me. All of the lights in the establishment had gone out, and I found myself walking through an uncertain oblivion. The thought crossed my mind that the two assailants were waiting in the shop, somewhere between the arcade and the thirty or so feet to the exit. My throat went dry, and I froze in place, but an emerging light caught my eye near the bell above the exit. In bright pink neon, scrawled in some sort of effulgent marker, were the words, '*Strike 1*'.

Outside, Vincent's friends were walking around aimlessly, puffing on their vapes. Shook up with hollow eyes, the boys talked about the weather, and 'how crazy it was in there'. I leaned against the wall opposite the entrance and lit up a smoke before a terrible wind blew all about, sending a subzero chill through the air. Vincent's friends looked at me for a moment with guilty eyes, kicking the ground at their feet and continuing to whistle, before looking back at me once more with an acidulous glare that suggested *I* didn't do anything in there either. Doubtless, Vincent would never tell them the truth. Turning the voice off in my head was tough. But it was getting easier.

The door opened and a silhouette appeared in the entrance, masked by the surrounding twilight. The boy, whose 18th birthday had become more of an affair than he had wished, stared at the ground as he limped toward his friends, his eyes catatonic and devoid of anything that once made him human. Making certain to evade his friends' eyes, Vincent rubbed his shoulder nervously. "Let's just forget it." He said, the tremor in his voice no longer there.

LeResche

He walked down the road as his assailants laughed and taunted the young man from a nearby Taxi while his friends quietly consoled him and patted his back. Vincent ripped his arm away from one friend. The wind nearly blew out the ember of my cigarette and the two men stared into my eyes, heckling, "You enjoy the show?" as I walked down the street.

The stars above LA had become extinguished under the city's omnipresent lights, forcing the will of the city onto the once starry sky above. Those sidereal, interstellar idols of nightfall, eternal and incandescent, fought the moon and the city lights for the locus of the sky, but lost and, for this one night, even the North Star was nowhere to be seen. The city was little more than a concrete tyrant, raging against the presence of nature, caring only for itself, forming the bowels of an iconoclastic land, meriting little more than corruption of spirit and soul for the price of glamour. And as the world was filled with the embers of its malevolence, the city thundered with fire, fed with the kindling of the spiritus mundi.

I walked the remaining sidewalk of Alameda, passing a gas station and more than a few project houses set up as makeshift brothels. A coterie of prostitutes under illuminating streetlights followed me with their eyes. Each one became increasingly suspect of my presence there, watching intently with narrowed eyes as I feigned a smile, waved awkwardly, and made my way closer to the I-10.

The Call of the Void

""Hellloooo tall, dark and handsome." A sultry, jocular voice said with a wolf-whistle, "You gotta light?"

I stopped on my right foot, pulling out my lighter without looking, and walked toward the voice that was blanketed in a sheet of shadows beyond the sidewalk.

"Thanks man." The voice said sotto voce, emerging from the darkness as a pale call girl, wearing a little green sash around her otherwise scandalous outfit, "Haven't lit up in about an hour."

"No problem." I said, leaning toward her with my lighted zippo, "Seems like no one has a light around here."

She laughed. "Yeah."

As far as prostitutes go, she was the most well-kept I had seen that night. She was young and seemed to be well-spoken, considering her lack of the occupation's choppy vernacular.

"How old are you?" I asked.

She glanced at me with the eyes of a superior looking down at their lackey who had just asked an asinine question. "I'm as old as you want me to be." She laughed again, composing herself more seriously this time, "That's what I'm supposed to say, right?"

"I'm not looking. Got my fill at the G-Spot."

"Clearly." She said with a hint of curiosity, exhaling smoke out of the corner of her mouth, "You look pretty shook up. I'm 20, by the way. So, what're you doing here?"

"Walking. Trying to get to the Convention Center."

"Ya know, they made cabs for just such an occasion."

"Right," I laughed, shrugging a little, "Just like to walk I guess."

"You like to walk?" Her right eyebrow shot to the top of her forehead as she pivoted her weight to her left hip. "Well, you picked a terrible place to do it."

"Apparently so. I was trying to pass the time so it wouldn't be one, long boring walk."

"I have a few things we can do." She shimmied backwards, making a cheeky dance out of her saunter.

"You don't look like a typical prostitute. No offense..."

"You don't look like the typical clientele." She pursed her lips and moved her eyes from my sneakers to my head. She inhaled her cigarette, holding it tightly with her index and middle finger while moving closer to my face as I lit another one for myself. "No offense."

"None taken. I think..."

She laughed again, this time turning off her sultry voice for one more practical, more genuine. "I'm over at LACC."

"Community College. Nice." I said, nodding my head in honest praise, "No job openings at the bookstore on campus? Target is at capacity?"

"I'm not going to dignify that with a response." She said, trying to laugh, obviously holding back a chord of shame. Her eyes shot to the ground, and she tapped her foot testily. "Now! If you want to know why I chose this over stripping, it's because I'm less likely to run into people from my class down here. There's about the same number of drugs but there's way less exposure. Of course, fucking hairy, middle-aged, middle-class beer bellied men is none too fun. And I can't do porn. Once again, too much exposure. Plus, I'd like to get married one day." Her gaze left mine momentarily as she gave a curt laugh, as if the thought alone was absurd. "I'd like to think that I can put all this in the past. A little difficult when your 'sexcapades' are all over the internet." She gave a resigned sigh. "Sex is eternal. There's no getting around that. Once it happens, it happens forever. But at least I can control who knows that."

The thought of doing something reprehensible—or at least ignoble—because the alternative is less lucrative was incredibly abject. I looked at her, loosening my face in woe. "I'm sorry."

"Can I be honest with you?" she asked.

"By all means."

"I hate sex. I hate it. I'm just good at it. Sex, to some, can be their sole virtue, and that's truly depressing." Holding back a tear, she moved her eyes around the top of her head listlessly. "Anyway, that's why I need this job. I need to pay for school. I want a degree."

"What're you majoring in?"

"Is this some sort of kink you're trying to act out?" She laughed again as her voice cracked, "Knowing my back story?"

"I told you, I'm not interested. You approached me."

She clicked her tongue and bit her cheek. "Classics."

"Get the fuck out of here."

"Well then!" she said, swatting her hair and turning around, "Ire in Gehennam"

119

"Whoa, sister!" I laughed, grabbing her elbow and spinning her around, "I'm sorry. Okay? So, you know a little Latin and I believe you about majoring in Classics. Why Classics?"

"That's the stupidest question. Everyone always asks that. 'Why'd you major in this?' 'Is there a reason?' What the fuck do you think? My Dad ran a big Classics factory and was waiting for me to join the family business? Stupidest fucking question there is."

"Just asking. Just asking." I assured her, "I'm sorry, but what's your name?"

"Candy Su-"

"Your real name."

Her eyes swelled a little, as if she were near crying and I had made her feel worthless. "Lily."

"L-i-l-y," I said, sounding out each letter, "Well, Lily, tell you what, if you ever transfer over to-"

"Bitch! Who the fuck you talking to? You been talkin' to dat john for five min. I ain't runnin' a fuckin' talk show. Bitch you think this da View?"

A Caucasian man draped in velvet with a purple trench coat secured tightly around his waist began walking towards us. His right hand brandished a bible with a vile of clear liquid on top of it. He waited on his right foot and leaned to the left with each step he took, strolling down the sidewalk like Frankenstein's monster.

"Shit." She exhaled as she extinguished her cigarette on the bottom of her leather boot "It's my pimp."

"Him?" I asked, trying not to laugh.

"They're not all black." She hissed.

"I'm aware of that Lily," I said, eyeballing the approaching pimp "But, even you could smack him up."

"Bitch, I ne'er like to call a trick bitch but damn. You out here talkin' to this Johnny date lately. This John pay more than what I got your ass set fir or you goin' in? Is he the looker? Another looker?"

Lily whispered so only I could hear, "There has to be a different word other than 'bitch' that they can use, right?"

I smiled, thinking for a second. "*Tramp? Skank? Harlot?*"

"I'll take *bitch*." Lily whispered before inspecting me in front of her pimp. "Yeah. The John wants another party."

The pimp studied me, his gaze carefully moving from my shoes to my shoulders. He sneered begrudgingly before turning back to Lily. "That freak payin' extra to da champ. Room 6523."

"Whatever." I said, flicking my cigarette into the empty gutter nearby and pulling out my flask, "I have to get a refill. I'll meet you up there."

I walked back over to the gas station across the street. The clerk, a Hispanic man with a 5 o'clock shadow, was watching old show tunes behind the counter. My gaze had gone impatiently from him to the mini-tv set a few times before I rang the service bell on the counter. He turned to meet me with wide, bloodshot eyes that seemed to fill his entire ocular cavity. Dazed, I took a step back, noticing that he never blinked his eyes. He had that thousand-yard stare seen in trauma patients with the eyes of the Kayako ghost from Japanese myth.

"Pint of whiskey." I said, matching his fixated eyes, more curious than terrified at that point.

He turned at the waist almost immediately, never moving his feet, and grabbed a bottle of cheap whiskey from the shelf before swinging his body back toward the counter and placing the bottle on it. He moved like one of those wind-up, animatronic mechanical doll shows at the park. I reached in my wallet to grab some cash, but by the time I pulled it out, he was already turned back toward his TV. I grabbed the bottle and left the money on the counter.

Outside, I finished what was left in my flask and broke the seal on the new bottle, spilling it every so often around my fingers as I refilled the flask. After tightening the lid, I began finishing what was left of the pint before heading up to Room 6523.

A flurry of confused noises, both sexual and aggressive in nature, were emanating from inside Room 6523. I lifted my hand to knock on the door but, after some contemplation about ruining the party, decided to open it slightly and peer in instead. The room was filled with masked men, storming around from side to side as Lily and another couple spoke tenderly from the bed. The bed, positioned in the middle of the room, was covered in iridescent cloth. The older couple had decided to situate themselves on the adjacent couch. Their faces, molded awkwardly like wax, were frozen with uncanny smiles and dull, widened eyes. They were comely, middle-aged, trim, and well-tanned individuals. But their faces, injected quite clearly with Botox, had a smooth, almost burnish, sheen without any trace of wrinkles, and their eyes, harboring a slice of mischief, were impossible to ignore. There was an almost perverse, Norman Rockwell aesthetic to them.

The woman, wearing a diaphanous robe with nothing underneath it, walked over to the bed, patting it as she stared at Lily. A projector screen was hung opposite their bed. I looked over my shoulder and down the hallway, its corridors growing frighteningly caliginous under the dying light.

The man, sliding across the bed and smiling like a deviant, pulled out his phone and began to dial a number. He spoke softly at first, his voice barely reaching a whisper, before nodding rabidly and speaking so the whole room could hear.

Lily, jolted by the man's outrage on the phone, jerked her head back, a hint of unease creasing across her brow, before snorting a line of white powder on the nightstand. The woman beside her laughed, speaking almost incoherently, going on and on about family stories that made no sense, and mixed a bag of white powder with another bag of powder, and presented Lily with another line.

The woman liberally sprinkled the powdery concoction on a bent spoon on top of the nightstand. She placed a lit zippo lighter under the spoon as the powder turned to a molten liquid that bubbled at its surface. They each filled a needle with the dope, smacked their forearms, and shot up. I sat still, drinking my whisky, as the older gentleman grinned at his phone's screen, his teeth baring themselves like a wild animal's chops, and the girls slipped back onto their pillows. After some time, Lily took deep, concerned breaths, and itched the sides of her arms while the woman next to her embraced the high and began masturbating. Lily stared at me as if she were trying to concentrate and ask for help, her eyes distant yet troubled. I furrowed my brow and lit another cigarette before taking a sip from my flask. The man kept interacting with the phone lovingly while taking intermittent bumps of cocaine.

I opened the door a little more, careful not to get involved in the unfolding scene. A noise, like the creak of a floorboard being stepped on came from the darkness to the right of me, just inside the room, but I paid it no attention.

Lily laid flat on the bed contemplating the invisible stars above her head. Two men, completely naked, walked out of my peripheral and stood next to the projector, stroking their gear in the process. The projector turned on and, after a few minutes of warming up, a face appeared on the screen.

A sound from down the hall gave me a start and I jerked my head to see what it was, careful to close the door gently, not slam it. Silence ensued. The hallway was almost completely pitch black, save for the flickering emergency exit sign that intermittently lit up the stairwell. I swallowed the lump in my throat, cracked the door open once more, and continued to watch.

While the man embraced his wife and Lily on the bed, the surrounding crowd of masked men began to disrobe. They lifted their hands to the air, twisting their wrists gently in centrifugal motions, before letting out heavy, throaty, breaths that seemed to modulate into a minatory hymn. As the man prepared himself on top, I peered my head in a little closer to get a glimpse of the screen. At first, it looked like a young girl, but I couldn't be certain. She was in a bedroom being forced closer to the screen by an entity behind her. I narrowed my eyes to get a closer look, uncertain if it were a live projection or some sort of prerecorded film, but one of the nude men stood in the way.

I turned my attention back toward the bed. The man was thrusting and thrusting with irate aggression, turning around every so often to look at the projector screen, his smile that of a raving madman. A chrysalis of frenzied delirium was forming across the room, injected, for better or worse, into the minds of everyone as the scene unfolded. The man's eyes filled with redoubtable madness. He flung his head around wildly and yelled indiscriminately, as if seized by a veritable palsy. "O, swear by the moon!" He yelled, pushing out a climax like he might a kidney stone, with discontent, as if piqued by a terrible endeavor, "That constant moon!". He climaxed with an almost fatal grunt.

It was getting hard to tell if people were in danger or if this was just some kind of outré kink.

Rather than call it a night, the man, his back muscles throbbing the atrophy away, filling with blood once more, rose like Lazarus from his tomb, smiling and walking with a confident saunter over to the two naked masked men.

Feeling uncomfortable, I turned to leave but was met with a pair of eyes staring at me from the darkest corner of the room directly beside me. The eyes, feral and brutish, stared at me with wild intent, motioning the swarthy mass of its invisible body back and forth before staring back up at the projector.

I panicked and let out a terrified shriek, slamming the door shut as I did so. Not wanting any unwanted attention, I moved quickly down the adjoining hallway, fumbling through its darkness. Finally out of sight of room 6523, I heard 'Lunatic Fringe' playing from the room across the hall.

The door was wide open, an invitation for anyone to walk in. I supported myself in the door's frame, taking notice of the foot or so of darkness that covered the room's entrance. Across the room, a man, relaxed and in a state of dishabille, sat on a couch, staring at himself in a mirror that stretched the length of the room. Under the shade of the room's entrance, he could not see me. The computer monitor on the shelf above his mirror was projecting a woman disrobing by herself on a bed. But he never looked up. He just kept his eyes glued to himself in the mirror, smiling a confused smile every so often from the corner of his mouth.

I moved in closer and, once I got under the light, his eyes shifted slowly to meet mine, keeping his head perfectly still. Moments went by without a word.

"I know you." The man said, speaking to me through the mirror's reflection.

"I don't think so." I answered to his reflection.

"I do. But I can't stop."

"Can't stop what?"

He lifted his chin in the direction of the computer monitor.

I shrugged casually. "If that's the worst you're doing tonight down here, you can rest easy."

"And then," he blurted, almost comically, "if too much of this is seen and people start seeing porn as normal, people will start having polygamous relationships."

A little confused by the statement, I rubbed the back of my head. "Well, so what? Let people choose."

His voice and movements were inhuman, nearly robotic. "I agree. Only the people wouldn't be choosing; they'd be led there by influence. It's like saying to a drunk person, 'Go ahead and get a tattoo. It doesn't matter if you're drunk.'"

"Excuse me?"

"Do you feel it? The pangs of lust, tearing at the mind, pulsing in acrimonious desideratum, becoming human. Those tendrils latching on to the mind, breaking down its natural, congenital barriers, for a life of servitude, whimsically captive to the will of many. When was it last I saw myself? My mind is flooded with the Gehenna of simulation. That first inorganic exposure to sex, not with warm flesh and blood, but with a cold, careless machine. The inchoate adolescent's wandering eye, striving for nature, for ambrosia, and landing in an abyss, leaving the adult helpless in a hollow tomb."

I laughed nervously. "What?"

"We're at an impasse."

"Okay..."

"Goodbye."

He didn't say another word. His eyes, through the mirror's reflection, walked me all the way back to the shaded pass of the entrance. As soon as I reached the darkness, they moved immediately back onto the reflection of his face.

Back in the hallway, before the exit, there was a garish sign in front of an open door with multicolored balloons scattered across its entrance. I moved in closer, taking notice of how the sign was decorated with a multitude of colorful confetti and ribbons. The inscription on the sign was smeared in red marker—or at least what I hoped was marker— *Come See the Whore.*

I downed a little more from my flask and took it as another invitation. Once again, a very similar room; white, barren, and accompanied by the nauseating smell of day-old ejaculate. A bed laid the centerpiece for another one of the projects' finest rooms. A woman was lying prone on the bed with her bare ass sticking up in the air. A glimmer of what appeared to be an eye peered at me from around the corner. Startled, I took a step back as a man with lipstick in his right hand emerged behind the countertop. He slouched and moved with a subtle slide. "You're here for the queen, right?"

I shrugged, darting my eyes from side to side, before exhaling a languid sigh. "I guess."

"Come," the man said, waving a hand to the seat next to him, "Everyone is entitled to the deification of her royal majesty."

I sat next to the man, maintaining a distance of at least five feet. He gently pulled out a mirror from the side of his chair. Glancing at his reflection, he pulled up the roll of lipstick and began to pull it closer to his face. He painted his lips with the lipstick before carefully bringing it to his forehead. With precise strokes, he painted letters from right to left. His jaw was open, and a slight moan punctured the air as he finished.

"What'd you think?" He faced me, showing the word 'PIG' spelled backwards on his forehead. "Good?"

"Good." I said indifferently.

I stared at the woman's spread buttocks for a few moments as the man began to pleasure himself over his pants. He pulled out an enormously durable dildo and chuckled while wobbling it in the air. It had a black overtone with a base pair of testicles. Anticipating the start of the show, I placed my elbow on the arm rest and rested my chin atop my closed fist. He looked at me and shook his head.

"This isn't for her. A level of worthiness needs to be attained for that purpose. Char is-"

"It's *Charlotte*! You piece of FUCKING meat!" The woman screamed into the pillow.

The woman turned her face, still pressed firmly against the pillow, towards us as she smiled slightly, barely in our range of visibility.

"Charlotte is on a certain level. I'm not."

"What?" I said, completely puzzled.

"She can only be with men of a level higher than her level. Get it?"

"No. Who are you?"

"I'm her husband." He smiled as I looked at him with concern. "Look! These are our kids."

He pulled out his wallet and flipped out an accordion of photos with the woman on the bed, himself, and several children hugging.

"And you're not going to fuck her?" I asked, looking around the room in confusion.

The man's laugh was ephemeral yet intense. Sweat pooled on his forehead as he began to smear the word 'PIG' with his forearm.

"My station is not there. I'm not... 'worthy'" the man said making air quotations with his fingers.

"I'm just curious, and I'm not trying to be funny or an asshole or whatever but, do you see a psychiatrist?"

"I see one routinely, yes. Charlotte makes me visit him once a week to ensure any willful desires are kept in check."

"Ah... Jesus. Okay. What do you talk about? What does he tell you?" I asked, still concerned.

"This and that," the man said, twisting his head with a tick like Stevie Wonder, "He asks when I started getting these desires..."

"And..."

He was like a child when he spoke, batting his eyes and playing with his fingers. "And I tell him it's in the porn I watch."

"I watch porn. I don't feel the need to- to- well, whatever this is."

He pulled out his phone and unlocked it, showing me the last video he had watched. He started the video again. It was an interracial couple having sex.

"So?" I said, begging him to get to the point.

"So. So it's so good to see white girls starting to turn to black men at such a young age."

"I see." I said, not really seeing anything at all.

"He, my shrink that is," the man started, a sliver of normalcy trickling down his face, "He says that-"

All of a sudden, a pair of black men appeared behind us on the couch. One was svelte with nothing but jeans and timberland boots on. The other was rather large, burly, and fully clothed, wearing all denim and a beanie cap that barely fit the top of his head. They rallied and cursed, accosting the man on the couch with a raspy urban dialect. Both demanded silence from the man beside me, asking him what he was talking about.

"Nothing." The man said, pushing his chin into his chest.

"My kings have arrived." Charlotte squealed from the bed.

"Ay, shut up." the larger man said, laying out a baggie near the bed.

The thinner man eyeballed me for a second in an attempt to intimidate me, but my eyes remained steady and unevasive. When he grew tired of our staring match, he moved his gaze down to the man with 'PIG' etched on his forehead and lunged forward at him, feigning an attack. He kneeled down to his level and slapped him hard across the face.

I knitted my brow. "What the hell is going on?"

"They're just-"

Cutting him off, the thinner man cocked a fist back in an effort to scare the timid weirdo on the couch. The man nodded as his accuser rose to look at me cross once more.

"Like I was saying," The man beside me whispered, "he says that there is some deviation in my head from listening to my mom get fucked by the mailman. He also suggests that I may have a 'deep-seated' stark resentment towards my own race for what it's done to the African American population. Of course, the ultimate realization, he says, is that after watching pornography for so long, I have grown accustomed to watching others copulate. It isn't enough to have sex with a woman. I must watch. I need to witness. Intimacy is learned. So, it comes in two-fold. I like to watch the woman I love be the centerpiece for something I've loved my whole life. And her promiscuity is a major turn on. Being with a woman skilled enough to bring men to climax is a major turn on. And, finally, the idea that our race has ruined another race, it gives me insurmountable pleasure to think that the, as my psychiatrist would say, 'forbidden fruit' would finish inside my wife and possibly get her pregnant. It's an enormous turn on. And now I can't even close my eyes at night without a visual picture of my wife sucking a cock or getting a money shot."

I cracked my neck from side to side, my eyes wild with bewilderment. "It isn't enough to go to a civil rights rally or something?"

Both men began mounting Charlotte, one at each end of her. The larger male mounted her anally from the backside. The thinner man shoved his erection into her mouth without a moment's hesitation.

"Civil rights?" The man beside me whispered as he began to masturbate.

"It sounds to me-" I paused, mortified, as the man simultaneously stroked his cock and shoved the dildo in and out of his mouth. "It sounds to me that this act, in itself, is in fact a form of racism. What you are doing is putting a race of people on a platform for nothing more than sexual gratification. This is hardly an atavistic desire. You are, in essence, using a race of people for your own personal, sexual exploitation. There is no difference between masturbating to these men using your wife and seeing blacks as inferior. You've reduced the humanitarian essence of an entire race of people to a singular, sexual benefactor. Perpetuating this will lead to a communal desire that, will in turn, lead to the segregation of African Americans as nothing more than sex objects."

The man ejaculated all over himself.

"Look at this porky white bitch! Lick it up faggot!" the larger man said from the bed as Charlotte laughed at him.

"The fuck you laughing at?" the thinner man yelled, "We're gonna play slut roulette with you. I'm calling up my boys after this and we're all cumming inside you and you'll never know which is the father."

"Hey," I said, nudging the man beside me, "Are you listening to me?" The man glanced at me briefly before licking the semen off his chest and stroking his flaccid penis. "Never mind."

LeResche

Philosophizing probably wasn't going to get me anywhere tonight. I lowered my head, exhausted from the night already, staring once more at Charlotte getting spit roasted. I took a deep pull from my flask and lit a Spirit before standing up and leaving the project house.

Walking down the road and toward the I-10, a qualmish rumbling had erupted inside of my stomach. Saliva began to form in the corners of my mouth and, though I fought for a moment, I jerked over the nearest railing to retch on a bed of flowerets, frozen in nocturnal chill.

Adjusting my shirt and wiping my mouth, I pulled out my notepad to make an entry.

First, I'd like to thank a certain Dr. Felix for this night. Without you holding that imprimatur over my head, I'd be comfortably numb in my two-bedroom condo, happily nescient of the concupiscent rites of Alameda.

It seems there has been an incursion of kinks that have pushed the boundaries of acceptability lately. A slippery slope is one thing, but a clear view of the proximate horizon is another. In his more well-known essay, Big Red Son, Wallace had quite aptly remarked on the final resting place of the porn industry—perfectly mirroring the themes surrounding Ballard's Cocaine Nights—which we find ourselves presently.

The Call of the Void

One of the more interesting fetishes has become spouse sharing. While Nietzsche, and others from his school of thought, might see this as the natural catena out of religion's dominant stranglehold on monogamy, I can't help but think it is different somehow. For one, it seems to only advantage one spouse—though admittedly, it does seem to derive pleasure for both parties, just in different ways. We see it most often with the male partner lusting over the female partner to 'experience' other men. What happens behind closed doors between consenting adults is none of my business, but, from a particular observation I've made tonight, it would seem that men who have become too exposed to pornography wish to see their wife as the center of the sexual experience the only way they know how—as voyeur. As for the female, it seems to go one of two ways; one, that this is more about having multiple partners than actual love for their partner, under the pretense of promiscuous anonymity, or two, their love for their partner is so great that they would reluctantly take on such an endeavor for the sake of their significant other's pleasure. Though I will admit, I have a newfound respect for a call girl's line of work. And here I thought educators had it tough.

The clock on the Coca Cola billboard over the interstate read 7:18. There was an intense pressure in my mind to turn back, drink the night away, and call up Cheryl. Yet the strangely surreal chill of the November air thrusted me forward. A male and female couple were canoodling nearby as I walked closer to the bridge under the I-10.

135

LeResche

Getting closer, I noticed the female was much larger than her male counterpart.

"Yeah. How much for the night baby?"

"40 for a bareback blowjob. 100 for everything."

"Damn. You know how to get me hard huh?"

She shrugged and gave a coquettish smile.

It was getting hard to listen to any more of this. I previously would have thought it quite odd to see a man groping a woman' genitals in the middle of the street before, but after an hour out here, I didn't know what to think. Probably that it was the least unsettling thing I witnessed tonight. But, as he groped harder, and the call girl motioned him away more and more, his face filled with repugnance.

"The fuck is this?" He shouted.

"C'mon baby. I'm the only one out here now. You wanna wait for the rest or get a real woman."

He bent her over a railing nearby. I stopped to watch, exhaling my cigarette and leaning against the closest car.

"You Goddamn tranny whore. You think you were gonna trick me? Huh? Straight guy gets tricked and you still get dicked, is that it?"

"You could just leave." She said, cowering a bit in front of the man, his hands balled up into fists at his side.

The man pressed his left forearm on the transvestite's back as he undid his belt with his right hand. He was breathing fire and his nostrils flared with a sense of virulent rage. And even after the show he put on, he still pulled his penis out and lifted her skirt without relent.

"Oh no. This is happening."

"It's a hundred, baby. It's a hundred."

The man slapped her across the face before reaching into his pocket and throwing bills onto the back of her head that bounced off and onto the street. He rolled her skirt up and the transvestite struggled for a minute before capitulating. A shooting star passed through the sky. I watched as it went from east to west before turning back with a marked aversion to the odd scene unraveling in front of me.

"There's your money whore. You really had me fooled. But that's all you trannies are good for though huh? Getting fucked."

Out of the corner of my eye, a shirtless drifter was walking back and forth on the interstate above the precipice of the overpass. The man, standing still with his arms stretched wide in opposite directions, pointed his face to the sky, the tunic around his waist whipping in the wind. One of the Recusants. He stared down at the street below, watching for the headlights of a moving vehicle, his arms spread out as far as they could to each side, like a beacon, as if to guide the way. A semi-truck was picking up speed from the north side of the street. The Recusant took notice, looking toward the sky once more before closing his eyes and taking a swan dive off the interstate.

"No!" I yelled out of instinct.

He seemed to float, if only for a moment, as his head made contact with the truck's windshield. The driver screeched to a halt, his eighteen wheels sliding perpendicular down Alameda. I weaved through stopped vehicles to get a closer look, rushing to see the line of blood the Recusant had left on the street. His body was mangled, and

137

his arms and joints reached clear across his back on each side. His foot separated from his leg, hanging by a tendon near the shinbone, and his right shoulder was twisted around the back of his head as he laid motionless on the ground.

The driver ran toward the Recusant, anxiously wringing his hands. When he noticed him on the ground, mangled beyond recognition, his tunic covering the lower half of his body, the driver exhaled with relief.

"Fucking idiots." He said before getting back into his truck.

I walked down the remainder of the boulevard before glancing at the expansive streetlights that enhaloed the base of the city. A man painting portraits below the overpass was seated directly beneath the off ramp. The canvas he was working on painted a picture of Mohammed getting sodomized by Jesus. Buddha and Vishnu were in the background twisting each other's nipples and masturbating. Moses was painted defecating over the Torah with an erection while Odin watched on with delight. The man, wearing thick, wavy glasses, forcing a creepy smile across his face, pointed toward the bridge and uttered under his breath "I'm just doing my part." My eyes followed to where his finger pointed; the words 'For. I. Matter.' were scrawled above a graffiti portrait of a three headed dog with blossoming flames behind   it.

IV

A bumper sticker, crassly placed on the pillars beneath the overpass, read:

"*Eat beef. The West wasn't won on salad.*"

And, quite humorously, the graffiti underneath it read:

"*But it will be lost on it.*"

At the Jack in the Box across the street, hordes of corpulent men and women, most likely coming from their Thanksgiving dinners, moved in and out of the fast-food chain. Jack's marquee board had a message that read:

'*Didn't have enough turkey? Grab Jack's new bacon wrapped mozzarella sticks!*' And right below that was a tiny disclaimer that was barely visible to the naked eye. '*In light of the recent mold scares with our bread, our health facility has assured us this is due to negligence on the part of our quality-control department, and not the bio-emissions of a select few employees. Please continue to enjoy Jack in the Box regularly.*' The caveat ended with a tiny, smiling clown emoji.

I stepped over a berm of discarded thirst busters slatternly littering the underpass before narrowing my eyes to study the other side of the street. I pulled out my notebook, licked the tip of the ballpoint pen and made a note.

Is that you Deleuze? Haunting me with the specters of schizophrenia, running your desire machine to the tune of delirium, in order to make a point on societal thought? Casting me off from a realm of depraved prurience to the icon, the ballast, of all-American woes; the cheeseburger.

Nothing new here, I suppose. Fat people are unhealthy. You're an asshole for pointing it out and, wait for it, counterargument, it's unhealthy to argue that.

I sympathize with the overweight. Not because, as plenty of people have shown us, there is a national permeance to their vice, but, rather, because the world around us praises the consumption of products that are counterintuitive to our well-being and natural balance. I should talk. I'm nearly half in the bag already and this past year I've been double bagged most of the time. But there is in fact a fallacy in the direction of marketing towards unhealthy and 'healthy' foods. It isn't the cliché 'You're killing your loyal supporters by feeding them this' or even the 'Blatant Bandwagoning will blow up in your face'. Rather, I've always seen it as, 'How long until the dopamine receptors burn out?' Again, I should talk. I haven't had a lick of serotonin since I was 18 and even a whiff of dopamine since last year. But the question remains, how long until the novelty wears off? Or is this it? Have the corporations truly found the cure to human reason. That mysterious panache they've molded that bludgeons the human mind into either burning out or killing itself. There aren't F.A. meetings. But the underlying concept of the poisonous sustenance, whether it be drugs or food, has not a conditional property but rather an ontological property.

The Call of the Void

This is where my thesis counters Searle and Nagel; Ontology is not as 'subjective' as we believe. It is not a 'first-person ontology' but rather a collective, objective one. Corporations have embedded themselves into the minds of generations not yet born. It isn't based on the statement 'I've always been around it.' But rather an excuse of 'It has always been a part of me'. You could give children benzoylmethylecgonine at the age of five and continually feed it to them day after day and the addictive, and possible health, effects would not deviate from those of fast food. Sugar, and salt to a lesser degree, taste too good. However, cocaine gives an effect of bewilderment and, under the influence of alcohol, belligerence. Conversely, sugar and salt do the opposite; they make one lethargic and torpid. The idea of free will comes to mind almost immediately. Yet, the departure from our reason and sanity came not from will but rather deceit. That is the devious purpose of the fast-food chains. They are a symbol of society's abundance. Once a McDonalds was placed in front of Alexander Pushkin's statue, it was all over.

The payphone next to me rang. It vibrated with each *brrinnngg brrinnngg,* jostling itself back and forth on the receiver. I walked up to it and read the collect-call advertisement, boasting of five more minutes talk time for just ten cents. As if anyone ever used a payphone for that long. I reached in slowly while the phone was finishing its fifth ring. Something inside me—call it a voice, a premonition or daemon—told me that the phone would ring forever. Looking around to find no one nearby, I answered.

141

LeResche

"Hello?"

"You know where you are, don't you?"

"Wrong number."

The voice on the other end let out a joyless sigh. "Perdition's road is arduous and caustic but not as eternal as one might think. That road is paved by the death of many young men that would rather embrace Heaven than manumit themselves from Hell."

"Who is this?" I demanded, trying to distinguish the familiar voice on the other end.

"Have you ever heard of Philosophical zombies?"

I closed my eyes and shook my head, tired of the back and forth. "Can't say that I have. Now, who is this?"

"The theory goes that a good portion of the human race lack conscious experience. If you've ever dissociated or done something and don't recall—driven home but have no recollection, your brain acting on auto pilot—that's what they are like. They do everything required to be human, they ape emotions, go through life without thinking. They simply lack sentience."

"And?"

"*Wellllll*, I'm beginning to wonder if the same can't be said for people that overthink things. What do you think? Think. Think. Think." He said, ending the last few words in rapid succession.

The voice on the other end giggled at first, almost like a whisper, before bellowing out a deep, orotund laughter like that of a madman. I slammed the phone on the receiver and walked on.

The Call of the Void

The rotund patrons leaving the Jack in the Box looked dazed, staring up at the sky insouciantly, and skipped—if it could be called that—out of the double doors and down one street toward North 14th. A once abandoned building, the 'Big Green Monster'—which had become its unofficial sobriquet in previous years—was now a spot of increasing infamy across the west coast for having every food known to man. And though its putative claim to fame was probably an exaggeration, it wasn't too far off.

The establishment was called 'Big Matt's Factory of Fat'. The canvas above the restaurant's sign had a large, personified worm licking his lips and holding a spork as his distended belly stretched out across the building's roof. Interestingly enough, it never really deterred customers that might otherwise feel shame from the moniker. In fact, most wore it like a badge of honor. Larger patrons were often seen walking joyously down the streets, swinging their arms with a wide grin and proudly wearing shirts from Matt's that read '*I'm fat. How bout' dat?*' and, to their apparent confusion, '*The Eighteenth Article hasn't been amended yet. HANDS OFF MY BACON!*'. Matt's 30 second commercials lauded their vast culinary accomplishments which included, but were not limited to:

- Brisket
- Elephant's Ear
- Deep Fried Oreos
- Hot Cheeto Crusted Pasta
- Mountain Dew Fritters
- Rocky Mountain Oysters

143

- Cheesecake
- Brown Bettie
- A Bowl of Nacho Cheese
- A Bowl of Ketchup
- Whatever is left over after draining the fryer from the night before at a discount

An assemblage of large, Rascal bound consumers lethargically made their way into the enormous diner that hugged the cross section of Alameda and 14th. The restaurant's lights were dull, and, in a dust storm, it was scarcely visible from even five feet away. Still, despite its grotesqueries and my better judgment, I decided to grab a bite.

Inside Big Matt's, there was a 50's diner bar top that curved around the length of the restaurant, arrayed with black and white checkers. A few patrons sat atop the barstools, buying coffee and bear claws, the cheeks of their asses spilling over to the chairs next to them. The unoccupied booths were filled with families gabbing about Thanksgiving dinner, and 'how it was always so much better at Matt's'. Families that, despite their debilitating languor, insisted on having another meal that night. Couples, topping the scales easily at a combined 700 pounds, sat with their brood, destined—in an inescapable sense of the word—for a life of taking their own children here, all for the privilege of saying, 'My parents used to bring me here. I wish you could've met them.'

I settled myself on a nearby barstool, allowing the air from the red cushion on my seat to slowly deflate. The man next to me was checking his phone, a grimace of indignation promenading his face, mumbling something about losing to the Washington Generals in a bet. The waitress, ensconced in red and white striped kitchenware, was surprisingly thin. Most, if not all, of the wait staff were. She grasped her checkbook tightly, her knuckles nearly bursting out of her skin. She couldn't be older than 30 but the paucity of tight skin in her face made her look like an adolescent in a geriatric mask. Her hand moved methodically underneath her name tag like a television personality presenting a grand prize to the audience. Becky, as her name tag read, handed me a menu while her grip on the checkbook shakily enervated.

"What'll I get ya sir?"

"Got any alcohol?"

"Beer. It's all we got."

"Coors Light?"

"16, 24, 28, 32, or the Big Matty's 44 ounce?"

The customers to my left and right were shooting me ignominious looks. I assumed it was for not asking about the special.

"When in Rome." I shrugged, "The 44-ounce works."

"Gotcha."

"Don't take this the wrong way but uh, I didn't expect the wait staff to be so, erm, how do I put this?"

"Thin?" She asked with an exhausted huff.

I managed a coltish smile. She cocked her head quickly to the side.

"Big Matt won't let us eat on the job or after without paying," she chewed her gum and blew a bubble, "And I ain't payin' to eat here. Sometimes, if the staff are lucky, they'll get someone leaving behind their food and they'll devour it like some pack'a wolves. But let's face it mister, that hardly ever happens around here."

Becky slapped the side of my face gently and pinched my cheek, mimicking my smile before frowning once more and moving to the kitchen.

I took a deep breath and placed both my hands together over my nose and mouth. A large, yet seemingly docile, man sat beside me as soon as the seat opened up. His stomach protruded well past his belt. On top of his midsection girth, his arms were flabby, and it looked as though he hadn't lifted so much as a pencil in years. He had no edge, no rancor in his eyes, just a soft, flabby, asthenic demeanor. His hair was styled like that of a marine with a two-inch shave on the sides and back, and a gelled, flipped bang atop his head. His breathing was extremely labored. He wasn't *morbidly* obese per se but was incredibly morbid—or at the very least awkward— in appearance. When no prompt service was given to him within the minute or two that he sat there, he began to flail about, clasping his hands over his face in impatient fury. He stared at me briefly with an expression like, "*Can you believe this?*"

My beer came shortly after that. It was poured into a novelty pint glass, taller than my head sitting down, with sparklers attached to the handle. I extinguished them in the water cup to my right.

"Finally!" the young, Hispanic, beer bellied man, who had probably never had a beer in his life, professed.

"Hello to you too, Richard," the thin rail of a waitress sighed, "What do you want tonight?"

The Call of the Void

"I'm going for it tonight sweetie! I'm going to actually do it!"

"No, you aren't Dick. You nev-"

"It's Richard!" He yelled, pounding the table with both fists before throwing his water in Becky's face, "And I am!"

What a horrible excuse for a human being. He floundered his arms around in the air as if to draw attention toward himself. I drank my beer, remaining calm through his puerile outburst.

"Fine. Richard." Becky rasped under her breath, wiping her face perfunctorily, as if this happened every night, "It's impossible to finish this challenge. That's the point. You pay the extra money to try and eat the meal and... oh Jesus Richard! What the fuck is wrong with you?!"

The sack of overindulgent calories sitting beside me known only as Richard—though I prefer Dick—had begun to sob uncontrollably. His fists pounded the framework of a once stable bar top. His cries were unlike those of a normal human that are concealed, profound, and emotional. Instead, his sobs were that of a sign flipper or street performer that begged the attention of everyone within a 20-foot radius.

"Just bring me the meal bitch," the fat, imposter of a human being said firmly.

The waitress rolled her eyes and moved toward the kitchen. I finished about half of my beer.

"You want to yell at me for being a horrible person, don't you?" the mold of blubber that filled the seat next to me said, looking in my direction.

I shrugged and finished the beer. Becky brought me another one.

"Well, this is my livelihood," he conceded in an almost somber, singsong voice, "Eating as much as I can."

His voice had an odd inflection that mispronounced certain diphthongs and a lisp that made his antics twice as unbearable.

I scanned the bar, looking for anyone who may sympathize with me and give me some sort of reprieve from the situation, hoping someone may recognize I wanted to witness this buffoon but, if at all possible, from afar. Nothing. A woman with green acrylic nails, green hair, green eyelashes, and a green glass of soda sat alone in a booth, rapidly filling her mouth with what looked like crab legs. A rather slender Asian man and woman in the opposite booth were promptly served an enormous chocolate cake. They held one another's hands for a moment before smiling, their gaze lowered like robotic predators onto the cake in front of them before lunging full bore into the pastry and devouring it without utensils or even their hands—face first into the calorically dense monstrosity. A family of rednecks in the back corner of the store ordered an entire onion, fried, for each member of the family, with a pizza for the main dish, posited right in the middle of the table like some monument to their pride in finishing the fucking thing. One rather morbidly obese black man had a basket of fries on his table. It was the only solid food he was eating. A diet perhaps? Nay; merely an appetizer to the six 44-ounce cokes he ordered. A spectacle for the masses to fathom at while he gulped down one after the other in an astonishing 73 seconds. His belch, at 9 seconds long, was mystifying and had to be seen—or heard rather—to be believed.

Richard, his moist breath fogging the table's acrylic laminate, was staring me down. I could feel his beady little eyes gazing at the back of my head, entreating me to turn and meet him so we could continue conversing about *him*.

"Oh well!" he jabbered on while flailing his arms in every direction, hoping to catch the eye of any individual that would walk by, "This is the life. No?"

He perched his hands underneath his chin almost seductively. My aloof expression must have thrown him off because he pouted his lips and acted like he was going to cry once more. I finished half of the new beer I was given.

"Can I ask you just one, little, tiny, *eensie* thing?" I remained quiet. "I need someone to film for me."

"Film what?" I jeered, recoiling in bemusement.

"'Film what?'" he imitated "Film me silly. I need to make a new video and if I geolocate this place it drives revenue through the roof. It's like what Heart Attack Grill used to be for Youtubers before it shut down. Only here, I get to hit all of the food groups. Not just, um, burgers?"

He took a seductive bite out of a French Fry from the man next to him. The man didn't seem to mind or even acknowledge his existence as he wolfed down the rest of his Velveeta fondue.

"Sure," I hesitated, grabbing my beer and standing up.

LeResche

What compels a person to eat in front of a camera for money is beyond me.

We moved toward the booth on the eastern corner. The waitress appeared next to the table to serve this kid his feast. She placed down two chicken sandwiches, with pickles slipping out from under the bun, an order of onion rings, an enormous plate with bread cheese and meat that—I believed—might be a cheeseburger, an order of three chili cheese footlong hot dogs, six king crab legs, breaded buffalo wings coated in a film of nacho cheese, a steak with a twice baked potato *and* mashed potatoes, a tub of fried chicken topped with fried cheese curds, bacon-wrapped mozzarella sticks, and, for the coup de grâce, a footlong burrito wrapped in a quesadilla. I grew nauseous just from the scent of it.

"Well, you can't *not* have a burrito wrapped in a quesadilla. I have to ask though," I croaked, "Is all this really necessary?"

The Buddha statue of a supposed man looked at me vacuously for a moment. He finally composed himself and brushed a hand underneath his chin, tightening his lips in the process.

"Oh, this isn't for me darlin'. My fans want it. I put it online and people watch it. I, in return, get money from ad revenue. Which reminds me, will you press play and point that camera at me."

I puzzled over the words 'ad revenue' before his phone slipped out of my hand and onto the booth from the grease it was covered in. Placing his hands on his love handles, he began to puff his face out with a grim expression.

The Call of the Void

"Hello fanboys!" he said, imitating the immature, boyish voice of a latent homosexual, "This is Richard, your king. And I am especially mad at what is happening in the world right now. Did you know that one man, every hour, of every day is diagnosed with testicular cancer? And that several, uh, thousand people die from diabetes every minute. Today's broadcast is brought to you by Sonic y'allll and their alliance against many, shit- I don't really know. Many diseases okay. Be sure to like and subscribe to stop this madness."

His insincerity was palpable. His insecurity was not.

"So, then, is this all for money? This is-"

"Oh no," he laughed, "This is because I loooove chili and cheese."

Grabbing one of his footlong chili cheese hot dogs and using it as a microphone, he began to harmonize.

I love chili and cheeeeese I do
Far more than the average boo

He stood up from the booth, his arms jutting in every position through the air, as his beloved chili dog fell violently onto the table.

And what's the worst you take
From every other steak
I came dancing and strutting
Hoping this restaurant will start price cutting
So... I... may...

151

The entire restaurant stared at their meals as if this were the rigamarole one had to endure in order to eat copious amounts of continental cuisine at Matt's.

Eat a little

Chug a little

Pass my gut for some ham

To find out who I truly am

Dick flailed around the restaurant singing his song and dancing at a sluggish pace, pulling at others and trying desperately to get the patrons to join in, hoping that some communal ballad from the restaurant would make his videos better.

What's that?

A tasty cat?

There must be a system glitch

Too many tasty sandwich-

"Richard!" one of the more austere waitresses interrupted, "Enough. Let the people eat in peace for Christ's sake."

"I was done anyway," Richard enunciated in such a childish tone it almost made me throw up. He turned his head quickly to a table with an onion ring fondue fountain and rushed over to cozy up with the customers.

As Richard stuffed his face, I took the opportunity to write in Felix's notepad.

Richard was most likely a product of his environment. A human being once faced with the inescapability of life itself. A sound

152

The Call of the Void

upbringing—in Richard's case— would be dubious at best, and one must wonder if, like most of the patrons at this feeding hole, he ever had a chance. At one point, he made a decision to turn himself into an unrecognizable member of our species. And yet, would direction have saved him? Would a strong household have revived his consciousness from almost certain slovenly annihilation? Or is free will, at this point in history, too despotic? Too obsessed with annihilating himself?

Maybe Konrad had a point. There is a point in life where we humans must 'take responsibility for our actions' but this does not seem to apply here. He's become largely 'self-sufficient' despite his lack of dignity. Not to mention, his purported million viewers will watch as he tears away, cell by cell, at his physical body. Perhaps that was the point of watching; to observe man's greatest ability for self-destruction and denigration.

And still, why weep for his physical body when it is his consciousness that he has lost? His impression on this world is nothing more than that of entertainment to those who believe they are free. Free to watch Richard eat himself into an early grave. Free to be subliminally penetrated with advertisements on Richard's channel that they will, inevitably, download and play or watch. It is a perpetual cage that the human race has willingly and happily put itself into by trading virtue for vice. Trading vice, in turn, for vice. One must wonder then when one must 'transcend'. There was, until recently, a moment of transcendence that almost every human being experienced. This was either through the acceptance of captivity through childbearing or through the destiny of creation. Now, it would seem, captivity is merely *in the form of whatever is most comfortable to our faculties. Maybe Dr. Piper was right about the death-drive...*

"So, anyway..." Richard lisped while raising an upturned hand, suggesting I raise his camera once more.

As he sat back down in the booth, he eyeballed his food hopefully, savoring his first bite. Poking the food with his fork, his scowl grew longer and larger.

"Something wrong?" I asked, not too keen on hearing his response.

"It's cold," he waved callously, "That's okay. IHOP is just as good. I'll find someone there."

"Fine. Just as well. The wait staff here could use a meal."

"Ew," he heaved, "I touched my food already. That will disgust me all night if I think about someone eating food I've touched. I'm not kidding. It's going out."

I sat, trying to not let my bilious expression explode off my face and into a combustible rage, as Richard put all of his 15,000-calorie meal onto one tray and pushed it into the trash can. The wait staff watched on, their dejected expressions eyeing the food as the gravy from his plate slid down the wall and into the trash.

Outside, it began to rain. I grabbed a newspaper from a nearby bench and fashioned it into a roof over my head. I rushed to the awning nearby, took the newspaper off my head and waited for the rain to die down. The article in the middle had a picture of a fatal car crash and a title that read, "*Father and Son's Drunk Driving Accident Places Southwestern America at the Top of Fatal Car Accidents.*" What a shame.

A homeless man in the alley nearby asked me for a smoke. I lit two in my mouth, handing him the other. He walked slowly to the side of Matt's, clutching his hand to his collar for warmth as he moved. He sat beside a row of other homeless men and a shopping cart with a fire underneath it. They huddled around it, cupping their hands over their mouth and then back near the flames. One of the men was diving in a dumpster and pulled out a slab of raw meat thrown away by the kitchen staff. The homeless men all hissed in delight. The man with the raw steak used the bottom shelf to start another fire and the top shelf as the grill, placing the raw steak over the shopping carts grates and cooking the meat, flipping it every couple of minutes with a makeshift pair of tongs made out of tinfoil. The group looked at me once more, their eyes telling me a story I'd heard far too many times before.

Across the street, on the western most side, there was an alleyway that extended well past any of its surrounding buildings. I inched closer to the alley's entrance and lurched my head around the corner, watching as a line of patrons with poor sartorial taste, dressed in everything from dazzling opera gowns to bolo ties with ratty jeans and half opened flannel shirts, lined up underneath a dimly lit sign that read, 'Teatro Del Macabre'. I moved to the back of the line behind a woman with opera glasses cackling her head off in a way only a

LeResche

Dickensian aristocrat could. When I got to the entrance, the bouncer waved me through carelessly, never asking for so much as an ID or cover charge.

Near the inside of the entrance, a man, garbed in a red tuxedo, locked his gaze onto me. His eyes lit up and, before I could move any further, he rushed to my side and forcefully grabbed my hand, shaking it vigorously with a smile that stretched from ear to ear. I pulled my hand back in shock, but he reached for it again and continued to shake.

"Dr. Killian! What a surprise!"

"You could say that again." I said, looking around the lobby, a little confused that he knew my name.

"Oh, I'm- *we're* so thrilled to have you, doctor." He said, his smile growing so wide as to see his molars, standing with his arms behind his back like a soldier at attention. "I'm Mr. Jill, the theater's manager."

I nodded, unsure of how else to respond. He stood silent, his eyes pinned to my face, moving his head with mine even when I peered over my shoulder and from side to side.

"Will there be anything else?" He asked, his smile never wavering.

"No. Thank you. You're very kind."

He remained frozen and silent.

"Is there, um, something you need from me?" I asked.

The Call of the Void

Mr. Jill looked as if he had swallowed a lump in his throat, and the defining features on his face—his mechanical smile, the deep valleys of creases in his nose—twitched nervously. "Well, sir, if I may."

He moved one hand from behind his back and handed me a book. I grabbed it from him and observed the films of dust layering its cover, running my finger across the front, making little lines that resembled racetracks on the cover. I leaned over, took a deep breath, and blew the remaining dust from the glossy cover. The book was *Odium Fati*, a diminutive philosophical exegesis with satirical undertones about the negative depiction of predestination in literature that I had written some time ago. It was picked up and published for a series of courses at Stanford University.

"How did you get this?" I asked, examining the interior cover, unsure if *I* even still had a copy, "This was a very limited publication from the University's press."

Mr. Jill shrugged with a modest smile before handing me a pen. "Would you be so kind?"

"You want *me* to sing *this*?"

Mr. Jill twisted his face a little. "Who else?"

"No one has ever asked me for that before." I whispered to myself.

"What's that, sir?"

"Nothing." I responded, signing the interior cover with a brief smile.

He took the book back and opened the cover, raking his fingers gently across the page. "If, sir, there is anything—and I mean anything—I can do to make your experience more comfortable, please don't hesitate to ask."

"O-okay. Thank you." I said, pointing behind me to the theater, "I'll just go enjoy the show."

"The show?" Mr. Jill said with a hint of fury in his voice that only lasted a moment, "Of course, sir, the show. Well then, I'll be right here, waiting for anything you may need."

"Don't do that." I said, "I'll be just fine. Please, resume your, uh, duties."

He pointed emphatically to the ground below. "Right here."

"Um-"

"In case you need me."

His complexion had begun to turn a pale gray and his once amiable facial features had disappeared, growing dour and sullen the longer I stared at him.

"Okay." I said.

"Right here."

I lifted my hand to stress the effect. "I heard you."

"In case-"

His gaze trailed from my eyes to over my shoulders mid-sentence. I turned to find a woman in a red dress—the only other person in the lobby—walking toward the theater. When I turned back around, Mr. Jill had turned his back to me, and remained frozen in place.

Inside the theater, past about fifteen feet of dark, empty space, there sat two large men, identical in girth, at a table in the middle of the stage. It was a smaller theater with the capacity of around a third any regular theater. There were two balconies, one with a couple of opera dressed fanatics adjusting their ornate opera glasses and laughing intermittently, and another with a group of poorly dressed gentlemen, burping obnoxiously and drinking out of their brown bag coolers. The stage was adorned in velvety red drapes, cascading at the bottom like an ocean's wave onto the stage. The seats were sparsely occupied, leaving a space of about five chairs in between each patron. I sat near the middle as the lights dimmed and a man in a tuxedo came out with an empty wheelbarrow. A violin strummed lightly over the speakers as the master of ceremonies lifted the wheelbarrow to the table and hoisted the invisible contents in front of the corpulent men. Moving enthusiastically behind the table and MC, a ring girl, kicking like a Rockette as she shimmied across the stage, held a white card above her head with the number '1' written on it. The MC rang a bell and the two men, pantomiming their every move, began devouring all that they could of the invisible feast. Patrons clapped and others laughed as I looked around for a 'No Smoking' sign. Realizing it wasn't that kind of theater, I lit up, propped my feet up over the seat in front of me, and slung my left arm over the seat next to me, trying to get comfortable.

A smell, strange and foreign yet somehow familiar, floated across the room. My heart raced a little and my breathing grew deeper and deeper. I examined the room, attempting to parcel some sanity out of the insanity unfolding before me. I looked over my left shoulder and was met by the eye and grinning face of a woman wearing an all-black, skintight dress that flushed past her feet. Her right eye was canopied with a strand of latex material that extended out of her dress, covering the right side of her face. The encounter shocked me, and I sat upright immediately. Had she always been there? I took a drag from my cigarette and tried to concentrate on the show once more. How much time had passed? The ring girls were already on card '3' and the invisible feast on the table had—according to their mimicry—piled up beyond the actors' heads. I drank from my flask and let the liquor warm my brain. It helped, if only for a moment.

By card '4', the players on stage unzipped their rubbery flesh suits and emerged as thin, frail old men. An impressive legerdemain, no doubt. I was feeling more uplifted, more euphoric. Had my senses not already been marginally dulled, I would have recognized the shift in my mood sooner—or at least the clamminess of my face. The first thing that hit me was the sickly-sweet smell of styrofoam burning. Then, a howling in my mind burst open my frontal lobe. I panicked for a moment and turned my head over my left shoulder to see the woman with one covered eye blowing smoke in my face. She, inhaling from her device once more, reached out, her hand covered in a silky, Victorian glove, and caressed my chin, pulling me closer to her face, her cheeks pregnant with smoke. I let her pull me in, closer and closer to the darkness inside of her mouth, until finally, we kissed, the smoke from her lungs going through my lungs and back out through my nose. But, when my heart flushed and pounded irregularly, I turned back around and shot my eyes upwards to the ceiling. No mistaking it; she was freebasing cocaine; crack most likely. The mad bitch.

The Call of the Void

No. Maybe it was paranoia getting the better of me. But the focus of a cocaine high coupled with the smell of a crack rock was distinctive. Shit. I wasn't prepared for this. Was she trying to dose me? What if it wasn't crack? Meth? The questions rattled around in my mind like a salvo of anxious bullets, fueling my paranoia. I leapt out of my seat and ran for the exit, listening as the one-eyed woman screeched a laugh hoarsely in the background. I'd done coke before. I could get through this. But the high was intense, forcing me to focus on every small minute detail. Cocaine was easy, smooth. This was a delirium of epic consequences.

My heart pounded like the slow strumming of a guitar string as I walked briskly back out onto the street. I raked my fingers over my thumbs nervously, darting my eyes from left to right, hoping no one would look at me. I wished there was someone at home waiting for me. Someone I could embrace, who would take all this madness away. The thought of an isolated life was becoming an even more formidable dark cloud that I could not escape. For some reason, suicide, which I previously thought of us as a reasonable escape, was too frightening of a concept. Scared. I was scared. I needed someone for something. I needed to speak to someone. This was bad. And then it dawned on me, the woman with one eye was going to try and kill me. That was it. She'd follow me down the road and, when the moment was right, she'd lop my head off. Or, worse, she'd follow me home and do it in my sleep. No one there to console me. No one there to stop her. Never another waking image, simply death in a dream.

Come on, old boy. I thought. *You can do this. Steel your mind.*

After some time in my head, while chewing my fingernails to the base, I lifted my head up and snapped out of my psychosis, picking up where I left off, more than embarrassed by the experience.

I leaned against a wall and sat, my hands still trembling, before reaching in my pocket to write in the notepad.

I think the city is trying to kill me. I've reached the shores of downtown, and things have never been so morose.

The walk down North Alameda was filled with plenty of brash 'super saver' type stores that pandered only to the lower class. The vulnerable types that had a child at a very young age because 'feeling good' was far more paramount than 'planning for the future'. The type, blinkered by their unfettered testosterone, that pursued a life of fulfillment, searching his potential as a dime store Casanova, which would stop at nothing to champion his dream of becoming famous, at the ill-advised counsel of his family, that inevitably became a heroin addict and never meet his son or daughter. Meanwhile, the single mother would monotonously shop at such stores labeled 'Exports and Wholesale' in the hope of her own serenity. And, as her hips grew larger from Big Matt's inexhaustible and inexpensive food, she will pray to dear God above that her child will become an enormous success in the NFL, or even possibly get an education that might take him to a level above her own station. All the while, growing exhausted from raising a child that curses the fatherless world he was born into,

The Call of the Void

she envelops any form of distraction she can in front of her child. No toll of electronic entertainment can sate the young, increasingly fattening, boy's appetite for a distraction from the world slowly suffocating him into adulthood. The mother, distraught, begins to search for programs at the local school that the tired teachers and counselors roll out for fear of being sued. And if, in an alternate universe, an honest conversation was to happen it might sound like, 'Your son is a real asshole.' 'He doesn't have a father cunt. He's been an asshole his entire life.' 'I want to teach kids who actually want to learn. I take pride in struggling kids, but your kid just doesn't give a shit.' 'So, what should I do bitch?' 'Well, you fat, toddling cunt, I think you ought to send him to reform school where he can properly mature and receive a proper education and, oh, maybe get a strong male role model. You know, the type of education and role models we, as a public education system, tried to instill before you fucking, troglodytic, imbecilic, absentee parents threw out the window because your kid was too stressed, or we started to take over as the parent and your insecurity as a bad parent made you rebel against. Something like that, twat...' 'Thanks bitch. I'll look into that.' 'Cheers'. Instead, the conversations usually go something like, 'My boy is not concentrating. My friend told me about an IEP for him.' 'Ma'am, what does your son do after school? How long does he spend reading and working on homework?' 'Oh, I don't know. He's in his room a lot. I try to take his phone away, but he gets so upset when I do and, honestly, he's the only man that is in my life that matters, and I could never imagine upsetting his sensibilities toward me.' The entire staff looks at each other in such

163

a way that only patients on suicide watch glance at one another. 'Sure, ma'am, we can give him an IEP.' 'Oh, Thank you. I just know he will be able to turn it around now.' And then the mother, filled with alacrity at her son's chance at a better education, goes back to work to make a better life for her son. She works the long hours in order to work her way up the proverbial food chain at her 9-5 in order to better provide for her son. And still, her dreams of a better life are veiled by an enormous secret that was her illusion of 'movin' on up' before her son presents to her a failing report card with five F's and a D in gym before succumbing once more to the television. He simply tells his mother 'Don't worry ma'. I'm getting pretty good at this shit. I can just stream for it.' The mother, with a lachrymose sense of sympathy at the boy who could never escape her, hugged him and simply said 'I'll take care of us buddy. We made it either way. The American Dream isn't you getting some education, but us being able to afford the luxuries in life. One day, you'll find your way. You take your time baby. Momma brings in close to 80,000 a year. We're good.' Meanwhile, the boy's father has died not long after that from a hot dose. In due course, one must still wonder if, had the father not left, it would have been better for the boy considering the mother's ambition was sparked solely on the father's exile but then the father and mother together would have been toxic and-

"Hey boss." A homeless man announced, breaking my frenetic concentration, "You got a light?"

"Huh? Oh, uh, yeah. I need one of those too." I said, examining the butt of my last cigarette between my fingers.

The Call of the Void

The homeless man pulled out a second cigarette before I waved it off.

"I just meant... never mind." I said, handing him my zippo. A violinist, smoking his own roll, was playing for quarters in the background. "Is this the way to the convention center?"

"Yeah. You can get there by going west on Olympic. You in town for the conference?"

"In a manner of speaking."

"Well," the man said, tossing me my zippo and inhaling his cigarette, "Fuck you."

I waved amiably. "I hear ya."

The cross streets of Alameda and Olympic had a quasi 'walk of the stars' type sign at the corner. The sign read:

James Woods BLVD due West

Brad Pitt RD due East

Bob Hope LN due South

Tom Holland Ave due North

Saoirse Ronan Ct due Northwest

Tom Hanks DR due Southwest

Cate Blanchette Ter due Northeast

Hugh Grant Pl due Southeast

I took the man's advice and headed West.

The city was clustered and dark, impregnated by the same ordinarily white, post-industrial buildings that had made LA such a banal, yet flamboyant, city. Those with a lobotomized sense of hope often said, 'There are so many more beautiful parts to see. There is the walk of stars. There are the few and far between restaurants that might make you wait for an hour for a foamy mayonnaise induced pâté that is drizzled with Sweet Baby Ray's Honey Mustard reduction for a mere $107.75.' All anybody could see down here though are miles of abandoned buildings and contumelious people begging for a chance to dull themselves, to escape from what it's like to be human. To forget they even once had a consciousness, while they pace the street like an endless track, stuck in some acid trip on a vibrant hellish landscape.

Nearly a tenth of a mile down the street, a sign read 'Sammy's Hot Brew' and was completely fenced off from the rest of the street. I walked to the front and showed the bouncer my ID. The doorman looked me up and down with a concerned glare, scrutinizing my attire. I looked down at my jeans and white sneakers before staring at him again and giving him an awkward smile. He reluctantly waved me in.

Inside the parking lot, as CCR's 'Bad Moon Rising' played on a jukebox, there were numerous ersatz casino tables surrounded by the local denizens, anathematizing each lost hand or foul roll of the dice. Near the entrance, blackjack tables made of overturned bar stools and lawn turf were filled with both Caucasian and Asian males. The roulette tables, cheaply made out of inferior bar tops with drink umbrellas for each marker, rested in the middle of the lot, filled with cars abound on every side. I smiled at the makeshift craps table near the entrance of the steakhouse and wrote a quick blurb in my notebook.

The Call of the Void

Craps had always been my game in Vegas as it has the highest odds for the casual player. Only a fool, unless counting cards, trusts his fortune to blackjack. Craps is nearly 50/50 odds if, that is, one knew how to play right. Betting the field is no good, and neither is the Big six and eight that is invitingly flashed to the novice better. Betting the pass line is a sure go, even for veteran betters, as long as one plays the odds. I believe, as any levelheaded gambler might, that the Don't Pass Line is the way to go. Place a minimum chip on the don't pass— assuming the shooter isn't some rogue offspring of St. Michael himself—and wait to make that bet back two times over. Then, when the house's chips are stacked up, start placing on the 6 and the 8—the two most hit, and lucrative, numbers outside of the unspeakable number '7'. In cases where neophytes want to place on the—gasps—'7', they must abide by strict parlance at the table by calling said number 'Big Red', lest he be dragged off kicking and screaming by some vindictive band of over-the-hill bettors trying to beat the 'bad luck' out of him.

As the smell of freshly grilled ribeyes from the nearby steakhouse perforated the air, I bit my fingernails in anticipation. Truthfully, betting had always been my most treasured vice. I had bet on education, my job, my livelihood, and even the fool-hearted journey I'd taken on tonight. Above all else though, Craps was my game. I might not make it to the end of the line tonight if I go on a heater.

I could smell the intoxicating aroma of cigarettes, liquor, and sweat against die. The one thing that might make me break the façade of nihilism tonight just might be the thrill of fighting, arguing, rolling, and winning. An overwhelming impulse to shred my shirt, go to an ATM and drink myself silly on the table had suddenly come over me.

A man, watching as I approached the table, squatted his legs widely against the ground and began to hiss, "Interloper!" He watched me for a second more before rushing off behind the parked cars against the wall.

"Shit house mouse!" a voice from the half-full table screamed.

"Fucking boxcar that I already had on the God damn table before that roll. Rolled twice already!"

"I'm always getting fucked out of a good roll. God damnit!"

I stood over the table as the stickman pulled the dice back to himself. The leftmost dealer placed the puck on the 'Off' side. I took my opportunity and placed 200 dollars on the table. The stickman, directly beside me, eyeballed my cash for a moment before looking me over.

"I don't know you."

I gave a mocking wave toward the cash. "My money isn't green?"

He stared at me, then my money, then me again, before looking over my shoulder at someone in the distance. "Whatever. New shooter!"

I looked over my shoulder to see who he was looking at. Nothing. I shrugged and pulled the second and fifth die from the five on the table. Each die needed to have the same number on top as its opposing die. A ridiculous superstition but one I never broke. The key was to have each number for each side opposite the top to display a-

"Hey! New bitch! You shootin' or what?"

"Hold your fucking horses!" I yelled, "You're cooling off the table!"

I swept my wrist to the back of the table and cut the die through the air like buckshot against the wall. A five and two landed. Hollering from half the table drowned out any jeers from the 'No Pass Line'. A quick estimation put the median age at this table around 45 but there were still a few men around my age. A man with a wizened face, wearing a Nirvana shirt, spat tobacco into his empty whiskey tumbler. Another man, far older yet far comelier, stood staring at me with glazed over eyes as he sipped his hot toddy. He only placed five dollars on the pass line. His eyes, cold and white, followed my every move. Beside him, a boy, possibly a freshman in college, dressed in his finest polo, laughed as he put a nominal amount of his father's fortune—in the sum of 300 dollars—on the pass line. The older male beside him had all of a sudden disappeared. His spot was quickly filled by a middle-aged man with thick, horn-rimmed glasses. I grabbed the die in front of me and threw a six against the board as the ambrosial smell of honey made my nose twitch.

"How's the night?" The elderly man beside me whispered. "Enjoying yourself?"

I gave him a blithe look before grabbing the die. "Fine. Just fine."

I threw an 8 which I covered with the Come bet.

169

LeResche

"Sure. And I suppose you don't realize that some here see you as an outsider?"

I broke on a Lil' Joe which I had wagered with a 10, scoring 100 instantly. "Are you running this game? Is that what you're talking about? I'll fuck off. I don't want any trouble." I said, paying no particular attention to the man.

"Yes. I run this game. But that is not what I'm asking. You can stay here all night and I'll even run you a credit." The man gave a resigned sigh. "If that might assuage you from moving forward tonight, I can certainly make that happen."

I looked over my shoulder to meet the man's gaze, a little confused by his sudden generosity, before throwing a six against the board. He trailed back into the deeper, darker recesses of the parking lot, urging me on as he curled his extended coke nail. I collected my winnings and tipped the stickman. Standing beside a Volvo and a Bentley, the man waved me on once again. I walked toward him, the poison of uncertainty coursing through my veins.

"There is nothing out there for you Sam." He said, snorting a bump from his nail.

"You're telling me."

The hissing man from before ran up behind the elderly gentleman and locked his grasp around the man's left leg. The elderly man patted him on the head and began to walk away.

"I'll be just a few minutes." He said, patting the man on the back as he trailed off.

The Call of the Void

The alcohol was finally taking effect, warming my brain and giving me a fleeting sense of euphoria. With a false, drunken sense of ingenuity, I took yet another opportunity to write in my notebook, as it was all I had to pass the time and stay sane.

"The human consciousness has the ability to transcend the current reality we live in. It is, by all measures, the most powerful tool. It is the most powerful tool we currently have in this world. It has the ability to shirk pain, depravity, poverty, and decadence of the soul. Yet still, the collective human consciousness has imprisoned itself into a box of seemingly worldly pleasures. How could one not surrender themselves to the thought of infamy, riches, and self-gratification. It is a dopamine far greater than we could ever imagine. From the moment we are born, our survival instincts force us to subvert to the will of immortality. Our conscious minds, which are far too evolved, neglect the simple pleasures of a day at the fair and a walk in the park for an undying desire to have our words and our name last the ages. And what ages? The ages of a hundred years? A thousand years? A million years? All our names will compact into metaphorical dust after the big star in the sky that gives us light ceases to be. And, for a moment, let us entertain the idea that the sun never fades away and earth is eternal. Let us give weight to the idea that human consciousness will live forever. Will we not eventually be buried by the simple idea of obscurity. Our ideas will only last for as long as they are relevant. The idea itself is crippling to the common man as they live under the façade that their 'name', which is wholly immaculate in their own minds, may be passed through the ages. The thought of non-existence is only

frightening to us because of our own evolved consciousness. We fear the thought of never being born because our current consciousness is so pleasurable. It is these very people that weep over the thought of trillions of semen ejaculated daily that they may never experience a life like ours. A life that is little more than an aberration of nature in which a daily schedule that is only tempered by the flames of drinking, fucking, and passively negating the reality of its own conscious thoughts gives us peace. Why then, with the luck of the draw in the human reproductive system, do we not surmount our blessings by remaining completely passive to pleasure and enjoy what biology has given us? Simply stated, it is because we desire pleasure and entertainment to distract from our looming doom. That one day, a thousand years from now, you will be referred to as 'great-ancestor' rather than your first name. Every human being on this planet shares a conscious reality that they may never change. If you are a billionaire or a street dweller, you are still completely beholden to ideals and laws set upon you by men that are no different from yourself. The greatest struggle of mankind is not accepting this but, rather, accepting the reality that the individual is nothing more than an animal. Yet, our consciousness brought about a great responsibility that we seem to neglect. A responsibility that we cannot come to terms with. A responsibility that we throw away for the principle of 'You can do this but not that.' In lieu of 'We are conscious beings that will not be conditioned to believe another conscious being's will.' At what point will man think for himself and understand the trifles of the modern world are hardly worth a moment of thought in its own mind? Nature has its paradoxes as does everything else. Nature's

The Call of the Void

greatest paradox is man's evolvement of consciousness. As we break the intellectual dimension that holds us prisoner, we broke through to another, more sophisticated, dimension that keeps us just as imprisoned. We are, by nature, meant to be more entertained, more well fed, more in power, and more captive than any other species on earth. Instead of belaying such atrocities to our DNA, we instead choose to stay in our prisons of self-gratification. No other animal on earth accepts captivity with such happiness than we do. The Lion fights. The gorilla rebukes. The man loves."

The elderly man came back as I was putting my pen away. He squared himself up in front of me. "You're obviously not an idiot. You can make out that I know enough by now. This journey, this... odyssey into the city, is foolish. You can't convince your students to listen to you. What makes you think you can make yourself listen to you. I can make it better. For you, that is. I can let you score, legitimately, as much off the craps table as you'd like. Afterwards, anything else you want, whores, steak at the steakhouse, drugs— psychedelics I presume? More alcohol? It's yours."

"Wait." I said, holding my hand up, "Have you been calling me tonight?"

"You still sound like a boy, you know that? The great brilliant, perennial boy wonder of Western Philosophy, who sounds no different than the average talking head." His head tilted and his smile shriveled. "I meant no offense. You're simply a paradox. That's all. A mind of found potential that is interacting with a world that has forced you to diminish any sense of consciousness you fight to preserve. That is your forte, is it not? Consciousness? I've read some of your theorems. You're too personal and too scathing in your climaxes. You push a train of thought that you, and only you, take as an axiom of the human mind in the hopes of changing the collective human consciousness but you fail to understand humans as a whole. You, like myself, are an observer. You're extremely well-read but you fail to echo the axioms you have studied. Instead of reiterating or even incorporating your ideas, you create new ones. It's too frightening to mankind. Once more, too personal and not personal enough."

"You work at the University?" I said, scratching my head, "Wait, do you know Felix? That's it, isn't it? This is a test."

"Not hardly." He laughed, "And I don't need to work at a university. I am everywhere at once and it is severely within my power to ensure you are not 'born posthumously' as you might wish. You are what we cannot have in this world; a man who flouts the idea of inequitable power between man and the powers that be. You are a man that was far more common amongst your heroes but must die outright amongst your peers. Each creator is a threat to the power that is currently held in balance. You are inspired but you do not reiterate. You move the conversation forward. You cannot, in this new world, be allowed to continue. So, I offer you this one-time reprieve from your own consciousness. I will put you at the head of the department of Humanities and you will be able to teach the extension of your knowledge on consciousness, metaphysical translations, phenomenology, and any other trifle you wish to ponder."

The Call of the Void

My eyes fell on his open hand as he stretched it out. I looked back up at him and noticed, under the streetlamp's light, that his eyes were different colors and one of them was a prosthetic. He had the eyes of a fractious and acrimonious animal, green and blue, that shined dully in the moon's light. His left eye, green and glossy, moved vacantly amongst the night's sky, scanning for something in the distance, while his right eye remained fixed on me sharply. His face was that of a man that had weathered nothing but tragedy his entire life.

"I'm not too sure just what's, uh, being implied here. And, meaning no offense, I doubt you have that kind of pull at the university. So, I'm going to head out."

Closing his eyes and cracking his neck, he breathed through his nose with regret.

"You are nothing Killian. You are a drunk. You will fade into the void upon your death and will be nothing but a blip in a seventh edition philosophical index. Your greatest desire is immortality, like every writer and philosopher before you, but you will never be remembered, and you will become nothing more than drivel on a footnote. Your ideas and writings are nothing more, I must say, than absolute shit. You are the reproductive fluid in a porno. You fucking fool, you-"

I snorted and smiled. "I believe it was Lucretius who said, 'Man's greatest wealth is to live on a little with contented mind; for little is never lacking'. Now, give me the front and I'll think about it."

He stared at me with narrow eyes, taking the time to consider my offer. His outfit was cheap and probably from a pimp's thrift store.

175

He wore silk, paisley pants that cuffed around his white Reebok's and his shirt was pressed with extra starch that made his collar stick out from side to side without any other support. He was bald with a prominent cul-de-sac and had the mustache of a walrus, starting high on his nose and moving well past his lip. By the time he opened his mouth to answer, the anticipation had made me impatient.

"Thank you, Sam. Thank you for proving my point; that drunk as you are, you can still recite pablum ad nauseum."

"No," I said in a serious tone, "You're right. I am a fool. I have the worst case of imposter syndrome any psychologist has seen. I am a fool for believing this walk tonight would make even one iota of difference. I'm a fool for believing my colleagues would ever take me seriously in academia. They see me as little more than a novelty act because my parents worked sinecures and remained in the middle-class. I use a vocabulary I've known since the eighth grade in the hopes that it will equivocate and mask my perceived inadequacies as a 'precocious professor'. I do so in the hopes of being seen as smart. And yet, existence is nothing more than delirium and failed maxim after failed maxim. But I have to ask, why do you care? Why do you offer me this bargain?"

"I offer you this, Sam," he sighed, glancing down for a moment, "because your 'walk', as you put it, is inimical to our future. You WILL refuse my offer and any other and will inevitably write about tonight and cast a nasty aspersion around a system that has to operate in order for mankind to continue. My desire for power aside, you must think of mankind as a sleepwalker. I know the old myth is not true but for comparative measures, stick with me. Mankind is a sleepwalking giant and if you are to wake them, they will severely harm themselves."

"Whose future? What power? What are you talking about? I don't give a fuck about any of this-this-"

"Neither do they." He made a grand, sweeping gesture at the casino tables behind him, "But, eventually, as time corrodes the edges of our control, your words will resonate with a few before finally, exponentially, germinating to the once believed immutable masses before an unavoidable uprising happens."

"Plenty of philosophers have pontificated on the restraints of mankind."

"But, Sam, none of them have experienced it the way you will tonight. You are the microscope on mankind in the 21st century."

"So much for my theories being too 'personal'. Thanks for giving me a big head but the truth is that I'm not that powerful. Or influential. And honestly, I'm starting to like it. The idea that every thought of care and concern is truly superficial is enlightening on some level."

"You'll be seeing me Sam. This isn't over."

I lit a cigarette and sauntered back down the main road. "*This isn't over*" I japed in a mocking tone, "The night beckons me, and the fettering of my soul must never be... fettered. Whatever. I'm not a fucking poet."

LeResche

The path ahead bifurcated into two directions from North to South. Cesar Chavez Avenue was littered with shopping malls that were abandoned years ago yet still had the lights on inside. Parking lots, halfway homes and cash for gold stores were all a constant reminder of the perceptual frailties to the unfamiliar thought of what it means to be human. The buffet, opposite a dim sum restaurant, simply named 'Buffet', had a line going out the front door. My stomach growled, chastising me for nurturing myself with beer and whiskey, so I went in.

The entrance was inviting, draped in a myriad of shaded purple and gold colors with a red carpet to its doorway, beckoning the eye of anyone with twenty dollars to spend. A Recusant was sitting on the outskirts of the parking lot while an employee sprayed his face with a hose. With a fairly brisk windchill, the temperature was dropping into the mid-40s, approaching a record for Los Angeles in November over the last decade. The employee, wearing a backwards visor and the company's uniform polo, laughed dully as he sprayed the denuded Recusant in the face, pressing his finger on the nozzle to widen the stream and hit the rest of his body. The Recusant's eyes moved from the employee to me. They were wide and confident, shouting to the world that he would die tonight, and that he would hardly regret forfeiting his life to the city.

"This fuckin' idiot has been out here starving himself for five days." The employee's laugh turned to a cough.

"Spraying him is obviously working." I said.

The teen, his face pocked with acne and turning a dark red, faced me and twisted his facial features in resentment before laughing once more at the Recusant.

"Management says it sends a message."

"Sends a message? This is a buffet. What the fuck do people coming in here care about him?"

"Cause' we can."

Inside the restaurant, the smell of pork, burnt tallow, and fried bread was nauseously intoxicating, brusquely battering the air without mercy. Oddly enough, in stark opposition to Matt's, the establishment harbored more than just corpulent patrons. Humans of all shapes, sizes, and ages enwrapped every booth of the restaurant. The walls were lined with orange fabric and the booths were covered in red velvet. The smell of MSG poisoned the air and threw off a pestilence of noxious malaise.

I took a seat in the only open booth and grabbed the plate in front of me. Moving toward the tables of copious meat and bread products, I overheard a man, who was clearly an environmental nut, speak.

"I am so glad this place has cage free chicken. Have you seen them in those cages? I would never."

A waitress walked up to his four-top table, placing waters on each of their paper coasters.

"Oh! Congratulations!" The waitress said to a pregnant woman at the table.

LeResche

The woman scowled at the waitress, taking another sip of her cocktail. "I'm not keeping it."

I placed a roll on my plate before moving down to the 'Mexican' portion of the buffet, which was little more than congealed, refried beans and brown rice—a travesty for any native Mexican to see. The seemingly infinite number of patrons found themselves scraping every single bean out of the steam pan and tapping their toes in anticipation while the chef rushed out to bring another pan for them to heinously fight over. I grabbed a few slices of carne asada.

The tables were endless, holding inexhaustible heaps of meat, starches and limp vegetables kept warm by heat lamps and steam tables plastered from wall to wall. A rather large woman began to shift her hip forcefully into mine in an effort to move me down the line. Her partner, from the look of it, began to rev the motor of her rascal scooter into my ankle over and over again until I was forced into yet another unnecessary cornucopia of human despair; the seafood section. On one, unexplainably large steam table of human megalomania, there was a platter of boundless crab legs. I walked closer, trying to get one of the legs, as a slew of patrons with two plates clamored over the horde of red, crustaceous meat and dug in with one plate, which they used as an improvised shovel, before placing it onto another.

"With apologies to moderation..." I whispered to no one.

"I need energy for tonight." A voice yelled out before breaking a plate over the head of another diner.

The Call of the Void

A leviathan of a woman sat on her rascal scooter, driving herself madly into the mob of hyperventilating buffet goers before flying just a foot short of the front line.

"Need them legs, Sarah." She breathed.

To which the bovine woman nodded. The hungry, unrelenting eyes of every human in line pierced me with a sense of fear I had never known. There seemed to be no sign of magnanimity anywhere in the establishment. And yet, amongst the bestial rabble, there was a sense of ovine-like abeyance amongst the crowd. Any sense of tact or savoir-faire had fled the diner.

The side-by-side room that filled eager customers was constricted only by a lattice barrier that was merely a cage to keep the beasts off of one another. A man with three plates in front of him let out a bellow, like that of a javelina in heat, before scarfing down the most varied continental dinner known to man. His children, aping their father's gustatory interests, followed their patriarch into the trans-fat ladled tables. The only thing missing was an anthropologist to record the data.

Behind the latticed cage, a swirling of shrimp shells and sesame seeds began flying wildly in the air. Breathing fire, the gaunt, almost rail-like man, who opposed the hybrid boar family was inhaling food at an even faster pace than any morbidly obese person in the establishment. A din of grunts and sloshes had commenced amongst the buffet goers that seemed to consist of the incredibly corpulent and the incredibly cadaverous. Chicken wings flew and gasses, which would most certainly put a hole in the ozone, sprayed amongst the bordello of beef as patrons that identified with their own body types cheered for their respective champions. One such large male, mashed potatoes still glazing the outer parts of his mouth and stuffed tightly into his cheeks, demanded the head of the skinny, endurance eater, as another, far more flaccid, buffet goer, with a lemon water, began to decry the woes of the obese amongst the thin. The boar's offspring guzzled down grits, cream corn, and ranch dressing in incredibly fascinating succession. Not to be out done, the thin competition eater began sucking down crab legs two at a time. However, the nightmare was abruptly ended by a bus boy that came in to commence damage control by saying:

"Please! There is enough for everyone who can pay!"

With a snarl, and another bite of roast beef chewed by both parties, the men went back to their respective booths.

Not long after the mayhem, many of the thinner man's devotees—himself included—began to make the trek toward the bathroom. I needed to take a piss, so I trailed along behind them. I opened the door to hear sounds of retching echoing off the walls. Each set of heaves had a unique tone of its own, rhythmically playing off one another. Noisome bile and vomit flooded the floor, spilling under the stall doors, forcing me to rush back toward the entrance, my package still in my hand, as the men's fervid purging reached its climax. One by one they came slouching out of the stalls, gripping one another in triumph, content that they would never be like *those* other men out there. They would never defile themselves the way those men had. And as their smiles grew larger, more men rushed through the door, disgorging the night's repast into every receptacle in sight from urinal, to toilet, to trashcan. I walked back over to the toilet, stepping on any clean, dry surface there was, like playing some childhood game of 'The Floor is Lava'. When I turned around, the men, woozy from lack of nutrition and an abundance of conceit, began to hold hands in a séance of sorts just outside the open bathroom door. I narrowed my eyes and focused on the group, noticing one man shushing the crowd as he pulled out a Klondike bar

"Anybody care to partake?"

The group of men became giddy, transcending to an almost ethereal state, as they each took a single, molecular bite out of the bar.

Back in the buffet's arena, there was a cacophony that would raise the gods of Crisco on Mount Hellman's. A crowd of both round and thin alike created an aisle of sorts to a table of screaming trenchermen.

"Oh Jesus! Is there a doctor here?!" The woman yelled, looking at me directly.

"I'm not a doctor! I-I mean- I'm not a medical doctor!" I corrected.

"This man is choking!"

A man, eating by himself at a nearby table, was scratching violently at his neck as his face became increasingly inflated and red. He jerked his neck from side to side, crashing the sides of his face into each side of the booth as though his head might leave his body. His face was turning blue.

"Hurry! Does anyone know the Heimlich maneuver? This man is choking!"

"I got it!" a young man announced boisterously, holding his phone up in the air like a triumphant knight in King Arthur's court.

He began to scroll through his phone, swiping up on the screen a hundred times to close out of the apps he had open in order to get to YouTube. The entire audience looked over his shoulder like a group of medical students in an operating theater watching brain surgery. The savior of this house of beef flew his hands into the air defiantly, shaking his head as he watched his phone.

"Damn it! YouTube has an ad. It'll take another fifteen seconds."

The asphyxiated man began to pound the sides of both men on his left and right.

"Just another second pal! We'll have you back here in a jiff!"

The purple-faced man was flailing his arms aggressively.

"Hey." I said pointing an open palm toward the choking man, "I don't think this guy is choking."

"Have you looked this up on YouTube?" The young man asked, "No? Then fuck off!"

The purple-faced man, whose head was now the size of a basketball, was motioning toward his pocket.

"Almost there! Only 7 seconds left."

"Hurry up man! This fucker is choking!"

"It's running an ad!"

"Just skip it!"

"I can't! It's a 15 second one!"

"Go to another video sometimes they don't have ads."

The Call of the Void

"That would sink time into another video that may or may not have an ad and-"

"It's starting! Skip ahead to the maneuver!"

"I think he's having an allergic reaction." I said, walking toward the man as he did his best to nod with what little neck he had left.

"Here! Got it! Heimlich maneuver!"

Both men grabbed the man by the sternum and began to dry hump him into a state of apoplexy.

"He isn't choking! Where's his EpiPen?!" I wailed, searching through his pockets and pulling out the pen, "He's allergic to something!"

"You know how to use this?" The local hero demanded, swiping the pen from my hand.

"No," I said, thumbing toward the nearly dead purple man, "Ask him."

"Okay. Open YouTube again." He ordered, throwing his buddy the phone.

The two men watched another thirty second advertisement anxiously. The crowd meticulously stroked their egos with shouts of '*You can do it!*' and '*Save him boys!*' before I put two fingers on the man's neck.

"Hey! We got it. Hold on there's another ad."

"He's dead." I muttered

"Wha- How do yo-"

"I'm not a medical doctor, but he's fuckin' gone. Look."

185

The group of onlookers took a moment to console the men that attempted to save his life. They crossed their chests with the sign of the father before calling an ambulance.

"Shit!" a voice behind me shouted out "I think I was supposed to put up a sign about peanuts or shellfish or something. Damn..."

I looked over my shoulder and saw the young man that was hosing down the Recusant earlier. In his hand, he had the Recusant firmly in his grasp, frozen like a trussed Butterball turkey, dragging him across the marble floor. The Recusant was lifeless, his eyes thoroughly glazed over.

"Damn." He said once more

I walked outside and exhaled deeply before searching through my pockets. A thin, elderly man sat alone, his head moving slowly in the direction of each passerby. Some of them dropped money while others ignored him completely. His mouth hung open as if he had forgotten how to close it. A needle stuck out of his right arm with the plunger pushed down halfway, his tie off still dangling loosely around his bicep. I pulled out my flask and sat beside him. When I did, his head turned to meet me.

"I remember you." The old junky whispered. "You once carried ashes, but now you have fire."

"How's it going?" I said, lighting a cigarette and ignoring his previous statement.

"That's the first time someone has asked me that in a long time. I'm high, so, I'm good."

"Mmhmm."

The man gripped his limp left hand with vigor and gritted his teeth before falling backwards into the wall, bouncing his head right off the bricks. "What do you think this world is?"

"Oh, God. Not another deep conversation."

"Hmmm, well?" He smiled, revealing gaps in between most of his teeth.

I rested my head against the wall behind me and exhaled a jet of smoke that sprawled out amongst the stars. "I've been trying to figure that out tonight."

"There's nothing quite like watching Leaving Las Vegas with a big, fat cocktail in your hand; watching Super-Size Me while eating a Big Mac. It's always changing but our job is to assess whether it is change for better or worse. I guess we can look at the opposition to this world as 'reactionary' or even 'old-fashioned' but isn't there some give? I mean, don't we sometimes see entities as monosyllabic, purple, people eaters of-"

"You lost me, old timer."

The elderly man snapped out of his stupor and eyeballed me carefully. "Sorry. I just think that everyone enjoys a vice but eventually traverses that vice for their own individual desires. We were once individuals that abandoned our reason for-" The old, heroin filled sage took a moment to stare at his own hands. "For... for comfort."

187

"Shit," I laughed, "You should teach at UCLA, and I should do heroin."

His shrunken face looked at me momentarily before sinking into a garbage bag pillow filled with trash. "I did teach at UCLA. I used to be the head of the department of literature there."

I felt like fainting.

V

LA's sky had turned a light burgundy, a color most Californians associated with seasonal fires plaguing the rural lands. But it wasn't the season. November was far too late in the year to see something this bad erupt out of nowhere. Nature's wrath had finally broken its arrangement with the city and was fiercely devouring the heavens, fighting desperately for control of the sky against the moon's tendrils of light, which had already consumed the stars.

It was already 9:30, but the sky lit up like judgment at Sodom and Gomorrah. Particles of ash floated in the air, dancing around from side to side like smooth, rhythmic angels, misting the welkin above with an indissoluble gray blanket. Even so, the surrounding fires made no impact on November's gelid air. I turned my head, shivering mildly and stifled by the freeze, to find a billboard thermometer close by—it read 22 °F. It had to be Celsius. I was certain it was busted. Still, it was becoming impossible to tell whether the visibility of my breath was from condensation or cigarette smoke.

Downtown LA had an informal entrance—off the radar and free from prying eyes—near 9th street. I approached the street to find it barricaded with a bulwark of camera flashes and a mob of yelling maniacs. One of LA's many prominent theaters was contrasted against a seedy apartment complex, the terrain consisting of strung-out tramps and lifeless entities trying to make their way home. That very theater, which poorly attempted to mimic Grauman's Chinese Theater, had prided itself on spiritual decadence and imperiousness. Still, in recent years, the theater had garnered a large crowd from its 'celebrity' guest list, filled with the new age stars of streaming entertainment. YouTube royalty and Social Media influencers, often donned in tacky and ostentatious apparel, were frequently invited to attend the premiere of several B-movies. Accompanying them were an onslaught of voyeurs that desired nothing more than to live in their presence. Living vicariously through their modern-day heroes, these proselytes of the digital age, whose demographics ranged from pre-adolescents to squat, balding middle-aged fellows, watched as the world was set ablaze in the decay that their own heroes had conjured for them.

I moved in closer for a glance at the future of entertainment while avoiding the blinding flash from an onslaught of camera phones. As I lowered my hand from my face and got closer to the purple carpet, a photographer in his mid-30s stopped me abruptly and began to shout.

"Father! Father adversary!" he yelled, placing both his index fingers pointed upright on the back of his head, "Bringer of subterfuge that would uproot our ways!"

I inched forward as he hopped on each foot, bouncing from side to side while an unsettling grin formed on his face. I pointed to the middle of my chest and mouthed, "Me?" The photographer's camera dangled around his neck as he nodded and pointed at me with his right index finger, keeping his left positioned above his head.

The Call of the Void

"I invoke you God! Strike down our adversary! Father! Come no further!" he said, hopping again from side to side on each foot, his right index finger placed behind his head once more.

Confused, I froze in my tracks. A man on the distant purple carpet, wearing a suit far too garish for his own good, began curling two fingers in my direction. "Yo! He's good my man. He's with us. That's my boy Brad!" The man on the carpet gave me a mawkish grin, opening his arms and begging me to come in for a hug, like we were long lost friends.

"Brad!" the man slurred, bringing me in closer for a hug, "Brad, you gotta stick by my side."

His breath hit me square in the face—a distinctly repellent aroma of bile, cheap wine, and female genitalia—and penetrated my nose, forcing me to jerk my head over to the side and glower back at the flashing cameras.

I lit a cigarette and looked from him to the floor humorlessly, deciding to go along with the mistake. "Sorry pal. I think the bright lights got the better of me."

"Brad," the overdressed man said, making a *tsking* sound "Brad, you can't smoke in there. And I mean that with a 'T-H-E-Y-R-E' Braddy. A real fucking drag to smoke in there man."

Whatever this idiot was on, I was going to need something even stronger to get through this walk with him.

"Right," I exhaled "How's a big YouTube star like you-"

"Twitter." He corrected.

191

"Of course," I said, smacking my forehead playfully, "Twitter. And death to any detractor of- what was your name again?"

His look was so vacant I would have guessed his conscious mind was lost somewhere between Fentanyl Boulevard and Margarita Lane.

"Look Brad," he said, leading us further down the carpet, "I pulled in a big favor bringing you here. Do you realize how accomplished these people are? How accomplished I am?"

"Right," I said, holding back a laugh "And, pray tell, what are your polished laurels? Any accolades to mention, hmmm?"

"Acco- um. Wait..."

"Your accomplishments, buddy." I said, flicking the ash from my cigarette into the air, "I always forget."

"Look Brad," he slapped my chest with the back of his hand playfully, "My advertisers cannot know this but between you and I, I run the secret account that promotes my tweets. It's far more money than just advertising through Twitter. It's really fucked up man. I feel like I betrayed.... I betrayed a lot of people doing it."

"What?"

"Braddy. If I continue on this path, I may lose followers. The trademark 'Lance Bishop' will be nothing more than a.... than a-"

"Superficial title?"

"I'm already super my man." He answered, his eyes nearly rolling in the back of his head every time he dropped his shades to look at me, "Look. Look at these people taking pictures."

The Call of the Void

The crowd was practically wetting their pants trying to get to this meretricious fool who was so obviously obliterated. Fandom had always been an unfortunate verity amongst the masses, but there was some point in recent years where it folded in upon itself, and those who are now the most zealously followed are the most talentless.

"Braddy," Lance whispered, rubbing his eyes underneath his shades and letting out a burp, "You'll always be my friend, right?"

I stood there for a moment eyeballing the inebriated lout. I wanted to ask him, 'What's the definition of abnegate?' or even 'Do you know what city you're in right now?' before telling him 'No, Lance. We aren't friends.' But something deep in me resisted the low hanging fruit dangling directly in front of my face. In that moment, staring into his empty eyes, watching as he slouched closer and closer to the ground, something inside me felt pity. Something, or someone, was behind his obviously undeserved infamy.

"Yeah," I muttered, "Friends 'til the end pal."

"I love you Braddy."

Lance gave a smile that left his face hanging like a stroke victim. He hung his arm around my shoulder.

"Yeah. Let's meet your friends." I said.

Flashing strobe lights pulsated synchronously as we entered the theater, forcing Lance and I to shield our faces with our arms. The lobby was draped in velvet cloth and costumes were displayed in glass cases with plaques underneath. Ushers were moving walls and snack stands out of the room, revealing a larger, more hip, atmosphere with dance floors, a bar, and a DJ booth. It happened almost too fast, too instantaneously, for me to even comprehend. Attractive influencers and chiseled internet stars flooded the room, a rapt cupidity forming amongst them as they groped one another carelessly, never recognizing the theater transforming right in front of their eyes.

I raced over to the drink cart with my hand outstretched to stop the waiter. I grabbed two of the shots on the cart and took them in stride, wincing at the bite of tequila. The waiter regarded me with repulsed eyes as I gracelessly fumbled my flask out of my pocket and asked if I could get a refill. He shook his head shamefully and filled my flask.

Lance took a moment to vomit in the faux palm tree near the eastern part of the nightclub as hordes of 'journalists' with phones in their outstretched arms bombarded him. I thought about helping him, but my pity had its limits. A rather surly, buxom blonde approached me. Her nails were longer than her fingers and her dress was blindingly golden, like a fulgent sun breaking at dawn. She wore platform flip flop heels much like the women in those old Steve Madden commercials.

"You're Lance's friend, right?" She asked, her voice nasally and tinny.

"Sure, I guess."

"Would you be an angel and tell him I'm mad at him?"

"Look, I really don't-"

A slew of 'paparazzi' began to focus their attention on us.

"He knows I'm mad. But, if you told him, he might get a little more upset."

The Call of the Void

"I see." I said, trying to figure out just when it was that I became embroiled in these people's drama, "And what do you do?"

"Wow. They just let Lance bring anyone in here nowadays I see." She huffed, "I started on YouTube but, I mean, it's not even a big deal, but, I mean, I pick fights with reality TV stars, sleep with them, and then post it to my Only Fans account."

"Lance is on reality TV?"

"No. He's my boyfriend."

"So, he-" Both of her pupils were moving oddly, shifting from right to left, struggling to maintain eye contact with mine, "Never mind."

I pushed my way through a ravine of silicone breasts and a cloud of Brut cologne to find the door. Frantically, I felt as though I may be drowning in a sea of obfuscated existence. Faces and bodies blurred together, destroying any recognizable feature of a human being. Freeing myself from the mob of glamour driven hysteria was a task that had become nearly impossible. I moved closer to the exit, reaching out to grab the door.

A blanket of darkness covered the room. I fumbled for the door handle, slashing my hands through the blackness, like a kid rummaging around on the floor, looking for his lost glasses. A low murmur transformed into a stridency of cheers as purple lights, covered with smoke, dimly cut through the darkness. I slowly stood up to find Lance and his curvaceous girlfriend standing on opposite sides of me. Their eyes were glued to the purple lights, hypnotized by the modulation of beats and strobes. I looked at each of them, moving my head back and forth from Lance to her, wondering how I got back to the center of the club. As if in a trance, their eyes widened, and their mouths went agape, controlled by the low cadence of electric drums in the distance of the club. Every member of the crowd was now staring at the purple strobe lights, drool trickling down the corner of their mouths. It wasn't long before I found myself looking at that light and—I must admit—it was a magnificent sight to see.

A sound, much like the static white noise of a speaker, drilled the air of the club. At his booth, the club's DJ was slowly motioning his index finger downward, repeating the motion over and over again, his eyes, staring off into the distance, were hidden behind his dark shades. I could feel my head become heavy, struggling to turn it from one side to the other. A dark mass was forming on the middle of the dance floor, becoming larger and larger with each stroke of the DJ's finger. Within seconds, a finger manifested at the peak of the black mass on the floor, and then a hand, until finally an arm threw off the black sheet covering a group of seven dancers. White LED lights covered their appendages in vertical lines with a larger, more effulgent light placed directly on their foreheads. The DJ made his final downward motion and a digital ticker read the words 'Unknown Brain x Rival - Control feat. Jex', moving from left to right.

An angelic voice blared from the speakers and the dancers, now in a straight line so only the front dancer was visible, rhythmically grasped the air above them, maintaining perfect synchronicity with their peers. With each beat they moved their arms in perfectly choreographed fashion, making the front dancer look like a fourteen-armed Durga, hypnotically swaying their arms in slow and rapid succession to the song's cadence. All eyes watched as the troupe squatted, slid, and gamboled across the floor. And as the beat to the song picked up, the ground pulsated, sending a vibration through each muscle in my back. A louder, more aggressive beat initiated the lights on the dancers' bodies as they came together in a circle once more, incising the air with precision to the beat. And as the beat slowed, like the mixing of a record on a turntable, they switched direction, creating a mesmeric display.

I could feel my brain freeze and my heart warm and I struggled to move my head in any direction. Winning the fight against my own body, I was able to turn to both Lance and his girlfriend for only a moment. Their bodies were stiff, their arms cemented to their sides and eyes to the floor.

As the singer recited the verse at the beginning of the song, the dancers began their choreographed motion once more, starting a slow pound before hammering the floor and our minds at the breakdown, almost as if there were unforeseen forces controlling them. The song reached the chorus once more and, as the climax started, the dancers' lights began to illuminate madly.

"Impossible..." I whispered, watching as the dancers created an enormous flapping eagle with their lights before transforming into a monolithic blinking eye.

I caught a flash of movement out of my right peripheral. Struggling even harder to move my head, I was able to inch myself over to see Lance seizing on the floor, his shades bucking wildly with the

197

sporadic beat of the song. But as the song lost control, becoming more afflictive, a jet of liquid sprayed from Lance's mouth. His tongue was hanging loosely over the front of lips as his teeth sunk in harder and harder, gnashing through the median membrane. With one final bite, his mouth relaxed and his seizing subsided, a flaccid tongue falling down and resting below his chin. He began to motion slowly with the beat, lightly moving his head from side to side. His eyes were constricted, circular discs, moving confusedly around the room like an overstimulated baby.

Feeling stuck, I forced one foot backward and then the other. I could feel my limbs loosening as the song began to fade away. I closed my eyes, searching behind me for a door to open, before finally grasping a handle behind me and pushing through.

"Over there!" the madness cried out, following my every move.

"I'm nobody!" I pleaded, rushing out of sight into a nearby ally.

I ducked behind a trashcan and peered into the street. The mob ran past my mini sanctuary, flashing their cameras and live streaming any movement within their range of vision. I grabbed a cigarette and rubbed it between my index finger and thumb, trying to find my center, trying to feel normal. I strained my eyes to concentrate, my vision still blurry from the club. I lit up the cigarette and exhaled, resting my outstretched arms across my knees.

"Why did you leave?" a phantom voice asked.

"Gah!" I roared, hitting the side of my head against a nearby trash can.

A thin, adolescent, black girl stood with her hands clasped against each other, resting over her midsection. Her hair was straightened and elongated well past her lower back, parted on the left side of her head, with a tiny bandana hair clip placed directly down the part. Though her teeth were incredibly straight, her two front central incisors were very prominent—almost to the point of being cartoonish. She bit her lower lip a little and creased her upper lip as her face grew more and more anxious. I held a finger to my lips in the hopes that she might not attract any attention our way.

"I'm Princess!" she announced.

"Jesus," I whispered, getting up and examining the street "Your folks named you Princess?"

"Folks?"

"Your parents God damnit." I said through my teeth.

She nodded with a simple smile. She had—as I suppose most adolescents do—a charmingly gauche demeanor, evidenced in the way she walked and talked. But she exhumed a great deal of self-confidence, no matter how risible her personality was.

"How old are you anyway?"

"16"

"16?" I scoffed with my back turned to her, checking the street once more for paparazzi, "Your parents allow you out at 10 o'clock at night? In downtown LA? Right after Thanksgiving?"

"Uh huh!"

Princess had an imponderable look about her. She had this almost natural congeniality, locked away in an immured intelligence, behind a facade of tween virtue. Her innocence was obvious, but she held something back, something almost recherché.

"Great." I mumbled sarcastically, "Do you live around here?"

"Yeah!"

"Good," I whispered, leaning back against the wall and letting myself slide down, "Very good. Do you know a shortcut to the convention center? I usually don't come around this part of town."

"Use your phone."

"I don't have a fuc-" I stopped myself, "Princess, *sweetheart*, I don't have a phone. Do you know a way there? I'm a little drunk and disoriented right now. I'm going to need some help, Princess." Princess shifted her eyes anxiously, possibly a sign of fear or processing. I couldn't tell which. "Princess?"

"Sure!" She agreed, "But you have to do this one little thing for me."

"What one little thing?"

"It's easy." She said with a nod and a smile, demonstrating her bubbly personality, "I'm going to ask you what you saw in *there* and you tell me. Fair enough?"

"I, uh- in there?" I asked, flipping my thumb over my shoulder toward the pavilion.

"In the theater!"

"Uh, alright. Sure, sister."

"Do you have any social media? A handle maybe?"

"I, uh- I used to. When I was a kid, ya know? I haven't in years though. I was your age the last time I was active on there. I used it as a way to keep up with the trends, I guess, and my friends were following me but, well, there's a tolerance level with me there." I shrugged, "Sorry, I guess you can't tag me."

She placed her hand on her hip and cocked her left eyebrow, imitating my sullen scowl. Trying to hold back a laugh, her cheeks grew tumescent from the pressure of holding in her breath. She finally relented, letting out a staccato burst of infectious laughter. I couldn't help but join in.

"You don't tag on this one, silly."

"Okay," I said, composing myself once more, "on what one?"

"Look."

She put her phone up in plain view of both of us so I could get a good look. She smiled and nodded, waiting for my approval, as she slid down the brick wall and planted herself next to me on the concrete. The first video was ephemeral, no longer than a few seconds. A man, possibly cross dressing, lip synced a popular Brittney Spears song.

"See, this one got almost a million likes."

"A million people liked *that*?"

"Ya know, you say it like it's so hard to believe." She wagged her finger. "I didn't like the video, but is it so hard to believe? Or do you just like to shit on everyone's parade?"

"No, it's not. I mean, no I don't." I whispered, a little ashamed of being read so easily, "I guess sometimes I should roll my eyes rather than open my mouth."

The other videos were not much different. Collaborations between obvious pederasts and teenagers were the most popular. Most videos were merely self-aggrandizing bouts of vanity, but some were just downright embarrassing. It was like falling down a spiraling hole, viewing the insanity that people thought other people needed to see. As the lip sync videos waned, the far more personal videos manifested. A woman, who was clearly psychotic, announced her pregnancy to her estranged spouse for the whole world to see as her hostile husband became more uncomfortable and pleaded to talk with her privately. She would not acquiesce. The next minor treasure from the recesses of human consciousness was a man who pepper sprayed himself, and ate a banana. That's it. And just as I had nearly had enough, the final video showed two lovers—who insisted they were not cousins but quite obviously were kin—yelling relentlessly at the camera and threatening anyone with a 'ban' if users kept accusing them of an incestuous relationship.

"Princess, for the love of God, what is this?"

Princess giggled, holding her hands over her mouth gingerly. "You're so old. Everyone is on this."

"Christ," I hissed, raising my hands and dropping them instantly, "it wasn't three years ago people said you were old for using Facebook. I'm not even in my fucking thirties yet." Princess jokingly cupped her hands over her mouth in feigned shock. "Yeah, well, if you're wandering the streets at this time, I'm sure you've heard worse."

"Yeah," she nodded, "It's not Instagram. It's the latest in social media, but this one will never get old."

"Ahhh, to be young again. To believe everything you hold dear will stand the test of time."

"It won't! But my teacher said they steal our data and it's, um, 'banked'? Is that it?"

"Banked? What are you talking about?"

"Like they give them money?"

"Bankrolled?"

"That's it! He says they're bankrolled by China and stealing our data or some shit. But so what? China owns the app. Who cares? He's an old idiot anyways."

"An 'old idiot'." I said, with a ponderous glance toward the sky, "Brilliant."

"I know, right?" She responded with an over-the-top parody of a smile, doing her best to imitate an old person's voice.

"I think you should listen to your teacher. Social media is tacky anyway, Princess. I used to see pictures on social media of people literally photoshopping themselves out of reality. They don't even look human anymore." Princess looked at me blankly, giving me the impression that she could care less. I rubbed my forehead and flicked the butt of my smoke, lighting another one. "And what's more, everyone looking at these overt displays of vanity are apathetic toward this because they believe these are fringe people. They think that because they don't do this, they are immune to its foolishness. Yet, they interact with it all the same. Not criticizing this kind of behavior is what turns fringe groups into social norms."

"What the fuck ever loser." Princess laughed as she pointed the camera at herself "Get ready."

"Wait a minute God damnit, get ready for what?"

"We're going live." She said with a jaded tone, as if I needed to get with the program.

"Live on China's Most Wanted?"

"That's not even funny," she said, giving me a remote look.

"Alright, well, it's been a long night kiddo. These are the jokes."

"I'm using this for my vlog."

"Your blog?"

"VLOG! V-L-O-G. VLOG! Video Blog!"

"So, you just talk? You don't write anything?"

"Writing is for losers."

"I hear that."

Princess adjusted herself and made certain her face was proportional to the phone camera facing us. She pouted her lips and made a kissing motion to the camera, placing her hand over her head as if she were posing to no one. After she was certain all angles were felicitous, she began to speak.

"Hey y'all! This is Queen Princess here with another hot take!"

I laughed. "Oh for Christ's sake. Not you too!"

"I have here a person from the guest list of tonight's YouTube Movie Premiere! I'm here with-" She paused, looking at me in anticipation.

"Uh, Sam."

"Sam?"

"Sam Killian"

"And Sam, how do you know Victor DeLamonte? That is his friend y'all!"

"Um, actually, I don't know him. I know Lance. Actually, I don't know Lance either. I should say-"

"Sam is a little lit from the party y'allllll. He was there and brought in past security by Vicky. He DOES know him. Or at least Lance."

"I don't know him. I don't think 'Lance' knew himself tonight. Hell, I don't think Lance knew the difference between an inflatable sexdoll and his mother tonight."

"And you were telling me you hooked up with Vicky, is that right?" Princess shoved the camera two inches from my face, showing me a video reflection of myself.

"What, I never said that!"

"Rumor is, she's having a baby. Is it possible you just may be the father?"

"Princess..." I pleaded, rubbing my eyes with my thumb and forefinger.

She stopped her feed abruptly. "Sam, if you want me to direct you to the CC, I'm going to need a hot take from you."

"Do you know what hot take means?"

"Something interesting."

"Princess, I'm really proud of you for having a blog and- what am I saying, I don't even know you." We sat in awkward silence for a moment, me thinking of what to say, her pushing her bangs out of her face. "Look, it's great so many people want to see what you have to say, but you're 16 and already practicing yellow journalism. Plus, to be honest, I probably shouldn't be on camera right now anyway. I'm already on probation and God knows how it'll look talking to an underaged girl about celebrity 'hot takes' in a seedy alley.

"SAM! I need you to give me some of the gory details of tonight. My reputation, literally, hangs in the balance."

"Hangs in the balance?"

"Sam." She sobbed, cupping her hands over her eyes, "Sam, I- I..."

She began to cry lightly, her shoulders popping up and down with each sob, goading me into consoling her.

"Princess, no."

"Sam..." Her crying persisted.

"Fuck this. I can find my own way."

"And leave me out here, all alone, in downtown LA?!" Princess forced her hands away from her face. She was beginning to well up, revealing pools of tears resting on the corner of her eyes, as if they were waiting for the right moment to race down her face.

"Now, see here young lady-"

"Sammy!" She pleaded, mumbling my name as if she were a child on the verge of tears.

I sighed. "Alright. I'll-"

"Good!" she said, her eyes drying instantly.

She pulled me back down to her level, smiling and sniffling. Princess raised the phone to our faces once more. A text notification flashed on her phone with a message from 'Steve'. The preview of the message read:

I've got my hand on my cock right now. Waiting for you to eat-

I twisted my face, revolted. "Awfully precocious sex talk for a 16-year-old. Is that your boyfriend? Steve?"

"Yes. And he isn't 16. He's 32."

"He's older than me. He's twice your age. Are you-"

Princess dropped her phone between her legs and looked at me cross once more. No doubt trying to convince a 16-year-old girl to stop dating an older man was as fruitless as convincing her to switch from video to written journalism. Not giving a shit was getting tiresome but, I'd made it this far.

"Am I what?" Her left eyebrow cocked once more in grave curiosity, shooting me a look of indignation that reminded me I was not her father.

"Nothing. Fair enough. Let's finish this."

Flipping her bangs, she resumed her broadcast. "Sam, what was it like in the green room?"

"Well," I said, looking like an absolute creature on camera, "I didn't make it to any green rooms, but I did meet Lance's lover. Or, rather, paramour, I guess."

"Marissa? Or Pauly?"

"Um," I tried not to laugh, "I couldn't be sure. She was a little overweight, blonde, big fake tits, and, uh, had a general apathy toward anything outside of her own, immediate solicitations."

"That doesn't really narrow it down, Sam..."

"Yeah." I said, laughing, "I figured as much."

"What do you do for a living Sam? Camera work? Are you a dealer? An Agent or manager?'

"I'm a professor of philosophy at the University of California Los Angeles."

"Borrring!"

"Tell me about it."

"Do you do drugs, Sam?"

"At this point, every chance I get."

"No, seriously."

I pinched my lower lip and extended it, contemplating my next answer.

"Drugs are ultimately something we would have never come up with had it not been for a litany of travesties that we must face on a daily basis that makes us want to escape reality. Our exodus from a bucolic way of life has made even the most common man look for a respite in the form of-"

"Sam... Sam..." Princess interrupted, looking at the camera with a reassuring smile, "What drugs do you like?"

I rubbed my eyes with my right hand. "Ketamine is pretty good."

"You heard it here first, folks! Sam Killian, best friend of Victor DeLamonte and prominent professor at UCLA, is addicted to ketamine. Is Victor? Will Paula have an abortion? More on tomorrow's broadcast!"

"I think my career in academia is over..."

"Hey! You did good!"

"I did 'well'." I corrected.

Princess's expression grew mordant. "Mhmm."

"Awfully short for a VLOG though, isn't it?"

"Not really. The shorter the better. Gotta keep people's attention. Recent empirical evidence has shown that most consumers choose more aphoristic, almost pithy, VLOGs over the exhaustive ones."

My face must not have betrayed my amusement at her bookish response since she held her hands over her mouth while her eyes lit up in affected horror. I nodded and smiled, looking toward the sky, admiring its crimson tint.

"Look," Princess said, tugging on the side of my shirt, her head tilted upward at the sky "It changes from red to black depending on where you stand."

She showed me the sky from the West then the East, scooting around on the concrete. The sky did seem to change color depending on the direction. She looked at me, a troubling glance growing on her face.

"Well," I said, a little perplexed "I'm sure there's some sort of scientific explanation for that."

"Is there?"

"There must be..."

"Alright professor," she said, shimmying her way up the concrete wall, "Let's go. A deal's a deal."

"You know Princess, you aren't bad in front of the camera. Have you ever thought about a career in journalism? Broadcast journalism that is."

"There's no need. If I hit it big enough, I can make a career off my vlog, or social media or whatever. Maybe, one day, I can make it to the YouTube Premieres. It's my dream."

"Your dream is to be a part of that shit show I was just at tonight?"

"But of course."

Princess soured with contempt at my question. Clever as she was, I couldn't help but feel a little pity at her myopic goals. Her whole world was nothing more than a tainted medium of which she had no control over. Like a moth to the flames of obsolescence, Princess would make it to that purple carpet one day and drug herself into partial infamy and forget where she was even from. But, I supposed, that was the point.

"Look, I'm sorry. I'm an idiot. That's why they kicked me out of UCLA. I've gone on my whole life talking to myself and almost no one else, thinking I'm so smart but, I'm really just miserable."

Princess's frown healed a little. "You're not so bad I guess."

"Thanks."

From down the alley, a sound, much like the terrible wailings of a dark, nightmarish funeral reverberated toward Princess and me. The back of the alley was a pit of hazy darkness, swallowing any light that dared escape its jaws. Yet it was unmistakable; the sound was approaching at a rapid rate, waiting to pounce as Princess took position behind me and grabbed tightly to the back of my shirt. And just as the apparition made itself seen and Princess shouted in fear, a man, draped in baggy clothes so excessive his face became a black hole, rode his bike down the alleyway behind us as shopping bags hung from his handlebars and a speaker bellowed some somber tune that went on repeat:

Ya da da. Ya da da. Ya da da da.

"That was... weird." Princess said, loosening her grip on my shirt.

"Was it?" I asked, watching the dark mass tilt from side to side as he rode off into the night.

Princess and I walked and talked all the way to Olympia Street, discussing trends in her life and faults in my own. The streets, renaming themselves at each stop sign we reached, seemed to appear and disappear over the embankments of the hunchback roads. Princess assured me this was normal and that we will find the way once more. I showed her—or rather told her—about the video that went viral in my class. Her face warped from awe to hilarity.

"Ya know, for a guy that's drunk, you talk pr-"

The sound of a human making dog noises halted our conversation. Just outside of the Starbucks across the street, Princess and I came across a man walking his female companion mimicking a dog. They had just left the Starbucks and his odd sex slave began to nudge at him with her nose. He obliged by lowering a small cup filled with whipped cream. I crossed my arms and leaned against the wall as Princess stood there in bewilderment. The worst part was just how natural they seemed—to walk around shamelessly like that. But this was LA. I would imagine it would take the average Midwestern couple years to work up the fortitude, or lack thereof, to pull off a stunt like that. And yet, here they were.

"I'm sorry you had to see that." I said.

Princess gave a bemused shrug. "Meh. I've seen worse."

"I'll bet."

Just as the roleplaying couple walked off, it became clear that something was wrong. At first, the pebbles on the ground vibrated, making a light clacking noise. Then, the building made a rumble, shaking the windows. Finally, as the worst started, a violent tremor shot up from my feet to my spine like a massage chair in overdrive. The asphalt and cement made a wave like an urban ocean, convexly moving down the street as Princess and I took cover in a nearby alley.

The Call of the Void

"The fault!" a woman shouted from her fifth story window, hanging her entire body out with arms stretched to the sky, "The San Andreas Fault! It's come! It's broken! The Faultline is broken!"

"T-tt-ttt-ttthhh-hhhh-eeee fff-ffffaaaa-uuuuult? Iiiiss iii-iiittt rrrreaaaalllllyyyy?" Princess chattered, attempting to ballast herself on the wall.

"Wwww-wwweeee'lll-llll knoooowwww sss-ssssooo-ooooonnn ennnnnouggg-hhhh." I rattled.

And then, nothing. Motionless. It was hardly my first experience with an earthquake in LA, but it was definitely one of the heavier ones.

"We're here! The road to the convention center!"

Olympia had reappeared in an almost supernatural fashion. The journey, which seemed like hours, had lasted mere minutes. Up ahead, a Target was flashing strobe lights that motioned from North to South in anticipation of the big night. Princess looked on in absolute amazement at the vastly expansive line of customers camping outside that created a morass of pitched tents and barbecues. Her head turned to meet me.

"I don't really... I don't ever get presents. I've never been to a Black Friday sale."

"I'll save you the trouble. There isn't anything more than greedy, sub-conscious beings in there. Bestial at best... they would trample you in a minute."

"Not really thou-"

"*Really* though." I interjected, raising a stern eyebrow to get my point across.

"Alright." Her disappointment was palpable.

"But I have a few bucks." I said, trying to palliate the tension from my comment.

"There is this new purse that Target has on sale, and it would really push me further in, well, social circles."

"Sure." I said, slurring a little more than I intended.

Princess stopped and looked at me with concern. "You said you were drunk. Why do you drink?"

The question was a knife in my sternum I had to carefully pull out.

"I drink because, when I'm sober and conscious, my life is a bleak husk of something I had always hoped it would be. A husk of my dreams. I drink because, when I am actually drunk, the difference between life and death becomes so obfuscated that death is not so scary. Going the way I am now, a stroke, heart attack, lung cancer, or even liver failure is quickly creeping in on me. At best, I'm at the midway point in my life. In the morning, when I'm sober, it scares the shit out of me. But, during the night, when I can enjoy a bottle of whiskey, I can rest easy knowing I am nothing, and this world is not worth my petty fears of fraud and ennui. Because the night, I live. Because the night, I laugh at the world."

Princess lit up at the end of my monologue, almost as if she hadn't heard the rest of it. "Because the Night. That's one of my favorite songs."

"Shut up. The Patty Smith song? Her version?"

"Yeah. Patty Smith. What other version is there?"

"There's... like one other rendition I think."

"I love it! It came on while watching an ad and I reverse listened to it so I could find it. It spoke to me!"

Princess took a moment to open her phone, pressing a button that played the song we had both relished over. The song came on slow and Patty Smith's vocals blared amongst the small circumference we had made for ourselves on the grassy plain just outside the Target parking lot. And as the chorus blared out, Princess and I danced awkwardly in the night. The full moon shone down upon us, lamenting its presence amongst the stars. And as the hordes of midnight shoppers stood in line a quarter of a mile away, we shook our heads and pranced like animals in a field, shirking inhibition and laughing at our clownish dance. We conceded to our station of being nothing more than children of the night, and we knew that, because the night, we were born again. Nothing more than passengers in life.

The song ended and Princess cupped her hand over her mouth as she laughed. We moved up onto an enormously grassy berm that peaked about twenty feet above the parking lot and sloped into a concave down to the cars.

"I'll never get to the purse if we don't get up front."

"Good fucking luck. These animals will rip us apart. Look at the size of that fucking guy!" I pointed to a man in his rascal scooter, looking more ursine than human.

"That bariatric punk?" Princess said as she placed a hand on her hip and craned her neck up at me.

"Bariatric? That's a big word there."

"Fuck off." She laughed.

As we approached the bottom of the slope, a gang of ten Recusants converged into the parking lot. The crowd, clearly irate at their presence there, began to hiss. They stood there in the hollows of the concrete basin, whispering horrid anathemas under their breath, praying to a god that might grant the Recusants' untimely deaths.

"Oh, God," I said, shaking my head, "Not now."

"Why do they hate them?" Princess asked.

"Because," I began, exhaling deeply before answering, "They remind them of what they should be. They remind them of a life worth living. Of what austerity and sacrifice really mean. They are, quite literally, an embodiment of their own hypocrisy. They are a reckoning to these people—and all people—come tenfold."

The Recusant formed a circle in the middle of the western most parking lot. They sat like monks in a state of tranquility, each leg crossed over the other. The only Recusant standing walked around with a jerrycan. He went Recusant to Recusant, like a game of duck-duck-goose, throwing a little liquid over their heads while chanting something unintelligible in Latin. He forced the container over his head, chanting still into the wind, his biceps rippling with each douse of the can.

"Princess, don't watch this."

The Call of the Void

Princess, clearly intrigued, began to pull her phone out and film. I put the palm of my hand lightly on the top of her phone with concerned eyes. She reluctantly, but understandingly, placed her phone back in her pocket.

"But they are!" she said pointing over the hill at the obese, handicapped customers.

"Let them."

"Fine." She whispered, "But I'm watching."

The lead Recusant finished the bottle off on top of himself, shaking his head fiercely as the gasoline jutted from the stocks of his hair, almost in slow motion. The oily liquid smeared his face until it was a smooth sheen. The rest of his crew remained cross legged, watching as he stood above them in the center of the circle.

He turned to face me, as if he knew I was there all along. "Got a light?" He asked with a confident smile.

I sighed before reluctantly tossing him my zippo, his dire smile still tattooed in my brain. He caught the lighter mid-air and stared at the moon, smiling defiantly like a mad man. Pushing the zippo to the top of his closed fist, he lifted his right hand. The lid flicked open as he peered up at the moon through the fulcrum of the lighter and, for just a moment, a flash of hesitancy formed on his face before he shook it off. With a quick motion of his thumb, his body became engulfed in a searing flame, blossoming like a great marigold flower from his head to his feet before spilling onto the seated men. I stood in disbelief, my jaw so slack that my cigarette nearly fell out of my mouth, as Princess gripped the inside of my flannel and whimpered pathetically. I placed my arm around her, keeping her face pressed firmly against my abdomen and away from the immolation. It wasn't the screams of the Recusants that frightened me, but their stagnancy, their nearly unworldly ability to stay completely still through the inferno. My zippo, engulfed in flames, came shooting out of the circle, landing directly at my feet.

After stomping my zippo out, and with a sense of urgency, I moved Princess closer to the line at Target, hiding out behind two vehicles. As we approached, an eerie tintinnabulation manifested in the form of Christmas bells from across the parking lot. With great difficulty, I lit a cigarette with my zippo, jumbling it like a hot potato from my right hand to my left. A vehicle, very similar to that of the popemobile, came swerving through the Target parking lot.

"Christ," I said, exhaling smoke and narrowing my eyes, "what now?"

Sure enough, a completely pellucid, bullet proof popemobile approached with Santa pantomiming a celebrity wave to all those in line. A duo of men masked in balaclavas, armed with rifles painted like candy canes, stood on opposite sides of the crystalized vehicle, flipping their guns in the air and catching them like a close order drill.

"Santa!" Princess shouted.

I grabbed her left arm just as she rushed off. She looked back at me, confused at first then understanding, as I vigorously shook my head.

The vehicle, moving no more than 5 MPH, made its way toward the Recusants' circle before crashing right through their charred, still burning, bodies. Before Santa could emerge, a blinding light revealed itself from the Northern parking lot. Each addlepated patron waiting in line genuflected with alacrity. A vivid, wide screen appeared showing Santa in a corporate suit. The Santa from the popemobile emerged from his safe haven and looked at the screen before glancing back at the crowd and giving his best 'Ho, Ho, Ho!' to which the crowd cheered. At the foot of the telescreen were two Recusants dressed in old Nazarene garb like Jesus and Joseph, dramatizing a still motion work of the creche. In front of them, a sign read 'Pray this Christmas' with 'Sponsored by Your Reckoning' underneath it. There was an outcry amongst the consumers in line as Santa waved inanely at anybody and nobody. The crowd shouted out in joy as Santa pointed at the Christ figure and cupped a hand behind his left ear, begging the crowd's approval.

"Are you okay?" I whispered to Princess.

"Uh, well, I guess." She answered, a little dazed, "Are you okay?"

"Honestly, as heinous a night as it's been," I said to Princess as she waved smoke out of her face, "it's the most alive I've ever felt."

We shared a smirk before looking back at Jesus.

Santa moved carefully toward the holographic display with a wide gait, looping both thumbs under his belt, a brash maneuver to establish dominance. The Recusant stood up, pressing a button on the projector to reveal a life-like hologram of Christ in a Pantocrator pose, his two fingers raised up high to his chest, that glitched and simultaneously switched back and forth between Jesus and Baphomet in the same pose. Both Santa and Jesus met like professional wrestlers in a ring, the Jesus-clad Recusant standing stoically and Santa cracking his neck from left to right.

"This has been a long-time coming, fat man." The Recusant Jesus laughed, "Why don't you show these people what you're made of?"

Santa bellowed another 'Ho, Ho, Ho!'. A great exultation roared from the crowd, cheering Santa on, as the Recusant dropped to both knees in defiant submission at Santa's boots. Covertly, Santa grabbed two, thickly portioned, candy canes out of his back pocket and tied them together with a piece of twine, making a cross. Pinching it between his thumb and forefinger, he tilted the rood made of candy from left to right, pointing it directly in Jesus's face, asking once more without words to take his peace offering and absolve himself. Jesus merely looked on with a recalcitrant smile, shaking his head as Santa cocked back his arm and pushed the cross into his right eye. The crowd, drunk with the adrenaline of their neighbors, cheered the cataclysm as phone cameras from behind the velvet rope flashed and flashed.

Princess raised her hand gently to her mouth. She watched, mortified, as Jesus struggled to keep his composure. He knelt, gritting his teeth for a moment but, when the visceral white and red fluids began to trickle down his cheek, and the realization hit that his optic nerve was damaged beyond repair, he lost it and began to scream. I placed a hand on Princess's shoulder, watching her as her eyes welled up and she looked from Jesus, to Santa, to the crowd, to me.

"Stop them. Please!"

I looked at her with disappointment. "I can't."

"What do you mean you can't?" Princess whispered, before raising her voice to a yell, "You can't, or you won't? Are you afraid of Santa? Huh? You big- you big pussy!"

"Yeah. Sure, kid. I'm afraid of Santa. Let's leave it at that."

"You said you accepted death! You said you weren't afraid-"

I grabbed Princess, more aggressively than I intended, by the crook of her arm and shook her out of her hysteria. "Listen to me God Damnit! They want this! What? Did you think that little 'demonstration' back there was an accident, Princess? Get a hold of yourself and don't get involved. With either group! This is not the place, and these aren't the fucking people. I told you already, stop watching!" She exhaled, nodded, and stared down at my knees, a little defeated. I handed her my handkerchief out of my back pocket so she could blow her nose, which she did. When she lifted her arm to hand it back, her face still solemnly staring at my knee, I lowered her arm. "Keep it. And Princess, I'm sorry." She nodded lightly and moved in closer to my side, as if to tell me it was okay. That maybe, she would forgive my outburst.

Joseph, clearly concerned with the health of his son, rushed in to help Jesus before being leveled by Santa with a faux, lawn candy cane that had the insignia 'Sponsored by Target' on its side. Santa, intoxicated by the rabble, grabbed Jesus by his ponytail and began to swing him back and forth, hitting each car that he could with his lifeless body. Santa picked Jesus up and secured his head in between both of his thighs like a vice grip before dropping all of his bodyweight backwards and piledriving the crown of his head onto the asphalt. The mob rushed the parking lot and picked Jesus up, crowd surfing him with extended arms to the front of the lot. They moved him lightly, almost as if they cared deeply for him, to the forefront of the parking lot where the Target emblem was bolted in shining bright lights. Jesus, with only a modicum of life remaining in his eyes, looked back at his father before being thrust, headfirst, upon Target's enormous, neon lit symbol. The blow must have broken his neck. His eyes were colorless orbs, staring up at nothing in the sky, and his eyelids were beginning to lose life, crashing like waves with each closing motion.

The crowd began to move on Joseph. He took off his coat and dropped to his knees.

"Now's our chance," I said, pulling Princess toward the empty entrance of the store.

The onslaught of shoppers, whimsically captivated by the aesthetics of festive decorations, were hardly conscious of their own family members, let alone themselves. Those singular minds that had fled the sanctuary of reason and frugality had come tonight in the hopes of saving a relationship with their son or daughter, or wooing a coworker, or even, out of self-interest, to get a bargain on whatever device might be trending at the time.

As we went deeper into the store, the distinct, sonorous and gentle stringing of violins from Camille's "Danse Macabre" played lightly from behind a tarp as a man draped in purple velvet, standing in front of the covered display, heralded to every belligerent shopper within his range. Princess watched in eager anticipation as the man's rotating display moved faster and faster. Like a child hauling her parent through the store, she pulled on my arm to slow me down, jumping up and down with nervous glee when I finally stopped. The man smiled wide at the growing crowd, performing outré dance moves as he flamboyantly slashed the air with his cane as if he was fighting off an invisible demon. He paused and silenced the crowd with an extended finger, his eyes paying no attention to the army of frothy mouthed consumers racing around behind him.

"At Target, our prices will never cost you an arm and a leg," he said, pursing his lips together and nodding with an odd sincerity, "But how's about a finger?"

The orator reached back, grabbed the tarp, and ripped it off, revealing a standing violin orchestra of men and women in red shirts and khaki pants masked with a translucent vizard that blurred their faces. In front of them, on display, was a roulette table with poorly scribbled notes on its felt cloth.

"Any takers?" he asked, scanning the crowd.

I grabbed Princess's arm just as she was about to jut it up into the air. We made a bit of a scene—me shaking my head fervently, her nodding with ardent resilience, the orator watching on with a capacious, toothy grin.

"How's'in we possed to know what we takin' if'n we don know what's we doin'?" a woman asked.

"Spoken like a true philologist," the orator said, pulling out a roulette ball, "Tonight, and only tonight ladies and gentlemen, Target, a subsidiary of The Vanguard Group and State Street Global Advisors, welcomes you to try your hand, quite literally I might add, at Rota Fortunae, for a chance to win an hour-long shopping spree."

The crowd moved in closer, hyperventilating and raising their hands in the air toward the orator as he slinked back.

"On the condition," the orator amended, "that you actually put some skin in the game for once. Two players enter, one may win. One black. One red. Just place your right hand here on the table," The orator tapped the table with his cane rhythmically. "Black or red it makes no difference and buckle in for a shot at an hour-long shopping spree. Don't be shy, step right up. Step right up!"

The crowd muttered under their breaths and kicked the toe of their shoes against the floor. Some raced off toward the electronic section. Others wandered off casually. I eyeballed the two restraints on the table closely, unsure of where this was going. Two females took their places on the chairs near the table, shrugging their shoulders insouciantly at the orator, while one slid her hand in the black restraint and the other in the red.

"Now, you understand the rules?" the orator asked intensely, allowing them a chance to realize their mistake, "And you understand what's at risk?"

The women both brushed him away, an unusual smile forming on their faces as they stared one another down. Princess's focus was narrowing on the ball in the orator's hand as he shot it through the roulette wheel. The ball hopped around the wheel, bouncing from green to red to black. Princess gritted her teeth as I leaned in closer, a beam of sweat sliding down my forehead. The ball's momentum slowed, rolling it lightly from red to black before landing on green '00'. In an instant, a crimson stream launched from the table. The women rattled their heads violently in the air, screaming and panicking, as they tried to remove their fingerless hands from the restraints. Instinctively, I covered Princess's eyes and rushed us away from the table before Princess had a chance to realize what had happened. The howl of both women slowly faded the further we moved. The orator's cackling did not, lingering in my mind indefinitely.

"Now!" The orator shouted as we moved further down the store's corridors "Bear witness!"

Psychosis and bedlam had made their masterpiece. Middle aged women, with cries akin to javelinas in heat, began toppling the rows of TVs that paved the aisles. It was all TVs. TVs everywhere. Mankind's soul was eternally mired here amidst plasma screens, filling the aisles with abundant heaps of hollow boxes. Some game consoles, fridges and tablets were pulled into the appalling abyss of human technological lust, but it was the TVs that had equivocated human reason.

The lack of formal etiquette had become jarring. And while we shoved and squeezed our way past a sea of bodies that floated over red carpets, Princess and I watched on in horror, our mouths agape, as the crowd itself became a self-aware, sentient being all on its own. The faces of pure malice formed within the crowd as the great beast turned on itself and began a full-on assault to eliminate its own entity.

A mother and her two children, one strapped to her stomach and the other gripping tightly to her hand, accosted a black couple over who had the rights to the last TV. The couple was certain that they did as they had seen it first, but the mother would not relent, insisting she was next in line. The mother's eyes grew wide, addressing the couple with asperity, demanding they put down the device. The imbroglio that ensued was absurd, at best.

It began with an obstreperous yelling match after the mother took it upon herself to arrogate the TV from the couples' hands. This ended with the wife biting down on the mother's hand, drawing blood as her young son grappled himself onto the other woman's leg. Pratfallen by the counterattack, the mother attempted to maneuver herself upright by grasping onto the towel rack nearby but was thwarted by the husband of the black couple who began kneeing the infant clad mother in the temple and swiftly hitting her son with a right cross, knocking out three of his teeth that went sliding across the varnished floor. The bludgeoned mother arose, lifting the TV over her head awkwardly and cocking her left foot back to kick frantically at the air, missing everything in her path. She began to fall backwards once more but, by some divine intervention, was able to graze the temple of the other woman with the side of her foot. The woman gripped the TV with such force that her knuckles whitened, even as she began to fall flat on the floor. Outrage tattooed the face of the husband as his choice between the TV and his wife was easy. His long, outstretched arms saved the TV, leaving his wife supine on a clearance rack. She rose once more, the look on her face softening, fearing for the well-being of the TV.

"Fucking niggers are always stealing shit!" the child yelled.

"What did you say?" the black woman said, grabbing him by the collar.

"Don't you fuckin' touch him, bitch! He's only seven years old! That's my bloodline! I'll kill you!"

Princess and I shared baffled expressions.

"White trash bitch!"

"Spook!"

"Inbred white bread cunt!"

Interest from the surrounding mob, with its own malevolent squabbles unfolding, had begun to focus on the couple.

"Did that boy say 'nigger'?"

"Is that a 125-inch Toshiba?"

"I'll attack the white kid," one Caucasian man shouted to the black woman beside him "If you'll split your share with me."

The crowd was a mercurial shadow, swallowing the aisles of the store. It was self-aware, sentient, and out for its own destruction. The mass of people, aimless and distraught, let out a cry like the bleating of a downed animal, their eyes turning a dark vermillion, coiling their fists into balls of pizza dough.

A look of disquietude was drawn across Princess's face. "Jesus. What the fuck..." she gasped, backing herself into the accessory aisle.

I took one look back at the melee. "Let's hurry up and get out of here."

Princess nervously fingered through the purses on the colander in front of her, shooting her eyes back and forth between me and the mob. Shame filled her eyes, and, for only a moment, tears began to trickle down her face.

"I, uh, I don't think I'm in the mood for a new purse. Maybe later..." she said, discreetly wiping her eyes with the back of her hand.

"Okay." I said, patting her gently on the back, "Yeah. Whatever you want, kiddo."

"Yeah." She grumbled, "Thought you might be a little more proud of me. But who cares, right?"

"I am proud of you." I assured her, squeezing her shoulder tight, "Of course, it should actually be 'prouder' but, who cares right?"

Princess looked up at me and tried to fight off a smile. "You know what your problem is?"

"My problem?" I laughed, ignorant to the balmy bloodshed unfolding behind us, "What?"

"You think you're better than everyone else." She sniffed, "And you might well be a bit smarter, but not better."

I feigned shock. "Awfully trenchant tonight madam. But I don't think that. Actually, I-"

"Okay, you might not think it, but you act it. Drop the holier than thou act. You fit in perfectly here in LA, and it scares you, doesn't it?"

The Call of the Void

A wave of sincerity washed over me, and I had to reflect on just how right she really was. "It terrifies me." Princess looked a little disappointed. I patted her back lightly once more. "But it's been nice to talk to someone. Finally, talk to someone- someone... I respect."

"Thanks-" Princess faltered, taking a moment to respond, "Sam."

"Anytime kiddo."

I stared at her for a moment and saw a young me. For a brief moment, I regretted never having a child.

"Come on," I said, waving my hand toward the back of the store, "I have something I want to show you."

We swam through leagues of women's underwear and traversed the mania of digital goods before ending up in the emptiest aisle in Target. The book section. A strand of gossamer was yoked to the ceiling from the books, and sneaker footprints were etched onto its the dusty floor.

"Books?"

"Yeah. Ever read one?"

Princess shot me a look of indignation before playfully slugging me in the arm. "So what? This is some Boomer lecture on the 'powers of reading'?" She lazily air quoted the latter part of her statement.

"No. No! I just thought, since you weren't getting a purse, I might buy you something else."

"Something *you* want me to have."

"No, I- well, I didn't really know what else might mend the situation. We'll be stampeded anywhere else."

"I thought you said you were in trouble because of books anyway."

"I'm not in trouble because of books. I might have misrepresented that statement a little."

"Well, I've never read a book." Princess's face flushed a little.

"Don't worry about it. You're still young. I have students close to my age in grad school that still haven't. They've actually prided themselves on the fact that they made it that far without reading a single book. I'll still never really know *why*. But what's worse, I'll never figure out how we've gotten to this point, and if there's a way to fix it. I'm just looking for a little wisdom here."

"That's what you want? To make me wise?"

"No. I only thought I might guide you to a good book. And, to marvel at how empty it is here."

"Well, no one buys books on Black Friday."

I snorted a laugh and looked up at the ceiling. "I swear, kids your age are the most keenly observant scatterbrains this world has ever seen. You're like that kid, in the story, that ignores the metaphor in the book for the most obvious answer. Honestly, reading fiction must be impossible for you kids."

"Whatever you say, Boomer." Princess said, smiling coyly before humorously skipping away.

"We used to have debates on the superiority of writing over orating. Now we just have Vlogs. And constant stimuli."

The Call of the Void

Princess snorted. "We used to shit in the woods too."

I broke out into a wild cachinnation at her response. "And I'm not a Boomer." I said through my teeth, "I'm twelve years older than you. And to be completely honest, I really don't give a fuck anymore. I'm growing steadily accustomed to not giving a fuck as the night moves on. I've yet to see any redeeming qualities in anyone. Or myself, for that matter." I gave a resigned sigh. "But I did want to look at ground zero. Believe me, I get it. Your 'Boomer' teacher lectures you about how important reading is. She, or he, tells you that this generation is glued to their phones and falling apart but she still cannot explain *The Old Man and the Sea* to you properly because the only books she has read are the *Harry Potter* and *Hunger Games* series and slept through her Comp Lit class in college." Princess stared at the floor in silence. I drank generously from my flask as my tone grew more somber. "Bonus points to her for trying. I love teachers because at least they take the plunge, but I know there are far too many that don't belong there. They were inspired by another teacher in high school because that teacher was 'cool', but the truth is that first-year teachers forty years ago would have run circles around even the most seasoned teachers today, me included. I'm not immune to this. Regardless of my distance from reality and my immersion into literature and philosophy, the inadequacies I feel, and experience are symptoms of the world we live in. Don't become a part of the abyss the powers that be are plunging us into."

"I have no idea what the fuck you're talking about," Princess blurted, her head shaking with a smile "But, I will pick out a book."

231

"Then," I said, smiling for what felt like the first time tonight, "I am truly proud of you."

"What do you suggest?"

"Well," I said rubbing my chin, "The old adage 'Don't judge a book by its cover' is arrant bull shit. So, what calls to you?"

Princess thumbed through the books in the YA section. "Do your friends read as much as you do?"

I rubbed the stubble on my cheek. "I don't really have any friends anymore. But, if I did, no. I don't think they would. As a matter of fact, I used to write opinion pieces for AP and Reuters in my early college years and I doubt any of my friends even glanced at them. They weren't any good, but still."

"Poetry?"

"Poetry what?"

"A Poetry book?"

"Do you like poetry?"

"I don't know. Who is your favorite poet?"

"Hmmm." I considered her question for a moment. "Probably Hart Crane. But I doubt they have any of his stuff h-"

"Here! Hart Crane." She exclaimed "Unless, there was something else I should grab?"

"No, that's good. It might take a little work though. His-"

"What else should I read? What's important to read?"

Her sudden interest in the books warmed my heart, and a smile slowly formed across my face.

The Call of the Void

"I don't know if there is a predominantly *important* piece of literature since it's all about opening up your soul; as cliché as that sounds." My mood was raised, and my tone lightened at the conversation. "Though, a colleague of mine always told me that art is something beautiful created from nothing. In my early years, being the assured prick that I was, I used to deconstruct what 'beauty' actually meant and what 'nothing' actually is and if the two were not inherently born from one another already. So, I tell my students that literature is not what you put into your prose, or what ancient allegories and references you can cram into your book but rather, what you can write that scares people. What can you write that makes people run away and never want to read you again? That's art."

"Who's this?" Princess asked raising a copy of *The Idiot*.

"That," I muttered under my breath, holding back a bad case of whiskey indigestion, "Is Dostoyevsky. He's one of my favorite authors."

The edition cover was trite and looked like something the publisher excreted for an extra buck. Princess looked at me endearingly.

"I'll read it." She said shrugging nonchalantly.

"Wait," I stopped her, thumbing through his other works, amazed that Target had his entire oeuvre, "Start with this one."

I handed her a copy of *Notes from Underground*.

"Is it better?"

"I don't know. It's-" I took a moment to think. "More your speed, I think. A little shorter too."

As the crowd dimmed and the shouting had evaporated, Princess and I walked toward the register by the entrance. The store had gone silent, save for the few employees sweeping the aisles.

"I think I'll try a written blog. Like you!" She kept her head to the floor. "I've been... kinda self-destructive. I think change is a good thing."

"Self-destructive? How so?"

"Nothing." She answered almost immediately. "Never mind."

"Ya know, you'll probably lose some followers."

"So?" she laughed, jerking her shoulders into a shrug.

"Cool. Hey. Maybe you'll be the match that hits the powder keg."

"Whatever that means."

We checked out at the register. Princess grabbed a pack of gum from the nearby stand and took a piece before putting it on the belt. I paid in cash and Princess began to skip playfully toward the exit.

"I'll tell you what." I said, raising my voice a little so that I was in earshot of her. "If you're switching to a written blog, I can help edit it for you. I'll promote it on campus too. What is the-"

And just as Princess's eyes lit up with the sting of adrenaline, the intercom announced the arrival of the second coming. A wave from perdition. My eyes widened with horror. I grabbed Princess by the arm to force her toward the exit. The flash of an eye cannot begin to describe the swiftness at which the mob ferociously grappled toward freshly stocked televisions. I pulled once more on Princess's scrawny arm as the impetus from the crowd's current thrusted me into the whitecap of shoppers. Reaching deep into the current that pulled us like the undertow of the sea, I scraped and clawed to pull her out, but only her face emerged. Tears pooled in her anguished eyes as I began to shout out to her. "Please, no! Princess! No! Hang on!" I could hear the futility in my voice, knowing full well how this was going to end. I pleaded with her to hang on, to be resilient. I locked on to her eyes as they slowly became lost in the flailing arms and heads pulling her under. In a last-ditch effort, I pushed myself closer to her outstretched arm in the hopes of grabbing her. Our fingers touched briefly before she was lost amongst the chimerical mass. I screamed, "Please! Please stop!", but in vain.

I waited impatiently for the crowd to disperse, darting from side to side and ripping out my hair, as I shouted her name endlessly with what little lung power I had left. There was nothing once the crowd had fought, bought, and separated. But, as I lowered my eyes, I could see a sight so vile it nearly made me vomit. Princess was laid out on the slick floor with her head caved in, fractured pieces of skull and bulbs of gray matter covering her otherwise unrecognizable face, her innocent hands grasping for dear life to Dostoevsky's canon. I breathed shakily in shock, gasping for breath, stretching my arm out to grab on to whatever was closest.

"Poor dear," a morbidly obese woman beside me gasped, "Did you know her?"

The woman picked up her Clydesdale hoof of a foot and casually shuffled the remainder of Princess's brains from underneath her shoe. The Target crew acted quickly, sweeping up her body and wiping down any remaining blood, before moving her toward Target's medical tent.

"No." I muttered, releasing my tensed muscles and lighting a cigarette, "No. I didn't."

"I, um... I don't think you can smoke in here."

"Then call the fucking police."

The moon outside was taunting me. It illuminated the night, reveling in the ire of Los Angeles. The moon was a fraud. The night was a pursuing Dullahan, chasing me through the corridors of hallucinosis, never stopping to call my name.

This whole thing started off as a black and white endeavor, but there I was, running through the prisms of human consciousness. For a moment, I thought of where Princess was now, and pondered infinity. It was what drove mad men insane in the twilight of their psychotic breaks, moments before killing themselves. The image of life, and where it started. The thought of the beginning, of genesis, of life itself, was frightening—the Big Bang and how it was insufficient to describe life. Something had to come from something. God. But who created God? There always had to be a beginning.

Being there was a mistake. I began to reminisce on the cold laws of nature, never giving my mind, and the past, a chance to breathe. My dreams had always been nightmares, a labyrinth of twisted desires and hopeless ambitions, swelled by a tempestuous incubus. But what's obvious in a dream will never make sense after the awakening.

The Call of the Void

It took quite a few minutes and three cigarettes to calm my breathing back down. I rested my hand on the transformer outside, rubbing my eyes roughly until the tears had dried and there was nothing but blackness. I looked down at the graffiti on the transformer. It read:

Finn:

I gave you

Space that

You asked for

8 PM

Sunday

There was a red arrow next to the writing pointing to the other side of the transformer. In red ink, it read:

Babe, I was here

Call me

623-555-0055

Finn

Out of my peripheral vision, a crowd was gathering further down Olympia Street with a mass of bodies forming a circle around a man on top of the eight-story complex nearby. Police helicopters shone their spotlights onto him from above. I got closer, moving quietly behind the crowd. The man on the building was erratic, jumping from one foot to the next, holding himself in position with a mocking grin on his face. He had a noose around his neck and was walking back and forth from east to west along the rim of the roof's balcony, tugging on the noose and laughing madly every so often. He wasn't a Recusant though—just an average Joe. Each move was a slow, defiant step closer to his death, and a certain ecstatic delirium overcame him, as if he wished to leave the decadent world behind. On his megaphone, the police chief was attempting to bring him down to safety. Common phrases such as 'You have so much to live for' and 'Think of your family' were shouted liberally, as if a suicidal man would suddenly snap out of it at these remedial 'lifesaving' revelations. With each platitude the police chief shouted, the man grew more frantic and laughed, forcing a raspy, almost ominous, tenor into his cackles. The crowd grew to over a hundred people, steadily staring through their phone's camera as he moved back and forth. I supposed, at that point, there was nothing more to do than to document the event. Still, the man looked down and wildly laughed a jarring screech that kept tugging at my soul.

Up above on the building's ledge, he inhaled deeply before yelling from the top of the building. "The first one who can post this to their social media will have the great privilege of being haunted by me until the end of your days!"

"But," a faceless voice from the crowd shouted, "It's already on social media. I'm streaming it live."

The man on the ledge finished the remainder of his bottle of Thunderbird and threw it into the crowd, wiping his mouth forcefully with the sleeve of his shirt. "And with that, my fellow cavities of existence, I bid you adieu!"

He didn't so much fall off the edge as he did thrust himself off. If the rope didn't kill him, the force with which his head bounced off the brick building surely did. His leap was a statement; a statement that this was all he could take. It was all he could take of debt, debauchery, draining, indifference and a raw deal he never signed up for. So many people find it insane that a person would rather experience nothingness than the movie playing in their head. Insane that the thought of missing out on so much would be preferential. All the while, they never realize just how negligible their time is from his.

As the group focused their cameras on the hanging man, I moved in to get some answers.

"Excuse me. Excuse me! What happened here?"

The crowd stopped abruptly and slowly moved their eyes from their phones to me. One man answered. "The man killed himself. Probably depressed."

"Yeah but, did he say why?"

A woman, two rows back responded. "The man killed himself. Probably depressed."

"Fine. I saw that. I just was curious if any of you knew specifically why. Did anyone know him?"

As the woman's head went back down toward her phone, three more heads rose up to meet me, speaking in unison. "The man killed himself. Probably depressed."

"Anyone want to tell me why?"

"The man killed him-"

"Enough. Don't bo-"

239

"THE MAN KILLED HIMSELF. PROBABLY DEPRESSED."

Growing at an unsettling rate and encircling me, I tried to reason with the crowd, their eyes slowly rolling into the back of their heads. "Listen to me! I-"

"THE. MAN. KILLED. HIMSELF. PROBABLY. DEPRESSED."

I bolted through the space between two men with their cameras upright, making my way farther down Olympia.

The time was 11:57 and Olympia had turned into 9th street. Nearby there was a textile and fabric store. I lit a cigarette and leaned against the nearest wall. Just past San Pedro, it became hard to focus and the remainder of the street appeared like a mirage, made purely out of evaporating water. A sign for a flower shop floated by amongst the mirage of a street and clashed with a QQ café sign before submerging into the lake of asphalt.

"What'd 'ya think of that?" a voice behind me murmured.

"What is this?"

"Happened a little while ago. Traffic isn't closed off though. Too many cops at the conference tonight."

"What happened?"

"Don't really know. I think a demolition went bad. Fault line maybe? The whole street is flooded."

I turned to the man as he was packing a bowl of black weed from a purple container into a blue pipe. He wore a poncho and tattered jeans. He wasn't wearing shoes and his feet were painted with soot from years back.

"But why is the street flooded?"

"Are you retarded? I said I don't know."

I sighed in defeat and sat beside the man. His eyes were scanning my face, carefully examining my features. I could feel his gaze like some sort of sixth sense.

"Ever hear of Acute Stress Disorder?" He said, eyeballing me wearily.

"Yeah, why?"

The homeless man looked me up and down. Opening his mouth to speak, he closed it before looking at the ground and answering, "Nothing."

"Okay."

"Want a bump?" he asked, holding out a pinch of blow on his hand's purlicue.

"Awfully generous of you," I said, staring back at the flooded street, trying to figure out how to cross.

"Don't get much company."

I nodded and took the hit, wanting to dull the pain of the night anyway.

"Let me get a swig of that too," I said, pointing to his malt liquor. I took a sip and spit it out almost immediately. "Jesus! What is this? Wine?"

He nodded with a sheepish grin. I shrugged and drank some more, letting the effects of the cocaine warm my mind.

"What happened with the crowd over there?"

"Crowd? Where? Crowd?" I asked, tapping my feet spasmodically, "social media. All for social media."

"You haven't sniffed in a while, have you?"

"No," I said, trying to focus on my heart rate, "I haven't. I'm fine. I'm fine. I'm-"

"You said something about social media?"

I bounced around on the concrete, pulled out my notebook, and wrote feverishly.

"Social media has become the hotly debated generational issue of the last fifteen years. Ironically enough, both sides seem to agree that moderation is the key to this dilemma. Yet, as the two sides of opposition shake hands in parlay, they immediately indulge in their vices they had previously rebuked. Like a heroin and meth addict agreeing to keep their habits in check before privately over consuming their respective products. Yet the very existence of social media will never be eradicated. For now, within these last fifteen years, we have at least three generations hooked by the dopamine of self-importance. Of validation. And in this, we have children growing up believing the sky is made of pixels and their words truly matter. That is categorically the 'why' of social media's predominant control over human beings. It satisfies their three most base desires. First, it gives the mind a platform to extrapolate any idea, no matter how mundane, clever, intelligent, witty, or insane it might be. This has now become a primal need for all humans; to be heard. The need to feel your voice heard. And, above all, it takes no more effort than typing on a keyboard or phone.

The Call of the Void

Humans, more than anything, hate diligence. Second, it eliminates the anxiety of facing your peers with controversial or, for lack of a better word, moronic opinions. Humans dread, more than anything, the idea that they would be considered a fool and a fraud. And, while they very well might be considered that from a picture or aphorism posted online, they can delete it. They may also run damage control in the meantime, giving them time before confrontation of their folly. Finally, it gives humans their most basic desire; a form of escapism. This idea, to any man, may seem trite. However, it is the one true reason we connect. Mankind can transpose himself on to any new life in an instant and have conversations in his own head about how important he is. Rather than proactively changing one's own life, one must rush to those equally vacant souls that have done it better than him. And escapism isn't merely the escape from reality that is bleak, but it is also an escape from what is boring. It makes us feel important. And we never have to break a sweat feeling important. The only thing users need to accomplish is a state of superficiality. Flash some ass. Preach a highly misinformed political point. Criticize a new TV show. Eat copious amounts of food. Break the news that you are dating your sibling and that you are happy so fuck everyone else. We cannot stand being ourselves. During the day, as the sun reprieved the human race of its hardships from the night, man walked, defecated, copulated, and so on. It was only during the night that he might ever even hope to understand himself. A dim light crosses our souls, and we are never to question just how meaningless and alone we are inside. We act and feel similar to animals. The only reason we are at the top of the food chain and different from animals is because we convince ourselves we are important, and that our deaths are tragic."

The homeless man shot me an odd look. "You gonna talk to me or just write in your notepad?"

I lifted my head up from the notepad with an expression that wasn't entirely human. "Sorry. I have to- never mind. It doesn't matter. What are you smoking?"

"Salvia." The man grunted.

"A man of class." I muttered.

"Not really." He said, putting ELO's 'Fire on High' on the boombox behind us, "But it's better than any drug on the street."

"Salvia is a delirium though. Not really a drug. I don't think I've ever had a good experience with it. Neutral maybe. But never good."

"No one does. Only, as you said, neutral or bad trips. Still, it's the most eye opening and strongest drug there is, and it only lasts a few minutes. I take a rip of this, and I'm set for the night. I don't want hooch, coke, or anything else. Keeps me at peace by rattling me. Makes me realize I'm really not all that important and any life I might live is not worth it. It helps free me from my mind. So, you can hang onto that bag of nose beers right there. Ain't gonna need it. Want some?"

I raised my eyebrow in suspicion. The homeless man smiled wryly, knowing full well how shady it was to offer someone a bag of coke, regardless of how little of it was left.

The Call of the Void

He waved a red pipe in front of my face. I shrugged, grabbing it and the purple canister, before pocketing the coke. "Just don't expect me to babysit you." I said, packing the bowl.

"Done it fine without you for years, thank you very much. Now... Geronimo!" Inhaling as deeply as he could, the man rested the pipe beside his knee. He sat there, babbling incoherently for a few minutes before opening his eyes wide and looking directly at me. He bobbed his head around mine, examining my eyes like I were some foreign matter he had to study.

I wasn't far behind. I took a second to refamiliarize myself with the process—hold in the smoke as long as possible, close my eyes, and get fucking ready. I held the smoke in for as long as I could, letting the divinorum particles loose on my lungs, knowing what to expect, praying for a merciful trip. The final repetition of 'Madness' yelled from the boombox, as I exhaled, and that old familiar world began playing tricks on my mind. Time lost all meaning in a way that is inadequate to describe with words. Within an eternity, the man's head beside me was resting calmly on his shoulder. As the last remaining memory had become the smoke leaving my... mouth...

"Greater levels of consciousness my ass..." I whispered. I think I whispered. I think it might be the last thing I said. Ever.

I've been here before.

A breeze cut leaves through the street, but it was the world, formed like a scoop of ice cream, so familiar, so bizarre, that made me turn my head to the angel, similar to one from an old 90s VHS, forming right in front of my eyes.

LeResche

The man pulled me to the ground, his face and entire body turning into an animation made out of a flip book, begging me not to leave this world. My face and hands, now visible to myself, like I was watching out of a camera, were also a flip book animation. I yelled for help, but my mouth grew longer and longer until it consumed my head backwards.

Legos were next. It was all Legos. Always has been. Plastic army soldiers dropped out of the sky, painted in Lego architecture. And it was then, I realized we have no conscious experience for inanimate objects. There is nothing that feels like a road or a chair. And yet, here I am, experiencing the qualia of impossibility.

I can no longer use the word 'I'. It has no meaning here.

Sam sat still next to the homeless man. His face was dull, and it was obvious that he was experiencing eternity in an instant. That is how one experiences eternity, in an instant. Sam has done this many times, but he never learns from his mistakes. So he must experience eternity infinitely. It is his curse. And if one were to look at Sam, behind his head, just out of the peripherals of human consciousness, they might see, here now, in his delirium, an entity floating behind him, working him like a maestro works an orchestra, or a master controls his puppet. And Sam is so close to solving that mystery that has haunted him his whole life. But he will never find it. And he seems so familiar... So much like a facsimile of identity. Identity. I.

I'm looking for a word. A verb actually. I'm looking for a verb in a sea of words, floating aimlessly in the sky. The verb I'm looking for is 'look'. It was always look. And I know this now because looking at me is the city. I am looking at the city. The city's look is a mask. I look from tower to tower as the city looks at me. And as the city looks, Bald Mountain watches, silently, invisibly, from behind. It looks at the lightning forming around the crown of its ever-looking eye.

Outside the walls of perception, the clarity in Being reveals itself.

But then it comes to me. To I. The colors of all beings are truly where I sit and feel the dysconnectivity of... words. Words are nothing but physical beings that have been placed solely into our minds to speak phantasmagorically through our mouths. The colors of all beings within my sight have become moving and passing like waves over my sight until they become nearly corporal, manifested beings of carnage that beg with me to stay. They plead with me that this is reality. This is where home is. Do not leave us behind. You are eternal here. You are everything here. Waves of colors speaking, crashing, yelling, pleading. A feeling of anxiety not entirely possible to human beings has gained hold of me. I am not truly me. I am not truly anything. This is life. 'Stay! Stay!' they cry 'He wants to take you away from us. That world is bad. That life is wrong. This, here, is reality! Stay!' No one could discern the pressures of a reality beyond their comprehension. Like infancy. Yes! Infancy! Like a baby, trying to comprehend a world of new shapes, concepts, ideas, all without the possibility of language.

Konrad's face manifested on the moon. "The fates have their eye on you," His face said, disappearing almost as quickly as it appeared, "but we're going to kill them."

Fading as life begins to get another meaning. Half of my sight began to see again as the colors faded into a washing machine rotation and a faceless demon with a crown firmly infused upon his head grew out of Bald Mountain before toppling the buildings of Los Angeles and began to tap a conductor's baton. His face was nothing more than flesh smoothed over itself. As he motioned for his symphony, demons pooled out of the sky riding other demonic entities. The crowned conductor began to motion more emphatically as demons danced through the air. The demons approached closer as I made a dive to my right and began to regain consciousness.

"I'm... I'm me." I said, anxious and harried, as if I had just survived a near-death experience.

"No. I'm me." The ragged man whispered.

"I-I'm Sam. I'm a professor. I'm... I'm a human." I narrowed my eyes as the physical world began to rematerialize. "A human deception. I'm no one."

"Alright, Sam."

"I'm not supposed to be- I'm not here. That wasn't Salvia."

"I always say that after I come back."

"I... I have to keep going. But I don't want to. I've seen enough. I'm not smart. I'm not anybody. Cir-cum-lo-cu-tion." I stuttered, sounding the word out syllable by syllable, as if I was hearing it for the first time, "I-I've talked my way around and into everything in life. I'm not important."

"None of us are."

The Call of the Void

"It's all just abstract thought. It's all ju-" I breathed deeply, gathering my thoughts and realigning my mind, "just abstract thoughts manifest as numbers and shapes." I looked at the homeless man, awaiting his response. He rolled a cigarette and turned his head away from me. "Jesus... what a calamitous eternity. Just," I paused once more, peering out at the moon, "abstract thoughts. And concepts."

"Eternity?"

"I mean, if that is our soul."

He laughed quietly, as if he had seen this a hundred times. "We can probably suffer an eternity of abstract thoughts. We've had a lifetime of practice." He lit the cigarette, inhaled and exhaled. "Sam. I can call you Sam, can't I? Sam, just talk to me like a human. What is it like? What do you feel is most wrong with this so-called 'reality'?"

I closed my eyes and shook my head, ready to placate him. "I don't know man. It's like there's a world that you left, and they still watch you as you try to make sense of this world and you're so close, but you can't quite get it. Like, you told the old world, 'I'm better than you and I'm going to prove it.' And then went into a pit of despair to try and complete this equation that seemed impossible to them, but you have your finger on the pulse, and you're almost there."

"Now you're talking my language."

I sat still for a moment, wringing my hands as my sight began to stabilize. "I'm not. I'm... not."

"Relax, Sam. You're fine."

I took another moment to wipe the sweat from my brow. "Yeah," I gasped, looking back at the flooded street, "I have to get across there."

"You could swim. Don't think you'll want to in this cold though."

I stood up and stared across the sewer water crashing upon itself as the windchill picked up.

"You could ask him though," the man said, pointing toward the bay, "He looks like he knows what he's doing."

A Recusant with a sign and a ferry was perched up against the wall nearest the bay smoking a cigarette. My hands shook, both from nerves and the cold. The night's sky blew a wrathful wind as I lit up and walked toward the shore.

VI

LA's once mesmerizing skyline had become engulfed, yet again, by a blinding fire in the sky. Where the crimson tint of the fire had previously teased the lower edges of the horizon, it was now moving across the middle of the firmament. Stars fought against the moon's oppressive luminance to make themselves visible. I stared at the sky, my hands buried deep in my pockets, admiring the dark cloud of smoke that was growing out of the southern vista, an enormously dark pall, illuminated briefly by bolts of lightning amongst its backdrop, like a terrifying presage from the gods. The wind had picked up and blasted cold air against my cheek, sending a frisson through my spine. The sky was red again and embers blew in the wind, bouncing lightly off of my face before turning to dust.

The few flooded blocks of streets in front of me remained entirely dark under the absence of streetlights. Just by the bank of the sewage river, there appeared a crowd moving and shouting frantically in the night. As the crowd opened up wider to capture any passersby, it became obvious that two men were fighting or, at least, grappling along the bank. The men wrestled each other, their shirtless backs lacerated from the coarse asphalt, persistently gnawing at one another's flesh before sharing blows back and forth. The disheveled, homeless pugilists were balding, and sweating profusely. The crowd shouted, jeered and roused around the men like predatory animals watching their prey fight for survival. Atop the flooded buildings, people were watching the spectacle and shouting their cries of approval.

The young Recusant approached me from the ferry just outside of my vision.

"Hey." The kid said at my side, staring at the boxing match by the shore "I'm Jack."

"Sam." I answered, keeping my gaze trained on the homeless fighters, "A little young to be a Recusant, aren't you?"

"We take all ages, races, genders, and creeds."

"Sure, sure. So, what's this all about?"

"They pay the bums to fight," he muttered absently, "Most of the time to the death."

A wild-eyed, young frat boy, his face the color of a cherry, had a wad of hundred-dollar bills in his hand and was flashing them like a fan around his head.

"That one! That one!" the boy shouted, as one homeless man sat on the back of the other and began to pull violently on his chin "That's the one that looks like my dad! An extra fifteen bucks if you kill him!"

A sharp whistle curled off the lips of a Hispanic man standing nearby. "¡Pinchè Chinga madre! ¡Estas loco como una cabra!"

"I'll add to that." His buddy remarked with a half-smile.

The man on top picked the felled opponent up and virulently slammed him onto his face before yanking on his chin once more, bending his spine to its limits. When the assailant finally released his grip, his opponent was twitching on the ground, his face marred with confusion and his mouth agape in roiling pain. His arms had shot to their sides as he began to twitch. A look of concern fell across the eyes of the downed homeless man, the presence of death forming behind his pupils. The man behind him showed no remorse and even a smile crossed his lips as he sneered and pulled harder and harder on the man's chin. With no escape in sight, the subdued man's eyes began to fall into the back of his head as he shed a tear and locked eyes with me briefly. And with a moribund look in the gleam of his eyes, I could see the life slowly pour out of his body. He had accepted his end, but there's nothing more unnerving than watching a man die when he knows he's going to die. The snap of his neck was harrowing and unlike any sound any man at the shore was likely to have heard before. His neck, now elongated to twice its size, rested limply on the back of his spine, like a hen whose had its head spun around and snapped. The assailant groveled at the feet of the crowd, begging remittance for the entertainment he provided.

"That was his brother." Jack, the young Recusant, pointed out to me.

"Sure," the young man laughed, "But what do you say to double or nothing?"

The man eagerly nodded his head in agreement. By the looks of it, he hadn't eaten in a month.

"Cool," the boy said, waving casually to the crowd "Let's get two on this one!"

The boy motioned toward the bay and two heads slowly began to emerge from the flood. Two well-fed, discalced individuals walked like colossal titans out of the water and made their way through the crowd, shouldering the frat boys as they barreled toward the center of the circle. More likely bodyguards than vagrants, they outweighed the other man six to one.

"Can you get me across that river?" I asked, turning away from the madness.

"That's my job." He sighed with an air of resignation.

"Hey. Hey faggots!" the frat boy slurred, "It's fifty to watch!"

Jack thrust his middle finger in the air as we walked off.

"Go jump into traffic you piece of shit!" the drunken frat boy yelled, "Do the world and your *family* a fuckin' favor! Your mother should have swallowed you!"

Jack's boat was makeshift, formed out of the discarded detritus from LA's deepest cavities. It was a good twenty feet long and, despite the materials it was made of, seemed sturdy. The stern was little more than taped and banded beer cases and his oar was a 2x4 filed down into a paddle. Jack, no older than nineteen or twenty, had a boombox playing the end of the fourth movement of Beethoven's 5th. I couldn't be certain, but my guess was that the boat was made of pine, probably from an abandoned stagecraft class. Corpses littered the bay, washing up onto shore from the tide of the sewage water. As Jack began to push the boat out, white-eyed transients breached the surface of the water, resembling wraiths of the underworld, wading through shit, litter and sewage to get aboard the Recusant's ship and make sail for the other side. A motion began to rock throughout the bay's restive, stygian and mysterious water; first came waves, then came the rats. They popped out of the water, two at a time, rushing the shores and over the bodies of the dead and dying homeless. I lifted my legs in an attempt to avoid them but there were too many.

"We have to go." Jack said with a tremor in his voice "Now!"

With both our legs in the ship, we pushed on the stern to give it momentum against the fractious, fetid waters. I could hear Verdi's "Dias Irae" starting on the boombox. I pushed harder as homeless men on the shore and in the water began to ambush us. Thrashing the water and clamoring amongst the artificial wakes, the homeless surrounded the boat, their heads barely above water. I extended my foot out, swinging it wildly, in a vain attempt to frighten them off.

"Don't let them on!" Jack yelled, "The ship can barely hold us!"

Screams and imprecations polluted the air while Jack paddled with one hand and swatted off the homeless reaching for the ship with his other. The wind rocked Jack and I back and forth in a violent flurry. A loud boom accompanied by a blinding flash from the sky rattled me to my core, but I recovered quickly. From out of the water, a hand forced itself over the bow and grabbed a hold of the young Recusant's arm. Watching as it nearly pulled him overboard, I rushed over to Jack, grabbed him around the waist and sat down with all of my dead weight, pulling him back in. He stood up and dusted himself off before making a beeline to the bow. Jack pulled madly on the wheel from left to right, overcompensating his steering to keep us from capsizing. I took a second to catch my breath, kneeling down and bracing myself against the floor as the roaring symphony berated my mind. Standing wasn't an option. With water filling the vessel at an alarming rate, I began slipping and sliding involuntarily toward the stern. I looked back, shocked to see a handful of wraiths clawing their way up to the boat, their weight forcing the stern underwater. Forming a massive, human bulwark, they stood upon each other's shoulders like a human wave made of flesh. I began sliding closer and closer to the mouth of the beast, clawing the boat's deck madly for anything to grab ahold of, as the balance of the boat shifted.

"Jack." I shouted, "Hey, Jack!".

Jack jerked his head around from the wheel to the stern. A look of dread flushed his face as he instantly kicked up his oar from the ground. From the pressure of the tremulous wakes, I fell again to one knee and lifted my forearm up to my face in yet another vain attempt at blocking the wave of homeless ready to crash down upon me. Jack leapt through the air and over my head, suspended briefly in time, and froze for a moment, his torso stretched out as far it could, before thrusting the oar over the top of the mob's heads. He flailed around on the stern, swinging at everything that moved but the waves were growing immense.

In one final, desperate move, Jack emptied an unlabeled bottle on the stern and overboard the ship. The fighting stopped for a moment as he lit a lighter and stared at them with careful awareness in his eyes. His eyes dragged across the surface of the water, begging the demons to call his bluff. I gulped anxiously, knowing full well he would drop the lighter without a second thought. Bereft of any courage, the horde relented back toward the middle of the river. Jack scoffed while he lit both of us a cigarette. His knees wobbled slightly, and he exhaled in relief, throwing the lighter overboard as it erupted a hedge of flames ten feet back.

My chest was rising and falling as I stared at the flames in the distance.

"I uh-" I breathed with a weary and raspy voice before coughing and lifting my cigarette. "I thought Recusants weren't allowed to indulge in any 'earthly' vice."

Crossing his arms, he sized me up momentarily with waxen eyes, his quiet face like something out of Picasso's Blue Period. His eyes were determined and decisive, the eyes of a man twice his age that had seen too much. He looked down at the floor of the boat and flipped his cropped hair that accentuated the frame of his jaw to a point. His skin was pale, but oddly tan around his face and neck—most likely the result of a farmer's tan. The tattoo on his forearm was a skull that broke off at its teeth into a sitting man with four heads. He had the look of a leader. The look of someone who knew what he was doing. The look of someone who was going to get the fuck out of LA one day.

"They don't. Why do you think I'm driving this fuckin' boat tonight?" He said gruffly.

"I don't know. Why *are* you driving this fuckin' boat tonight?"

257

He shook his head for a moment and looked at the moon pensively. The clouds stifled the moon like a broken sheath, their intermittent breaks attempting to suffocate the light that might shine upon us.

"The Recusants need this ferry open for the Values Voter Summit tonight. Business I guess..."

"Actually, the VVS is held in DC." I corrected, "This is more of a- well, I don't really know actually."

"Yeah."

"Look, don't take this the wrong way but you seem a little less zealous than the other members I've come across tonight. I wouldn't call a Recusant enthusiastic per se, but-"

Jack leaned on the starboard side. "I'm not... as adamant about the cause as I once was. I think that I reached a point where I realized it can only go so far. It started off so strong. Standing up against the decaying West; pissing everybody off and doing it legally; complete, fraternal harmony. And, on some level, it's as strong as it has ever been, but I feel like we're treading water."

Jack let out a deep sigh as he continued to paddle the boat from starboard.

"I understand." I said, crossing my arms and leaning against port, "In some way, every cause is ultimately doomed in our day and age. I've been following you guys since the start and watched as every different cause there was toed the line to grab for media attention. I also watched as all of those movements fell by the wayside. But persistence is the only factor that drives a movement. Persistence is what embeds your movement into the culture. If you burn out, you will fade away."

His eyelids drooped and he let out another sigh. "I guess. It's just that, we used to be taken seriously. We used to be on the big ten for domestic terrorist groups. Now what? We flagellate ourselves for the amusement of the public. No matter how long we persist, we will never be seen as anything more than madmen. No amount of self-mutilation is going to change that. What force in this world is greater than pleasure?"

"Well, I share your cynicism. I do. Still, I think the Recusants' cause is a hill to die on; ostensibly so from what I've seen tonight." I laughed. "We might not agree ideologically but, uh, well, they are the most proactive group for change I've seen."

"Still, I gotta get out."

"Get out? And go where?"

"Probably somewhere in the North. Can't stand it here anymore and, honestly, I can't much stand the Recusants anymore."

"Can't run from your problems."

"My problems are the whole country. And we're literally killing ourselves to send a message that will fall on deaf ears."

"So, you think there's a problem with the country, that doesn't-"

"Don't you?! I saw your video. I saw the tirade. Don't you think so?"

I lazily blew smoke out of the corner of my mouth and flicked the ash of my cigarette over port. He had a point. "I think," I said, pausing a moment for reflection, "There are too many conflicting zeitgeists in the country. I think we'll never see eye to eye again as a population. I think we may have lost our way."

"Yeah, well, 'til Konrad actually acts and puts some fuckin' skin in the game, nothing will change."

"You don't think he has? I saw some pretty gnarly scars on him. And honestly, I've never seen anything like what I've seen tonight. So many... deaths."

"Scars? Deaths? He's getting guys like me to join and then he sends the word."

"You think he's a chicken hawk?"

"I think he better start putting his dick on the chopping block tonight or he's going to have more than just a bunch of dead Recusants to answer for."

"You don't think he knows that? Let me ask you this, does Konrad strike you as the type of guy to ditch his own crusade? Does he seem like some dime store grifter to you? Does he even collect money?"

Jack nodded begrudgingly in agreement, leaning against a cockpit made of debris. His mouth twitched and his nostril curled up, not fully convinced of my argument. "I used to be one of your students, ya know."

I examined his face subtly, hoping my mind would make the connection. "I see." I said, a little embarrassed.

"Yeah. Philo 101"

"I never taught Philo 101." I said, a little relieved.

"Then 150 or whatever I don't really remember."

"Right. Sorry, I just don't recognize-"

"It's alright. I dropped out after the Spring semester to join the Recusant. I was a 'B' student at best so, ya know, either way."

"Quitting a school like UCLA is a pretty big commitment. I hope it wasn't for nothing."

"Me too."

"I'd hardly call what I do nowadays teaching though. Maybe years back, but not now."

"Then what would you call it?"

"Musing, I suppose. I guess the best definition of what I do is 'musing'. Though, after tonight, I'm running a little low on inspiration." Jack snorted a laugh that was either sincere or forced. "So, why'd you pick me up tonight?"

"Saw you on YouTube last week. Then I saw you walking. Figured you were on your way to Skid Row and could use a ride."

We shared a laugh.

I flicked my cigarette into the water. "It's interesting though because, I could swear, it felt like I was being followed by the Recusants all night."

"Not likely. Tonight is '*in noctis iudicii*'. A night of finality. Death by our own hands or any other. Not all of us. But enough. It's happening all across the city. It would be odd if you *haven't* seen a few. Konrad rang the beacon tonight. Very abrupt. Totally unforeseen. But when the signal was given, there was no doubt. Tonight was the night."

"And to think they left you on boat duty."

A radiance off the bow of the boat, like a beam from the sun, pierced the moon's net of darkness. A massive circular complex was ahead in the distance. Its signs were demolished yet its lights were blinding from even 250 meters out.

"Can I ask you something Dr. Killian?"

"Yeah. Shoot."

"Why'd you go off in class?"

"I was drunk, didn't you hear?" I sighed, hoping to buy some time for an answer, "If I had to put it on anything it would be that I'm not well equipped to teach in today's world. I don't know who is, but it's not me."

"I always enjoyed your class. And if it's any consolation, plenty of students were like that, and even worse, to just about every teacher on campus."

"Well, it's not." I snapped, my tone rising in agitation, "What is class for then? Masturbatory self-indulgence? To hear myself talk?" Jack nodded his head and bit his lip, looking down at the lake of sewer water. I shook my head and looked off the port side, ashamed to have snapped at the kid. "I didn't mean to raise my voice."

"It's alright. You're right. It's half the reason I left anyway. Half the reason I joined the Recusants." He laughed to himself and swept his hand across his mouth, "You think it's bad at university? You should have seen my high school."

"Yeah, well, I know there's nothing I, or any of the other teachers can do. I get that. I once said, 'If only we could get High Schools to teach rhetoric and critical thinking', but I know it isn't what's being taught. I know that when I was in college, it wasn't nearly as hard as it was, say, 50 years ago but I got into higher education to teach kids who wanted to be taught." I began pacing from side to side, gesticulating wildly with my hands, as if possessed with a fury I didn't know I had. "I just thought college would be different. And it's all lost. I see that now. There isn't a thing we can do. And I sit up at night, anxious and speechless, wondering, 'Is this really it? Are we truly at the precipice of the dark ages?' And I know! I. Know. Others think that I'm being hyperbolic and think that it's just because I have a few 'rotten apples' but it isn't! The time that has elapsed from when I left graduate school to the time I started teaching graduate school was less than half a decade. The time for chaos is nearly around the corner."

"I'm sorry..."

"Me too."

I leaned against the port side to scribble notes in my notepad.

"The more the night goes on, there seems to be an almost entropic push in, not only our city, but our human nature. Philosophers have been talking about a phenomena, a world outside of the physical world, for centuries. And here we are, embracing it... It's a shame really that-"

The oar Jack was rowing pushed the notepad from my hand and into the sewage morass. I watched as it sank below the surface.

"Oh, sorry. Anything important?"

I paused before shaking my head and finally answering, "No."

263

"Well, we're here," he murmured, slowing the boat with the pine oar. "Pandemonium Square."

"Ominous name for a complex."

"Yeah." He said, fighting off a smile. "Just wait 'til you get in there."

After docking at the nearest bay, I jumped off the cardboard ferry and turned to wave to Jack. He pushed off from the shore with his wooden paddle, a look of resignation crossing his face, contrite to return to his post.

"Hey!" I shouted, "I might have given up but, keep your head up. You're a part of something special. If not now, soon."

"We'll see..." He said, a faint smile drawn across his face, as Erebus blanketed the surrounding area in a shadow of wrath.

And in the cloak of the night, he disappeared.

A poignant darkness had swallowed the city and my mind. What was once a dimly lit, promising night, had been extinguished by a swarthy mass of menacing dreams and hollow malisons. Pandemonium Motel had become a shell of acceptable life in America, decorating its exterior with the decaying sinew of 'better times' and brown, shit-like matter. A testament to the soul of the city. A mausoleum of the unrelenting wrath that harbored racial divides, infidelities, and self-hatred. The architecture was like Bruegel's Tower of Babel, immense in appearance, wrapped around in a spiral to the 10th story roof with gateways every few feet. I took a step back to take in the crisp air, trying to shake off the surrealism of the night, as an organ hauntingly played from the chambers.

A tall and slender ticket agent with a Clark Gable mustache, eloquently dressed in a pinstriped quartet suit, worked the entrance booth that was designed to resemble an arcane cinema. His left cheek was festered with a skin disease, like formaldehyde had kissed his face. Above his head was a sign that read:

Hourly-25

Halfday-225

Daily-500

Monthly-1200

Forever In Madness-1500

?-2000

"What's the question mark?" I asked.

"Pay 2000 and find out. Do you have 2000?"

"Not on me."

"Then you won't find out." He finished, raising his hand brusquely.

"One hour then." I passed him the 25 dollars and lit a cigarette. He narrowed his eyes and creased his forehead while examining the money. "Problem?"

"Room 237" he hissed, sliding me the keys.

The complex was a vision from a mentally ill Baroque period painter; ostentatious and grand, yet terribly morose. A burial chamber would be a more apt description. Near the easternmost wall was the origin of the music. Fused to the wall was an enormous organ, twenty

265

feet by twenty feet, with a plaque, so morbidly bedizened, so terribly funereal, it couldn't be missed. Its letters were fading, and I strained to read the message.

Imp— Mu—

"World's... Emperor. Empress? Empress... world? What?" I mumbled under my breath, trying to translate the Latin.

The organist, shirtless and bald, had taken a quick break, his back bare to the entire courtyard, showing a tattoo of a yellow frowny face with graphically gouged out eyes painted across his spine. With a jittery pumping of his leg on the swell pedals, the organist began to play the first movement of Liszt's Hungarian Rhapsody No. 2, taking a moment every few seconds to experiment with the stop knobs, before switching seamlessly, and almost comically, into Bach's Toccata and Fugue in D minor. Methodically, the organist picked up the tempo, hitting the B sharp over and over again, switching rhythmically from Liszt to Bach's Fugue in G minor. And finally, as sweat had painted a glossy canvas over his reflective dome and smooth skin, he slowed his tempo, pulling gently on another stop knob. His final tune was background music for the damned, an even paced yet somber and eerie melody one might expect to hear out of a lamenting drunk's basement.

I moved toward the middle of the grassy courtyard. Toilet paper rolls were flung from one direction to the other up above, some engulfed in flames. Unsupervised adolescents, so cross-faded on grass and wine they could barely see straight, were standing near the organ. They sized me up, throwing gang signs and aping my every movement with square shoulders and puffed out chests. Moonlight illuminated the courtyard from the sky above. I walked into the illumination and looked up to see a vacant space where the roof of the towering motel should have been.

The high rise was constructed ten stories tall, each level projecting furious hollers from its denizens, those inescapable testaments of rage. The stars were the only natural light in the courtyard, a saving grace of the humans that still resided within its walls. A disturbance on floors 5-10 caught the eye of the nearby residents. Each door from the upper floors had opened up and a clamoring was shaking the foundation of the complex. The northernmost side had been filled with white men, wearing black ski masks and Kevlar vests with assault rifles slung over their shoulders, stomping the ground vigorously with their feet. As I turned to face the southernmost wall, I saw, at first, the same thing before inspecting the crowd closer. Black men, donned in white ski masks, Kevlar vests and assault rifles, stomped the floor as well in synchrony. The stomping echoed through the halls, quaking the complex to its core, as a dream of chaos was born amongst its inhabitants, a dream eternal.

Abruptly, the gonging of boots on asphalt had ceased. The two groups of Whites and Blacks stood silent, staring at one another without so much as a movement or word. Dwellers of the night glared at the individuals intently, waiting for their next move. I stood squarely in the middle, staring up at them like an imbecile who stares upward at an icicle, fully embracing the danger, praying it might be his last

267

moment. Nothing. The groups eyeballed one another maliciously, but without a word.

As I began to look down, a bottle of malt liquor came flying out of the air. It crashed against the left side of my face, breaking on impact. I howled out in pain, holding the left side of my face, watching as trickles of blood fell to the grass beneath my feet. Turning to search the area, I found the teenagers laughing and running off into the distance, their stuttered laughs like the braying of a donkey.

"Oh, you mother fuckers!" I yelled, "You better hope I don't fucking find you!"

At a nearby vending machine's reflection, I lowered my hand to examine my face. The blood was sparse, gently dribbling from my nose and mouth. The impact had left me with a bluish, crescent bruise about two inches wide, stretching from my lower eye to my cheekbone.

I moved up the stairs to the second floor and to room 237. Next-door, outside of 236, there was a woman, hunched over and silent, carving something with a letter opener. She was humming some unrecognizable tune and rocking a little on the porch of her room. I leaned in, careful not to disturb her, and peered over her shoulder to get a better look. I instantly shot back. Her hand was completely awash in blood, its appendages trickling the visceral fluid in droplets onto her dress. It was difficult to make out, but I distinctly saw the word 'Yule' etched into her skin with lines crossing every which way. Finally turning to meet me, she smiled shyly before resting the back of her head against her room's door. The room behind her had an eerily enchanting hymn coming from it; a devious canticle, like a pheromone to the ears, played over and over again, singing to my soul. Her laugh, barreling out of a toothless, black-tongued mouth, snapped me from the trance as a black cat jumped onto her lap.

"Piss off." The woman scowled.

I opened 237, still uncertain why I rented the room. The shag carpet was either filthy with stains and dirt or terribly designed. The walls were plastered with green wallpaper from end to end and a red balloon was thumping back and forth against the air conditioning vent in the corner of the room. I sat at the foot of the bed and turned the TV on to the evening news before cleaning up in a nearby sink. The picture was fuzzy, and the frames of the TV looped wildly before pausing on the newscaster's face. He was still, paused like a mannequin, but the clock continued to run in the background.

Lighting a cigarette, I threw the 8-ball I got from the homeless man on the counter of the nearest desk. My head was becoming swollen from exhaustion. I had reached the apogee of my body's limits and was at the point where my brain was telling me to slow down and get some sleep—or suffer the consequences. And yet, that old, long-nailed finger in the back of mind, scratched and scratched, demanding I persist; health be damned.

Despite the coke, I rested my head on the bed's pillow and closed my eyes. Visions, horrible and unworldly, like the animations of a madman, appeared in my eyelids. I opened my eyes to escape the insanity but found myself closing them over and over again as a hypnagogic trance arrested my consciousness.

LeResche

With my eyes closed, I fell into the hypnosis of sleep. Filled with abstract images and chimerical horrors beyond the mind's comprehension, I dropped deep into the abyss of my mind, surrendering myself over to the darkness, whose images began surreal before sliding into madness, like a gauntlet of Dali paintings that ended with Bosche.

I rose that morning—to my surprise—alone in her bed, the smell of Hazelnut coffee breaking through the air. The window was still propped open from the night before, and, flirting with the fragrance of the coffee, the light aromatic vestiges of the monsoon that had battered our town the night before fused with the elysian perfume of the kitchen.

She was staring at herself in the mirror, swinging and twisting her hips from side to side, observing her calf muscles at each angle. I shimmied myself backward onto the wall behind her bed, placed a pillow on my lap, and observed her without a word. Her hair was a tinge of orange, so light that it could have just as easily been fire. It fell naturally down her back in a voluminous, supple braid of wiry curls that she would comb straight for just such an occasion as today. Her bangs, in those early morning mirror sessions, always obscured her eyes until, finally, after the comb had revealed her face, those emerald orbs would divulge themselves and eclipse the scene.

Her body's skin, even for a ginger, was like pale milk, pocked with copious freckles that speckled her face into a dalmatian's hide. But her freckles had made her self-conscious no doubt. I could see it, even if she wouldn't admit it, in the way she covered up in front of new company, the way her face blushed whenever someone mentioned them. Hyperpigmentation they had called it. But it didn't matter to me.

When she had finished examining her lower body in the mirror, she reached for her pub skirt wrap, barely long enough to cover her knees, and slipped it up her legs, past her sinewy claves, before stopping just below her small, yet firm, cheeks. Hooking both of her thumbs into the lining of her green leotard, she lifted her wrap skirt over her backside and to her waist, flashing me a glimpse of her emerald eyes in the mirror.

With a smile that thinned her pale lips, she bent down—slowly and almost seductively—to the floor and slipped on her black reel shoes. The floorboard echoed a click from her taps as she shuffled and spun around and threw her arms into the air, giving a look of demure confidence. She tightened her white dress socks to her knees and leapt once more into the air, gracefully floating down with one foot arched out in playful dance. I laughed while she slipped her black, long-sleeved dress shirt, embroidered with green floral patterns across the front, and placed her braided headband over her head, turning once more to check her makeup. My eyes fell on the arras in her hallway. It was a late 19th century tapestry that depicted 2 satyrs drinking wine and playing lyres amongst a backdrop of interwoven designs in green and golden fabric. In the center, the tapestry read, 6/9/13.

It was hard to believe that our town's Annual Irish Folk Festival had already come again. Junior year. It felt like a month ago

271

that her and I, driving with my newly issued driver's license, were cruising to the nether regions of our town's bucolic environs, the wind wisping up in our hair, her thin, pale fingers gripping tightly to the cola bottle in her lap, my hand caressing her thigh lightly as I bared a sangfroid smile. She lifted her hand to my cheeks and passed it under my chin, but her face betrayed her true feelings. I could tell, after all we had been through that year, that this day—her first competitive entry into the Riverdance competition—was weighing on her mind more than it should have. Her hand squeezed mine twice before releasing it and staring blithely out the window.

At the entrance of the festival, past the graveled parking lot and near the green beer garden, she, standing no taller than chest length to me, held my hand tightly, nearly pulling it down to the side of her hip as sweat lubricated our grip's tension. I hooked my arm around her neck and kissed the top of her forehead to ease her troubled mind. People passed in droves, sometimes staring at the freckles, variegated with light red dots, across her face, looking at her, mouths covered in shock, as if she might have a medical condition. She had an amazing, sylphlike body, but most people—myself not included—couldn't get past her freckles.

When inside the venue, the canorous aura of flutes, harps and timpan fused together into an upbeat Irish jig. We walked toward the stage, her hand still sweating, eyes darting around to see if there was anyone we might know there. I assured her once more that it was alright and went to get some food from a nearby stand. She had two boxty cakes wrapped in wax paper and I grabbed a boiled bacon

The Call of the Void

sandwich with Blaa bread, topped with shaved cabbage and mashed potatoes. She ate one of the cakes and placed the other on a nearby table. Her brow creased and she seemed to stare off into the idyllic forest surrounding the dancefloor on the dais. Beech trees, so wide and unkempt they spread out into each direction, and White oaks, so tall they seemed to touch the sky, bordered us into the festival, like a fairy tale, a nirvanic presidio, a lucid dream, our own fulgent veld.

When the competition started and she went up, the crowd, first staring blankly at her freckled face, looked on in astonishment as she whipped through the air with grace, her legs staying in the air just long enough to make the dance look preternatural, animated, as if from a movie. She lambently tapped across the stage with deft precision, keen to match the harpsichord's rhythm with that of her feet as she executed a perfect entrechat over and over again. For a brief moment, she stared out into the crowd and our eyes locked. We shared a smile as she continued her gambol around the stage.

After it was over, she received third place. I figured she would take it rather poorly, but she leapt into my arms, sprawled out straight like a steel rod, her left hand outstretched with the third-place medal, and hung her right arm around my neck—no longer conscious of the rabble's critical stare.

The music playing all around us transitioned periodically from the classical to the contemporary. A song came on, introduced by a rigid guitar riff, and her eyes opened slightly in relief. I turned to meet her and smiled, raising an eyebrow in confusion, as she began to mouth the lyrics to the song.

"*Don't tell me you've never heard this song before.*" *She said, her voice mellifluous, a panacea to my soul, "Sammy! 'Can't fight the moonlight'? Leann Rimes? Come on..."*

"*Well,*" *I shrugged with a smile, "I've never heard it.*"

She passed the backside of her hand across my cheek before wrapping her arms around my waist as I picked her up and swung her around. Her eyes shut tight, and a smile grew wide across her mouth while she laughed and held me close. Behind the concession stands and looming oak trees, through the foresty borders and deep in the heart of the woods, we danced while listening to the distant tune grow more resonant. As we fell to the ground and embraced one another, I gently cupped her cheek and rubbed my thumb across her skin, irrorate-cerise freckles coating her face almost completely. And as the song played on, the opalescent firmament above shone through the forest as we took turns lightly touching one another, removing articles of clothing, and passing our fingers sensually over our bodies with tumescent desire. We became one and the world swallowed us whole, soul and all. The strands of iridescent light reflected off of her face, turning the color of her freckles the same light carrot shade of her hair, nearly blending in with her skin's complexion.

The sun reached the peak of Lion's Sunny Hill when we had finished. Her hand, soft and smooth, ran its fingers across my chest and her foot went up and down my leg as I stretched out, watching the sun lift over Sunny Hill.

"*Thank you.*" *She whispered.*

"*For what?*" *I asked.*

The Call of the Void

"For being here."

Life could have paused right there, and all would have fine. We had told ourselves we would never grow old; that our junior year would last an eternity. I had considered staying in town, shirking my intellectual desires at Michigan State, and getting a job locally. But the impetus of my yearnings had cleaved a gap into our joined hearts.

We never spoke again after graduation.

As the sound of a low bass rumbled through the air vents—SOAD's 'Spiders' I recognized—and a wave of terrifying chants from 236 pulsed through the room like a morbid cadence, I woke and rubbed my temples, dumping the rest of my whiskey into a water cup by the nightstand. I opened its drawer beside me and put a few lines of coke on the St. James Bible. I did a line and let the powder go to work on my brain. That first hit of cocaine is like a supernatural relief, like death had always been there and this was the release to the other side. After vigorously rubbing my face into a pulp, trying to exculpate the nightmare from my mind, I did another, drinking half the cup while chain smoking. I rested on the pillow with my hand behind my head and watched as the newscaster looped the same projector line over and over, as if he were a broken record.

The phone rang. It was a blaring ring that bounced off the walls and back into my mind, disturbing my momentary peace. I turned my head to the nightstand and let the phone bounce off the receiver fiercely from side to side. I extended my hand before jerking it back. It rang even louder. I grabbed it.

"Hello?" I said. A coarse static played on the other line along with the screams of unfamiliar voices fading in and out. "Hello?!"

"Is this who I think it is?"

"I doubt it."

"You might know what infinity is, old friend, but do you have any idea what eternity is?" I didn't answer. "I hope you're ready for eternity, boyo. Because it's always ready for you."

"What do you want? Quit playing phone tag with me and just tell me what you fucking want!" I finished my whiskey and threw the empty cup on the floor.

"People ask me all the time what it's like to receive that honor of youngest tenure." The voice said, mocking my tone, "I feel a bit like a sham. So many young protégées and tenured professors from ages 26-28 and they've already accomplished so much. I write pseudo-intellectual pieces in the opinion column of a soon to be defunct media company."

"I never- Felix? Felix is that you?"

"Felix?" The voice asked, now mocking a halfwit's voice, "Felix is that you?"

"Cut the shit!" I shot up in a rage, ready to slam the receiver down. "What do you want, asshole?!"

Silence cut the static and screams on the other end. "Do you read John Gray?" The voice asked in a serious tone.

"I- I do."

"He said, and I quote, 'Removing the masks from our animal faces is a task that has hardly begun.' Is yours coming off soon, Sam?"

The Call of the Void

His laugh—that old, gruff, cackling, madness laden laugh—revved up on the other end. My left eye twitched and my face flushed red as I felt the muscles in my neck tense up. More laughter came now from the others on the line. I slammed the phone down onto the receiver over and over again, breaking it in half. I stopped, leaned back to catch a breath and center myself, before lunging forward, ripping the phone off of the wall and throwing it through the glass of the front window.

A loud knocking shook the walls of my room.

"Bitch! Open the fuck up!"

I couldn't tell if it was my door or the neighbor's.

"Open the fuck up!" a voice screeched, followed by blows on the door outside.

"I won't hurt it. I won't hurt you. I just need... I just need... I JUST NEED YOU TO LET ME THE FUCK IN!"

I took a look out of my peephole and saw a young man in front of 238, kicking the door violently as his wallet chain bounced from one side of his hip to the other. Slowly, I creaked open my door to get a better look. A young, Native American man stared at me with murderous intent for only a moment before bolting down the northern most corridor and into the black of night. Against my better judgment, I knocked on 238's door. An extremely malnourished Hispanic man answered the door and slunk away. On the bed there was a Native American woman with a black eye. I nodded my head, quietly trying to empathize with the couple.

"I'm sorry about that." I said, "Look, if you need anything or if your boyfriend comes back, just knock on the wall and I'll, uh, open my door again."

The woman raised her hand and mumbled a little under her breath, trying to get me to stay. "No." she squealed, holding back a tear "He's not my boyfriend. He's my son."

I had no words. I leaned against the railing on the walkway and looked down on the courtyard. Three boys dropped a Molotov cocktail from the third floor onto the ground. I lit a cigarette as they tied up a stray cat and threw it off next.

A moment later, as the clouds above stifled the moon light illuminating the courtyard, shadows clouded the corner of my eyes, and a vast twilight swallowed the hall's fluorescent lights. Exhaustion had surely gotten the better of me.

"Are you angry?" a voice, dripping with inhuman makings, whispered from the dark corner behind me.

Staring into the abyss, I sighed. "I never used to be. It's kind of hard not to be though. Everyone keeps taking the path of least resistance and-"

"Time for that in a moment." The voice whispered, thick with an unearthly rasp, "Come forward. Just a little."

"Forw-"

"No, no, no. Not another word. Forward, if you want to see the light again."

The Call of the Void

I turned around to find the entire complex covered in a pall of darkness. The only light in the place was the moon's tendrils, beaming down from the roof into the courtyard. I turned back and walked forward slowly, placing my foot down carefully with each blind step, as the embers of my cigarette illuminated the way.

My knee hit a solid, marble table, and I sat down at it. A radiance—dull but visible—came up from the table to reveal a chess board. Noticing the white pieces in front of me, I looked around in the darkness for a moment before reaching down and moving my knight to F3.

A condensed breath plumed from the shadowed corner of the second floor. "Now, as I was saying; The path of least resistance is usually the path best taken."

A dark smoke engulfed the black pieces and moved the knight to F6.

"Sure," I laughed, moving my pawn to C4, "if we're in an action movie. But we aren't. And maybe that's our tragic misstep. We want to believe we are all entities of fiction. It's probably why we mourn our deaths at a young age so intently. We never take a moment to realize we are cosmic tragedies; not local dramas."

A moment of silence came once more from the abyss before the swarthy fog moved his pawn to G6. "You're angry at humans?"

"I'm scared, alright? Scared for humans, not myself." I moved my knight to C3. "There is a ceiling to our advancement and, at some point, we're just going to start picking each other off out of boredom." The dark mass moved his bishop to G7. "I am human.

279

But, sure, who wouldn't be? I'm pursuing a beast through a tempest on a daily basis. I'm the paranoid gopher following his next meal into a flooded wash fleeing from an owl. I'm cognizant enough to realize history has its own reflections but-"

"But?"

A line drew across my brow as I thought of the question. I moved my pawn to D4. "But I can't help but feel as though our progress has-"

"Progress?" The voice interjected, castling his king and rook, "Sounds a bit Ludditic."

"Hardly! Progress isn't met with responsibility at all. Do you know that we went from ground travel to space travel in a generation?" I took a moment to exhale and stretch my neck, while I pondered my next move. I went first for my farthest pawn, but switched to my bishop, sliding it to F4. "Sure, my greatest fear is that I've become a Luddite. I've always tried to balance culture, modernity, acceptance and tradition all into one. But it's hard not to recognize the industrial revolution as one of, if not the most, watershed moments in human history. It's led, at a rapid rate, to our dependence on machines. Technology now has stymied our emotional intelligence and intuition in a way that seems irreversible. Progress is only degenerate if it lacks artistic value. When we lose art, we lose our spirit."

The voice moved his pawn to D5. "You had the privilege to obtain an education that allows you to think that way."

"And I've been trying to pass that knowledge on for years." I hovered my hand over my pieces and analyzed the board, trying to steady my drunken vision. I moved my Queen to B3. "So, I ask you; if my privileged education affords me enough to examine the world the way it should be examined and I'm lambasted for the very privilege, what privilege do I truly have?" Silence. The voice captured my pawn with his at C4. "To answer your original question, yes. I am angry at the human race. I used to be so optimistic about everything. I thought knowledge would prevail and common sense would invigorate the most stubborn minds, but knowledge is scary today. Knowledge is a questionable offense. So, yes, I am a misanthrope. I am a pessimist. I hate humans. I hate myself but I can at least resonate with myself because I know I am trying." Flushed, I captured his pawn at C4 with my Queen. "And the most tragic truth that comes from all of this is that I never became misanthropic or pessimistic until I became an educator. I have to accept something that we have never seen in any century other than our own; a MAJORITY of students compliant with ignorance in favor of being sub-conscious beings that will never take reason or, at least, an opposing view in mind." The voice moved his pawn to C6. "I am a Doctor of Philosophy and, in two thousand years, even Socrates would not believe the level of denigration that plagues us. So, once more my shadowy friend, I am ready to face death and nothingness at the disgust I've found at the hands of the human advertence. No man, living or dead, would embrace the fate that all men must with such grace as I would at this point." I moved my pawn to E4. "We evolved ourselves into consciousness and we are currently devolving ourselves into primitive sentimentality. Which is fine! I just don't want to be here when it goes off."

The voice slid his knight to D7. "Which is just a long-winded way of saying you hate change."

"I'm angry," I sighed, lighting another cigarette and moving my rook to D1, "My criticisms are not biased. They are merely observations of the collective mindset that seems so ready to contradict itself. But my rage, my wrath, is unbiased. It is a pure rage that knows no discrimination. It is pure in its scope. If I lose that... If I lose that, I lose what makes me human."

"I see." The voice whispered, moving his knight to B6.

"God," I rasped, exhaling smoke, "that sounds terrible out loud."

I slid my queen up one to C5.

"Well," The voice started, immediately sliding his bishop to G4. "you've got a good head on your shoulders."

"Yeah. I'm talking to a fuckin' shadow, but sure."

Without thinking, I pushed my bishop to G5. The voice immediately responded by moving to A4, which made me pause and reflect.

"You like to hear yourself talk, don't you?"

I crinkled my nose and exhaled smoke through my nostrils, moving my Queen back to A3, contemplating the question I'd always struggled with. "I do. What professor doesn't?"

"No excuses." The voice answered, almost laughing, moving his knight to C3 and capturing my knight. "Why did you move your queen?"

The move was so obvious, so plain. I felt like a fool.

The Call of the Void

I stared at the table for a minute, trying to get it back into focus, as I replayed the move over and over again in my head. I moved my hand over my upper lip in an attempt to hide my dour expression, before responding, "I'm a little drunk." I clenched my fist and pressed it tightly against my lips, the white in my knuckles glowing through the skin.

"Excuses again. And for a man with such a penchant for indirect convolutedness and periphrasis. Like a politi-"

With a volatile rage, I reached back and backhanded the chess pieces into the abyss, shouting, "Fuck!" into the air, before sitting back down.

"That's what I'm here for." The darkness responded with a content tone.

A piece of paper slid across the table with indiscernible notes scribbled across its page.

"Now," the voice beckoned, as a light formed behind him, "Come through here."

I stared with exhaustion at the folded sheet of paper for a moment, taking note of the odd symbols present on the page, before raking my face over with both my hands.

"Tonight-" I said, exhaling smoke, "Tonight is not what I thought it would be. It's like watching a fucking vaudeville act and I'm on the stage and everyone, besides me, is in on it. Only, there's no resolution; no reckoning."

"Reckoning?" the voice laughed "Reckoning? You were hoping for a reckoning?" I didn't respond. "Sam, I *am* your reckoning."

I closed my eyes, then opened them, and found myself turned around. The complex was completely abandoned. The lights had turned on once more, illuminating the darkened corners. A warm zephyr blew my collar up as stale smoke permeated the air and the silence of the organ left a haunting impression over the complex. That curious feeling of oblivion was present. No sounds. Nobody. Just, for once, the wisp of air gently caressing my neck.

I lifted the paper from the ground and, this time, noticed the words were no longer in cryptic symbols but English.

Dead bolt, rotten key

Brass ring, eternal tree

Dark voice, visible face

Bring me to grace

248

Crumpling the paper and dropping it into the wind, I shook my head and moved toward the stairs.

Sounds of distant drums played softly from the street, taking their time with each beat. I jogged over to the elevator and pressed the first-floor button, jumping up and down in anxious anticipation. It stalled, displaying a digitized error on the screen above. A fire axe stuck between the handles of the emergency stairs blocked my exit. I looked down off the second floor's balcony, maybe fifteen feet or so below. The melodic humming from the street impaled my better judgment and called to me like sirens of an urban sea. Taking a deep breath, I calculated the fall before swinging over the guardrail and crashing onto the courtyard below, grateful my ankles didn't break.

A fire enveloped the barrier of the entrance like some ancient tribal ritual in the Amazon. The street was barely visible, marred by the legion of torches consuming the darkness. I slowly parted the wall of incinerates like a veil of beads to see the racial militias divided in the street. The army of whites maintained the westernmost portion of the street while an army of blacks garrisoned the easternmost street. The militias were lined up parallel to one another. And about twenty feet back, just south of the white militia, was a table with two well-dressed men with microphone headsets, talking back and forth like old pals and making play by play color commentary, clearly nescient of how volatile the situation really was.

A leader from each side stepped forward, meeting the other at the zenith of the gauntlet. Both men, wearing polarized sunglasses, stood stoically across from one another at six feet, staring intently at their natural born enemy, baring their faces for all of LA to see. The chanting from each militia grew unintelligible and coarse with every second that passed. I moved in closer, trying to get within earshot of the two.

"You know our terms."

"I do. And we need to renegotiate. Anything less would leave us vulnerable."

LeResche

"You know, I'd rather just have a challenge here and end this whole thing. I'd just as well prefer you went back to wherever you came from."

"And your men feel the same?"

"Undoubtedly."

The crowd burst into a frenzy.

"You people really are endowed with inferiority, you know that? A mephitic lot, too imbued with centuries of ignorance to recognize your own terrible smell."

"And you, a constant burden on society, whose only measure is to incite calumny against us with your newly found ideas of superiority, ossifying the vox populi against your own race."

The two men at the booth stifled their laughter, a mien of bafflement slowly overcoming their faces.

"Too proud, t-"

"Pride. It's embedded in our DNA. It's what makes us superior. I wish the same could be said for your kind."

"What is your biggest fear regarding my people? I'm curious. We've only spoken professionally. Is it our skin color?"

"It's statistically proven that 'your people' do worse in situations unfavorable to our race. That's problem number one and infinity."

"And when the system favors you and leaves us working our ass off for nothing more than scraps on the table, you could see where we've come from after all these years."

The Call of the Void

"You're afraid that our race will overcome yours, is that it? That we'll interbreed enough, and your skin tone will no longer be anything more than a page in an extinct textbook. Isn't that right?"

"You got that ass backwards. Our skin tone dominates any skin tone it breeds with. You're afraid because your women like us more than they like you, isn't that it?"

The crowd exploded, demanding blood.

"You're only saying that 'cause your wife left you for me, isn't that right?"

"That stings. It really does. It won't ever take back the fact that I fucked your little sister. It won't. But it stings."

"They demand it."

"Yes. They demand it."

"Peace is impossible."

"Like the dueling shadow of a man at dawn, it is impossible."

"I'm sorry brother."

"As am I..."

Both leaders locked eyes and drew back, raising their arms to incite their crews. The commentators sprung back to life, laughing and pointing at the chaos embroiling before them. I stood still, silent as possible, directly between the two militias, in awe of the inevitable slaughter and of the many sons unknowingly becoming bastardized that night. Both sides remained silent, awaiting their oppressors to fire the first shot or for their general's command. The two leaders, drunk on hellfire and angst, inured by a lifetime of hatred, had their hands raised far above their heads like finials atop a station, intent on killing the other. The music of the crowd swayed the souls of each group farther and farther into a rage. And as both of the captains began to lower their hands, a faint yell from behind me came tearing through the crowd. I turned my head to see a man rushing past me, dressed in a peace symbol hoodie with a bandana around his mouth, holding a ball of fire in his hands. He ran against the night with an inchoate lunacy growing behind his eyes, holding a ball of flame over his head as he moved swiftly to the front, galloping almost, as if seated on an invisible horse. He cocked his arm back to the ground and flung the Molotov clear across the street into the middle of the armies.

The petrol spread quickly across the street and hit most of the vanguard before germinating through the remaining ranks. Soldiers from both sides shot their opposition but with hardly any success. Both captains worked fiercely at their body armor, tearing molted flesh from their chest, revealing muscle, sinew and, finally, bone. The immolated captains locked eyes in the judgment of the firestorm and grappled at one another's throats. Falling to the ground, the pair never released their grip and stared into their enemy's eye until both were completely consumed by the flame. And, after the flames had swallowed them thoroughly, both men were indistinguishable—blackened flesh and blanched bone.

I juked awkwardly through the fusillade and rushed past the barricades off ninth street. When I got to the bus stop, I sat on the bench, slid down it a little, and relaxed my head on the backrest. A section of ninth street was caged off with construction of the zoo's remodeling project. A gelid wind roused goose pimples on the back of my neck as I popped the collar of my flannel for warmth. The confused and riled growls of animals, caged in close proximity, were audible from the street. I looked down over the precipice next to the barricade to watch as they howled at one another from cage to cage, fighting against the steel at a chance to escape.

A group of Recusants were sitting around a dais in the center of the zoo. On top of the platform was the vulture exhibit and a Recusant chained to a boulder within the exhibit. His hands were manacled over his head and his feet chained together along the bottom. One of the epigones smeared something from a bottle over the midsection of his abdomen. A vulture moved in closer as the chained man gave a withdrawn nod and smiled. The other Recusant nodded back to him before bludgeoning him over the head with a blackjack mercilessly. He took his seat with the rest of the group as lamentations and cries drowned out the sounds of the animals.

Back toward the Tower of Babel, through the carnage, past the cries, and beyond the growls, the sound of an organ played distantly.

VII

Around the corner of ninth, the detritus of empty doomsday food buckets glutted a vast street fraught with starving homeless men and women who flipped over each bucket, hoping, praying, that one may still have a morsel of food. The moon was caparisoned in November's dark clouds, its face visible but unrecognizable. More vagrants began to line up at the neighborhood soup kitchen and the city, a fire burning deep inside of it, projected itself onto the sky and shaded the clouds a ruby red.

"I haven't the time for such trifles," a derelict said in a nearby, inoperative phone booth "You can watch as many Jack in the Box commercials as you want but eventually, you'll come to terms with the dark secret of Jack. Monterey. The name that seized Jack of his identity before he could break through to the other side. A tragic day indeed." He was a cagey old man with sparse hair and a look in his eyes that clouded his true intentions, dithering from keen intellectual to psychotic rebel. "Damnit, Jim! I'm a doctor. Not a monastic!" His eyes caught mine and he froze. "Jim," he muttered, staring at me in bewilderment, "Get the car."

Further down the road, past the illuminated liquor store and smoke shop, another homeless man walked with his back to me. As his hair blew in the wind, he strolled down the street calmly, a flattened cardboard box filling the fissure between his left arm and ribcage. As he turned and smoke billowed from the cigarette seated in the corner of his mouth, he stretched out his right hand with a haggard thumb turned upward to hitchhike with any passing stranger. On his cardboard sign there was one word scrawled in red marker, 'Reality'.

Around the corner of the phonebooth, down a faintly lit alley, a yellow light flickered brightly from an open door, dimming and illuminating the corridor simultaneously, like the shadows of a flame. With the wind against my back, I walked toward the open door as the twang of a banjo tuned to the thumping drums coming from the area. The strums of a guitar accompanied the other instruments and, before long, a familiar folk song, "Wayfaring Stranger", was being kicked up under the plaintive acoustics of the entire band.

I walked the hallway to the source of the light, my steps congruously picking up and falling with the rhythm of the band. When I turned the corner, I found a band of Recusants, 25 or so strong, standing around a pit in the center of the room with yellow reflective lights flashing around it. The pit, which seemed bottomless, broke off near the eastern wall, inching closer and closer to the stage, until finally it was little more than an invisible crack across the ground. On the stage, an enormous tombstone, ten feet tall, was placed in the center, upon which a Recusant with a banjo sat, picking up the pace of the song's tempo before belting out the tune.

I am just a poor wayfaring stranger
Traveling through a world of woe

291

LeResche

Ain't no sickness, toil, nor danger
In that bright land to which I go

Stationed around the stage was a complete band of Recusants, modulating with the banjo player. The stand-up bassist tapped his foot to the beat. The fiddler pranced back and forth while stringing his bow as if he were some kind of life-sized wind-up toy. The guitarist, his feet dangling off the oddly crafted stage, raked his hands across his acoustic guitar, faintly showing a smile every so often.

I'm goin' there to see my father
Said he'd meet me when I come
I'm only goin' over Jordan
I'm only goin' over home

The surrounding crowd of Recusants danced around the abandoned room with little regard for the glowing pit in the center. They hopped on one foot before slamming the next one down abruptly, clinging to one another's elbows and swinging around, before leaping to the next person in the circle, like an impromptu Dosey Doe.

I know dark clouds gonna gather 'round me
I know my way'll be rough and steep
Yet beautiful fields lie just before me
Where God's redeemed their vigils keep

The stand-up bassist flipped his bass around and began thumping a percussive beat to the song. The other Recusants, unaware—or otherwise unconcerned—with the fulminating pit, began falling into the cavernous hole on the ground, blithe smiles still etched on their faces as their shadows faded away down the endless trench.

The Call of the Void

The warmth from its core was emanating waves of heat that hit me at the door to the abandoned building, forcing me to keep my distance.

I'm goin' there to see my loved ones
Gone before me one by one
I'm only goin' over Jordan
I'm only goin' over home

The lead singer yodeled the lyrics until his voice went hoarse. He stood atop the tombstone and swayed from side to side before leaping down to the floor and following the slight crack as he continued the song.

I'll soon be free from earthly trials
This body rest in the ol' churchyard
I'll drop this cross of self-denial
And go singing home to God

The band followed him close and, as the number of dancers diminished down the glowing ditch, they began to hurl themselves, one after the other, into the glowing abyss. When none were left, the vocalist strummed his banjo rapidly and stood at the foot of the hole, his body steadily engulfed in flames.

I'm goin' there to see my savior
To dwell with him no more to roam
I'm only goin' over Jordan
I'm only goin' over home

And with one final glance and nod, the singer fell forward and belted out the final lyrics, which echoed from the depths of their shimmering tomb. They were faintly audible as I left the building.

LeResche

I'm only goin' over home

Near the Western sidewalk, behind a parked car, the sounds of grunting and splashing echoed through the alley. A hand, clenched tightly around a brown book, thrust itself on to the trunk of the parked car, shaking it vigorously with each corresponding grunt and splash. I moved around to get a better look. A man, missing an eye, with melted facial features, as if bathed in acid, was thrusting a female Recusant into a gutter filled with sewage and fresh shit, submerging her face fully as she struggled to break free. He lifted his book in the air—a holy bible with the letters 'LY' and 'BIB' missing—and began to recite scripture. Struggling to break free, the Recusant convulsed, forgetting her vows in favor of life, in a futile attempt to fight off the man and gasp for air, but went limp after a while, drowning in the fusty sewers of LA.

Down the road, a line of people dressed in their Sunday's best filed into the CCOCC building near the middle of 12th street, its incandescent sign attracting the mob to its entrance like mayflies to a neon sign. The Church Commission of Christian Communications—commonly referred to as CCOCC—was a monument to the flight of human reason and home to finger wavers and pearl clutching apostles. Some time ago, Jim Bakker, Kenneth Copeland and Joel Osteen had subsidized the biggest Christian broadcast center on the West Coast, attracting most of the local Christian denominations. A now world-renowned broadcast station funded by what the media called, 'The Big Three', CCOCC was a bastion to the theologically lost, the spiritually bankrupt, and the perpetually downtrodden. The pinnacle of the cross at the top of the church tower's steeple blinked a dark vermillion light, emitting radio and television broadcast signals all across the globe. The church was an empyrean tower, visible well past the southern border of the I-10, and, on the front entrance, a sign was plastered over the translucent door that read "*Recusant need not apply.*"

"*Pssst.* Hey." A voiced whispered to me from the alley.

I turned around and squinted my eyes, trying to recognize the barely visible face emerging from the shadows. A giant white smile materialized out of the darkness before the rest of Konrad appeared. He crossed his arms and leaned against the wall, oscillating his head from me to the giant church steeple.

"*Konrad?*" I said in shock.

Konrad pushed his index finger against his pursed lips and pumped his open palm at me, insisting I keep silent. He fell back into the shadows without a word. If there is one thing Konrad and Jim Bakker have in common, it's that they both welcome the apocalypse with open arms.

I followed a line of people into CCOCC and opened the doors to its foyer. The smell of cheap hand sanitizer had arrested my senses almost immediately. The floors were freshly buffed, and the walls, so artlessly rococo, were positively charged with an absence of shame. On the dais, behind a safety barricade, a monumental, gold statue of Jerry Falwell was erected. In a triumphant pose, the statue had one foot placed on the back of a calf.

The coterie of church goers had begun to get antsy, and mutterings of salvation spread through the crowd like a virus as the scent of chewing tobacco slowly suffocated the air. Nudging my way through breaks of space in between each person, I moved through the sluggishly undulating rout to the front of the room. Spacious and august, the plaza was twice the size of any lecture hall at UCLA.

A cheer rippled through the mass as Joel Osteen barreled out of the green room with his hand raised. Waving from behind the safety of a barricade, he smiled widely from cheek to cheek, the effulgent pallor of his grin blinding the crowd. He remained uncannily quiet, even after the crowd fell silent. His hand waved and rippled with a mechanical twist. Kenneth Copeland fell in line just behind him. I looked on, from the preachers to the crowd, in morbid fascination.

"In a perfect world," Copeland said, "man would never have wanted for any institution. Man's ability to reason and survive would bear enough of the burden filled in by the middlemen of churches, politics, and other institutes."

"But this isn't a perfect world," a voice, husky and almost faint, said from behind a partition, "And no man but he who stands in front of God may say so."

"What the hell does that even mean?" I whispered to the man on my left.

He turned his head slowly to look at me askance. His eyes were hollow, willing me to shut my mouth and turn around once more.

Osteen was still moving his hand in a stilted fashion. The crowd was petrified, yet partially mesmerized, by his pale white teeth, and that thousand-yard stare was clearly beginning to frighten the good people of 9th street. Jim Bakker, emerging at last from the curtains, took notice and, with a mirthful smile, forced Joel's arm to his side.

"Covid 19." Kenneth Copeland said, breaking through the waning applause.

"Yes." Bakker added, almost as an afterthought.

Kenneth's face was almost unnatural. His eyes were sunk into the back of his head and bloodshot, their depth receding and elongating based on his level of excitement. His face resembled putty. One might first guess that he had had plastic surgery, that his face has been imperfectly molded, but it seemed more congenital than ersatz this close up. Merely a defect of old age that served no purpose other than to frighten the children in the galleria. His voice dripped with a heavy, thick residue of Texas twang.

"What a world we live in that the Catholic church can condemn sin yet get in bed with those who would, shall we say, forge that virus out of thin air."

"That's right!" Several members of the crowd shouted in harmony.

"And w-we, Ken, we d-don't know exactly, what, well here," Jim said, fumbling for the right word, "Whoever shall come to me will never go hungry. That's John 3:65-"

"5:36..." Copeland corrected.

"5:36!" Jim agreed reluctantly. "And I am the way. I am the way to God. But you have to get there yourself."

Joel Osteen remained stagnant with a frozen smile; his eyes catatonically glued to the back of the room like a lobotomy patient.

"And Jim," Ken said, "The young lions do lack and suffer hunger; But they who seek the Lord shall not be in want of any good thing."

"Psalm 13:40" Jim jubilated.

"40:31" Ken corrected once more, his confident gaze scanning the room but never meeting Jim.

Jim stroked his hoary beard with each of Kenneth's corrections. There seemed to be an unspoken, almost unsavory, competition between the men that Ken was apparently winning. Four years his senior, Kenneth Copeland clearly had the mental drop on Jim Bakker but what Jim lacked in Bible recollection, he made up for with senescent charisma.

"F-fine, 40:31. Thank ya, Ken."

Jim took a moment to regroup himself and his thoughts. His audience grew concerned, like a crowd watching two ancient wrestlers grapple against the ropes. And as Jim seemed defeated and ready to retreat to the back with a vacuous Joel Osteen and let Ken run the show, an array of colorful lights began to flash from one side of the room to the other. The display heralded the arrival of Jim's younger wife Lori. She was incredibly charming for her age; in a sense, they all were. She moved gracefully through the gallery and her smile never faltered, giving the appearance of a loving mother and dutiful wife.

Jim came back to life in an instant. It was as if Lori was his source of energy; an energy that could bring this crowd back into his good graces.

"And what we n-need," Jim said, "is a miracle. A miracle that has come from our prophets and through the vision of our most holy of oracles."

"Oracles?" I whispered to myself.

"What we need for this 'Dark Winter' that the mainstream media is punishing us with, is right behind these doors. Come, brothers and sisters, come and join us for the future. And make sure, f-for your, uh, for y-your coming here tonight, you pick up a pillow, but not just any pillow! A pillow from our own Mike Lindell."

As the doors to the viewing center opened, a light from above radiated onto a man with a sleeping cap wearing a pair of pajamas. The crowd awed at their host's generosity, nodding to each stranger in the crowd. I followed the throng into the main entrance and tried taking a seat near the exit but was propelled forward by invisible hands jabbing into my back. I sat down and studied the faces of the crowd. This was probably not the best place to test the limits of their smoking policy. I took out my flask and shook it up and down over my mouth, trying to manage out one more drop, looking like an absolute reprobate fresh off of Skid Row.

The stage was set, swathed in vivid red and green Christmas decorations, displaying garishly shallow tawdry. An enormous Douglas Fir, seven feet tall with crimson stars all intermittently hung around the tree, was placed, almost strategically, in the middle of the stage behind the televangelists' table and chairs. The crowd roared at the re-entrance of the 'Big Three' plus Lori. The Big Three forged their confidence on the indiscriminate cheers of the crowd. It was the thrill of an audience. And as such, their presence on stage was far more boisterous than pious. Joel walked pokily to his seat, his arms remaining motionless at his side with every step.

"I just want to say, of the best Christmas that has been," Ken began, raising his hands and closing his eyes while taking his seat, "we are just blessed. To all our cohorts, all our cohorts in Europe, and all our cohorts in Africa, all our cohorts in Germany, all our cohorts in Panama, all our cohorts in Papua New Guinea, all our cohorts in Switzerland, all out cohorts in Królestwo Dreamlandu, all our cohorts in Lagoan Isles, all our cohorts in Woodland Patchwork, partners, uh, the very blessed and most, uh-"

He paused for a moment and cupped his hands over his mouth. His eyes focused on the annotated bible directly in front of him. Silence throttled the air as those in attendance couldn't figure out whether he was deep in supplication or in the early stages of an aneurysm. Ken squinted his eyes shut as the tension grew deeper and concerned faces shifted their gaze from one side of the room to the other.

"The most anointed-" he began again, raising his arms up. A sigh of relief came from the back. "Cohorts in the world."

"My God is alive!" Jim interrupted, his voice cutting through the room with precision, "He will not die!"

"That's right," Lori said, nodding her head lazily in agreement.

"For He has satisfied the thirsty soul, and the HUNGRY soul He has filled with what is good. And folks," Jim pointed a hand to the ceiling, "w-we have got something good for you."

A stagehand operating a forklift brought out palettes of white barrels. The lift stopped abruptly, backed up to the stage, swung right once more, and lowered the cargo just beside the speakers' table.

"Now," Ken said, "I know it's late, and I know y'all are ready for a midnight snack after that Turkey you had tonight, but w-while it's cookin' we have something that all three of us have placed a sizeable invest-"

"Spiritual investment" Jim quickly corrected, "Spiritual, is what my colleague here meant to say. Yes, this was bestowed on us in, well, in m-more or l-less a dream. And I'll tell you right now what I saw."

The congregation nodded their heads as Jim tapped the microphone lightly. Ken slumped slightly in his chair, a moue budding slowly on his face.

"I saw days, slowly shortened by the Moon."

"That's right." Lori affirmed.

"And it wasn't just the days that were shortened, it was the, uh, the armies that amassed in Jerusalem and, well, children were running to the mountains."

"Yes" Lori said with distant agreement. She seemed to avouch anything her husband said, the same way a distant radio jockey agrees with his guest.

Jim took a deep breath and paused for effect. "And there were two Kings, one of the North and one of the South, and they were b-bad, no g-good, and, uh, one of these kings from the West had a floating goat with a horn in between his eyes."

I tittered and looked around to see everyone's reaction. Modestly surprised, most of the room was in awe of his prophecy, their eyes bulging and mouth agape sending the signal: 'Tell us more, tell us more!'.

Jim's face twisted into consternation. His eyes squinted, glowering at the crowd. "And, just before Christmas, Europe broke into pieces, and the kingdoms of man were shattered throughout the world. And then the sun bore us fruit that connected Europe back, it connected it back people!"

Resounding applause came from the apparent emissaries of the European Union.

"It's o-only-" Jim became distracted by another stagehand mixing water into the palette of buckets. "Uh, wuh, it's only the fruit of unity. For flocks of sheep and shepherds will go to find the Lord but they will not see him. And, well, there was a mountain of olives, and uh, two thousand years. Look, folks-"

"That's Luke 26:21." Ken interrupted, a swagger of splendor forming on his face, "Folks he is citing scripture."

The crowd heaved at the blasphemy.

"A-am not." Jim said.

Whispers began to circulate as confusion spread throughout the room. Jim and Ken sized one another up from their chairs. Jim took a step forward and protruded his jaw out in an assertion of dominance. Ken cracked his knuckles and stretched his neck from side to side, his clay face sneering with wicked intent. Joel stared directly at the stage light as a bit of drool began running down his chin.

"Oh look, the soup's ready!" Lori blurted, pouring oil over troubled waters.

Jim and Ken stood back and exhaled. Their muscles relaxed and their scowls turned to hesitant smiles as they looked around the room nervously and shook hands.

"A-all a joke folks." Jim laughed.

"A trick of evil forces." Ken corrected.

"T-that's what I meant." Jim added.

At that moment, I felt a bit of my own spirituality die inside. Had this all been the throes of senility? Or a possible attempt at a poorly produced revue? Or maybe, something much worse.

Previously, I had thought—myself a deist in purely teleological belief, but far from a religious man—they were a cohort of spiritual mountebanks assembled to line their pockets and commodify faith with ethereal remedies—a practice dating back to the antiquities of organized religion. But despite their superficial behavior, I felt a sincerity in all of their voices that made me believe. Maybe even—God forgive me—to have a little faith in them. Their eyes never wavered to indicate mendacity. Their fingers always on the appropriate annotation of their King James Bible. They believed every word of it. Or, maybe, they were just that damn good.

"This brings me to scrip- err, my dream for the cure. Now, previously, the FDA and CDC had cast its evil wing over the production of our Silver Slime."

"Bastards!" the man directly to my left shouted, "Nothin' wrong with it! My little Jessie ate it every day with her cereal. Never got sick. In- in fact, she got better."

"Well, that's just great, but our new solution to the next strain of the Coronavirus," Jim said, pulling something from behind the table, "is here. People look no further than the 'Green Gumbo'. Trademark pending."

"Silver Slime?" I asked to no one in particular.

"Colloidal silver," a woman near me answered, pulling money from her purse, "It's an antimicrobial. The government said it was a scam and wouldn't let Jim sell it no more. The media was talkin' on and on about how it was dangerous if we consumed it. Some 'ol Jewish bullshit. You know."

I nodded politely. "Right. Of course. Well, I doubt it would harm you, but, Colloidal? I thought they used to use that to filter water. And would an antimicrobial be effective against a virus anyway?"

"Yeah, cause it kills everything."

"Madam, if that were true, and it killed *everything*, it can't be that good for you."

"Bad things."

"Ah, I see. Odd that the FDA and CDC wouldn't endorse it."

"Very odd indeed." She nodded her head and gave me a look, as if trying to lead me to some answer.

"What?" I asked as she closed in on me.

"There's no money in silver solution," she whispered intimately, "the CDC and FDA don't want to ride the coattails of pastor Jim."

"How do you know it works?"

"How do you know it doesn't?"

I breathed through my nose, almost laughing, and slouched in defeat. "I guess I don't. This whole conversation is out of my purview. But why? Why buy this shit? It costs..." I looked over the shoulder of a man in front of me to see Jim and Ken locking hands next to a brightly flashing sign that read '49.99', "50 fucking dollars?!"

"Because he is doing God's work! I don't care what you think! 'They all gave out of their wealth; but she, out of her poverty, put in everything—all she had to live on and...'"

As she cited scripture, a tear formed in the corner of her eye, and I realized I was probably being an asshole. Who was I to trample on one's beliefs? Let her spend. After all, I'd probably be a Christian myself if it weren't for those three wags peddling horse piss on stage.

A troupe of men came in dawning WWI era gas masks. Each one had a different instrument under their arms. Jim and Ken attempted to introduce the band before being distracted by Joel. He had managed to get his head stuck in a soup cauldron and Jim and Ken were attempting to yank him free. The lead vocalist spoke into the microphone but, under the vent of the mask, he was completely inaudible. Hordes of patrons rushed the stage to meet a trio of soup bespattered televangelists. The band started with a slow melody. It was obvious after only a few lines that the band was doing a rendition, or possible parody, of Bette Midler's "The Rose" with the ending word of each line being a rhyme of some word found in apocalyptic scripture.

The woman behind me who I had previously chatted with had placed a paper bowl in front of me with some green substance in it. It was soup, verdant and thick, almost like pea stew with a spoon looping around the bowl. The stew wobbled with each shaking of the table. I looked up at the woman as she nodded her head fervently.

"I'm okay," I laughed.

A silence fell over the room at my words. The woman looked around in distress before her kind eyes turned callous.

"If you're one of us," she growled, "you'll eat it."

"Who?!" A bellow from the stage announced, "Who won't eat the stew?!"

"Soup!" another voice on stage corrected.

While gritting my teeth in distress at the mob slowly surrounding my table, I peered to my left a little and saw Ken and Jim back in their fighting stances. Jim yapped at the top of his voice while Ken walked around with his arms folded into his armpit, imitating a chicken. Jim thrusted out at him, and they locked arms and began to choke one another out like cartoon characters rolling around on the floor. The crowd was too busy upbraiding my abstinence of the stew to notice.

Jim and Ken rolled on the stage for some time before crashing into the Christmas tree. Both men used one another's shoulders to hoist themselves up. Jim curled his lip at Ken and smacked him across the left side of his face.

"Oooo my neck!" Ken howled.

Jim smacked him across the right side of the face. "How's it feel now?"

"Better!"

Jim smacked him with both his hands on each cheek. "Come on. What's the matta with ya?"

Joel's head wobbled lazily from side to side while he walked over to the duo as if his neck was anesthetized. He put his hands up and waved to them slowly in a futile attempt to stop the mayhem. Jim looked back at Ken as the star on top of the tree came crashing down on his head. He looked back at Joel, convinced that it was him who threw the star. "Oh, a wise guy. A head clunker, eh?" Jim smacked Joel across the chops, knocking him to the ground.

"He didn't do it!" Ken said, grabbing Jim's shoulder.

"Then you did." Jim extended his index and middle finger and went right for Ken's eyes. Intuitively, Ken placed his hand flat on the bridge of his nose, blocking the poke. He laughed a bit then placed his hand flat in a horizontal position under Jim's chin and fluttered it up to the top of his forehead as Jim watched with amazed eyes before Ken smashed his mallet sized fist over the top of Jim's head.

"Yuck, yuck, yuck." Ken laughed.

"Come 'ere you." Jim said, grabbing Ken by the collar and pulling him close. Joel was shaking his head from the hit as he positioned himself behind Jim. Jim cocked his right arm back in one quick motion, knocked Joel back to the floor with his elbow by mistake, and punched Ken in the face.

Joel got back up as Ken was coming for him. "Come on," Jim said to Joel, "Gimme a hand." Joel stuck out his hand to shake Jim's. "Why you." Jim smacked him across the nose.

Ken stumbled and knocked over a food bucket of pastries and éclairs that spread across the ground. He brushed his hands across his face angrily over and over again. "Look what'cha made me do."

Jim huffed and grabbed Joel by the shoulder. "Come on. Help me pick these up." All three simultaneously reached for the same pastry and clashed their heads against one another. Jim looked up, a rage building in his eyes. "One at a time." He said through his teeth. All three reached down again in unison and crashed their heads once more. Joel grazed Jim's eye on the way up, making him yelp out in pain. Jim pointed to his eye. "What's that?"

Joel looked at him absently. Ken answered, "An eye."

"That's right." Jim said, poking Joel in both his eyes, "An eye for an eye."

"And a tooth for a tooth." Ken laughed.

"Soitantly." Jim said, smacking him across the face.

Joel stood up with an éclair lodged in his throat. It protruded about halfway out of his mouth. Jim grabbed him by the nose and began to slap him across the throat to dislodge the pastry.

"I can't do a thing about it. You try something." Jim said.

Ken hit Joel in the back of the head and the éclair shot cream onto Jim's face. Jim was turning red. He punched Joel in the stomach and more cream shot onto his face. Ken motioned his hand wildly and swung once more for the back of Joel's head as Jim punched him at the exact same moment in the stomach. The éclair went shooting through the air and hit Lori directly in the face.

As the fight rolled along on stage, I laughed, forgetting the crowd had been looking at me the whole time. They dogpiled me and went immediately for my throat.

"Jesus Fucking Christ!" I yelled.

"Heresy!" A faceless voice screamed back.

"Stop!" a man shouted, running down the aisle, his arms flailing in the air. The mob's hands around my neck began to loosen as they listened to the kid. "They did it! They actually did it! Come quick!"

Confused glances went from me to the kid and over to the Big Three. The mob stampeded toward the entrance. Apparently, my death could wait.

Outside, the young kid had his hands on his knees, bent over and gasping for air. The entire crowd had surrounded him and asked what the fuss was all about. Jim and the other two made their way outside and demanded an explanation. The kid tried to talk but couldn't catch his breath, pointing to the door instead. A piece of paper was nailed to the door where the old '*Recusant Need Not Apply*' sign was. It had been nailed through the glass door. Kenneth walked up to the paper slowly and ripped it off. He studied it with precision, silently mouthing off each word as he read. Jim looked over his shoulder, his eyes widening the lower he went on the page. Joel supported his head against Ken's back, as if its weight was too much of a burden.

"Konrad..." Jim whispered.

"96 THESES?!" Ken shouted, "They're giving us a disputation? How dare they! How dare they Lord!"

"I want them dead. I want them dead!" Jim echoed.

And just like that, Midnight Mass had officially turned into a murder spree.

"The first one," Jim said, gathering the mob around him, "to kill a Recusant tonight, gets a year's supply of Green Gumbo for free!"

"And the one to bring me Konrad's head gets a lifetime supply!" Ken hollered.

An uproarious wave of assent penetrated the air.

"Hey! You!" a mobster declared, pointing at me, "Yeah, you!"

I looked around dazed, pointing to my chest and looking over my shoulder.

"I know you."

I shook my head.

"Yeah. TV guy."

"TV guy?" I asked nervously, "You have me confused."

"No," he said, smiling and nodding his head slowly, "TV guy."

He jabbed his buddies in the ribs with a mordant smile. I looked around at the icy eyes in the crowd staring me down. I wiped the sweat from my palms onto the t-shirt under my flannel and backed up slowly. As my hands trembled in anxious disbelief, I lit a cigarette, figuring it may be my last.

How fast could these fuckers run anyway? I thought. *My lungs might not be up to the task. Thanks a lot, Konrad.*

Before the man could make another move, Joel Osteen separated the crowd, a fierce expression bubbling over on his face. He lifted his finger, struggling the whole time as if it weighed more than him, and pointed to me. As he locked his eyes on mine, his mouth opened wide, a backdrop of the abyss prominent behind his uvula. I stared into it, waiting for it to stare back. He let out a scream that was more demonic than divine. I ran down the street in a hurried frenzy. When I looked back, the mob was still standing there, bouncing bats in their hands as Joel's scream swelled through the midnight air.

VIII

I ran. My reflection in the mirrored walls of the city looped endlessly like a magic lantern projection as the sound of my sneakers splashing through the puddles vibrated off the city's deep corridors and down the street through the concrete canyon of buildings.

I made a right on Olive, veering into an open-aired parking lot, and immediately placed my hands on my knees. They buckled, swaying my shoulders from side to side as I tried to catch my breath. With each inhale, the condensation from my breath bloomed in front of my face and hazed my weary vision. I felt drunk.

There was no way to be certain whether the mob was still following me or not, but I rushed to take cover in a sea of cheaply made Sedans at a nearby parking lot just to be sure. Squatting to the side of a Ford Pinto, my eyes scanned for any signs of an elderly mob hellbent on killing me for a lifetime supply of shit on a shingle.

Minutes passed and, as I began to feel safe, the sight of an old man at a nearby bus stop caught my eye. He didn't move. He sat there, motionless, staring at the abandoned building in front of him, plumes from his breath's condensation the only indication that he was alive.

"Hey man." I whispered. Nothing. No doubt he could hear me from this range, but it was possible that his hearing was gone.

"Buddy." I said, raising my voice slightly, "You got the time?" Nothing. He was frozen in his seat, but his breath surged up every so often.

I stood up and moved gingerly around the cars, walking a little closer to the street to catch a glimpse of the Convention Center. I was almost there. I turned to make my way down the street before an ancient voice cut through the air.

"2:17 AM."

I turned immediately to look at the bus stop, but no one was there. I jerked my head around to see where the voice came from, but there was no one in sight. Phosphenes had begun to smother my vision, regardless of whether or not my eyes were closed. Taking a seat on the trunk of a nearby Cadillac, I tried to gain my composure. Maybe it was the alcohol, or the cocaine, or the exhaustion, but the longer the night went on, the more a sinking feeling of self-doubt crept into my mind.

Self-doubt. Doubt of self. There's a time in every evening where conscious thoughts stop making sense and voices begin to tell you what's real. A time in the night when objective reality is hard to discern. I was beginning to near that coil. I was beginning to sound insane.

The moon was floating just above me like a theater prop, the clouds unable, or unwilling, to mask the veneer of its majesty. It was so much larger and more defined than I'd ever noticed. I began to get lost in its presence. Each crater was an event horizon, an ineluctable sight, sucking my eyes in until all I could see were the distant hollows of its malignant basins.

LeResche

I took a seat on top of the backrest of the bus stop where the phantom old man had previously been and spoke to the moon. "So, this is how it starts. Insanity. The nights grow longer, and the dreams become shorter. Your mind races, trying desperately to solve a puzzle it doesn't understand, that it never had an answer to in the first place. Your friends are distant, fading memories. Family is an evanescent silhouette of dust, floating through your mind. And, worst of all, your reason, your will, your mind, begin to evaporate into a chimera that you're slowly beginning to accept. Abruptness. Concentrated stress. The inability to assimilate to the vicissitudes of life. A lack of patience with loved ones. Finding cryptic meaning or life in inanimate objects. Tediously revising exegeses on inane topics that the world has long moved on from. Walking briskly from one end of the hall to the other, chewing your nails out, wondering how it all will end. Before finally, peace is made with new friends. The sun at 5AM on another insomnia driven night. A sense of dread that never leaves the soul. The feeling of isolation, of a desperate vacuum that no one can fill. Internment into one's own consciousness, never to be found again." I fought off a tear forming in the corner of my eye. "Why? Why..."

"There he is!"

The rabble had found me. Their clamoring and saber rattling had drowned out the silence of the night. I jolted off the bench and made a run for it down 12th street but had to double back as a multitude of holy warriors cut me off. Seeing no other recourse, I leaped onto the nearest vehicle as the crowd swallowed up the parking lot and moved in on me. Bounding from roof to roof, my foot making a dent on each car, I gained a bit of momentum and flew to the ladder on the nearest building's roof. The ladder broke off and fell to the ground almost immediately, but I was able to take a few steps and grab the ledge of the roof before it did. My grip on the roof's edge began to fail, and I took one look below at the vortex of people carrying bats, pitchforks and torches, ready to consume me at my fall. Feeling a heat at my pant leg and jabs underneath my feet, I made one last successful effort to pull myself up. Brushing the dust off my jeans and sneakers, I went back to the precipice of the roof.

I looked down and laughed intrepidly, mocking an admiral's salute. "So long, cock suckers."

An empty bottle of green gumbo flew from the crowd and nailed me on the side of the temple. My head went slack, and my chin slumped over my chest as I lost a bit of my motor function. Like a ragdoll, I was folding and getting ready to fall off the roof and into the crowd. With what little nervous system I had left, I twisted my torso away from the edge and tried to run but fell flat on my face.

I wasn't out. At least, not completely. My vision was a little fuzzy. I shook my head and held it up, forcing the blur out of my eyes, as the voices from the crowd hovered around below, making a perimeter on the Eastern side of the street. I stood up and, out of nervous desperation, kicked one of the antique air conditioning units that hadn't been replaced since the 80s. The yells from the crowd below were on the move, stomping from the parking lot to the other side of the building to cut me off. Without thinking, I shimmied down the northwestern side of the roof on a nearby storm drain and an apartment complex appeared like a mirage out of nowhere. A neon sign just outside the leasing office read, 'Luxury Apartments'. It was enormous, nearly 40 stories tall, with an aura of American ostentation. It loomed over South Park like a maleficent being, taunting the city for its social status, ensuring those that would sleep on the park bench remained there, so long as there were those that could spend 2,500 dollars a month on a one-bedroom apartment.

"Hey, buddy," a man nearby said, walking toward me with a bag from 7/11, chewing a stick of beef jerky, "You the one the crowd is looking for?"

I stared at him for a moment, trying to catch my breath. He wasn't one of them. I moved my eyes wearily from side to side, looking for the mob, before giving him a resigned nod.

"Hmmph." He snorted, "Wanna hide out at my place."

I lit a cigarette and looked him up and down. His eyes were almost inhuman, his smile like that of a snake just before slithering. He was probably no good. I raised my hand toward the complex, letting him lead the way.

The atrium of the complex was barren except for a kid sleeping behind the receptionist's desk with his feet kicked up over the counter. A familiar song, 'Through the Fire and Flames' blared out of his earbuds, audible to anyone within five feet. It was a shock that he was asleep at all. The walls were covered in a type of mustard colored paper. Muzak played lightly over the speakers to an invisible audience.

The Call of the Void

Other than the kid, the reception desk was empty, save for a few ornamental plants. Round circles adorned the walls, and the freshly waxed floors reflected an arresting light from the ceiling lamps. The man hefted his bag up to his chest, pressing a button for the elevator. Once inside, he pressed '7'.

"So, why'd you help me out back there?" I asked.

He stared at his image in the elevator's wall. His eyes flicked to mine in the reflection for a millisecond before looking back at himself. "The enemy of my enemy is my friend."

"If you say so." I said, still trying to catch my breath. "What's your name?"

"Greg." He answered, slowly sounding out each consonant of his name.

At his door, Greg leaned down to put the key in. I tried to glance over his shoulder after a few seconds of waiting. He snapped his head back and bared his teeth, snarling a laugh as he shook his head. Something told me Greg wasn't all there.

For all the shit I talk about the yuppies here in LA, I had to admit, their apartments are first-rate. Windows encompassed the entire room and each piece of furniture seemed to be in perfect harmony with the layout out of his pad. A little too perfect in fact.

Greg dug through his 7/11 bag and pulled out a bottle of malt liquor. Without acknowledging me, he tossed it at my chest. I twisted the lid slowly, making sure to hear the snapping of the protective barrier before drinking. The television was on, and an eyepatch clad Kurt Russel was talking to Stacy Keach and entering '666' into a remote. Greg moved with a dull torpor toward his TV, turning it off and staring at LA's skyline. He cracked his neck from side to side and rolled his shoulders back, freezing in an awkward position. I walked over to his thermostat that read '21 ° F' and began to tap it.

"Your thermostat is busted here, Greg. Can't be Fahrenheit. Not here. Not in November. Has to be cel-"

"Do you see it?" He said, moving closer to the window.

"See what?" I asked, following close behind.

"The ocean. The sea. The tides crashing all along the shore, raging for more."

I knitted my brow with concerned apprehension. "We're in the middle of downtown LA, Greg. You can't see the ocean from here."

He looked disappointed at my response and pressed his cheek firmly against the glass window, craning his neck back and looking up toward the sky.

"That's because it's night," he said, his voice becoming lower and more ominous each time he spoke, "And the stars are covering the water's majesty with their darkness."

I shook my head and pressed my lips tightly together, realizing too late I made a mistake coming up here.

"Tell ya what," I said, slapping him lightly on the back, "I'll take my chances with the mob."

The faint sound of a piano echoed through the room.

"There she is," Greg said with a smile, "Right on time. She plays every night, just like this. Do you recognize it?"

The Call of the Void

"Yeah," I said, picking up on the tune, "It's *Clair de Lune.*"

He said nothing in response, instead moving casually toward the sliding glass door to his balcony. I lifted a hand in farewell and began to move backwards toward the door. The muscles on his back strained as he moved something heavy back into the apartment. Greg heaved once more and threw a shivering woman to the floor. Her arms were tied behind her and a cloth covered the front of her mouth. She mumbled faintly. Both of her cheeks had turned blue, and her nose was a very dark purple. Ice hung down off her lashes and brows as her eyes pleaded for warmth. Her nose had loops of skin peeling off of it, revealing a dark, red sunken crater to the dermis of her skin. The front of her lips had turned a dark, almost black, purple. If she wanted to look at me, she couldn't. Her eyes were solid blocks of ice, but I could feel her watching me out of her peripherals. *Clair de Lune* played on plangently from the neighbor's balcony, unaware of this girl's existence.

"What is this?" I asked nervously.

Greg just stared down at the woman. He inspected every inch of her carefully at a distance, from her converse sneakers to her tight blue jeans and fresh, white, wife-beater style tank top.

A pain ripped through the back of my skull. *"Do something."* The voice in the back of my head called out, *"For the love of God Sam, stop this madness and do something. There is no going back from here. Enough. Enough."*

"When I was young," Greg said, moving toward the couch, "we didn't have much money. Dad spent a lot of it on booze. He was drunk most of the time. I always wondered how a man could drink so much and live to wake up the next day. But he had his sober days too. And his sober days were far worse than his drunk days."

As I moved back into a chair, drinking a substantial amount of the malt liquor, the voice spoke to me once more. "*Think of Kylea. Her seraphic smile. See her frostbitten face on the floor there. You will never live this down.*"

Greg disrobed and placed a ski mask over his face, leaving only his shoes on.

"It was only mom and me. Dad used to eyeball each of us. Just his look was enough to keep us quiet. He'd throw vases just over our heads, so they'd smash against the wall behind us. He'd pick up the dog by the scruff of his neck and lift him up, strangulating his every breath in front of mom's face. She'd wail and cry and dad would drop him at the last second, reminding mom that, 'I have no use for you or this mutt. When the time comes, you'll get the gun, and I'll put one right between your eyes'. I watched as she waddled the days away, cooking, cleaning, and preparing everything for father. She had nowhere else to go. More than physical abuse, dad loved to gaslight her. Fuck with her, ya know? He'd move things around the house and, when she asked why he did, he'd tell her he had no idea what the fuck she was talking about and that he had been gone all day. He'd tell her how stupid she'd gotten and that all that fat in her thighs had finally gone to her head. Mom was 80 pounds, ya know? He knew she was anorexic. He knew what would get under her skin."

Greg stroked the girl's head and became erect. He pulled a kitchen knife from beneath the couch cushions and stared at his reflection in the blade, gazing longingly as contempt consumed his eyes.

"Mom and I were never allowed to leave the house. I was home schooled by her, and she cried for hours at a time during our lessons. I just sat back and let her wallow. And every Sunday, like clockwork, dad would come home, smelling of cheap beer and cigars, so drunk the idea of violence had escaped him, and break down at my mother's feet. He'd beg her to forgive him as he showered her with fake jewelry and flowers. Told her, 'I know I've been a beast. But I love you Hun.' And he'd pick her up, mom laughing just a bit, and take her to the bedroom to plow her. And when the light of Monday morning pierced the windows of our house, I'd be woken up to the sound of my father's fist breaking her face in. Screaming the old trite expressions, 'Look what you made me do!' and 'If you had only done it my way, this wouldn't have happened!'."

Greg moved to his lounge chair near the window, staring blankly at the moon and back down again to the street below. His head oscillated up and down every minute or so as he pierced the arm of his chair with the knife and twisted it in circles lightly with his index finger.

"*Sam...*"

I exhaled an abysmal sigh as if I hadn't breathed the entire time. As my breath quivered with each exhale, I moved slowly toward the shivering girl. I wasn't cut out for this. I'll just cut her loose and go back home. I was foolish to take this journey to begin with. Hovering just above her, I reached forward and began to untie the figure eight knot around her hands. She looked at me vacantly before pressing her head against the floor, rubbing her cheek against the carpet for warmth. She started to squeal as the friction from the carpet opened up her frostbitten cheek and painted the carpet red. I clasped my palm over her mouth just as she did.

"He used to call her a bad mother. He told her I never spoke because she was too busy crying during my lessons. Said, 'The kid is retarded. He can't even read and he's 7! If you weren't so busy crying your fat fucking head off, he'd at least talk by now!'. And when we needed to go to the store, Dad would make her crawl on all fours to him while he dangled dollar bills just out of her reach. Same thing at home. He made her bark like a dog and crawl outside to defecate before throwing the bills down at her and holding me there to watch as my mother shit on the porch in front of the neighbors and picked dollar bills up off the floor."

I finally loosened the knot enough to ease her hands to freedom. Stupefied, she looked around the apartment, remaining in shock on the floor. I slowly reached for the throw blanket on Greg's couch before being interrupted by a loud stab. Still staring out the window, Greg had slammed the knife directly into the arm of the chair as my outstretched arm paused, waiting for his next move. He opened the window slightly and a gentle breeze caressed the room. The sound of traffic resumed outside. The echo of cars in motion and faint yells became prominent in the room, creating a symphonic amalgam of urban nightlife and sophisticated piano keys. I placed the blanket over the girl and urged her to her feet. She walked slowly toward the door and opened it, taking one last look at me, her eyes empty, her face nearly melting off, her expression completely devoid of any emotion. When she had left, I grabbed a rolling pin from the counter and sat back down.

"One day, mom finally got up the courage to leave. She began to pack her bags and move them to the living room. Dad walked in just as she was grabbing her keys from the counter. His eyes moving back and forth from the packed bag to her keys, he slowly pulled out his pistol from the back of his pants and rested his arm at his side. Mom gazed at him, waiting for his next move. He pulled the pistol up and pressed it directly against his temple. He looked at her and then at me before raising an eyebrow, letting her know, right there and then, that her son would see his suicide. She wouldn't call his bluff because she knew, deep down, he wasn't bluffing. Life meant nothing to him, and we meant the world to him. He'd never find another woman that stayed with him like mom and, if he lost that, life would become meaningless."

I slowly reclined back into the couch. Greg, once again, twisted the handle of the blade in little circles.

"One night, when dad had been out longer than usual and mom had gone to bed, I went into my parent's room and stood over my mother while she slept. I stared at my mother and saw a trapped animal, a woman confined to a life she could only wish to escape. I grabbed the pill bottle next to her nightstand. 'Prozac 50mg'. I knew mom wouldn't leave this life because that meant leaving me behind. With him. Alone. So, I did the only merciful thing I have ever done in my life. I placed a pillow over her head and pressed dad's pistol on top of it before pulling the trigger. The police believed me when I told them dad had killed her and ran off. The neighbors corroborated my story. It was the only thing they did for my mom, and it didn't come until after her death. I lived out the remainder of my childhood in foster care, knowing at least I had done that one righteous thing."

Greg slowly turned his head to survey the empty floor. A morose silence filled the room. He forcefully removed his ski mask and sat upright for a moment before reclining back down into his chair. Inching closer to the window and relaxing his muscles, Greg let out a sigh.

"*Et sangloter d'extase les jets d'eau*" Greg said, rubbing his face with his hand, "You've released my entertainment."

I remained silent as *Claire de Lune* stopped abruptly and the faint, familiar sound of a guitar and violin replaced it, creeping through the window from the street below. Greg chuckled an obscure laugh before looking up at the moon once more.

"Trans-Siberian Orchestra," he said, moving his head back toward the street, "Sarajevo."

He looked up, his eyes moving fiercely around the room. They fell on me slowly. The radiance of flames from the street below bounced off the walls of the apartment and Greg's look caught my attention almost immediately. He turned and faced the window once more.

"Looks like they couldn't find a chainsaw. A hedge trimmer will do just fine though. Even *I* recognize Konrad from the TV."

"What?" I whispered.

The Call of the Void

I rushed to the window and peered down at nearly a hundred men, women and children starting fires and placing makeshift barricades around Park Street below, like a mob chasing Frankenstein's monster. They had a person in their clutches, completely motionless, accepting each of their blows without so much as a restive twitch. I squinted to see who the man was, but I couldn't be sure.

"That's him," Greg said, baring a toothy grin, "That's Konrad. Look at the hair. Bakker's crew got 'em."

He was right.

I bolted through the door as 'Sarajevo' played louder and louder. I pressed the button for the lobby in the elevator, jumping up and down anxiously with each jab. When I got to the bottom floor, I rushed through the lobby doors and made my way to the crowd. Peering over the shoulders of the first row, I saw Konrad—next to a boiling kettle of thick, red liquid—being placed on an enormous crucifix made hastily out of the trunks of trees—each side of the cross displaying the numbers '289', '118', '305' and '134', respectively. Konrad looked up briefly, his left eye completely blackened and shut. He dropped his open eye on me and seemed to smile, if only for a moment. A man next to Konrad began to rev the engine of a lengthy, green hedge trimmer. The man to Konrad's left hefted a sledgehammer over his shoulder, his eyes ablaze with vicious intent. He began to swing and hit Konrad's feet, displacing his talus from his foot. Konrad screamed out in pain, gasping for breath as they placed giant railroad nails point down onto his wrist and feet, pounding the

325

hammer onto the nail congruously with the rhythm of the song. A man appeared behind Konrad, his smile reaching ear to ear, placing a circle of razor wire from a nearby trainyard over Konrad's head and twisting it from side to side. The man howled at the moon. "BEAR WITNESS!"

"I-it isn't... a-anything I didn't... promise myself," Konrad yelled, gasping for air.

His eyes went to me once more as anguish painted his face. Wailing with each blow, three more men pounded the nails further into his wrist and feet, finishing the job. A man with his ear placed flat against the speaker slowly raised the volume handle, smiling widely with each turn, his eyes staring into the void. The Orchestra became so loud that it was impossible to make out what Konrad was yelling to me.

"Don't tr-" was all I could make out as he mouthed the rest of it amongst a sea of discordant shouts. They began to elevate the cross with Konrad still attached, his head paralyzed and slumping over his chest as he tried to raise it up. I backed up slowly and out of sight from the crowd. For a second, and only a second, I stepped forward, considered throwing my life away, if not to save Konrad, to join him. Konrad saw my motion and shook his head emphatically from side to side, blood streaming from his forehead, turning to droplets with each shake, demanding I stay out of sight. He squirmed violently on the cross as the man with the hedge trimmer pressed it against his right abdomen. It didn't break his skin at first. Instead, it rippled his flesh like the skin on pudding before breaching through to his liver just underneath his right lung. He left it there momentarily, the trimmer chopping and mincing any organ it could reach. The spray from the cut splashed the crowd as a williwaw erupted amongst its members, their voices roaring and cheering the carnage. Konrad's face was twisted, his eye shooting up toward the sky, his mouth wide open with fury. I took one last look at him in those agonizing final moments before running off down Hope Street.

As I ran, a payphone rang behind me in the distance.

IX

The cries of a vindictive rabble slowly vanished the further west I ran. I couldn't be certain if they were following me or not, but I booked a right down 11th St from Hope. In a panic, I clasped my hands onto the raised railing of an abandoned building and swung myself in through the window. At first, there was silence. My breathing, almost instinctively, began to slow. I sat with my back to the wall and faced the opposite side of the street. A clattering of feet rustled around outside, and I pushed myself as far back as possible against the wall, hoping foolishly to blend further into it. The smacking of feet stopped abruptly just outside the window. I paused, waiting to hear from them, but they were off again, back down the road in an instant. Impossible to know who they were after. In LA, someone's always chasing someone.

I rested my right arm on my knee and lit a cigarette, trying to calm my nerves as they pumped what adrenaline was left through my veins. Faintly, Tool's "Jambi" was coursing through the A/C vents from a distant room upstairs. I surveyed the room I was in, looking at broken baseball bats, needles, paint cans, and other remnants of neglect. It wasn't until my eyes adjusted and the moonlight filled the deserted room that I saw a body directly across from me, sitting exactly as I was. His left arm was perched over his left knee, mirroring my right, and cigarette smoke came out of the shadow that concealed his face as I exhaled mine. Our smoke met in the middle of the room and plumed upwards as it clashed. As I reached my right arm up to take out my cigarette, he copied my movement. Craning my head to the left and then right, I tried to get a better look at his face, but the shaded barrier covered him regardless of where I was. My heart began to race again as I rolled my tongue around to salivate my parched mouth. The sound of heavy, nasally breathing filled the room and I was uncertain whether it was his or mine. I caught a glimpse of the white in his eyes, but only momentarily, as each move I made he mimed, making it impossible to get a clear view without moving forward—which I was not about to do. It was like looking into a mirror and only seeing a shadow reflected. I stood slowly, careful not to make any sudden moves; he did the same. As I got upright and made my way carefully to the window, his entire being, save for his shoes, vanished amongst the room's shadow. I carefully moved my hand toward the window, inching myself closer to it, careful not to upset the muted shade. And as I turned my head, I heard the shadow speak.

"Don't let them popularize my work. It does more for the few than it ever will for the many. If it's ever commodified or popularized, its meaning will be lost."

"W-who? W-who's them?" I stuttered.

"You'll see." The voice hissed, "Not far now."

"W-who are you?"

LeResche

The shade remained silent, deciding instead to stare at me from beyond the swarthy abyss. I waved my right hand in front of my face once more as he did the same with his left.

Leaving the building through the window, I made my way, as I had this entire night, toward whichever area was brightest. Cutting through the thick smog hovering in the air, the city's searchlights hovered above Hope St and 11th, swaying from side to side in the sky, waving the people in as if to say, 'Welcome to the wild spectacle of the night'. The convention center was just ahead but the way was blocked by a common plague in Los Angeles; construction. Slabs of concrete barriers underneath foot after foot of blue and green tarp stunted the streets. Parking garages built right next to more parking garages, layered in orange traffic signs, copied itself over and over throughout the vacant roads.

I noticed a sign for a bar called 'Saturday Drink Lounge Part 2' nearby. A few of its neon letters were dimmed, reading, 'S—t—r —i—k —e —2'. The lights from the establishment were all off and I looked at my reflection in its mirror. I ran my hand across my face where the bruise from the bottle was before noticing a dark, hooded mass running from a distant dark corner of the establishment into its backroom's oblivion. It was enough of a scare to make me pratfall and rush further down the street.

LA was so empty. I'd never seen it so empty. While I walked toward the base of the searchlights just past 11th St, my hand reached shakily for another smoke. Lines of people, manifesting out of thin air, were being heralded in by the searchlights, like moths to a flame. I could have sworn the place used to be a parking lot. The Horror vacui painting on the side of the building was reminiscent of some 90s urban, geometric shape art, with variegated symbols, and looked a lot like similar paintings commissioned by the city. The entrance to the building was empty save for two people, identical in size and uniform, that stood still outside its door. Their hands were firmly placed on a ball handle cane, each one donning a tuxedo, the coattails falling so far behind them that they curled up onto the building. The structure directly next to them was a poorly lit library. It was yet another building I'd never seen, appearing out of nowhere. The door had a '24/7' neon sign blinking. I took a look over at the crowd amassing and buying tickets to the show next door before walking through to the library.

The library's interior had an extravagance of antiquity to it. Rows and rows of books lined the walls, their massive shelves almost falling over at their peak and forming a steeple from one side to the next. Its roof and the adjoining walls were decorated by an ornate, cathedral-like glass pane window. The library smelled only faintly of human waste and the tables on both sides of the dividing purple line were nearly empty except for one person on each side. The librarian lifted her head slowly from her book, the rim of her glasses falling just below her nose and under her eyes. She dog-eared her page and placed both hands gently on top of it as I walked over.

"Good Evening," she mumbled thoughtlessly, "Welcome to Los Angeles's first privatized library. Would you like to apply for a library card?"

"This isn't the first private library."

"Oh, but it is."

"It's not."

"Is. Now, would you like a library card."

I waved my hand dismissively and nodded.

"Good," she said, bending over the desk behind her to grab some paperwork, "I'll just need a photo ID and a credit card."

"Credit card?" I asked, reaching into my wallet.

"That's right. For late fees."

She slid the application to me and watched my every move as I filled it out.

My mind fumbled around for the right words as I began to fill the application out, saying, "I, uh, never had to give a credit card for a library card before."

"Uh huh," she said, "And how will we charge you for late fees?"

"I understand, but you have my info right there."

She looked at me impatiently. "Sir, what part of 'private' don't you understand?"

"I see," I said, putting the finishing touches on the application and handing her the form, "Well at least librarians haven't changed much."

"Thank you, sir," she slid my ID and credit card back across the table to me with my new library card, "You'll be charged fifty cents a month as a service fee-"

"Fifty cents?" I responded in astonishment.

"In consideration of the administrative support services provided by the Divided Info Library, the card holder, that's you-"

"What? I don't wan-"

"Shall make service fee payments to that recipient monthly or at such other interval as deemed appropriate by the DIL, within 30 days of the end of each calendar quarter or other period-"

"I changed my mind. I don-"

"At a cancellation rate not to exceed 0.25% on a monthly basis of the average during the period of the aggregate net asset value of DIL's annual agreement with the cardholder, computed as of the close of each business day, constituting rental of one book per day owned beneficially or of record by the recipient or by his next of kin for a period of more than the minimum period."

"Lady," I said, moving my hip into the table and placing my hand down, "Why would anyone pay for this when there are at least ten libraries in Los Angeles? One right up the street from here I might add. And, and! Twice as many books. Look at this place," I motioned with my hand from left to right, "You have like 3,000 books in here. I probably have that amount in my own personal library at home."

"Sir, first of all, we are a private organization. Your fee covers our startup cost. As we get more suck- more patrons, we'll grow." She opened her book, pressed the dogear back and began to read. "Second, you are paying for the 'experience' of being in the first 'noeticly disunited information center' on the planet.... And it's open 24 hours a day, seven days a week."

Doing my best to keep a somewhat sober appearance, I squinted my eyes, hoping she might understand my frustration. "'Noeticly disunited'?"

She closed her book once more and made a steeple over her mouth, her eyes searching behind me for resolve. "Sir, this library is divided." She pulled out a two-foot ruler and ran it across the purple line in the middle. "It is separated by conflicting ideologies." I stared at her blankly, her patience clearly thin. "It's-" she stopped, looking at me honestly, "It's divided by political affiliation, sir."

I snorted a weak laugh. "Why?"

"There's a demand for it."

"Demand?" I asked, "What, is Barry Goldwater's autobiography on one side and *Rules for Radicals* on the other?"

I laughed a little, hoping she would share in my amusement. She did not.

"Amongst other things. Would you like me to look up a book for you?"

"No, no." I sighed, waving a defeated hand, "I'll just browse around."

I walked down the middle of the purple line for a second, placing each foot down slowly, making sure not to be outside of the line, as if walking a tightrope. I looked up. The kid on the right was reading a tome, one of his knees pressing against his chest, his bleached white shirt tightening around his torso with each uncomfortable twist in his chair. Noticing me walking closer, he raised a concerned eyebrow and placed his bookmark onto the page. He was reading *Atlas Shrugged*.

"C-can I help you?"

"No, I was just wandering around," I said, sharing an awkward silence with him, "*Atlas Shrugged*," I pointed to the book with a genial smile, "You like it? It looks like you're almost all the way through there."

He looked at the book, his shoulders slouching down, an indication that he had become more comfortable with me. "Yeah... no... I don't know. It's good and all but I don't think it's aged well. If you know what I mean."

"Sort of," I said, pulling up a chair, "There comes a time in every man's life when he grows out of his Ayn Rand phase. You're just doing it a little earlier than the rest of us."

He smirked, laughing lightly into his fist, and nodded his head in agreement. "You know, it's just, why go off on a strike and spend money and resources in a community cut off from the rest of the world, ya know? I-I'm at the part where Dagny finds out the inventors are in the Gulch and, the truth is, it sounds a lot like communism." I shrugged and nodded. "I mean, look, other than that, it isn't bad but the whole philosophy that she writes about seems self-fulfilling. I mean, I'm not a communist, but it does seem a little, I don't know, disjointed? Selfish?"

"Yeah, that sounds like typical Rand criticism," I said, trailing off at the bookshelves behind him, "So, kid, why would a bibliopole such as yourself come into a place like this?"

He pondered the question for a second before dropping his legs back down to the ground and anchoring himself there. "I don't know. Seemed like a cool idea. Divide books based on political beliefs. Read one here, read one there. Keeps me open minded."

I rolled my head back, unsatisfied with the answer. "Yeah, but how far back can you go? I mean, let's face it, no matter how reactionary or tendentious you are, I don't think you could ever put any author from over a hundred years ago into one distinct political category. Could you?"

"I don't know."

I stared at the floor, and he tapped lightly on his book as we shared another awkward silence.

"I like that it's in third person though. There's just something about first person. It's impossible to ever take the narrator seriously. But not, like, because it's supposed to be. It's just truly impossible to look at the story from their eyes and perception. Like, the author's message is clear but, I don't know. We all see things differently, right?" He might have been the first real human being I talked to tonight—other than Princess. He sighed and lifted his head to meet me once more. "But I do believe that one man can stop the motor of the world."

I nodded in agreement. "I'll catch you around kid."

Across the way, over the oppressive purple line, a man in a ponytail sat reading B.F. Skinner. He was paunchy and his face was swollen and red, his sweater vest doing him no fashionable favors. I searched the room for another person to bother, but he was the only one. The last reader in a ghost town library.

"I didn't realize B.F. Skinner fell on the left of the political spectrum," I said, sitting near him.

"Then you're a fool." He responded with a haughty, elitist tone. "What else would you put him in? A strong will to rush away from authoritarian, political control. A system of technological behavior emancipating the people from their oppressive chains. A society where resources are guaranteed."

He clenched and lifted his right hand each time he spoke. My eyes followed his fist with each thrust onto the table.

"I suppose you're right."

"Hmph." He snorted, whipping his ponytail from one side to the other.

"So, what do you do?"

"What do *I do*?" the man asked, emphasizing his last two words, "I do, the human mind. I am a clinical psychologist." He took a moment to dog ear his page before twisting his head in my direction again. "The best in LA."

"Good to know." I said with an agreeable nod. "Where did you go to uni-"

"Actually, I'm quite the breakthrough psychologist. You see, I'm studying the reverse effect of 'Abeyant Pathogenic Virile Plasmodium'."

"That's a mouthful." I laughed.

"You laugh now. Go ahead. They all laugh at Dr. Flibbertigibbet."

"Stop." I said with a light laugh, trying to get serious again, "Your name isn't Flibbertigibbet."

"Oh, but it is. I wonder, sir, would you laugh or question the names of colleagues who have the surnames of 'Weiner', 'Dickman', or 'Gay'."

"That's hardly the same, and you know it."

He waved me off. "The 'Plasmosis', as I call it, seems to be an extremely pervasive condition in 21st century males. It's never been recorded in any previous century."

"What is it? Where does it come from?"

"From me, of course."

"What do you mean?"

"Well, as I said, I'm a clinical psychologist. I don't deal in normal pathogens. I deal with diseases of the mind and so forth. The Plasmosis is a technique I use on particularly weak-minded individuals. I then proceed to lead them to answers, as if they are rediscovering memories from long ago. The truth is, and I found this out early in my undergraduate research, that the mind is extremely malleable. Are you familiar with consciousness?" He asked, smirking as he finished his sentence.

"Only too well." I answered with a threadbare tone.

"Well, early memories can be molded and even suggested to individuals. Things they've never even experienced. It's quite brilliant really. I have them remembering a pony they never rode on but, because they remember a commercial of a boy, happy with bright red cheeks and a smile, riding a horse at a time when they were especially sad or vulnerable, and they believe they were on the horse the entire time. And just when I have them eating out of the palm of my hand, I induce the Plasmosis."

"Induce?"

"Correct! I place a memory in their head of a family member—one that's close to them that I've researched from early questioning—and I have them believe that family member sexually molested them. Timorous and, almost always, frightened at the idea of their favorite family member stealing their innocence, they retreat. They won't accept the lie. The mind is funny this way. It recognizes that what I've said is a complete fabrication, a foreign invasion, a virus that must be expelled. Yet, as I talk them down and soothe their concerns, I convince them even more. They always break down, crying in fact. These once strong and impervious men break down wishing they had never been born. But that's only part one of the Plasmosis. I convince them, quite gently, that they are, in fact, latent homosexuals."

"You can't- there's not-" I rummaged around in my mind for the words, smiling in disbelief at his story, "It's not- come on, it isn't possible. The people believing this have to be absolute cases."

"No," he said, smiling at me as if we were on the same page, "Solid as a rock."

"If that's true, and it isn't, you're not even a doctor. You're a hypnotist. You're a- a- behaviorist gone rogue. At best it's medical malpractice, at worst it's psychological tyranny."

"Really? Well, I'll have you know that several large corporations have made generous donations to my cause. They're pleased with the findings."

"It would take some genius to master this, and I doubt some genius would be at the world's first pri-"

He cut me off by flashing his phone in my face with digital receipts from advertising executives around the country. "I'm, in essence, rich."

I stood up, my hands feeling for an invisible barrier, and slowly backed up in disbelief. He smiled at me diabolically as the smell of human waste began to fill the air once more. I shook my head, hoping to wake up.

"No," I said, trying to compose myself, "Why? For money?"

"No. Well, it doesn't hurt. But I do it for the advancement of science. All great experiments come at some ethical cost. Nothing great was ever discovered without a little bloodshed."

"This is fucked." I roared.

"SHHHHH!!" The librarian hissed.

I walked outside to a scene even more Kafkaesque than the one I had left. The air was redolent with the smell of popcorn as 'Thunder and Blazes' played faintly nearby. I walked over to where the entrance was with the two identical men in tuxedos still leaning on their ball handle canes. At the sight of me, they began to unravel in rapturous amusement, flipping their canes in the air and twirling them for show.

The Call of the Void

"Ladies and Gentlemen," they each said in unison, "The man that asks the questions to which there are no answers, the one, the only, Dr. Samuel Killian!"

Their showmanship was met with confused faces, light applause, and a farrago of subtle disapproval. In bright red and blue neon, just above their head, a banner read 'Locus of Amusement'. The two men fought for a moment over which of them would speak with me first. The man on the right rushed me, lifting my arm with his cane amusingly.

"My dear boy, it's great to see you. I was thinking, after, say, a few drinks and a healthy, cultured badinage, perhaps we can speak about your situation."

"My situation?" I asked.

"Your situation. Indeed. See, though those nasty periodicals have been having a field day scribing a small digest of calumnies in your name, I believe your issue, friend, is one of degeneracy."

"Issue? What do you mean?"

"Erm, well, that is to say, your, well, your williwaw of a performance in class. Bully. Truly bully. The papers would write you off as some Neanderthal but not after I'm done. As I said, your issue is easily written as the apotheosis of the West. The degeneracy of a few, breaking down the fortitude of the many."

"Now, now Sam," the man's twin interrupted, "You mustn't listen to Baxter. He lives in a fantasy world; a deceptive nightmare of revolting proportions, afraid of his own shadow one might say. No, lad. Yours is a tale of, well, triumph over the onerous task of education in

341

the face of free market profiteers. Imagine!" he yelled, grappling his arm around the back of my neck and sweeping his cane in front of us, "Professor, disaffected at student behavior lead on by predatory capitalists, turns to alcohol to numb his woes as a cloying confluence of external, ill-informed cognoscenti bait the rabble into-"

"Don't listen to Jasper! He's just-"

"Gentlemen, please." I said, putting some distance between us, "What's this all about?"

Baxter and Jasper looked at one another for a moment before looking back at me to start a more formal introduction.

"Well, I'm Jasper and this is my, erm, simulacrum, Casper."

"Baxter." The twin corrected. "I'm Baxter. You're Roscoe. Not Jasper."

"No. I'm not." Jasper said with a forced smile. "Your birth name is Casper."

"And yours is Roscoe."

"Enough! Your name is Casper."

"Baxter."

"Casper!"

"Bax-"

"Anyway! We know just how you feel."

"I don't think you do." I assured them.

"But of course we do. We know how philosophers speak, dripping with resentment for their fellow man, searching for their own private, inscrutable argot with which to confuse the incognizant masses. We know what it's like to have men look at you cross for using, shall we say, a more sesquipedalian vocabulary. And how impossible it is to teach them the inadequacies in the English language. If, just once, they would listen, they'd see just how important it is to inure their minds with those now inhumed words."

"I appreciate the camaraderie boys—really, I do—but I think you're getting the wrong idea about me. I'm not that pedantic." The twins began to snicker. "So, what is this place?"

"The, um, well, the Locus of Amusement."

"Yes." I laughed with a nod. "And what is that?"

The men shared the same addlepated glance once more, hemming and hawing, before Baxter cut in. "We're going to say a list of words and you tell us if they have a positive connotation or negative connotation."

I raised my eyebrow in confusion. "I, uh, words? I'm not-"

"Ready?" Jasper asked, not giving me a chance to finish my sentence. "Carnival."

Without thinking, I answered. "Positive."

Baxter wrote in a notebook before throwing the next word out. "Callithump."

I shook my head. "I can say with absolute confidence that I've never heard that word before in my life."

Both scribbled feverishly. "Arcadia."

"Positive."

"Circus."

"Neutral."

343

"Ahhhh." They exclaimed in accord, again writing feverishly in their notepad. "Spectacle."

"Negative."

"Hmmm, we see." They said simultaneously.

"And... lunacy?" Baxter asked a bit tremulously.

"Yes. Lunacy." Jasper whispered as a creepy smile formed over his lips, "Adjacent to lunatic. As in *lunar*. As in related to the phases of-"

"That's enough Jasper!" Baxter demanded.

This was too mad even for me. I brushed past both Jasper and Baxter and opened the double doors to the plaza with both twins right on my heels. The jingling of coins hitting the bottom of tin holders, like the entrance of an arcade, was prominently surging through the plaza as strobe lights that would kill an epileptic pulsed on and off, blinding me for the first ten feet. A cotton candy salesman was pressing freshly twirled sugar in my face as I struggled to read the 'Hall of Fame' behind him. Several accolades from CBS, Disney, CNN, MSNBC, Fox and Sony adorned the walls. Parents and their brood ran from amusement to amusement.

"What is this place?" I asked to either twin.

Baxter looked to Jasper. "It's erm-"

"The Locus of Amusement?" Jasper asked.

"Yeah," I said, exhausted by their evasive talk, "What is the 'Locus of Amusement'?"

"The Center of Entertainment..." Jasper replied.

"I know what 'locus' means, and I know what 'amusement' means. For fuck's sake, give me a straight answer. Is this an arcade or what?"

"Oh no, no, no, no, no." Baxter said sheepishly, "It's uh-well, Jasper?"

"It's, well-" Jasper said, looking nervous, "Look, we're just giving the people what they want."

"Right." I said, "24/7 library right next door to a 24/7 arcade. LA has it all it would seem."

The twins rocked on the balls of their feet with halcyon smiles. I shook my head and walked further down the arcade, stopping at a dated gallery game with pixelated animations. *Vertiginously Epicene Prevarication* was flashing in bright, fluorescent lights above the screen.

"It looks pretty dated." I commented, "Quite the name for an arcade game."

"Yes, but quite apt." Baxter admitted.

"Jesus," I mumbled, grabbing the joystick while staring both of them down, "Is that what *I* sound like?"

"Yes. Let's talk about you, shall we? My brother and I find you quite the amazing specime- erm, public figure. From what we hear you have quite the 'restive', shall we say, vocabulary. No surprise from a professor though. They're always going on and on pretentiously about-"

"Excuse me," I interrupted, "I'd like to think there is at least a bit of propriety in my vocabulary."

"Uh huh," Jasper said, crossing his arms playfully, "says the man that just used 'propriety' in a casual sentence."

"I, uh... hmmm." I said, looking down at the game.

The twins, possibly expecting me to fight back, looked at one another, confused once more. Baxter emptied a handful of tokens into my hand, and I started the game. 'Dated' may have been a bit lenient; the word I was looking for was archaic. Blotches of pixels in the form of two humans displayed on the screen and their mouths moved with a frogger sound effect.

"How old is this game?" I asked.

"We just made it, uhm," Jasper looked at his brother, raising his hands and counting fingers in uncertainty, "6 months ago?"

"So, what do I do?" I asked, grabbing the joystick.

"It's an RPG! Just... make choices." Baxter assured.

Back on screen, the little blotch of pixels spoke again, now with a dialogue box forming next to his head.

Dad, do you have a moment?

Sure son!

A dad, who raised his kid with love, understanding and knowledge, is bewildered when his son wants to impersonate black men and speak in Ebonics. After a heart to heart, the father convinces him that he is not in fact black by explaining that he will make a fool of himself. Unfortunately, much to the son's regret, he has already become a target of bullying at his school for such folly.

As the Father, do you:

A.   Mollycoddle the little wimp

346

B.   *Show him kindness and care*

C.   *Encourage the son to pursue his dreams of racial deceit*

D.   *Ask him for a beer*

"Seriously?" I asked with a bewildered grin, turning to the twins.

They were both scrawling on their notepads, hastily stashing them away after noticing I had turned around. Both bared their teeth in a phony smile. "Just... pick please."

Conflicted, and all of a sudden concerned with what the Twins might think, I chose B.

"Nah hahhh hah!" Jasper mumbled confidently.

Baxter rolled his eyes and scrawled more on his notepad.

The son, having another heart to heart with his father, tells him that he is transgendered. The father tells him he isn't and apologizes to his son for not distancing himself away from these things earlier. That, due to his lack of protection from the modern world, he has lost his identity. The son scoffs and accosts his father saying, "Dad no! I was transgendered all along!"

As the Father, do you:

A.   *Front the cash for gender reassignment surgery*

B.   *Kick him out of the house immediately*

C.   *Suggest counseling that may lead to hormone replacement*

D.   *Ask him for a beer*

"This game sucks," I said, rubbing my face impatiently.

Baxter pointed shakily to the machine. "Oh, but if-"

"Now we're talking!" I said, pointing to the bar at the back of the arcade.

My buzz was starting to wear off and that terrible migraine feeling I get after coming down was creeping into my skull. I leaned against the bar, flagging down the barkeep, as the twins separated themselves on either side of me.

Baxter cleared his throat. "I'll admit, it isn't as fun as Jasper and I's beetle game." Jasper and Baxter sniggered and showed one another identical boxes they pulled from their pockets.

I rolled my eyes. "Cute. Still, your game could use a little work. I mean, kids aren't going to want to play that. And there are four choices for-"

"You can't have a bivalence for such tendentious, ethical dilemmas." Jasper interrupted with an air of pretentious disgust.

I shook my head. "No. That's not- What I meant was, there are *only* four options. And one of them is just 'Ask him for a beer'. Which by the way..." I pointed a finger in the air to flag the bartender down.

"What can I get you sir?"

"We'll take three double whiskeys. Well is fine. Wait!" I turned to the twins. "This is on you guys, right? I mean, if you're taking notes and all, I figure you owe me a round or two."

The twins stared at one another and began to smile. Their dimples spiraled slowly against their cheeks, looking more and more balmy by the second, as if they were hiding some dastardly secret about the world. They looked at me and nodded.

"Make it three doubles of your best top shelf whiskey."

"Whiskey? Hmmm. I see." The bartender began to scratch his head childishly. "Well, we have a lovely triennially malted, mashed and fermented oak cask lain barley."

I swung my head to meet him. "That's what I said."

"Right." He smiled.

"And put one on ice." I said, turning back to the twins.

The bartender tapped me on the shoulder. "I, uh-"

Baxter looked over my shoulder to cut off the bartender. "Cryogenically. Stored. Hydrogenated. Oxygen."

"Right away, sir."

I looked at Baxter then back to Jasper. Their faces reverted back to blank canvases, telling me nothing. I half expected them to burst out laughing at any second. "Anyway, like I was saying, your game could use a little work."

"Jasper thinks the transgender movement might be a little out there but it's trend-"

Jasper shook his head. "Because they *do* eventually get over it."

"And by 'get over it' I'm assuming you mean 'stifle their natural identity'?"

"And by 'stifle their natural identity' I'm certain you mean, 'Purport the turpitude in the Intersectionality of an Oppressive, Pathological, mind altering-"

"And by 'Purport the turpitude-" Both twins were speaking incoherently over one another at this point, "I'm certain you mean 'a cissexist micro aggressive-"

Rolling my eyes once again, I put my hands over their mouths to shut them up. "Gentlemen, please. That's enough. I don't really give a fuck."

"It would cost too much money to fix it now anyway." Baxter sighed as he removed my hand.

Jasper shook his head. "You should be more on top of these things Baxter. How much they cost and all that."

"More than your alimony payments, Jasper?"

"I told you," Jasper cringed with balled fists and gritted teeth, "it's not alimony. It's post martial maintenance."

"Right." Baxter sneered, "And Stars Wars 10 isn't a remake. It's a remastering."

I stepped in once more. "Wait, I thought you were Jasper, and you were Cas- I mean, Rosc- Dammit! Baxter."

"No. He's Jasper and I'm Baxter." Jasper—or at least who I previously thought was Jasper—said.

"But earlier-" I stopped and smiled. "Oh, I get it. Someone put you up to this. Was it Felix? Dr. Felix? That motherfucker." I smiled, whispering under my breath. "He had it out for me as soon as I walked through his door. I knew it. Right?"

Baxter and Jasper grinned, pulling out their notepads.

"Tell us about this Felix." Jasper insisted.

"Yes! 'Doctor' Felix, was it?" Baxter laughed.

The Call of the Void

The bartender returned with the drinks. I took each of the twin's drinks, exclaiming, "Over the lips and through the gums, watch out floor, here I come." and downed them in one gulp before grabbing the whiskey on the rocks and bolting back to the arcade.

"Excuse me!" the bartender exclaimed in an almost mocking, burlesque tone, "That's dynamically gratifying crapulence!"

"Oh, Funk and Wagnalls! He's getting away." One of the twins shouted.

I took my time strolling through the eastern wing of the arcade. All of the games were labeled diffusely, as if from a surrealist's nightmare. At least, since the last time I was in an arcade they were. They all seemed to be named in a quippish manner.

Missiles for the Mugwump

Plaudits for the Politician

Minerva's Last Stand

Ring a Recusant

Political Pinkos

I passed them all to see a new room, heavily advertised with the arcade's most dazzling lights. *Opprobrium of Ignominious Characters* was lit up in little lightbulbs above the room. Husbands and wives packed the place with their kids, walking from table to table, getting a good laugh at the people seated at each attraction. One man was leaning over his son, sharing a laugh and pointing at a woman with a mop on her head. There was a man with clown makeup, pantaloons and a business suit at one of the tables. A camera was propped up right in front of him. I stood next to him, grimacing as the man's face torqued flamboyantly.

"I recognize you." I said.

"You should." Jasper said, rushing up beside me, "He was quite famous for some time. Until the *incident.*"

"Isn't that right, Tim?" Baxter asked, with a coy smile.

"Oh, Tim. Tim Downy." Jasper cooed, "Once famed, yet short lived, king of Late-Night TV. Where would you be without us? Without your act of contrition?"

"Contrition?" I asked.

Tim Downy hardly took notice of us, smearing his face instead with makeup before overextending the lipstick and eating it.

Jasper leaned in close to Tim's face. Tim was miles away. "What was it you said Tim? Oh, that's it! 'If only this stupid bitch weren't around'."

"'Bitch *kike*' I believe it was." Baxter corrected.

"'Pregnant bitch kike' if I'm not mistaken," Jasper said, "No accounting for philippic taste I have to say."

"This is... what? Penance for him?" I asked, "To be pilloried every night in front of these people."

"Not just these people, Sam." Baxter said, lightly tapping the camera placed in front of Tim.

"Hmmm," Jasper mused, looking at the gauge on top of the camera, "Quite the audience tonight. Over 10,000 viewers."

"Another week and," Baxter paused, deep in thought, "well, he can't go back to Late Night."

"No. No. Perish the thought, brother. We'll spin a yarn about alcoholism and maybe get him on the higher listed night clubs and stand-up acts. It's only momentary."

"So, wait," I said, sipping from my glass, "Everyone thinks that he's just livestreaming himself every night acting like a dotty maniac? After losing the Tonight Show over a remark he made?"

"Why wouldn't they?" Jasper blurted, puzzled I would even have to ask.

I lowered the glass from my lips carefully, my right eyebrow raised in shock. "It seems a little contrived, don't you think?"

"Do *you* think?" Jasper asked.

"Yes, Sam. Do you? I mean, honestly, it was all Jasper's idea. He said, 'Why not? They believe everything we say.' And I said, 'Not this.' And he said-"

Jasper banged his cane against the table. "Wrong. WRONG!"

Jasper and Baxter bickered for a moment before pulling out their notepads and leaning close to me, desperate for my thoughts.

"Dr. Killian, please, sir, you must be an arbiter here. I insist."

"Gentlemen, please!" I begged with a hoarse voice. "Don't get me involved."

Despite my outburst, both men began to write in their notebook, nodding in congruous agreement as they shared their notes with one another.

"W-wait, are all the people in here from TV?" I asked, backing up and pointing to the tables with seated clowns.

Jasper nodded. "Not just TV. But, yes, they are all in entertainment."

"Writers. Actors. Comedians. Producers." Baxter said, finishing the statement.

Jasper pointed to one of the seated clowns reading off a teleprompter. "Which reminds me. Colin. Colin! Did you work in that bit of covert advertising we talked about in the high-speed pursuit? You know, not making it so obvious, but shocked still that the man is driving the all-new Bentley. That he is making better speed than the police and that the Bentley is top of the line. Those lines. Did you get them in?"

Baxter nodded before turning to another teleprompter with a lever near it. "Ah, that reminds me! Put on the SpongeBob we talked about! The one with the pride flag and the non-binary anthem."

"No!" Jasper insisted, moving closer to the prompter's lever, "Like we rehearsed the one with the national anthem!"

Jasper and Baxter began fighting over the fulcrum, pulling on each end like it was a wishbone. It finally snapped, sending them both backwards onto the floor.

"All that work. Look what you've done!"

"What *I've* done?"

"Señor will not be too happy about this."

"No. No he won't..."

"I- I know you." I said, ignoring the twins and rushing to another table, "You're Steve Catwell. You wrote *The Embroiled*

Tontine a few years back. Wasn't it a best seller? I read every word and loved it."

"Critics didn't." He responded lazily, as if doped up on opioids.

"But it was well received domestically. I remember reading it in grad school. It was all we talked about for weeks. A jeremiad of linguistic inadequacies and the future of language. You said, 'Language is-'."

"Language is the great deceiver; it turns strong men weak and weak men strong. Language is both the brick and the brisance of our reality." He finished quietly.

Catwell looked up at me, dazed and lugubrious, his eyes, nearly catatonic, glazed over with a film of tears, attempting to speak once more.

"NO!" Jasper yelled, smacking his cane against the table as Baxter reared his threateningly in the air, "Show him what you have been working on."

Catwell pulled papers out from under the table, laying them flat in front of him.

"From the New York Times bestselling author," Catwell began in a forlorn voice, "Comes 'Double Trouble'. A brother and sister find out they were both adopted and begin a concupiscent tryst only to find out later on that they come from the same biological parents."

"Brilliant!" The twins shouted in unison.

Steve looked up at me. "B-but-"

"And over here," Baxter said, leading me to the next table, "Is none other than Dorothy Williams."

"Dorothy is best known for her 'hard-hitting' investigative journalism for the Times. But Dorothy broke the number one rule in journalism. Don't investigate your fellow journalists."

"Now she writes for a little-known periodical right here in LA. Don't you, Dorothy?"

Bags had formed under Dorothy's eyes. Her fingers and knuckles were pocked with bumps and scabs. She stretched her hands out and interlocked her fingers in the form of a bridge, cracking each knuckle in the process.

"Got the piece on the Federal encroachment of Amish land done." She said, handing Baxter the paper.

"Hmmm," he said, flipping through the pages carelessly, "No, no. This won't do. Less on the Quakers and more on their land rights."

"And change the title!" Jasper demanded, "'Amish in the Fight of their Life' is too, hmmm, what's the word brother?"

"Kitschy?"

"Kitschy! That's it! How about," Jasper said, thinking to himself for a moment, as he raised his hands and began to say each word one at a time like he was reading it aloud from an invisible paper, "'Feral Mennonites Strike Again: No one's oat cakes are safe'?"

The twins bridged their eyebrows and nodded at her with giddy approval.

"Whatever you say boss..."

"ENOUGH!" A voice bellowed from the end of the hall.

Baxter and Jasper grappled one another, shaking like children in a haunted house. An enormous screen widened across the hall nearby, projecting the large, ruptured green face of a bald man.

"I am the great Network! Who are you? WHO. ARE. YOU?"

I looked around, pointing to my chest listlessly, as the rest of the room looked on. I finished my drink and stepped forward.

"I am Sam, the drunk and loquacious. I'm not-"

"I'LL DO THE TALKING! THE GREAT AND POWERFUL NETWORK KNOWS WHO YOU ARE. AND YOU TWO! STEP FORWARD."

Wobbling their legs as they walked, Baxter and Jasper moved delicately toward the screen, dropping to both knees and bowing up and down.

"BAXTER, YOU DARE TO WALLOW THESE HALLS, HOPING TO BRING ENOUGH SCURRILOUS FODDER TO GAIN ENTRY TO THE LOCUS?! YOU SLINKING, SLIMING, SPURIOUS PILE OF MENDACIOUS JUNK!" His eyes moved to Jasper. "AND YOU, JASPER! YOU HAVE THE AUDACITY TO ASK FOR A SEAT HERE?! YOU EFFETIST, ENERVATED, BOWDLERIZING, CENSORING CROWD OF CLAPTRAP!"

"Yes, your honor." Baxter said.

"He means your excellency." Jasper corrected.

"We mean your majesty." They said simultaneously.

"SILENCE! I HAVE EVERY INTENTION OF BRINGING YOU TO MY TABLE. BUT FIRST, A SMALL TASK. THERE HAVE BEEN SEVERAL INDEPENDENT-"

"Jimmy, no!" A man whisper behind me.

I turned my head to see a boy skipping and laughing to the side of the room. He began to tug on a red curtain over and over before ripping it off, revealing a suited man with an earpiece and sunglasses in front of a microphone. Everyone's head turned to face him.

"ERM, UM, UH... THE GREAT NETWORK HAS SPOKEN!" the man behind the curtain yelled into the microphone, "PAY NO ATTENTION TO THAT MAN BEHIND THE CURTAIN!"

I shook my head and began to walk out. The twins raced to cut me off.

"Sam, please." Baxter said, walking backwards in front of me.

"Just one more thing," Jasper added, "We're going to tell you a list of words and we want you to tell us positive or negative."

"Felix." Baxter said.

"I'm out of here," I said, pushing my way past them.

Outside, the line for the Locus had died down and a cluster was forming near a table opposite the complex. As I got closer, I saw two Recusants with their eyes locked on one another, seated apart at the table. People were throwing money on a nearby bench and hollering back and forth. There was chalk drawn on the wall behind them with betting odds and a title that read 'Three Cylinder'. One of the Recusant loaded a revolver with three bullets before spinning it around on the table and sliding it to his comrade. The crowd grew restless, shouting for blood, before Baxter and Jasper showed up, flipping chairs and dispersing the crowd. Jasper grabbed the gun and pulled the trigger to the Recusant seated at the right hand of the table, exploding the top quarter of his head into a bright red mist. Baxter took the gun and pulled the trigger, cycling the empty chamber, as the Recusant to the left stared on in vacant amusement. Baxter's face was turning purple as he cocked the revolver once more. "Bear Witness!" Baxter shouted and pulled the trigger, blowing the Recusant's tongue out of the back of his mouth. The twins steadied themselves before putting a smile on once more.

"Come one come all ladies and gents! All betting debts will be paid inside..."

"The Locus of Amusssssseeeemeeennntt."

I lit a cigarette and walked down the road toward the Convention Center. At the corner, a group of four singers, dressed as the Mamas and the Papas followed me, singing 'California Dreaming'.

X

Nothing is more terrifying than reality. Everything in life has taught me that. Everything tonight has taught me that. My connection to mankind was a mere façade—a hollow mirror, reflecting and pantomiming the cultural milieu. And despite Felix's best efforts, abject alienation and discarded empathy were the only gifts bestowed upon me tonight, littering the highways of Los Angeles.

I'm worse for the experience. I could write a book about the anomalous horrors that are the sleeping mind, the collective human consciousness, the postmodern psychosis, but truthfully, by the time that book gained any recognition it would be a hundred years too late, and what is perceived to be ignorance now would be aptitude then.

A thought crept into my mind about an undergraduate professor I once had. One day, a cold morning in February, he had come into the class, his hands shaking and eyes glossy from the cold, and, right before taking off his gloves, announced, "I think of the greats. I weep for Wittgenstein." He paused as we all took out our notebooks and began to write excitedly. When I looked up to meet his eyes once more, he sighed and said, "The future will bury him." We all looked from one to the other, not certain what point he was trying to make, as he remained silent on the matter, refusing to elaborate any further.

The Call of the Void

I suppose he was right. A moratorium on identity came creeping through the night of the last century; humans have become so obsessed with adding flavor to their daily lives that they are unbearably insipid. Go figure.

In the middle of South Park, I checked a nearby clock to find that it was 3:56 AM. Looking no different than the local denizens creeping from one dark hole to the next, I pulled out my flask and drank what little whiskey I had left.

I craned my head back to look at the concrete colossus before me. The Los Angeles Convention Center was an empyrean monument to the city's facile preeminence. LA's sky was engulfed in flames, breathing fire, negligent of its own populace. The sky became awash in a robust red, its canvas a stark backdrop for a city on fire, a perimeter keeping its citizens prisoner around a border of flames in a labyrinth of a town.

The shade of a dying tree nearby, cast from the artificial light of a streetlight not far off, portended the auspice of a dark shadow world; a shadow world that reflected our own but was unable to communicate with ours. Theory: We are fully incapable of communication with ourselves and thusly have degenerated our consciousness to neglect the most basic elements of our environment.

I talk—and think really—like this whenever I'm nervous. It's the only comfort I've ever been able to find in myself. But why? I never had it bad. My life has been, by all accounts, completely normal.

I was feeling drunk and lost.

361

LeResche

The night was cold, and my frontal lobe was completely fried. I'd chain smoked and drank my way through the turpitude of Los Angeles, and I felt as though I'd passed through the tesseract of human-

"Sam!" a voice shouted, friendly at first before becoming concerned, "Sam?"

I turned my head as Jerry, my editor at Reuters, rushed up alongside me.

"Sammy, you okay?" Jerry asked, putting a hand on my shoulder, "What are you doing here?"

I rubbed my eyes hysterically, trying to wake myself up. I patted down my flannel, looking for my pack of smokes, grabbing a single and playing hot potato with it in the air.

"Beats me." I laughed, lighting up with a rough cough.

"You look, uh... beat. You alright?"

"I'm goof- Good! Good, I mean. Sorry, just been up all night. It's already four in the morning. Little tipsy too."

"Yeah. Yeah, I got ya."

Jerry looked me over. A crease formed across his brow and on the sides of his face, almost as if he were hiding something from me.

"It's good to see you man." I said, shaking his hand and bringing him in for a light hug, "Look, this might be totally out of line, but, well, I was wondering if you had any coke? I saw you using once at a party we were at and, well..."

"Um, yeah. Yeah, man. Sure. Actually, I do." He laughed and reached into his pocket, "Long nights usually call for it."

"Sorry. It's just," I paused and waved my hand toward the Convention Center, "I got a thing in there and, you know, I don't think a cup of tea is going to cut it."

Jerry pulled out a coke spoon and an ounce of coke, darting his head over his shoulders timidly in search of any police. I scooped and snorted before exhaling a sigh with muted virulence. I took one more, and handed the spoon back, feeling my head lighten, heart race, and mind clear. My confidence returned at last. I exhaled, smiling at Jerry and nodding in gratitude. "Some professor, huh?"

"Pfft, please. My boss was head of research at Columbia for ten years and he starts off each morning with a line and a highball."

"Oh, God. Don't say that..."

"Sorry."

"All good, I was half kidding." I said, dismissing him with a jocular wave, "Christ, that's better. I'll get ya back soon, Jer."

"Don't worry about it man. I owe you anyway. But uh, so, you said you had something? In there? Are you trying to get into the convention center?"

Jerry's brow and cheeks creased once more in awkward apprehension, indicating that he was either interrogating me or concerned about what I was doing there.

"Not really. I-I mean, yeah, I guess I came here to see it." I paused and looked down at my cigarette. The memories of that night faded in my mind second by second. The floor and the walls began to fume and melt as my concentration broke. "But, honestly Jer, I think I just might call it a night. Great blow and all but, it's going to get me home and that's it."

He crossed his arms and exhaled through his nose, lifting his chin at the convention center. "I've been trying to get in but it's almost impossible unless you're on an approved list."

Jerry's ash gray shirt read 'Press' across the front. His long sleeve black undershirt made his body look a little heftier than he actually was. I never really considered Jerry short, per se, but he was definitely below the average height. And he never did himself any favors wearing one-inch lifts under his boots. He had a cuffed beanie on his head and a tattered memo pad hanging out of his hand. No wonder they didn't let him in. I could see him now, waving his Press pass, trying to breach the doors of the center, looking like another one of South Park's lovely residents.

"Why? You work for Reuters. Senior Editor. Shouldn't be a problem."

Jerry nodded distantly while deep in thought, making an obvious attempt to avoid eye contact. I always thought he was a great guy but he's all thumbs when it comes to human interaction.

"Look, Sam, I'm gonna level with you. After I denied—or rather, deleted—your last essay, I've sort of been on the hot seat. And when you didn't answer any of my follow up emails..." He waved his cigarette hand in a circular motion. "This is kind of my only way back into the good graces of my editors. Though, they did make it seem like sending me here was some big joke." Jerry trailed off, looking up at the sky, as if he were finally realizing he was the butt end of some terrible prank.

"Wait, what essay? You mean the op-ed I wrote?"

"Yeah."

"That was drivel." I said with a sigh before sitting on the nearest park bench, "Drunk, unadulterated, maudlin pap. They should have deleted it."

"No shit," Jerry exhaled, lighting one of his cigarettes, "But 'pap' from a professor who went viral castigating the entire student body of UCLA before being put on leave."

"You hated it that much that you just deleted the email? I can't blame you I guess." I paused and scanned the street, trying to buy some time. "Anyway, how would you have known? I sent the essay in hours before that class, and a day before it went viral."

"Right, yeah, that's what I said. Still."

"That's weird... odd really."

"How so?"

"Well," I started, pausing to exhale smoke, slightly in disbelief, "Jerry, why would they blame you for that? It has to be something else."

"It can't be. I'm solid there."

I shook my head, puffing on my cigarette and trying to piece it together but nothing was coming to mind. "Just seems- I don't know, contrived? Manufactured maybe? Like they were set- setting... you up..."

"What? Setting me up? Sam, trust me, no one there is setting me up. I can guarantee it."

I considered the last thing I said, letting it rattle around in my mind, like a possible legend to a maze. "You said they sent you as a joke?"

"I didn't mean it like that. Look, I have friends there. Like, really close friends." Jerry said, crossing his arms in dismay, "Anyway, forget it. If you aren't going to the event will you at least help *me* get in?"

I sat on the parking curb, staring off into the distance at two homeless people fucking.

"Look, Sam, I know you're a little 'out of touch'" Jerry really emphasized the air quotes here, "But your rant was videotaped. It's permanent. Always there, looming in the digital world. And even though the public called for your head, it struck a little chord with some viewers. Plus, now that you've been rebranded as a high priest of the Recusants, the-"

"What?!" I heaved, snapping out of my stupor, "The Recusants? What the fuck are you talking about?" I sat still, shaking my head furiously at Jerry with my palms open, demanding an answer. Jerry gritted his teeth and grimaced like he'd just stepped on a nail. His awkward facial expressions were—in his own special way—an impotent means of communicating with me. "Jerry!"

"Sam... in an interview last night, a few of your colleagues commented that you seemed extremely sympathetic to the Recusants' cause during a party. Plus-"

"I wasn't sympathetic! I-"

"Plus! Plus-"

"I only wanted to discuss what just happened, that's all!" My voice was becoming more frantic by the word, "I-"

"Plus!" Jerry raised a hand to stifle my next outburst. "Quite a few people have recognized you from the news and have live streamed you talking to a few Recusants tonight."

"Talking?"

"Talking."

"I-I u-uh, well." I stuttered. Jerry shrugged. "Oh, don't give me that 'aw shucks' routine Jerry!" I stopped and took a deep breath, trying to find my center. "I'm sorry. I didn't mean that. It's just," I paused once more for reflection, ashing my cigarette and lighting another, "It's just, now, I-I... I won't- this was all for nothing. The fucking news is going to bury me. I'll be lucky to get a job at a Community College after this. And maybe, that's a big maybe, I'll find some independent press who'll publish my bullshit for extra cash."

Jerry nodded ruefully. "I'm sorry. I really am Sam. But the way the news has pushed it tonight- well, you've been playing with fire buddy."

I stood up, rubbing my tightly closed eyelids with my thumb and index finger, and grabbed Jerry by the shoulder. He jolted back a bit as I laughed like a lunatic with wayward, reckless abandon.

"Maybe we should sit back down..."

I waved an aggressive hand back and forth in his face, showing him I was fine, that I'd regained my composure. It was becoming fairly obvious that tonight was not about mere 'Human Connection', but something else. Something I didn't know. Something, I felt, I'd never really know. What good was the truth anyway?

Light wisps of wind bounced off my cheek and fluttered through my open shirt as I reached into my pocket to pull out the tickets I had. "You want in?"

"Want in wha-" Jerry said, stopping mid-sentence at the sight of the tickets "How'd you get those?"

"Work. So, you want in?"

"H-hell yeah." Jerry said, breathing a warm breath into his tightly wrapped hands.

I fanned out the two tickets like a poker hand, smiling as I revealed them to Jerry. I dropped my hand down to give him one before the writing on the ticket caught my eye, paralyzing me in place. I pulled the ticket close for inspection.

"You're a real life sav-"

"W-wait a minute. Shhhh!"

"Something wrong? Are they fake?"

"Shhhh!"

I had no idea why I was demanding his silence. My brain obviously wasn't working right. I pushed a long strand of hair from my eyes, looking back and forth from the Convention Center to the ticket. Jerry's face was growing red with concern. I stood silent, staring at the writing on the ticket.

"It can't be. No. I-"

"What?" Jerry asked, moving next to me to read the ticket, "Huh. So? Cerebral Ceremony. Clever. I guess."

"No, it- it's not what you-" A homeless man nearby sat atop a large rock and began to strum his acoustic guitar. He sang a near perfect rendition of Dylan's 'Masters of War' as the surrounding city crumbled, fulminating from its own ego. "Never mind." I said as we looked from the guitarist to the convention center, "That's our cue I guess."

The surrounding crowd of tramps, activists, and junkies were swaying in interpretive dance, entrancing us with a kaleidoscopic flow of movements. Jerry and I began to move through the street. The rabble, jumping from their seats and following close behind, turned their heads to meet us the further we went. Step by step, each pimp, vagrant, wino and hooker trailed onto our train, like a rafter of turkeys, ignorant of their pursuit to the axe. A pack of Recusants walked by in brisk pace, each with a cat o' nine tails whipping their own backs. A trail of blood followed their every move, flowing into a 'T' on the asphalt, as the gathered crowd pursuing Jerry and I shouted disdainful remarks at them and us. A group of hoodlums threw rocks at a felled Recusant whose head was caved in. Jerry shivered, gawking at the mayhem, and picked up the pace.

We walked past a trio of female Recusants weeping over a framed, daguerreotype photo of Konrad, his gaze staring off into the distance, that same old smile emergent on his lips. Time seemed to slow as they brushed their hands gently over his face. I looked down at

369

them and they looked up at me. For a second, a quiet understanding was shared between us. I looked at them mournfully once more with a nod before continuing down the street.

The air, swirling with fog and sand, turned thick with an arctic, bitter cold that made me close my overshirt. The color of the night's sky went from black to yellow to red and, finally, back to black again with each cloud covering of the moon.

At the entrance of the center, the lights flickered like those at a Halloween store. I stared up to the sky once more, marveling at its red tint. The moon, plastered against the red sky, had embers rocketing from its edges, like a halo of flames.

Only one doorman was working security at the convention center. A prototypical guard one might find at any night club here in LA, complete with chiseled biceps the size of tires, a bald head the size of a melon, a squared jaw, and over six foot six. Even I had to look up at him.

"You know what I just thought that's crazy?" Jerry announced abruptly, trying to break the tension, exhaling smoke and holding his hand over his nose as if to stop himself from snorting, "Amish people have never even seen 'Amish Paradise' by Weird Al. Blows my mind."

Sometimes I wonder just how Jerry was able to get a job as an editor at Reuters.

The guard halted us with an outstretched hand. "Passes gentlemen?"

"Right here." I said, handing him both of our tickets.

The Call of the Void

The guard looked over the tickets callously before casting his gaze toward me and then to Jerry. Anxious to get in, Jerry wrung his hands and flashed the eyes of a tame, submissive animal that could smell a predacious animal on his heels. The cigarette in my hand was half gone. I opened my pack and counted ten remaining. The guard never faltered his gaze and the shirt sleeves around his biceps were ready to burst. He eyed Jerry longer than he should have, like a man warning an intruder to leave his property. But after a moment or so, the bouncer's scowl ripened into a smile. His gaze fell upon me once more as he cocked his head to indicate the curtain behind him.

"Well," he said, fighting off a laugh and locking eyes with me, "You're really through the looking glass now."

And with the lifting of a regal red rope, we moved forward into a blizzard of madness. I passed the first veil and held it open for Jerry. Jerry stood in terror at first like the younger brother outside of a haunted house, awaiting his older brother's approval before crossing over. I nodded reassuringly as a strong wind from inside the convention center kicked up my hair and whipped my shirt in every direction.

We stood inside the atrium, staring at the veil twenty feet away that led to the next room. The ceiling had to be almost 200 feet high. But that couldn't be right. It wasn't possible.

"This isn't the convention center." Jerry said, "Sam, this-"

A faint and familiar sound began to emit from inside of the main hall. Loud. Very, very loud. An orchestra, somewhat common,

371

yet chilling and breathtaking. A song unlike any other. A song that could beckon the dead, whose chorus tattooed itself into my mind, almost supernaturally. 'O, Fortuna', in all its glorious, rhythmic chorus, was being played from somewhere deep inside the center. And, for the first time tonight, I thought, 'How appropriate'.

"Do you hear that?" Jerry gasped.

"Yeah." I said, moving cautiously to the next veil.

"Sam, this isn't the convention center."

"I heard you the first time." I answered curtly, opening the veil to the next room.

Behind the veil, a peculiar scene unraveled before our eyes. The room, spanning a football field's length, was filled from wall to wall with men in black tuxedos and women in red dresses, each one of them facing the opposite direction of the entrance, still as the dead. The architecture inside was wildly surreal, like something straight out of Piranesi's sketchbook. The interior of the Convention Center was incredibly garish, and the ceilings were plastered with floral printings and diamond encrusted ornaments, it's walls castellated with ancient stones. Past the curtain, the antechamber of the elite was more of a giant vestibule than a greeting room. It was decadent and something to truly behold. The ceiling embraced the sky and convexly pointed outward to a glass canopy that revealed the moon. Following the lead of the atrium, the convention center presented itself like an enormous ballroom laden with golden carpets, crystal chandeliers and swinging lights. There was one single bar toward the northwestern corner of the room but, before either Jerry or I could move toward it for a drink, the massive horde of well-dressed guests had all simultaneously began to shake with minor ticks.

"Great Zapffe's Ghost..." I whispered under my breath in shock.

At the sound of my voice, they turned swiftly to face Jerry and I, our mouths so agape a fist could pass through them. Their eyes appeared white from a distance as they stared directly toward the ceiling. Yet as they readjusted their gaze onto us, I could see the black of their pupils. Both Jerry and I, still frozen, were reluctant to take another step. No malevolence was present in their tremoring bodies, but an eerie ire of scorn coursed through the room. And, as the first verse hit its pinnacle and Jerry and I began our descent down the red carpet to the next veil, the room grew still, and each person had their eyes trained on us. With each step that we took, their eyes and heads followed as well.

"Uhm," Jerry whispered as the orchestra lowered just before its apex, "I feel like I've never been here before. But I have! Many times, in fact. This is wrong. This is all wrong. What is this place?"

"I've never been here but, I never thought it would look like this. I mean, it looks almost preindustrial in a sort of opulent kind of way. Like, a czar's ballroom almost."

Jerry, holding on tight to my shoulder, kept whispering, "I don't believe this. What the fuck is going on Sam?"

I didn't answer him. We moved forward, looking back every so often to see the mob closing in on the gap we made. As my cigarette lost its embers in its final drag, I decided to put the dogend between my thumb and forefinger and flick it at the face of one of the suited men. No reaction. Jerry noticed and ashed his dying cigarette into the scotch glass of the woman closest to his right. Nothing. I forced myself through the gaze of what felt like millions of unwavering eyes placed on my soul. By the time we got to the second curtain, Jerry had given up on taking pictures of all of them and ran back up to my side. The second verse of the song cracked through the air.

"Do you believe this?"

"I- I don't know," I managed to say, taking one look back at the group of men and women closing in on us.

"This isn't the convention center. This isn't any place I've ever been before. It's a mansion." Jerry's voice was practically trembling at this point as he wiped sweat from his brow, realizing that the surrounding mob may not be entirely altruistic.

I grabbed him by the elbow. "Let's go."

Ahead, just past the bar adorned with crystal, there was another partition similar to the one at the entrance. Jerry's pace was becoming more and more rapid, and the tempo of his shoes was the only sound in the ballroom—save for the symphony—clamoring in the air around us. Reaching the curtain, I pulled the partition back and stood aghast. Jerry had grabbed his chest with one hand and began to walk backwards, shaking his head in disbelief. Darkness as far as the eye could see. Like standing over the precipice of a mountain on a moonless, starless night, the corridor was a descending staircase barely visible to the eye and the darkness was as vast as space was infinite. The abyss was a maelstrom of umbra and wind, ready to swallow us whole.

The Call of the Void

It was an incredibly powerful work of legerdemain, forcing my mind to cede to its will. A glacial wind blew furiously from all directions inside, turning my hair and flipping it back and forth.

"This... isn't real." Jerry said in short, choppy breaths.

I stared down the descent of stairs. Each step down was a grim reminder of my journey to discover man, leaving me hollow inside. A terrible, subzero zephyr forced its way across me and suddenly my flannel wasn't enough. The chill made me pop my collar and nestle it tightly around my neck. Jerry continued walking backwards but ran into one of the men surrounding us. He bellowed out a "FUCK!" before running in ahead of me as I took one final look back at the lifeless beings, their eyes becoming black spheres that melted away in the darkness of the night.

I could barely see Jerry in front of me. The stairs we walked on swung from side to side as 'O, Fortuna!' still pierced the air, penetrating its way into our ears. A tempestuous wind kicked up and blew the stairwell back and forth, nearly bucking both of us off the stairs. It was the closest, I believe, I had ever come to death. And yet, a frisson kicked up inside me as I hollered aloud to the chorus of the song. I could hear Jerry yelling but could not make out any of his words. He seemed stuck in place as he reached for the partition to the next room. I could feel the warmth on the other side embracing me and pulling me forward, it's air redolent with hedonistic delights.

"Shit..." Jerry muttered, as we both fell forward through the sheet.

"Jesus Murphy." I whispered, examining the room.

The room was much smaller in length but at least another 100 feet high. The first thing to catch my eye were the twenty-foot-long tables layered with a lavender linen. Turkeys, chalices, fruits and desserts of all varieties decorated the tables from end to end. Towering figures that reached the ceiling stood on each end of the room, draped in crimson robes that covered their faces. Each stood side by side and across one another, like a Greek chorus ready to sing us our fate. Yet not a word. Their faces were eerily realistic. It was hard to tell exactly whether or not they were statues. The bottom of their robes washed against the floor like the tide rushing into the shore. Each of their sleeves was rolled up to their elbow and, much like the last room, their eyes became fixated on us—an almost human sheen running off the pupil of each eyeball. At the end, above the next partition, a colossal statue of a woman was cemented into the wall, nearly 250 feet high. She had a cornucopia in her left-hand and a till in her right.

Jerry began to hyperventilate. "This is like—shit—I don't know. How far down do you think we are?"

"I don't know. But it's freezing." I said, noticing how dense my breath had become.

Jerry started for one of the tables. "God damn! The fuckin' food is rotten!" He exclaimed, rolling maggot off of the fruit bowl, "All of it is. How long do you think it's been down here?"

"I don't know."

'O, Fortuna' continued. The stairs to the next room were easily twice as far down as the last set. Maybe 100 feet. The light from the partition at the end was flickering, visible only to a keen eye. The air was gelid, even for November, and I took a drink from a nearby bottle of bourbon before offering it to Jerry and lighting another cigarette.

"Sam, I can't."

My lazy eye—that only becomes prominent after I drink excessively—fell upon him with consternation. "Can't?"

"Sam," Jerry gasped, taking a deep skull from the bottle, "I'm not gonna lie. Th- this isn't right man. We'll be down another hundred feet and I don- don't- This is- something isn't right man."

"Don't abandon me now, Jerry."

"Sam, I-"

"Jerry," I said, yanking the bottle from his hand and taking another pull, surprised to be this sober, "I have no idea how many more layers we have to go through. But I can tell you this; this is the most intrigued I've ever been in my entire life. And the truth is, whether there are another three, five, thousand, million, billion flights left, I will go through it like Sisyphus in reverse. Because I have to see. I. Have. To. See."

Jerry remained silent for a moment. He stared at the carpet and listened to the verses of the symphony blaring out all around us. "Curiosity killed the cat, Sam."

Nodding, I stared down at the abyss. "So be it."

Jerry looked me over. We both looked back, in shock, toward where we came to see nothing more than darkness surrounding us. The room had disappeared into the dark shield of the night like a theater shutting off its lights for the show.

377

"Jerry," I whispered, barely able to see his face amongst the growing twilight, "more than anything, I need you right now. I can't do this alone. There might not be any cosmic reason for you to be here other than coincidence, but I need you now." And at once, it dawned on me, and I smiled. I didn't know why. Maybe it was because, after tonight, nothing really seemed frightening. Disturbing, sure, but never frightening. Maybe because I knew I was finally at the end, and what happened only twelve hours past seemed like decades ago. I moved in closer to Jerry, whispering confidently, "Don't trust your vision. Trust your mind."

He quivered his lip, trying to speak for a moment, but immediately stiffened up and lit another cigarette before opening his palm, indicating that I should lead the way.

We trudged through the next door, nearly falling over one another once again, just as "O, Fortuna!" was on its last verse. The third room was filled with an inescapable vibrance that the other two lacked, jolting with a tremendous jubilance and mercurial joy. It was a third the size of the previous two rooms but was filled with the most life. About thirty couples, each wearing masks and completely nude, were splayed across the room, humping one another's brains out. But, as soon as our presence was known, each male dismounted their female counterpart and watched us. They stood erect, pointing at us momentarily in suspended disbelief before their counterparts embraced them in a ballet like dance. The ending of "O, Fortuna" choreographed a massive cotillion amongst them, directing us to our final destination. The erect males and their partners danced collectively, making arrows of their bodies, as the final veil, unmoved by myself or Jerry, was split apart with phantasmal ease.

"God damn..." Jerry uttered.

Beyond the awning, a man, unctuous and sly, with a long horse face and pearly white teeth, smiled from ear to ear and held out an open palm, gesturing for us to sit. He was playing solitaire and only took a break every few seconds to look at us as we approached. His smile wilted almost instantly into some kind of invidious smirk. The room was far more diminutive than the previous halls, more of a study than a banquet area. Behind the man was a framed print of Francisco de Goya's "The Dog" as well as a makeshift bar just beneath its frame. It was completely barren save for two luminous torches that lit the room amply.

My head began to twinge with the fuzziness that comes from a mixture of too much liquor and not enough sleep. My focus was beginning to fade, switching between the host's smile and the Goya print, as we had a seat on the opposite side of the table. I put pressure on my eyeballs with my thumb and forefinger and rolled them about in a naive attempt to regain my composure. Blinking lightly to move the phosphenes out of my vision, I found Jerry in a stupefied state, his jaw slack and visage contorting in awe as he marveled at the man across the table. He jerked his head back toward me and then back at the man. I soured my face and shook my head at Jerry and his attempt to get me to care. The man stood and raised his hands up slightly, opening his palms outward.

"So foul a night I have not seen." I mumbled in jest to no one in particular.

"Samuel," the man said, "Bear witness."

He caught my attention immediately. "Bear witness to what?"

He smiled briefly. "To the end."

"You're senator O'Brien?" Jerry blurted.

"The same." He answered, folding his cards up and putting them under the table.

Jerry scrutinized the senator's face as he leaned against the table. "You look different somehow."

I caressed the stubble on my chin and cheeks to make it look like I was concentrating really hard. I even squinted harshly to give the appearance of awareness. Thrusting his hands down onto the table and breathing through his nose, O'Brien dropped his gaze onto me.

"What happened to your accent?" Jerry said, cutting him off before he could speak.

O'Brien laughed lightly before sitting down, placing both of his index fingers into a steeple and crossing it over the bridge of his nose.

"I'm a senator from Kentucky, born in Illinois. How else was I going to get elected?" O'Brien opened his hands, speaking now in a mocking, southern drawl. "I speak like a derrrnnn fool from time to time but 'spose that's to give that good 'ol southern voter a 'good 'ol boy' to vote fir. Plus, der's nothin' more disarming than speakin' like a damn fool." I raised an eyebrow, confusion painting its masterpiece on my face, as O'Brien committed himself fully to his mocking Southern caricature. With each word, he began to swing his cocked arms more and more wildly from side to side as if he were dancing a jig. "My, uh what's the word, treacle? Yeah, treacle. Treacle about the environment, and fracking are little more than fanfare for the voters. Political theater if'n ya will."

Jerry shook his head in wild amazement. "Do you mind if I record this?"

O'Brien swiftly switched his gaze back over to me. "By all means, there isn't much I can say that hasn't already been seen." O'Brien said, switching back to his normal accent as he dumped three ice cubes into a crystal glass and dropped three more into another glass, before filling it to the brim with a brown liquor, "It'll never make it to print though."

O'Brien passed me the glass and held his own in tight. He rubbed the rim of the glass with his index finger lightly before taking a drink. I looked up from the glass to find O'Brien scanning me carefully, his eyes filled with a luminous gleam.

"How about you Sam? How's your night been?" O'Brien said with a cloying frown.

I could feel the bags under my eyes weighing my face down. "Fine. Doesn't feel real I guess." I fingered the liquor in my glass, swirling it around and getting lost in its ripples before taking a sip.

Staring at me, O'Brien tilted his head, making his chiseled jaw and dimpled cheeks more prominent. "Do I feel real to you Sam?" His voice was smooth like honey, dripping with a dulcet tone. Exactly what I'd expect a politician to sound like.

Jerry looked at me then back to O'Brien. "If I could, Senator, I believe this could be a great opportunity to get a few prelimin-"

"Why are you here?" O'Brien interrupted, calmly staring Jerry down.

Jerry became silent as he slanted his head in my direction and leaned forward to get a better look at my head slumped over my chest with my chin digging deeply into my clavicle. I slowly lifted my head up and took a drink before flicking my wrist and shrugging my shoulders ambivalently. I gulped down about half of the scotch. It worked, waking me up but only insofar as to speed up my heart rate. My heartbeat, thrumming its pulse so that I could feel it in my mind, was like a pounding audio emission, begging to break free from my chest cavity. Still, I was able to straighten up.

"I have to be here," I said coldly, dismissing his question to Jerry, "I want to keep my job, so, I- well, I don't know. It seemed like a good idea at first."

"And now you're not so sure." O'Brien pouted his lips and nodded his head in understanding, the way a parent consoles an infant.

I laughed and looked around the room to break from his stare, shaking my head as I did so. I wasn't unearthing much confidence here. "Like I said. I thought it was a good idea at first."

"A good idea." O'Brien said in contemplative thought, "Carousing down the streets of LA and mingling with local malefactors. Is- is that what was going to give you your job back?"

The Call of the Void

I leaned over my whiskey glass, gazing through the translucent side. I lit a cigarette and shrugged. O'Brien finally reached a level of sincerity befitting a Senator. His body shifted and he sat upright, ditching his lightsome antics. Jerry sat upright as well, rubbing his cheeks and staring at O'Brien with staid attention as I slouched in my chair and swirled my whiskey. "It's a start..."

"You don't need to worry about him, Senator." Jerry laughed reassuringly, grabbing my shoulder and shaking me playfully, "Uh, Senator O'Brien, if I may, I actually feel like this is quite fortuitous... seeing you that is... as I'm tasked with writing about the Due Process Protections Act which would amend rules on criminal prosecution and procedure..."

O'Brien's eyes were tattooed on me. His gaze never faltered, like a hawk stalking a felled rabbit. I gave him a quick glance to let him know I could see him, but his eyes were stone, filled with a calm, indefatigable gnosis.

"... to issue an order confirming the obligation of the prosecutor to disclose exculpatory evid-"

"A story! Is that what you want? Something to give to your bosses over at Reuters. Is that it?" O'Brien blurted.

Jerry paused. "How did you know I-"

"I know more than you may think."

I snorted a pathetic laugh that seized the attention of both Jerry and O'Brien. "So fuckin' what? Some elite senator operating within some kind of weird cabal that's into-" I looked back and indicated the pitch-black room behind me with my drink hand, expecting to find one of the burlesque dancers, but instead finding an empty room. "Well, whatever. Paint the schizophrenics on the message boards surprised, we've just stumbled upon a senatorial conspiracy. Ni-nice touch with the stairways though. If I wasn't on the verge of some drunken neurosis, you probably would've gotten me." I raised the glass to my lips but shot it down instantly to finish my tirade. "Oh! And the media is involved too? Stop the presses! Or, don't."

Jerry looked disappointed and somewhat confused at the situation we were in. I shared the sentiment. He casted a glance over to me like the one a scolded dog gives its master, hoping I'd have answers. I didn't. My heart actually broke for a moment. I almost opened my mouth to tell him I was just as confused, just as... anxious. Instead, I gave him a quick nod to assure him that everything would be okay and that I'd be sure he gets what he followed me here to get.

"Fair enough. But do you really believe that tonight was about *that* out there?" O'Brien pointed at the entrance and emphasized the word 'that'. "That your 'journey' was about indemnifying the innate misanthropy you harbor. That this was a way for you to somehow free yourself from mankind and live like some sort of anchorite in the woods?"

I shot up. "So, what? You're responsible for all that tonight?"

"All of what tonight?" O'Brien asked, a little dithered, as if he had said too much.

"That." I pressed.

O'Brien reeled back. "What?!"

"That!" I shouted, pointing a finger indiscriminately.

The Call of the Void

"What're you talking about Sam?" Jerry whispered.

"You're gaslighting me." I scoffed, waving O'Brien off as he smiled incredulously.

"When was the last time you went outside, Sam? Surely you aren't that far removed from the collective consciousness that you haven't noticed that the shadow no longer wishes to merely coexist but rather consume. No, no, no, I'm not capable of that level of chicanery." He laughed warily, as if he didn't believe his own statement. "And you, Sam? Where is your shadow? Where would it hide? In what labyrinth might we find it? Or is it here, now, speaking with us?"

"What the fuck would you know about shadows? And me?" I croaked.

"Not enough. Not enough to get over on you, that's for sure. Your vision is opaque, but your mind is clear." O'Brien narrowed his eyes and deepened the tone of his voice the more he spoke. "Most Doctors of Philosophy are off on grants studying the consciousness of AI but not you; you are Samuel Killian, the youngest tenured Philosophy PhD in UCLA history, still trying to keep the kids up to snuff on rudimentary matters of life, death, the absurd, ethics, et cetera. You are what matters in this life, but you will never matter. How does it feel?"

"Fuck you." I slurred, "You and Felix put this together."

"Felix? Dr. Felix? Hah!" O'Brien roared, cocking his head back with an exaggerated guffaw.

I took a drink. "Whatever y-you cocksucker."

"You think of that one all on your own Dr. Killian?" O'Brien shifted in his chair, clearly growing impatient with my responses. "Sam, all I want is to talk. To give you the Socratic dialogue you've never had. To convince you that this way, our way, is the only way. I know you've had a frightful night and the burden of proof is on me, but I assure you, this was the only way. I've been watching you for a long time Sam. A *long* time. Youngest tenured professor of philosophy at UCLA? Now how on earth did you accomplish that? By being such a precocious young lad with a penchant for Phenomenology?"

Perspiration from the scotch glass dripped over my fingers and onto the table. I eyed it for a while, hoping he wouldn't say another word, that his body would evaporate, and I could leave without looking him in the eyes once more. I took a long sip from the glass, hoping once more that he'd disappear.

"Do you remember that article you wrote for the Times when you were 16? That's when I took notice. And that last article, so fluffed up with jargon and bombastic pomp beyond the average man's comprehension, that they wouldn't even publish it?" O'Brien pointed at Jerry with his free hand, "That's when I took action. The only great thing you ever wrote was your first and last. For as laden with fustian and sanctimonious probity as they might be, they were hardly bereft of substance."

"So, that's it? What you're saying is I'm nothing? I'm a nobody? You've given me everything? I'm a-"

"A fraud?" O'Brien interjected, his smile an odd farrago of equanimity and bewilderment, "No. I would never waste my time on a fraud. No Samuel, the truth is, you got cocky. You got lazy. You let your knowledge of people listening get in the way of what is truly in your mind. You began writing, not to give the audience your forethought on the world, but rather to write what you thought others wanted to hear. You missed something in the middle of your graduate education somewhere. Erudite? Yes, always. Perceptive? You're the nonpareil. A genius? Well, there's still time. But a pioneer? A freethinker? Not lately. You needed me to get you forward. For although you may have lost something in the middle, you never needed academia to bring you forward. All your best thoughts are right there, deeply imbedded in your consciousness. Your ability to reach only a few was what mattered all along. You owe these people nothing. They're nihilists only so far as that they have no care or direction, not in the sense that principled nihilists recognize absurdity. Their nihilism is strictly born from indifference, and the price of their nihilism is slavery. As pessimistic and spiteful as you are Sam, you still care. I can hear it in the tremors of your voice. I can see it in your self-destructive drinking and smoking that will surely send you to an early grave but will give you the respite from watching your fellow man kill himself. With us, Sam, *you* can make a difference." O'Brien's sincerity washed over the room, and I couldn't help but feel a tinge relieved. "I know the choice is difficult but tell me Sam, how will you navigate your vessel through the Scylla and Charybdis of the modern world? Will you choose the side that controls, or will you dwell amongst the lower consciousness, feasting and cannibalizing itself with its reptilian mind?"

I looked up and pointed to him with my free hand. "That's from my lecture. F-from-"

"I know. You referenced Nozick, who you had previously cited largely in your Graduate Thesis. That happiness and escape are not everything in life." O'Brien eased back into his seat, "I've always been here, Sam. The father you never had. The direction you've always craved. You needed me and I was there and now I'm here and I need you."

I propped my elbows on the table and stared at the ice melting away inside my glass and the thin film of tap water it left behind. "For what?" I asked blandly, rubbing the exhaustion from my eyes.

"For this," he answered, motioning with open arms around the room, "I need a successor."

It took everything in my power to steady my hand as I raised it to my face to light another cigarette before answering him. "What is 'this'? And w-why me? I mean, don't you have a family? A son or daughter? Someone else closer to you?"

"No families. Never. We always go outside of our lineage. It's one of our few rules. Some look for talent at private schools. Others look for their initiates in orphanages, or hell, even spelling bees."

"I wasn't... any of those."

"Quite right. But do you know who oversees all publications of Time magazine? That's right Sam. It's been a long time coming and I'm here to provide you with a little context in the hopes that it might persuade you to," O'Brien paused, swirling the ice in his glass, "see my side of things. Context is everything after all and, without any context, humans would wander aimlessly through life. We provide that context, not to show that we're right, but to change the world as it befits man. People are now hopelessly dependent on our information and will never go back to thinking for themselves."

I laughed, still in disbelief, moving my hands to the back of my neck.

"Tonight, was about three things Samuel," O'Brien raised his right hand showing his thumb, index and middle finger, "Truth, Power and Slavery."

The torches near the door flickered, making a whipping motion that flashed over his face, shading and illuminating him simultaneously.

"Do you know what we-"

"Who's we?" I interjected, "You keep saying 'we'."

O'Brien paused to reflect on his answer. "Fortuna Imperatrix Mundi, of course. We are, quite literally, the tethers of Fate. Dedicated to order. In service to mankind's one God. We are the imperialism that still exists in every country. Whereas we used to colonize gold, rubber and anything else, we now colonize the American mind. We are the demiurge of this modern world. The order it needs and the direction it so desperately craves. Now, personally, I believe your word 'cabal' is a little derivative. Cadre is a better word. Of course, 'we' never thought to deign ourselves with such a moniker. But we did coin a term, years ago, to accurately describe the hoi polloi out there. It isn't known in any textbook and escapes modern usage except for those of us in the purview of its argot. It is 'servusluxus'. Slave to luxury. As long as the people can have the nicest commodities, or at least the ability to 'Keep up with the Joneses', they will live in servitude to us. To Fortune, that is. They'll remain whimsically captive and do it with a smile on their face. The greatest irony ends up being that what they search out to free themselves from boredom, ends up being what ultimately enslaves them... Luxury is the ultimate primrose path."

I slammed my glass down. "Fortune? Really? You're fucking with me. Cut the act."

"Act? What act? When man prays at night to God, or Allah, or Jove, or whomever, he's really praying to Fortune. Man has always been praying to Fortune because man is always praying for something more or better for himself, making him incredibly easy to control."

"Fortune," I said, trying not to laugh, "is just a concept. A mythical invention of ancient polytheists. She isn't real."

"That's incredibly foolish. What makes something real? Physical manifestation? A thoughtless observation for someone such as yourself to make Samuel. What then of consciousness? No. Fortune is more than an idea."

"Your idea."

"No! An organic idea, born long ago, that refuses to die. People don't have ideas; ideas have people. You of all people should know that."

I had almost forgotten Jerry was sitting next to me when he stuttered, "W-what is this?"

O'Brien sighed through his nostrils. "Okay. Tell you what. I'll put it in terms you can understand Sam. Plato's idea of forms was entirely accurate. However, there is no way to ever truly reach the form, right? The form is merely an ideal state of being. We put forth the closest thing to a form. That's what I need you for. I need you because I need unfettered, forward thinking into human consciousness. Everyone always questions what the future will look like; floating cars, instant meals, abundant resources. The truth is that what we want is a working consciousness in the future. Not to instill some authoritarian dystopia, but for the betterment of mankind. We want to eliminate free will so that we may actually travel forward in time. Not, as many think, like some sort of sci-fi time travel machine, but a possible future that can be seen. Without free will, forward time travel, as we see it, becomes possible. I need you Sam. I need what you know."

"Plato's- t-this isn't." I sighed deeply, "You're misinterpreting Plato's forms."

O'Brien pounded the table with both his fists. "How fucking dare you tell me I'm misinterpreting the mind that made all this possible!"

I cut back at him sharply. "I doubt that very much."

"And what of Plato's noble lie Sam? What of the philosopher kings? You're to tell me this thought, that democracy is a farce and humans need a watcher, has never crossed your mind? And you're telling me you'll dwell amongst the lower forms after they fall?" O'Brien inhaled through his nostrils, composing himself once more, "I need you Sam. Because it is Philosophy, not psychology or sociology or even anthropology, that makes the human mind tick. It is Philosophy that is the root of all human endeavor."

"Because I'm just that damn good, is that it? I don't buy it. There are others in my own department better-"

"I don't know them. I know you. I haven't read their work. I have read yours." An almost honest smile made its way to O'Brien's face as he explained this. "Consider it a reprieve, Sam, for years in servitude as an educator."

"But, why?" Jerry asked, finally adding something of substance to the conversation, "Surely society can thrive outside of this- well, whatever this is."

"Because man needs it. Because WE spin fortune. Because, especially today, the only thing you have to look forward to as a distraction for your tremendous failures is whether or not a package from Amazon is waiting for you at your doorstep. And when it's all destroyed, when society has had enough, man's only luxury will be the loss of his sanity. The fickle nature of the Rota was a concept invented by man. Man's actions are capricious and random; that is the Rota Fortuna. We may plan the *world's* fortune, but *man's* fortune is left entirely up to his unpredictable nature."

"Not all of mankind is as you describe though." Jerry said, looking at me for approval. I drank from my glass.

"But they are. Similar to the cat that stares out the screen door in the hopes of reaching the outside world before the sliding glass is shut, it needs a master. The cat stares endlessly, in the hopes of meeting that one slice of life it may never capture under normal circumstances. Even under the threat of death from the uncertainty of the unforgiving outside realm, it wishes to experience something other than itself. That is man."

"And so, your purpose is control?" I asked.

"*Control?* Who is in *control?* Control is in the mind of the fool. Control helps people sleep at night. People have not been in 'control' for some time."

"Plenty of people are active dissidents to many forms of control." Jerry said, "Average Americans always fight for what they believe is right and just."

O'Brien raised his right eyebrow, a look of sinister delectation growing on his face, as he stated simply, "And fight though the tide may, the moon will always control it."

Jerry snorted lightly out of his nose, fumbling to find his next words. "Dissent is comm-"

"We filter dissidence the same way we control the counterculture movements of the world. We commodify them. Not for the money but for the pervasiveness of it. We put their slogan or flag or cause on a shirt and it just becomes normal, and the message is lost. We humans have a terrible desire to wear our cause on our sleeves."

"It's no secret that politicians make decisions and pacts behind closed doors," Jerry continued, "but the idea of a unified group like the illuminati is just so trite and-"

"Quite right, but was it not Umberto Eco who perfectly stated, 'Everything that happens in Troy was plotted the day before on the top of Olympus by the gods.' Conspiracies are as old as the earth itself. And here I thought you were smarter than that. 'The Illuminati'" O'Brien made a waggish gesture with his hand, waving Jerry off, "The word itself makes me shutter. Ya know, for being a secret society, there sure is a lot of information on them. But when was the last time you heard of Fortuna Imperatrix Mundi? Don't make me laugh, Gerald. That's an old bromide that helps paranoid people sleep at night. If they can believe that there is a force truly evil that is the harbinger of their woes and they can speak out openly about them, they'll consider themselves 'in control'. More than anything, these ideas provide precious little other than wish fulfillment. The paradox here is that the strongest altering of reality comes from conspiracy theorists. They see circumstances that are unexplainably, terribly out of their control and immediately go to secret societies and conspiracies to construct the reality around them. They've lost the perception to even think what's in front of them is even real. They hear voices and think people are following them. I suppose, in a sense, what we do is just that, but on a far more diminutive scale. You're truly a fool if you think that Rothschild or any of his constituents are nothing more than lower-level players in this. Rothschild? Rockefeller? They deliver my pizza and shine my fucking shoes. We're past that. There is no illuminati. There is no secret society. It's just us, out here in the open. We've been here as long as time has been measured, and we'll be here long after. Not me per se but us. The term 'illuminati' invokes an elicitation of evil. We are not malevolent. We just... are."

"Still, what is in a name?" I asked, "If what you say is true, then conspiracy theorists have to be on to something here. And if you're 'out in the open', why the ardent opposition to elitist conspiracies that come from the public?"

"Simple. First, people fear that which is too true, which they won't face. And second, people, so long as they feel they are in charge while talking about politics, feel that they are, well, in charge. Anything else would undermine and uproot their world. We aren't the ones ardently opposed to theories. They are."

"Too thin O'Brien." I snorted, waving his answer away, "Too thin."

O'Brien sighed with a loss of patience, rubbing his eyes with his thumb and forefinger, telling me that I just don't get it yet. "These are inveterate truths Sam, surviving since the West was born. The problem with conspiracies, for the theorist, is that theories are never put together until after the fact, and after years of effortless research that may or may not yield positive results. It's this tedium that wears on the human mind. The world will move on; it always does. Some theorists even get arrested doing what they believe is the 'right' thing by going on a vigilante hunt or searching for unattainable info, but the world doesn't care so they move on with the status quo—whether they were right about the theory or not. Conspiracies are not merely controlled opposition; they are engineered into an algorithm to make you watch and read more. You may start off watching some fanciful video on DIY projects but we will slowly start recommending crazier shit for you to watch and buy into just so we can get on top of it and get more views from the public. But, yes, you are right. There is some weight to the theories. Just not in the way you're describing it. And even so, the public perception of them will never bother the cause." O'Brien stared at me intently and shifted uncomfortably in his chair as an impatient scowl washed over his face, "Well? What other theories do you have?"

"I don't know." I sneered with an uncaring shrug, almost offended at the question, "Do I look like I follow that shit?"

"Depopulation is one we work at debunking at the press a lot." Jerry answered like a nascent student trying to convince his teacher that he's worthy of an audience.

O'Brien smiled. "Here's an interesting fact; 2000 years ago, the world's population was 150 million. A thousand years later the population was 310 million. Today, a little over a thousand years later, the world's population is 7.8 billion. Sam, you can't-"

"That's true," I admitted "But maybe the world is capable of having even thrice that populace. Science has shown-"

"Thrice that populace?! Shall we tear down Stonehenge to make room for duplexes? Bulldoze the pyramids for a Starbucks? Sam, look outside! Are you mad?! All good things must come to an end eventually. Modern medicine and surplus have bilked Mother Nature. Death was the one element that formed a pact to allow humans the ability to live here on earth. If it weren't for our consciousness, this would never be an issue. Instead, we have a world where everyone lives, and the lowest minds overpopulate, forcing people like me to take action and bring about collapse only to restructure in a way that will accommodate our surplus population."

"Bah humbug..." Jerry muttered.

"You said it!" O'Brien yelled in agreement, defiantly turning Jerry's remark on its head.

"So, what's your solution?" I asked.

"I don't have a solution per se. We're talking in theorems here after all. I'm just entertaining the question. Let's say that someone higher up did in fact conspire to insidiously depopulate the planet and bring us back to a reasonable population. Wouldn't-"

"What's reasonable?" I asked.

"Less than a billion I suppose. But let's say they did; would that be so bad? Would the painted pictures of them in your minds be the same if you realized that their initiatives were truly noble and virtuous and not vituperative? That they were the invidious boogeymen of a time, and the public knew it and could not prove it, but the true viper was the human race all along. Would you not have an understanding for who they truly were and are and what they are doing?"

"Okay, fine then." I capitulated, "What word would befit Fortune's cadre? Intelligentsia?"

"Oooo," he said, feigning a grimace, "That's a frightening word. It puts a lot of pressure on us to be smart."

I shifted in my seat, thinking of a way to get the upper hand on him. "You seem happy about all of these perfidious theorems. Why? What pleasure do you get from the treachery of your fellow man?"

"The why of our mission is the easiest answer. Most people come to that conclusion easily enough and with little help. The how is the hard part. And yet, it's made so easy. Why doesn't communism work? Why do we need an economy? Because humans can NEVER say no. Servusluxus. The bare minimum will never be enough. So, what's the solution? An agrarian society you say? No. That'll never work. Even if we reverted back to our pre-industrial economy, someone, somewhere, would find a way to spoil it by hoarding lumber, or stockpiling produce, just for a little more of the good life. But why do we do this? Why do we lord power over the masses? For their own good. And why, you ask, do I find it hilarious? On some level, for entertainment. I suppose we all have a nasty case of schadenfreude." O'Brien laughed, "The better question is why do people not have an even worse case of weltschmerz after everything we've put them through?"

"And that's why you picked my field. That's why you need consciousness."

Jerry cut in, trying to piece it all together. "What you do is similar to subliminal messaging then?"

"What we do is nothing like subliminal messaging." O'Brien sneered, seemingly upset with his question, "We are the demon Descartes metaphorically spoke of; we are a hypnotic suggestion, bludgeoning the world's mind into submission."

I scratched my head. "It doesn't make sense. If Fortune wants order, why the chaos out there?"

O'Brien's face turned bitter at the word 'Chaos'. "That's chaos? That's not chaos. That's Fortune manifest. An artificial chaos, maybe. But one that is acceptable. The world is the true form of chaos that, thanks to us, will never be seen. It is completely unhinged, and our objective is to simply find some order. So, which will it be Sam? Chaos or order? Madness or comfort?"

"And what about the Recusants? Konrad has-" I paused as the image of Konrad's face, his eyes bulging, and mouth twisted, covered from head to toe in blood, made its way into my mind. "Well, *had*, organized-"

"Konrad?! Organized?!" O'Brien laughed and shook his head, "Konrad couldn't organize a rape in a brothel. Amazing that he would dare make any tenants considering he's so keen to enliven a chaotic revolution. He was in over his head."

I sat in pensive silence before answering, "So, Konrad really has made a difference."

O'Brien's face turned to stone. "Konrad understands." He rasped plaintively, "And that's as much as I'm willing to say on that matter."

The three of us sat there quietly, our silence sundering an invisible line between the table.

"You need more. I understand. Shall we start with the *truth* then?" O'Brien mused, rubbing the stubble on his chin "Truth is everything. Truth gives power. Truth turns brother against brother and truth equivocates itself. The first truth is that we have been here forever. You see, the basis of history is dubious and nothing more than a set of fictional accounts starting as far back as Plutarch. The easiest thing to do is write a narrative. We can, essentially, contrive an equivocation based on a historic event and pay or even ransom to have that billed as the accounting of what might have happened. A civilian in ancient Rome or Greece, sequestered from the battlefield, would have never truly known the outcome of such events had it not been for historians. The truth lies in history, yet history is easily manufactured. The idea of manipulation struck a small group of patricians in early Roman civilization, and it grew from there. Ask yourself this; what made historians credible to begin with? And conversely, what made the populace so desperate to believe them? Initially, the trial period of altering history, which today seems like nothing more than an Orwellian fiction prompt, was a test run. A Caesarian demise here, an Etruscan King's death there, and the next thing you know we've driven directly into the heart of the Western world and Christianity the ideas we see fit. We began altering history at the Council of Nicaea and never stopped. The Gnostic Bible was something our ancestral benefactors could never allow. The Renaissance, the enlightenment, it was all us Sam, and all of these historical inaccuracies, no matter how small, are taken as maxims no matter what. Time flowed. Like a leaf down a rapidly convulsive river, time flowed. And, as time and technology progressed, we had to muddle the meaning of the word 'history' so future historians might look at it and say 'Well, that's not technically true but it's good enough'. And that was all we needed. If the older generations who had seen the spurious historical claims we manufactured could just die and their brood would listen, only marginally, to our version of history, it wouldn't matter. We would have already won. It only takes a small minority to pitch the ideas we have created to embolden a conflict amongst the masses. Most of history is apocryphal at best. The history books of the future will be filled with absolute fodder. They should have thousands of pages of intelligence, strategy and discourse but they'll instead be filled with partisan squabbles. Just like your history books now. A whole century covered in ten pages."

Jerry, shaking his head a bit with perplexity, snorted to announce his skepticism of the situation rather than his outright disbelief of the information. I leaned forward, my chin resting between the fist of my propped-up hand, begging him with silence to continue.

"Which brings us to my field of expertise on the situation of Truth; America. America. The great Mother of Liberty. The great freedom machine." O'Brien made a mock spitting sound on the floor just beside our table. "America is the embryonic example of chaos. America failed. The founding fathers tried, and their plan never came to fruition. It's time to realize this simple truth. It's time to realize that America never 'flew too close to the sun' but rather 'flew too close to itself'. America is not a Greek tragedy; America is a biblical nightmare. America is Babylon. America is no longer the land of opportunity but is rather the land of perdition. America is like a great skyscraper built by a stage designer; it's beautiful, large, and looks powerfully preponderant, yet inside, it is hollow, decadent and ready to crumble at any moment. With the world not far behind, America is the land of dishonesty. She is the motherland of 'coerced compliance'. What greater truth in 'coerced compliance' is there than the American constitution? The doctrine in which America believes it supersedes all other countries. Its very own global supremacy clause. The doctrine that is pissed on by all of your leaders and actively consumed by the populace. There is no Truth in America; not any more at least."

Jerry shot forward. "I know there are still investigative journalists out there who care about the truth, here, in America."

"Really? Now? Today? You believe this?" O'Brien's eyes lit up with an incredulous, mocking expression, "Investigative journalism used to be a virtue; something the bold would risk life and limb for to independently publish the under dealings of the elite to the public and swift action would be taken by the people. Now, everyone works for the system."

O'Brien idly sipped his scotch and placed the glass back on the table, the look on his face suggesting he enjoyed revealing all of this.

"Go on," I urged, "You have my attention."

O'Brien rested his index finger on his upper lip, his eyes deep in contemplation on what to say next. "Okay. Let me give you boys a deeper understanding of the 'Truth' at a local level. The notion that 'the government' or 'Big Brother' or any major bureaucracy is in charge of America is laughable. You two know full well that language always has and always will dominate the masses. Tell me, are you familiar with Zipf's Law?"

Jerry bared his teeth in a confused grimace, shrugging meekly as he looked at me.

"To an extent." I answered, "I read a book once on the principles of it, the frequency of words and what not. Seems to be a natural phenomenon."

The Call of the Void

"Natural, yes, but far from a phenomenon. Linguistic conditioning has created the world around you and there is no realty save for language. The idea of regressive usage in language is truly where it all begins. It's all in language. Always has been. Language is what developed consciousness originally. There is a place, right there in your mind, that you can bypass anything you see. Physically, you are blind, but mentally, you are the absolute epitome of thought. Some call it 'enlightenment'. But the truth is, language is slavery. For years citizens believed that censoring language was a form of control. It's quite the opposite in fact. Bloating the language is control. Here are some words; Racism, Lust, Rape, Violence, Greed, Gluttony, Kill, Hell, Death, Homophobia. Each time I say a word, a thought pops into your head. It is only by condemning one word and praising another collectively that you fall into a spell of emotional trepidation. Before these words existed, before you could call one thing this, that or the other, they were nothing. The action didn't invent the word. The word, and its definition, invented the action. You know this, don't you Sam? You've always known this."

I shook my head forcefully. "No. That's ridiculous. None of what you are or do is possible without language. Even if we reverted back to Latin, and made it universal, it would be impossible to review every nuance in modern philosophy and every intricacy in mathematics or anything else. Our evolution, our progress, isn't possible without an advanced language. What you're describing is poisoning our language, not bloating it."

"Who's poisoning who here? Every jape, criticism, commentary, and 'good point' written out on social media is followed by an image or—Fortuna help us—*meme* because people cannot properly convey their ideas and thoughts anymore without a visual aid. Language has failed us. And yet our collective intelligence breaks no boundaries other than that of simple aphorisms. 'Don't be the chaser, be the chaseé' and 'You're the tequila not the lime', amongst others, are symbols of our fruitless desire to seem intelligent without understanding intelligence."

I nodded my head reluctantly. "That's an obvious one for the modern era though. It hasn't always been like this. An image or a meme still needs language to operate."

"Why? Memes have reflexivity. They have the ability to become their own language. They can be wordless and still convey a meaning about the self, regardless of how miniscule. In the digital world, images will have no use for language. Memes are simply the grandiloquent semiotic communication tool for the lazy. Think about it. The human brain processes images complexly, and the more it discerns these images, the more they become symbolic, rather than objective. The more complex the image, the less your mind thinks critically about it, leaving you caring less about its representation. Abstraction makes the genius, as we say."

"So, which is it?" I asked, "Are you bloating the language or destroying it?"

"Both. Can't have one without the other. The bloating of language is far more effective though. Think on what your great progenitor said, 'The misuse of language induces evil in the soul.' It gives birth to a world of misinformation and ignorance, vastly more so than eliminating a language can." O'Brien paused and took a sip of his drink. "Now, most linguists—outside of the postmodern thinkers—will tell you just how deleterious the deterioration of language is. But they will end the conversation there. They won't move on to say how, over history, language has been picked at until it's the monster of Frankenstein we see today. You take a word, you add a negative connotation to its definition and then, eventually, you remove any portion of its original meaning. Language displacement, gentlemen. The hard part is removing the definitions in language. That's hard. You know what isn't hard? Getting people to give a shit. Some Ph.D. in linguistics starts mouthing off about which dictionary is compromised? We don't need to worry about it because everyone will shrug and say 'Who gives a fuck? The way I speak and the definitions I use don't affect my day to day!' and they're right. But over time, this becomes the new consciousness. The new culture. From the day you're born, you're cast into a world of foreign patterns and objects that are frightening and incomprehensible. Until, that is, language is introduced."

"So," Jerry began, thinking carefully about his next words, "This is, like, the 'deep state' run language program?"

I gave Jerry a mildly disappointed look.

"If you think for a second that the 'deep state' is organized or lettered enough to put even a polysyllabic word together in the right context, you're sorely mistaken. The government is an upside-down pyramid scheme. Academia, corporations, mass media, intelligence agencies, think tanks... these organizations, under our auspices, are what 'control' the truth and, consequently, you. Think about it, Gerald. When did you first hear the word 'Deep State'? Is there truth to it? Or is it simply another linguistic swell that has driven you into the world's new consciousness?" O'Brien passed his hand through his slicked back hair and took another drink. "And it all comes simply from wanting to get ahead and be immortalized in history. Take for instance the universities. Every single sycophantic PhD professor—present company excluded of course— feels the need to reinvent the wheel rather than take the best lessons from the past that they themselves were students of and move it forward. They use this solely to our advantage. We use these talking heads to push forward any chronicle we wish, government be damned. Because that is just it; your freedom of speech, which we utilize to our advantage, is marred only by your lack of education and your inability to think for yourselves when presented with a new idea or new theory from an 'expert' or what have you."

"Yeah, well, I don't see a lot of that going on. In fact, I can't get most of my students to read their chapters."

"Of course not Sam. That's because you look with your mind, not your eyes. You're not part of this. But that's what has lulled your students into a sense of security. Their ability to be brash. In fact, it's what's lulled EVERYONE into a state of hypobulia." O'Brien swung his arms wildly to emphasize his point, "America is already a third world country. We're just better at concealing it from the people. The only difference between America and a third world country is that in America you can hector the dictator. Your freedom of speech, while a tremendous privilege, is ultimately what pacified you against tyranny. Your ability to speak your mind to upper management is what makes you think you're in control, but you aren't. You see, like I said, we're not as procrustean as previously believed. Making proscriptions is the fastest way to dissent. Freedom, like everything else in this world, can be used as a means to an end."

"You love this don't you?" I asked, shaking my head in disbelief, "Explaining all this. About how terrible the country you use for your subterfuge is."

"It does give me great pleasure to see America's confidence in their democracy erode, considering it's the most obdurate country in the history of the Western World. It took 250 years to break it down, piece by piece. But people will cheer democracy's flight, for democracy is nothing more than an illusion. And what, might you ask, comes from this illusion? America's problem arose when it had too much faith in human reason. It was only a matter of time before human indolence consumed the very idea of critical thought and left a vacuum in its place. If you want to see the difference between what America could have been and what it is, look no further than the Walmart off Figueroa. Recusants standing in obeisance to the life they've given up juxtaposed with the hyper obese patrons waving flags and jousting on rascal scooters. For comfort seals the mind and pain opens it."

"What did you mean about freedom of speech?" Jerry interjected.

LeResche

O'Brien shot Jerry a chilling glare, his eyes categorically displaying to us both his contempt for me bringing him there. "Honestly, most people are starting to recognize that Freedom of Speech has run its course. Your messiah may have been Voltaire, but do you put the common good against individual liberties? Some say yes. Some say no. Most are too inane to even comment on it. And it's because of 'most' that 'some' will decide. Either way, it's inevitable; the first amendment will be amended and amended year after year until its final amendment calls for its disapprobation. And it won't be to the benefit of your congressmen, your president, or even your local governments. It will be to the benefit of the people. Or, so they think. When the truth strikes you hard in the face, it's only natural to try and reject it. What better way than eliminating people speaking about it. Idea 'A' is too scary? Censor it. Counterpoint 'B' is even more frightening? Censor it. Sure, both sides may argue they're opposed to censorship, but as civil discourse becomes more and more obsolete, they'll all fall in line. It will just be easier for people to have a force majeure censoring everyone. Both sides will fight for this in the hopes of raising their side, but it will ultimately bury them, and they'll be happy in their graves." Reaching down beside him, O'Brien rocked lightly in his chair and brought up a closed fist. He opened up his palm to reveal a sand-like substance. He began making a circle around the table as he moved his arm in a circumference. "There are two basic cycles in which the world is run. The first is scientific and relates to more evolutionary functions. The second is philosophical and explains the fleeting nature of democracy. The latter of which conservatives usually like to fit into some talking point, but it is truly all encompassing. Tytler observes that we have nine major cyclical steps in our 'democracy', which isn't even a true democracy but rather a bastardization of the word. Its parts include, in order, Bondage, Spirituality, Courage, Liberty, Abundance, Selfishness, Complacency, Apathy, and Dependence. And just as nature has a natural cycle, so too does civilization. Think of civil collapse like a forest fire. A controlled burn that is necessary to grow back better." O'Brien took the time to draw the first letter of each word around the circle of sand. "You are here." O'Brien said, pointing to the giant 'A' for Apathy. "America is not far at all from here." O'Brien then swiped his finger forcefully toward the giant 'D' at 12 o'clock.

I stared at the clock made of sand, considering my response carefully. "So, this is some form of dialectic?"

O'Brien waved me off. "No. It's a cycle. The dialectic—the historical one that you're familiar with anyway—can never truly come about so long as there is collapse and rebirth. Society stays in a cycle of oppression, never truly reaching the synthesis of the dialectic."

Jerry stared at the sand on the table with nervous hesitancy. "If societal collapse is coming, that means that civil war really is inevitable..."

"Ah yes. My favorite topic of doomsayers around the country. But no, Jerry. There won't be a civil war. Americans believe that a civil war is just around the corner, but the truth is that if anything were to happen, it would resemble more of an internal cold war with shadow governments playing the part. The populace would never hear a word about it. The populace would never risk its abundant supply of food, media, and dopamine triggers to fight for what's 'right'. A civil war does not happen organically. Usually, a mandate will be processed in which one party agrees and the other doesn't. The dissenters will boycott and eventually march on their state's capital and win. They will see that, through sheer force and will, they can win anything, and they begin to do this regularly. The other side will not abide and will eventually lash out, sparking your civil war. But as I said, that will not be happening anytime soon in the United States of Alzheimer's. Your collapse will look more like an agricultural blight, or something else natural, that'll require people to band together or die. And you'll die. But who knows? Gaia always cooks something up."

"How did we get here?" Jerry asked, a compunctious quiver growing in the back of his throat.

"We'll get to that in a second, *Jerry.*" O'Brien mocked. "But to put a final pin in this section, consider the *Truth*, in our day and age, like professional wrestling."

Jerry gulped. "S-so, the Truth is fake?"

O'Brien's eyes narrowed on Jerry. "Wrestling isn't *fake.* It's *scripted.*"

"Okay, okay, okay. So, you're essentially the *éminence grise* of some shadow government?" I asked dourly, "The voice in the emperor's ear compelling humans to submit to this... duplicity?"

"Me?" O'Brien mockingly placed his left hand over his heart, "Samuel, there are thousands of us. Worldwide in fact." There was another moment of awkward silence as Jerry and I shifted in our chairs, the frigid air in the room becoming almost unbearable. "It doesn't stop at human endeavor and historical malpractice; Truth, that is. It bleeds over into fiction. Into novels, movies, plays and, yes, even poetry. All those dystopian novels sold to young adults are, how you might say, 'controlled opposition'. The authors sell their souls for a book deal, they hand over the final copy for editing and we make it as bland as possible. People think they're so impervious to control after reading this excrement but it's all just misdirection to distract you from what we want. If you'd like an actual representation of our world, look no further than one of Dr. Killian's favorites; Plato's Allegory of the Cave. The world we let you experience is nothing more than a parcel of reality. What's more, everything I'm telling you has been said before by people who have figured it out. Books, movies, video games, the truth is right in front of your eyes. True creators and deft observers have been begging you to listen for centuries; people just never wanted to accept it. They prefer the realities we paint for them. Your argument about your students is actually quite astute Sam. Their disassociation with reality is the, uh, what's your generation's word for it?" O'Brien paused, searching for the word. "Oh yes! Norm. It's the norm. They'll miss out on amazing novels, short stories, poems and even movies that would drastically improve their lives and give them meaning. But they will never care. Our messages in the media are not for the older generation like I said. We don't care about voters, Sam. We care about the future. Vote for whoever you want! They all belong to us. The distinctive 'data bites' we drop in the media is a way to socially engineer the adolescents, not the adults. They'll forget you and leave you for a more favorable herd mentality. The world is changing Sam, it's a new generation's turn."

"I'm 28..." I said.

"Mmmhmm," O'Brien nodded, "But the younger the generation, the easier the exploitation."

"How?" I asked, staring at him intently, "How can you possibly accomplish this? And for so long? There are 7 billion people in the world and a thousand of you. How?"

O'Brien sipped his drink, maneuvering his eyes nonchalantly from Jerry back to me. "The greatest argument against free will is that we are inherently taught everything we know and see. We have no organic knowledge. We are cajoled into a direction to believe only what we are taught. From infancy, we are taught how the world works but we can never experience it without parental consent based on the fear that we may die. The only true organic thoughts of the world come from feral children that cannot even communicate with us. This is so real that there no longer happens to be a difference between externalism and internalism. How certain are you of any one thing? Do you remember what you did this morning Sam? I mean, you're the Doctor, and I'm certainly no expert but, what truths are there out there? Are there any? Or are people far more concerned with doubts? Doubts are what we live on. Doubts are what keep the wheels greased and spinning. Earlier, you had thought that we belonged to the illuminati. We want that. We want people believing conspiracy theories because it keeps them ignorant to the Truth. We want people to believe that Jews run the world, and that 5G causes pestilence and whatever else. And that isn't because we want to hide the fact that we are some evil empire, but rather to manifest doubts that keep us within the range of plausible deniability. And please don't be concerned with the information I'm giving you. Your misgivings are nothing more than the accumulation of knowledge you've been handed by your parents and us."

Jerry wrung his hands nervously. "And that's where your power comes from? Conditioning since birth? Built around some sort of post-truth hyperreality?"

"Power. Power is an interesting word. Power suggests that we force you to do something. We don't. We have never forced any citizen's hand. Period. We merely use influence and context to, say, change the world's blueprint. You see Sam, influence is what is turning the world's consciousness from dualism to physicalism. By influencing truth and desire into what is said and accepted rather than what is mathematically justifiable, we can transform the free will of consciousness into nothing more than a biological, or mental, imperative. Through language, we can make will an impulse rather than a choice. Take for instance, the means in which knowledge and epistemology is constructed today. Following the 'We cannot be that dumb' argument, Google has become optimal in becoming mankind's newest form of heuristic rationale. Cut out any long-term problem solving, and you're left with one database for all of your 'short' answers—our answers. It's really that simple. We take advantage of mankind's biggest vice, indolence, and we use it to our advantage. Simple as that."

"So, Google is part of this?" Jerry said, writing intently on his notepad.

O'Brien let out a little air that I interpreted as a scoff. He ran his right hand into his herringbone vest's pocket and pulled out a gold cigarette case. Grabbing one of the five remaining cigarettes, he lit it with a gold-plated zippo. "I don't think I'm making myself clear," O'Brien sighed, spitting little pieces of residual tobacco on the table, "Google's influence is the least of your concerns. It's YOU that you should be concerned with."

O'Brien's cigarette was gripped tightly between his forefinger and thumb as his accusatory, pointing hand remained on Jerry for a few seconds. His eyes were tattooed squarely on Jerry's nervous countenance as the smoke built up so much that it masked his face. I took the opportunity to light another cigarette as well before answering him. "Aren't there any real investigative journalists that find this kind of stuff out though? I mean, the whole Facebook and Google trial was in the news a while back."

"And yet," O'Brien began, pointing his finger at me now with a sly smile, "Not a single man behind bars. Not a single man who cares." O'Brien's eyes waited for my response. "Jerry, how much follow up did Reuters do on the story?"

"Not much." Jerry answered coldly.

"Why not?"

"I mean, uh, there were other-"

"Not likely. It got killed the day it hit the floor. A circus act was put on to mitigate the raised eyebrows, but it was dead from day one. My point being that, without Truth, those who serve will always serve."

I leaned over, extending my glass out so O'Brien could fill it with more whiskey. "But still, how do you maintain such a high level of power?"

"It's not easy. One man watching a million ants is dangerous enough. But 1,000 men watching 7 billion ants is lethal. It's one thing to control the Truth and have people vote against their best interests, it's another thing entirely to get people to not look your way. However, it is easier here in America than anywhere else."

"Why here?"

"It goes without saying. Patriotism. Political patriotism, that is. If most people were patriotic toward their country and not their party, we'd never be able to get away with what we do. Politicizing issues is key in maintaining power and influence. By doing so, we can get the majority to vote against their own self-interests, no matter how unreasonable. American citizens have long forgotten the path of communality in life, and individuality in politics. As I've laid out for you, your world is controlled by special interest groups so cagey they never see the light of day. Your world is veiled in a way to keep you docile and obedient. The thought that Donald Trump, or Obama, or even Bernie Sanders is going to save you is uproarious. The president has long been nothing more than a figurehead of control to misplace any theories of *elitist* control. You, the American people, are the only ones that can save yourself. But that'll never happen. Every measure taken against this has been tattooed in your brain from birth to make certain you buy the next thing, watch the next show, vote for hope. And so many Americans fear globalism while never realizing international political power vacillates like the ball in a soccer match. One century one country is on top, the next another has taken control. China, Russia, and America are unequivocally the world's superpowers, but give it a hundred years and it'll be four different countries. The middling countries vie their time, search for data, and then transfer and seize power when the opportunity strikes. Still, it's laughable to me that Americans fear another Global power because we are actually trying to globalize the world into America. We want 7 Americas all around the world; ignorant, decadent, and blinded by obscure political patriotism. But blind patriotism is nothing more than a psychological effect of familial relations to keep everyone, or at least the majority, in line. In a true twist of wicked irony, you can see that the voters who don't vote are actually truly enlightened for they have accepted the inevitability of the system. They recognize that it is the corporations and special interest groups that control the politicians and, no matter who you put in, they will get their way. And if, by some small, divine chance, a true candidate presents himself, the parties of those respective candidates will never let them succeed. It doesn't bother the GOP that a real up and coming ringer for the DNC has 'extreme' ideas because the GOP is fully confident that the DNC will extirpate them from the system."

I nodded in agreement. "Right. That's always been a criticism of politics. It's obvious that voters vote against their own interests but why go as far as to supplant the epistemological process just for a skewed ontology?"

The Call of the Void

"There's the Sam I've been waiting to see," O'Brien smiled, his jawline jutting from ear to ear, "To answer simply; perception. Ontological control is the cornerstone of our mission, but it is wholly impossible without values, substance, structure, relationships and all other tenets of knowledge that make up our epistemology. Epistemological manipulation keeps people in their head. Ontological control makes them powerless. More specifically, epistemology is used to stop people from changing their minds with new information and ontology is used to keep it that way."

"I'm sorry. But what you're saying is- it's just- just fantasy." I finally blurted, hoping to sound somewhat cognizant, "There may be people that are under the influence of your," I moved my hands around, buying time to think of the right words, "'manipulation'. But not that many. I mean, how is it possible to change the nature of reality to this extent?"

"How? Simple. Make certain everyone lives the unexamined life. Make certain only a few can see through the veil. Make it so people preoccupy themselves with frivolity rather than critical thinking. We can say, write, censor and just plain create whatever we want and tell you it's fact. We merely have the power of influence; people make with the info what they want, and it is often backed up by whatever media they gravitate towards. They will quite literally create a reality out of fiction. Seem impossible? Look at it in the form of body dysmorphia, or even illusions of grandeur. You see in the mirror what you want to see, not what is actually there. And it's all riding on the backs of cultural hegemony. As long as we can convince the populace

417

that THEIR values are normative and eliminate any critical thought that would in turn allow them to see alternatives, people will believe whatever they've been told to believe. As an example, political partisanship is far from the actual party's original values. Partisanship reinforces basic values from any one person's upbringing. That's why it is so rare to see a person disagreeing with their parents politically or even philosophically. Philosophies, sciences, and even core beliefs are all entirely subjective and malleable, but with a reinforced idea of values, people see an attack on their partisanship as an attack on themselves. Remember, the biggest issue with partisanship for the servusluxus is the idolatry placed on public figures. Presidents, senators, justices, doctors, inter alia are all the new professional wrestlers on stage to be booed or fawned over depending on your party. And the one thing the left and right don't realize is that their acrimony toward one another is a linchpin to their own ideological beliefs. They may want the other side dead, interred or repatriated, but their lives would be terribly bleak without the other. They're the true bivalence of the system. A terribly, tragic love story. A perfect world isn't one without conflict. It is one deeply seeded in disharmony. That's human nature."

"I don't know what to believe. I mean this is all- this is-" I tried to fight off my stammering but in vain.

"Sam?" Jerry asked, concerned after watching me down my drink and vigorously rub my temples.

"Sam knows all of this because Sam is the leading expert in his field on this. Samuel Killian, the last of the great hermeneutics! But let's start off small, shall we? Given the present company." O'Brien motioned his palm to indicate Jerry. "I want you to think right now. Think about who you are. Think about identity, Sam. And now I want you to admit that your identity is as much a mystery as consciousness itself. Your name was given to you. Your beliefs were conditioned upon you. Your thoughts have never been your own. There is no grand, technological, microwave, sci-fi beam that tells you what to think. It is every day that you are told what to think from pre-programmed truths."

"It isn't that simple!" I yelled, slamming my fists on the table.

"Of course it is." O'Brien stated sternly as he leaned across the table before calmly resting back in his chair, "You think it isn't because you've lowered yourself to *their* standards. Look at you. You're resisting everything I'm saying. Just. Like. Them. You know it's true. You know that our culture is a paradox of itself. Again, just take a second to think about it. We condemn child porn but openly sexualize children. Still, decades ago, when we were more 'conservative', porn was frivolously cast aside as harmless and part and parcel of that era, but God forbid a woman wear short shorts. And the media plays right into this. Ironically, the media was made to make tyranny and malice harder to accomplish, and the truth a preserved asset. Yet they themselves perpetuate a level of malicious subversion that the World can do without. The even greater irony is that people understand this as a universal truth but will listen to whichever media source fits in their own system of values. Look at the dynamic of the Conservative and Liberal. They've completely changed. The Liberals stifle freedom of speech and have become quasi crypto fascists while plangently rebuking fascists. For Christ's sake! They've lost all common sense, gravitating to whatever empathetic cause rolls through the news that week. And most people wouldn't mind voting Republican if Republicans actually represented ancient, conservative Christian values, but they don't. They represent some bastardized version of 'freedom' which is solely concerned with helping the big business tycoons and getting the upper hand over their opposition at all costs rather than resorting diplomacy. They've been tossed around so much in the washing machine of 'Power' that they've lost any and all identity. They don't even remember where they started or what they ever truly believed in. Their history has vanished into the abyss. It isn't one side's unity that we fear, it's the bivalence's accord that would immunize our plague. Revolution and collapse will need to come before any real change can be enacted. There is no way around it. Contrary to your own personal beliefs Sam, enough people still read, and they read history and there are at least a small few that are not arrogant and patriotic enough to not see this happens to every nation no matter the size, power, and influence of its constituents. But it will never happen. We've created enough racial, partisan, and cultural conflict to keep everyone distanced from the only conflict that matters; class warfare. If we can popularize one group's oppression, we can delegitimize any other form of oppression that we throw at the American people by contrasting it with a seemingly banal connotation of equality until the entire state of the nation is nothing more than one large imbroglio. Our own self-interests tyrannize us. They always have."

"Maybe," I said, "But there are still those that question their own party."

"We want you to second guess politicians and those in charge until, finally, you're second guessing yourself and have no idea what to think. Do you take the pragmatic approach of the democrats that wish for progress and a better, cleaner, safer tomorrow that won't be run by imbeciles? Or, do you take the staunch, robust position of the republicans that wish to eradicate any tyranny in this world and live as individuals? You'll turn yourself upside down trying to figure out whether you want to live in a world of waning intelligence or foreign meddling until you decide to sit back, become passive, and recognize the meaninglessness of the entire thing. And these political parties allow the politicians to stymie their motivations. The Left lets identity politics drown out Marxist theory and the Right allows a type of Stockholm syndrome to swallow up any one of Adam Smith's actual principles. What people fail to realize is that politics were a gateway to diplomacy. Now, they are our mainline to conflict wherein we only care about our tribe being *right*. Political Parties are there for the specific purpose of being the bête noire of the opposition. Not to actually get anything done. Which leads to the most intransigent people this country has ever known."

"How do you do it?" Jerry asked, "How do you keep people from recognizing this?"

"Easy enough. Once the population has been manipulated into believing what we say, or at the very least fighting amongst themselves over what we say, we begin a very simple process of counterculture. If we can create the movement, we can employ it however we see fit. The Tea Party, Antifa, you name it. We use counterculture movements to our advantage. A counterculture movement gets out of hand, and we set up a boogeyman—see Obama, see Trump—for the counterculture movements to hate just so we can put our own opposition in there for them to vote for. When he's elected, we have them run the same shit. It's all cyclical."

"This means that journalism doesn't even matter then, right?" Jerry looked at himself in the reflection of the table briefly, "What I do is... what everyone does, is- it doesn't matter?"

"Spoken like a true nihilist." O'Brien sipped from his glass so quickly, it wasn't even apparent he answered Jerry at all.

Jerry's face grew pale. "But you're telling us all this. Sam and I could just write about it and-"

"And who would listen? What little repute Sam has will be washed away and you'll join him. Do you think Reuters would really publish this? And I'm not saying that like 'I'll kill the story before it hits the executive desk'. I'm saying that because it sounds like the palavering of a mad man."

"But it's the truth!"

O'Brien's smile left his face for the first time since he began speaking. His eyes soured and he pinned Jerry down with his glare. "What is it about what I've told you tonight that has left you confused about the 'Truth'?"

Jerry fell back into his seat before looking at me once more. "Sam?" He rasped pathetically.

The Call of the Void

"Frankly, Jerry," O'Brien began, pouring more brown liquor into both our glasses, "I don't really give a good God damn what you do after this. It's only Sam I need."

I gave Jerry a look of encouragement to settle him down. A look that let him know everything was going to be okay and we'd walk out of there together, even though I knew that at least part of that was a lie.

"Go on." I urged, "You wanted me here, let's hear the rest. I want to hear it."

O'Brien nodded his head, glad that we could continue. "As I was saying, we don't brainwash; we encourage. That's true power. Youth is always the best candidate to change the world; they'll always see their elders as officious reminders of what they must become, and any deviation from that is always welcome to them. We encourage young teens to be insubordinate and make a joke of authority by making it look cool. We encourage obesity through body positivity movements. We encourage strife—even amongst family members—by integrating politics into everyday life. And we encourage ignorance through abundance. The greatest kind of abundance; informational. Kiss critical thinking and even heuristic knowledge goodbye. The information age is the final step in America's cycle. Old Glory is living on borrowed time. Society will collapse and be rebuilt but we'll never need to worry about what information people find. Even how to find it. Hell, even dating apps now hire 'professionals' to tell you how to become more marketable. More. Marketable." O'Brien pinched his thumb and forefinger together and stabbed them through the air twice to emphasize the phrase. "Having access to unlimited information at the tip of your fingers immediately diminishes your drive and long-term thinking ability. You'll never need to retain information because it will always be right there. Google started off with nothing but good intentions, but once we got our hooks in them, it was never the same again. We capitalized on man's unquenchable thirst for indolence. We mold it until we're at the stage we are now; running to Google for everything. And, if you go to Google for everything, as, I'd say, over 90% of the world does, we can manipulate human consciousness without any sort of sci-fi, invasive surgery that was previously thought to be the only way. And even now, Google is two steps ahead of every counter search engine. When other 'private' search engines boasted of 'third-party audits', Google set up a monopoly of auditors to ensure they too were private. Of course, the majority's taste for Google meant they never had to go to such lengths. Most people are chillingly aware of their data collection; they just don't care. Google simply wanted to prove to the world they could. And did anyone ever stop and think it wasn't such a good idea to ask one source for everything? Or was everyone just happy with having access to unlimited information effortlessly? If you want to control man, feed his appetite for indolence."

"If this is all true, then is there even truly an endgame?" I asked, "Or are we nothing more than just numbers and shareholder value to you?"

"I'll reiterate Sam. What we are is not *evil*. Nor are we after any sort of monetary value. You seem to keep coming back to the idea that someone holds Power for the sole purpose of committing heinous acts. Humans believe that Power is such a bad thing, but we cede power to at least one other person in our lives. We grant a parent power to see the world as they see fit. We grant our bosses power to keep us in line. We grant politicians the power to pass our laws. Humans want civilization? They have to take the order that comes with it."

"But what you're talking about is control of Free Will." Jerry cried, "If consciousness and reality can truly be manipulated in this regard, our minds are not only someone else's but our will to resist is as well. You've taken away everything it means to be human."

"'Everything it means to be human'? Did you get that little aphorism off some inspirational poster from Facebook Jerry?" O'Brien scoffed before sipping his whiskey once more. "We aren't evil, if there even is such a thing. We just know what's best. Someone has to do it. Call it what you want. Bread and Circus. Instrumentum regni. Orgy Porgy. 24/7 News. It all comes down to one dynamic in the modern world anyway; money. Money is what turned the Native American soft and quelled their rebellion against their oppressors. Money is what made Christianity into what you see today. Money turned the world on its head. Don't get me wrong, you'd be no better under, say, an authoritarian communist regime. As a matter of fact, that would make all of this so much easier. But no, it isn't your economy that grants us power; its civilization. *Civilization.*" O'Brien paused, tasting the word on his lips. "A place away from nature where nothing, save your family, can harm you. Humans never stopped to realize just how safe they were there. Always looking for the next best thing."

"But *you* need money." I said, pointing to O'Brien. "You need it to make power possible."

"To an extent, yes. Money is fictious though. It's nothing more than paper. It may help grease the wheels but it's an illusory detail in the wheel of fortune. Which is more likely Sam? That all of us, here in our organization, have all the zeros we want in our account? Or that, since the dawn of civilization, Fortune has put society's best in charge to help mankind, backed merely by an illusion of power? Look at your titans of industry today. All of those multi billionaire CEOs. And that's nothing! They're nothing. There are trillionaires out there that we created, just so no eyebrows get raised when a currency crashes, or an empire falls."

Exhausted, I shook my head and rubbed the back of my neck. "I just- I doubt someone with that much money would not be-"

"Money?! God damnit Sam, listen to me and try to keep up! What did I just say? Have you not been listening? What makes one wealthy? Accumulation of gold? Property? Digital zeros? Certainly not just paper? That's it. Paper. We have a winner ladies and gentlemen! Paper!" O'Brien's face was one of disbelief and anger. I almost felt like I was letting him down. "How many people do you think pay to not be on Forbes's wealthiest list? Do you really think Oil Tycoons sulk at missing a paycheck for a day's work?! It's all numbers! Wealth is deceit, wrapped in illusory details, pitched to society in order to create a goal. Debt is no different."

The Call of the Void

I laughed. "You've created trillionaires, have access to unlimited cash revenue, and yet we're the slaves to luxury?"

"Don't say 'we', Sam. You're not one of them. You're one of us. And no, we hardly partake. And that is why we hold true power. It is our abstinence that keeps us in control. How many successful heroin dealers do you know that shoot up themselves? We live within our means yet have access to the world. At least, most of it. Where it counts. Myself? I live on a three-acre lot in a four-bedroom house in the foothills of Kentucky. Let the capitalists fight over life's greater luxuries."

"So, America's primary deficiency is in Capitalism?"

"Not really. Capitalism may be the best economic system to live in, but it will almost always become doomed from consumerism. You leave people to their own devices to let them buy whatever they want whenever they want and you are left in America, a country teetering on collapse with a national deficit that will never be remunerated. And again, it's part of the cyclical system. Capitalism leads to socialism leads to communism leads to capitalism leads to monarchism leads to... you get the point. Capitalism is, however, a useful means of circumventing the constitution or even the law. Check the social media wars. As I'm certain Jerry here can confirm, social media has become the staple of every American's 'intellectual' diet—pause for laughs—and if someone posts something that is a little too close to the truth or may even sway public opinion negatively, it gets removed under the guise of private ownership. And Money pushes us into the news and other media venues, not by way of bribes but

427

ownership. As of today, Jeff Bezos is worth over 100 billion dollars. He could live lifetimes over on ten percent of that in luxurious indulgence, but that money isn't about luxury; it's about Power. Take, for instance, the most recent pandemic. It was a major breakthrough for the 'oligarchy' or whatever you people call it. It diminished small businesses and allowed for bigger businesses to exploit the starving market. Bookstores like Barnes and Noble, which wouldn't have stayed open much longer either way, were beaten to death by Amazon. Amazon was able to, in fact, beat the living shit out of any competition; small or large. The phrase 'Moving Forward' that the news touted ad nauseum became America's moniker and the pandemic played right into our hands; make people hate moving forward, so you'll be grateful to go back to the way things were—and the way things *were* was to keep you dependent on distraction. That's how new businesses and trends get started. We hire a flock of people to run out to clubs, or bars, or concerts or political lobbies and we have them promote an idea while another alpha member of the group approves it. The people, feeble minded as they are, agree that the trend is cool. We take to social media with hashtags, make new products and make a fortune on the tacit influence that product pushes before rinsing and repeating. Do you really believe anyone would buy a normal white t-shirt for 200 dollars with a stupid logo on it without that? Advertising isn't there to plant a seed to buy our product or even to remind you to go to that specific store. It is there to remind you who is in control. Of whom you must serve. Of whom you must watch before every YouTube video. Of whom you must see before riding the bus. It is an expression of pure will. The common phrase 'I'll never buy anything that is overtly advertised to me' is completely fruitless. The deed is done. The purpose of us pushing products on you isn't to fatten our wallets; it's to demoralize you, to make you feel more hollow inside, to widen that ever-growing void in your hearts."

Jerry and I shared a look before I answered. "Meaning what?"

"Meaning the future is advertising. And advertising implementation in dreams will become much easier than previously expected. You see, the average American's dreams have been supplanted by what they see online and on TV. Nothing is fantastic anymore since the modern man—the last man, as you might call him, Sam—can find any phenomena at his fingertips. Dreams of other countries, dreams of exotic wildlife, dreams of the other part of town, all gone with the click of a mouse. And since dreams drive ambition, humans will passively accept the advertising playing in their dreams as fresh and interesting."

"This is science fiction. It's nonsense." I shook my head fervently. "You'd need something, or someone, in a person's daily life to influence that type of stimulus. There is no way it can be achieved through repetitive video watching."

"Who better to mold the future of advertising than educators." O'Brien raised his eyebrow and smirked at me. "*Public* educators that is. Teachers have become destitute and desperate for money and, if all goes well, will wind up advertising products in class. Those poor educators whose only wish and sole hope was to educate the students enough so that they could be independent and make a life for themselves, are now reduced to hawking subscriptions and memberships before, during, and after their class. These teachers, they live in Hell, but Hell isn't fire and brimstone. Hell is making a man or a woman desire nothing more than to change the world, make a difference, and then making them a teacher. Hell is hope in this world. Simple as that."

"You're fucked." I said, "This is a fucking pathocracy. You hear me?! A pathocracy God damnit! People throwing their lives away! Public educators-"

"Public educators what? Public educators should have half a mind to tell it like it is and they don't. They're stuck! They're stuck answering emails from parents about their daughter's nervous breakdown and their son's 'indoctrination', all the while trying to think of a lesson plan that won't offend their delicate sentimentalities or show them the real world that their parents have sheltered them from. Parents are so focused on whether public schools should or should not ban certain content and indoctrinate their kids that they forget to realize, with constant internet viewing, the damage is done well before they reach grade school. Their identities have already been solidified. But it isn't the poor public-school educators that have indoctrinated them, Sam. I sympathize with you there. It is the public-school system that has failed them by design. Many believe the public education system indoctrinates their children, but they do far worse. Indoctrination requires obeisance and attention. Rather, public schools let the students be their own bosses. And without leadership, discipline, character or care, students run amok. Instead, they let kids be the boss, and with that, we allow them to run a *Lord of the Flies* type situation in their own learning institutes. If parents knew the truth, they'd wish their kids were indoctrinated. For the indoctrinated can have their minds changed, but those that raise themselves in a vacuum will always stay the same. The ultimate simulation *is* education. Teachers stand around and make sure you don't kill one another. Is that education? No. We simulate what you think is an educational environment. But only *I* show you what's real."

"Fine," I said, throwing my hands up, "but there's only so much the nation can take before it acts against this. I mean, eventually, people are going to start to notice that their employees' inability to tie their own shoes and recite the alphabet is hurting business."

"Not if we all go down together." O'Brien insisted, shaking his head lightly with a monstrously toothy grin, "Who's going to care about the state of their employees when advertising can pick up the tab."

"No way. Advertising is becoming increasingly scant. The products are already there. Like you said, it's a system of ontology at this point." I said, lighting another cigarette, "Also, if advertising has already put the conditioning in motion, then you risk exposing yourself by pushing it further."

"How scant could it really be? You saw those people tonight. Did that seem like a collective consciousness ready to revolt against their oppressors? It's that time of the year Sam. The time for abundance. The time for people to actually think they are 'doing the right thing'. Ads push hard for Santa during Christmas because we need that illusion. Santa was the most brilliant idea ever propagated by Fortuna. If a household raises their child to not believe in Santa, we have lost a customer, but at least we've gained an individual that trusts their authority figures. However, if a family conditions their child to believe in Santa, like most do, that child will eventually find out the truth. That child will realize that their authority figure had lied to them but for good reason; that it's good for them or that they need those illusions early on in life. And while the child and parents think they have accomplished something great by teaching their child about the world and how it works, the child becomes far more passive to the idea of an authority figure lying to them and accepting the outcome when the truth comes out."

"But what you're pushing," I interjected, "from a capitalist standpoint, is nothing more than accelerationism. Everything will collapse if taken to its excess."

"Right. Yes. Exactly." O'Brien said, agreeing and nodding his head with fervor.

"I mean, at that point, you'll no longer have the ability to use capitalism to your advantage and-"

"Sam, the end game is collapse. I've been leading you to that this whole time. Capitalism helps line some pockets in the meantime and pay for whatever we need to, but the ultimate goal of any economic system is collapse. Like I said, money is merely a figment of our imagination, a prevailing yet artificial source of power. Numbers on a digital screen. I told you already, this isn't about money; it's about

Power. And Power comes from influence and exposure—the public's will to apotheosize those which they perceive in their consciousness as deserving of Power. If you don't know how the collective mind works, no amount of money will grant you Power." O'Brien's eyes were resting on me when he lit another cigarette. "And when the inevitable societal collapse happens, who do you think will be there to pick up the pieces? Who do you think will be there to rectify history? To educate the survivors? To provide essentials and be the savior of the human race? While children and adults who are too intellectually nascent and preoccupied with survival to usher in a new form of democracy, fascism, communism, or whatever—it doesn't really matter—begin to fight and distract themselves as they always do, we will restart the cycle. Society is, and always has been, built on that cycle. Freedom begets rights, begets acceptance, begets participation, begets collapse. Once collapse happens, a new totalitarian regime is installed, that regime is plucked from its tyranny and the ideals of prosperity through the form of a free market are made anew, with all previous generations being extinct or forgetting what happened to their society in the beginning or at least believing they'll do a better job. If we can get rid of those with historical knowledge—i.e. those with experience—we don't need to worry about the next generation; we'll be their parents."

"This is mad..." I whispered to myself.

"No. Quite brilliant actually. But Truth and Power are only the beginning. The key is in Slavery. Enslavement happens right here." O'Brien lightly tapped the left side of his chest. "Humans attempt to escape through vices everyday but what they fail to recognize is that they are placing themselves in a hellish state of captivity; one that is impossible to enfranchise themselves from. Many try, but much like Orpheus clawing his way out of Hell, they still need to glimpse at their phones, or a double cheeseburger meal or that incredibly infantile analysis of corruption at the White House that just so perfectly fits their own narrative. Being an individual takes hard work; not just from the metaphorical slings and arrows you'll receive from being a constant combatant of cultural hegemony, but because the herd will always choose the path of least resistance. And if you resist the urge to follow the path of least resistance, you will have quite a battle ahead of you. Americans, and humans in general really, never slowed down to teach themselves self-control and how to properly use technology. And the problem now, in regard to technology, is that it's never about what you need but what you want; and you will receive it freely. And yet those who resist are left with one burning problem; solidarity. The government and the corporations can only go so far. Do you believe the American people will have the perspicacity to recognize their own rapaciousness? The end of American intellectualism, if there ever was such a thing, is nigh. Slavery is only possible with ignorance."

"But surely there are people that have access to this. In the information age, it's impossible for none of this to come out."

"I told you before, all of this has been exposed for years. It makes for wonderful fiction. The truth is best hidden in plain view. What's the one book that everybody likes to use to describe authoritarian control? *1984*. Hell, we needed a book like *1984*. It gives everyone something to put what we are into perspective. Allow them to... well, complain if you will. Without it, a true, universal spirit, would emerge. But the information age is less about information and more about confusion. Social Media is the key to all information, relevant or otherwise. Here's an interesting piece of *information* that few are privy to outside this room. Around 10% of Social Media users make up about 90% of the content posted there."

"No." I shot back bitterly, shaking my head. "That's wrong. It can't be."

O'Brien smiled at my outburst. "I know, Sam. But it is. As of today, there are a little over 350 million people living in America. As of today..." O'Brien paused to reflect, as if he were checking the statistics in his mind. "There are under 75 million people in America using Twitter. That's less than 20% of the population. This is not including nuanced accounts. Now, to really fuck you up, realize this; factoring in my last statistic, less than 2% of America's population has the largest cultural voice in America. And then think about how they consume! They're tricked into believing it's the norm! That is why we created social media. To set up provocative events and have the masses follow some social media campaign or another just to 'out' anyone who goes against the grain. We don't have to be Big Brother. We've turned your peers into Big Brother." O'Brien laughed with glee, clearly impressed with himself. "What throws people for a loop is the commentary. People are never allowed to critically think for themselves. The mark of true intelligence is the ability to change your mind, but if you have users galvanizing your original thoughts and others accosting them, it'll only cement you further into your myopic mindset. The newest form of avarice is the one that wastes our most valuable commodity; time. Time wasted trifling over celebrities and social media fights and political debates and games that do nothing but rot our brain and trick us into giving the developer money. All at the tip of your fingers." O'Brien's smile widened as he rubbed the tips of his fingers together, "And, much like the social media of today, your voices, though heard by a small few, will be lost in a sea of insignificance. If you give every idiot a voice, true art and significance will never have a podium. Literature and philosophy, in our digital world, will fade into oblivion. Mankind enslaves itself on a daily basis whether through stereotypes, affairs or even just your response to another person. It's done by placing emphasis on their identity and placing them in a box that you have limited and created yourself. Like, say, if you meet a mechanic, you will now only respond to them as if they were a mechanic. You place them in a box, whether grand or diminutive, it makes no difference. That person will always just be that to you. A specter of the digital world. You all enslave one another; we're just better at it."

"And," I began, before pausing and drinking from my glass, "that's why journalism has shifted to social media?"

"Social media will in fact be the new mainstream media. Everyone their own journalist. And when everyone has become a journalist, the cycle of anecdotal expertise begins. Not only is everyone their own journalist, but they're also now their own doctor, their own scientist, their own teacher, their own everything. This is the consequence of social media a la the internet. All politicians will have a platform, and everyone will be able to refute or praise them. This barricade of frivolous information that enervates the mind will help bolster our efforts to eliminate any and all truth. And while the mainstream media sits on its hands and ponders the power of social media, they're never the wiser that they are being eaten up by the very thing they helped create; slowly fed to the human consciousness for ritual sacrifice."

"Okay." I said, pumping my hands to slow the conversation down, "But let's say that all this does come to fruition. Eventually, with regular people assuming the role of journalist, there will be a moment of self-awareness at what social media has become. It's only natural."

"Possibly. But remember, the parties will always be the establishment. Why do you think you never have any real progressive policies being pushed by Democrats? Why not have any real conservative principles flexed? The establishment has deemed it so. And any dissenters are seen as 'too radical' or 'dangerous outliers'. So, in turn, social media has become more about relationships than about politics."

"And because of its influence with relationships," I said, finishing his thought, "No one will ever delete it..."

"Therein lies the slavery of social media; it is nothing more than a propaganda machine that no one wishes to fight. What forwarded emails accomplished in days, social media accomplishes in seconds. Everyone knows it too, but they choose to consume their own brand of propaganda without having a conversation about it. So, when everyone is a journalist, they only fit what they view into a reasonable narrative that they have manufactured for themselves without hearing any other perspective other than oppositional propaganda. And what about Twitter? If I were to tell you at the start of the 21st century that a company could put every user's thoughts, as frequently as they wished, onto a screen and people would eat it up, you'd have thought I went mad. But look at its success." O'Brien reached into his pocket and pulled out a sleek black phone. "Tweets such as, hmmm, let's see here, ah, yes! 'If we had sex and you have no proof, we didn't have sex.' And my all-time favorite, 'Ate some period blood last night and 'ngl', that shit is taste'." O'Brien shuddered for a moment, "The man's bio reads, 'The smartest man in any room. Just cause I fuck don't make me dum.' Sic. Intentionally. So. Written. A room of one's own though, I suppose. And of course, this is not only liked but apparently celebrated as virtuous. It's becoming extremely difficult to be genuine and 'deep' in a world that gives everyone a platform. You've heard the old adage, 'Put a million monkeys in a room and one of them will eventually type *Hamlet*.' The internet has done that tenfold. But for every copy of *Hamlet*, a billion copies of *Battlefield Earth* arise."

"But there has to be some sort of competence in politics though. As backhanded and pernicious as politicians are, they have to have some semblance of," I paused again, whirling my hands around in the hopes of finding an answer, "I don't know! Articulation or decency. It can't all just be a circus for social media. Social Media was never set up for that."

"Social media is of course political. It has the power to sway the populace if you get the right people behind the keyboard. If, for example, we wanted to get a person out of their majority shareholding or even to resign from the Senate and they won't budge, we'll simply hire influencers and 'celebrities' to run a smear campaign, rife with racial inequality and language disputes so the chairperson has no choice but to resign. Conversely, social media is an enormous ally to politicians. For example, if the GOP or DNC needs to gain leverage over their opponent, or sway the vote in their direction, they'll open a satire Facebook page and progressively start to post articles that contradict their bases' points, making the opposition look effete in contrast."

"Jesus. I-" I paused and took a drink. My eyes were having a hard time adjusting to the room. "I mean, they've always had that tho-"

"We've always had that, yes. It's an old trick but quite potent now that anyone can access it. And it spreads with ease, no less. How many people do you think actually read the articles online? It's so much easier to look at pictures mocking the opposition than it is to understand them. Twitter, as the best example, has become plagued with memes and paraphrases of sentiments revolving around ennui, and even suicide. That life is hollow and not worth living. Americans think this is a new concept, yet it is merely new to America. To live an American life, one must maximize pleasure and minimize suffering. It is imbued in our advertising, education and politics. THIS is why the world laughs at us. The world, and very few Americans, are initiated into the lifestyle of true, daily suffering. It is America that thinks this is a new, apocalyptic concept. And what's the greatest escape from ennui? Fame. We used to see Faustian bargains where a person wanted fame, beauty or riches and they would receive them at great costs. Now, the same applies; only the people don't care about the consequences or great costs. Their dignity was never discovered, and they will do anything for the endgame of fame. A woman asks Twitter to 'Do its thang' so she can become famous and be on a Netflix series. Her wish is granted because everyone makes fun of her for being an idiot that would post that. The show is about exploiting her stupidity. She doesn't care though because she has finally 'made it'. Fame is fleeting; nothing more than a trifle of the 20th and 21st century. The concept of fame will be evaporated in the near future and only ideas will remain, if anything at all. And yet the populi eat it up. Social media is not an addiction. Rather, it is a parasite that leeches onto our sentimentality and drains us of our time, all in a century of narcissistic hedonism."

"And I suppose," I said, rubbing my temples once more, "there is no stopping this. This is the next phase in the evolution of mankind. This is the state of the world?"

"Stop hating change Sam. No one descends twice into the same river. The future is happening with or without you. There is no fighting it. You're an idealist and idealists always die at the hands of their own self-righteousness. Idealists believe they can change the world by being proactive and intelligent. The world doesn't change in the light; it changes in the dark. And change is perpetual. There is no hiding from it. We're in a state of massive confusion and civil unrest. All thanks to your founding fathers wanting to gain the upper hand over their own fraternity. And still, some believe America is a majoritarian democracy—that they have an actual voice in the decision-making process. Most believe America is a pluralist democracy. The truth is that it is entirely based upon an oligarchic dominion. Our best-case scenario has come true, and we are living it; politicians and CEOs are idolized and treated like celebrities. That's where the vehemence and vituperation come from. The political talking points nowadays are scant and meaningless to the average voter. The average voter wants chutzpah and their cultural identity to be represented, not their best interests that would otherwise bury them anyway. The great irony is that those in power on the 'left' are actually more in favor of conservative thinking with a predilection for money and power. They simply use the 'far-right' as a cover for their schemes. Similarly, those on the 'right' have many predilections for classical liberalism and use the social justice warriors and insane boundary pushers as their opposition to make their political points. If you stand on the opposite side and rebuke the opposition's extremes, you can stand on your true beliefs. You need an extremist to balance your ideas. Hell, say what you will about both sides' radical politicians, at least they don't break from their core beliefs and pander for votes. And thus, the country reaches its critical boiling point. Brother against brother. Child against parent. A tale as old as time, and America is finally living in it. People hate one another; they always have. But with the proliferation of media, the masses have multiplied their hate tenfold. And hate can only sustain itself for so long before it inevitably turns to collapse. All those flippant ideas the founding fathers so righteously progressed, flushed down the toilet for partisanship. I'm certain a finger on a monkey's paw went down in one of their graves."

I shook my head once more. "But that's- that seems... paradoxical."

"Paradox is one of the principal pillars of change. Paradox lays the groundwork for what you know in your heart isn't right but is just believable and tempting enough to accept. The right has decried identity politics so long they've created their own form of identity politics. Take, for another example, the left denying class in favor of a very small percentage of the population's feelings and acceptability. It merely demonstrates how tribal we are by exposing our ritualistic tendencies that seem almost counterintuitive to a homogenous America."

"But America was never meant to be built on a hegemony." I insisted, "The great melting pot is what gives us our principals. Different races, ideas, creeds, all of that is what make-"

"And it's what will kill you."

"Thanks only to you." I yelled. "The ideal America gives every individual a voice. There is no predomina-"

"Samuel, I'll stop you right there as this dialogue is growing tiresome and I am really not making any headway with you. Tonight, you've tried to analyze, as you always do, man's condition. You've attempted to gain access to the minds and hearts of those foreign to you. But in doing so have alienated yourself further from them, and in turn, them from you." O'Brien leaned across the table, his stony eyes transfixed on mine. "And brought you closer to me. You belong with us." He said finally, resting his forearms on the table.

"Belong..." I said, musing on the word as if it were some foreign concept.

"I brought you here so that you could be a part of this. You can create history. You can subvert consciousness. You get to stick it to those students of yours that are so dense, all it takes for them to get frazzled is to ask them to recite their times tables while smoke comes out of their ears. Consciousness, Sam. Be a part of what I'm doing here. Be on the right side of history."

"Perception, not consciousness, is what you are talking about. Consciousness is our ability to reason with a situation that is built on our-" I paused before saying the word as O'Brien's toothy grin grew wider across his mouth. "Consciousness is a state of thinking and being. It can't be altered organically. Only with substances."

"Not true." He stated plainly. "The mind is altered at birth to see what we are led to believe. That first day you're alive conditions you to see, feel, and act a certain way. From that day, you have a hole in which for us to hook our influence into. You prefer pacifism? We'll exploit that. You prefer capitalism? Communism? Patriotism? Christianity? Utilitarian? We have all the bases covered with every academic, politician and celebrity ready for you. Most people don't even know what consciousness is. They never realize just how precious and damning a gift they've evolved into. That's why they give it away so easily."

"It's not that simple. The bicameral mind will always be a mystery." I shot back.

"But we may find it. Consciousness that is."

"You can't. You won't." I insisted, shrugging my shoulders confidently, "It's impossible. No amount of science-"

O'Brien nodded slowly. "We're close. Wouldn't you want to see? To make history?"

"You can't!" I shouted, "There isn't anything on earth with the ability to extract or find human consciousness! That much I'm sure of. No amount of scientific progress, no amount of future technology can grasp it. It is the only, ONLY, thing magical and shadowy in us that will always remain a mystery. Consciousness. Ontology. These are areas which will always remain a mystery and never yield an answer with 100% certainty. It's in its nature to remain that way. And even if you could, why? Why would you?! You wouldn't. No matter how far technology progresses, the only thing sacred to humans here, on earth, is the mystery of life and death. And say we actually could transfer consciousness to a computer. Would our past memories come with us? If not, what's so different between that and dying? Between that and reincarnation? Our consciousness controls us, but our memories create our identity. That's why social science is complete bunk! You can take two identical beings and put them through the worst, most torturous, environment and still one will come out lively, spiritus and full of life and the other will be a shell, waiting for the sweet embrace of death. If nothing else, DNA gives us our identity more than anything. Our only real understanding from the mystery will be to wish that our higher selves are waiting there for us after death. That the dimension of time or whatever else can help us understand. Why? Why wallow here in this prison we call earth? And say now that this machine that harbors our consciousness, which is nothing more than an agent of control not unlike you, were to transfer memories, would we not eventually wish for our own demise? Would our consciousness not beg for deliverance? So, then the man who is about to kill himself, or the woman taking her last breath after a car accident, or even the couple dying of old age, should then say, 'take me, send me to the void'. For if it happens now or later, I have to say, 'What a beautiful, agonizing, and vexing life I have lived'."

O'Brien raised both hands just above his shoulder and clapped slowly. "Oh, Sam. You have no idea how much you need us."

I could feel my face turning red. "Answer me!"

"Because acceptance and complacency are the greatest psychological sedatives. Human minds are changing. They are seeing something objective and automatically giving a spin on it, no matter how wrong they really are. Engaging in our pathos—or bathos if you will—is where it all starts. Once we have you emotionally hooked, critical thinking is out. We don't force any information or reality on anyone. There are no top-secret brainwashing programs. There is only influence that people decide to build their reality around. A state of apophenia. Admit it, this is what you want. What you want to study. To change."

"But I want people to be free. To be happy! Even if it kills them!"

"Human beings were never meant to be happy. Whether that sounds insanely pessimistic or apathetic does not matter. They were meant to live, and only live, the life of an animal. But look where we are."

"Maybe." I said. I watched out of the corner of my eye as Jerry looked at me, concerned.

"But Sam, you must know that this is the only way. You're a student of history. You know that, even without our," O'Brien took a second to think of the right word, "'push', that this is an inevitability. The world needs us to make certain the transition of society, from collapse to rebuild, goes smoothly."

"What's the use in studying history if everything I know is 'apocryphal'?"

O'Brien's glare left me for the first time as his eyes trailed off and contemplated my riposte. "Hah. Okay. Okay. Sam. Listen to me. Someone is coming. Some rough beast slouching toward Bethlehem to be born. Soon. The time is murky, and it may not even be in my lifetime, but soon. Someone will be born that will transcend the human consciousness and will subvert the intellectuals, the talking heads, the politicians and the press. Someone is coming that we must stop. For the sake of order, and nothing else."

I laughed, bewildered at his apparent madness. "What the fuck are you even talking about? A prophecy? Yeats? You really are pushing your luck talking shit like that. What even is human transcendence? And why would you want to stop it?"

"Because it will usher in a new age of chaos far greater than man has ever known. Civil war and human wickedness will never stop what this transcendence will bring."

"It can't be worse than this..." I said, laughing a little.

"Let me ask you, since this is your field of expertise, what is consciousness?"

I shrugged my shoulders indifferently. "Consciousness is our ability to process and focus our thoughts outside of nature. Consciousness is what allows us to love, rationalize and, in turn, irrationalize. It makes us fear death but take risks. It's our computer... sort of."

"Precisely. Good answer. But how do you know that's what consciousness is? How do you know that our consciousness proceeds and evolves from what we understand of it?"

"It doesn't. Not that we know." I shook my head, "You've lost me."

"Let me break this all down as easily as I can." O'Brien sighed out of the corner of his mouth. "Your 'consciousness' is really nothing more than our will manipulating what you see. Meaning, we can change history to fit a narrative, but your consciousness allows you to question it. What we've developed, Sam, for almost a century now, is an ability to manifest and entice human consciousness to believe what we want. Your thoughts are your own. They're simply realigned with what we want you to see. So, yes Sam, you are a total fraud. And that's okay! You just need to realize that." O'Brien leaned back to let me digest everything he said. "I know you Sam. I know you study coherence theory in your spare time. I know you believe there is a missing link in epistemology's cycle."

"That isn't me. You don't know me."

"Not personally perhaps, but I know your type." O'Brien was speeding up his speech now, almost excitedly, as if he had me on the hook. "You were disgusted by what you saw tonight, no? The misanthrope, the polemicist, deep inside you couldn't wait to get to the end of the line so you could live under a rock the remainder of your years."

"I don't really care."

"Then you have become everything you hate. You've become desensitized to what you see. You've become, as you would put it, the 'coddled nihilist'."

With each waning whip of the torch's flame, a darkness began to envelope the room.

"I'm telling you all of this because you have influence, Sam. You are in academia. You've become a household name overnight. Drunk though you were, your message resonated with a large portion of the country. People have flocked to your cause. And it never hurts to have me on your side."

"My cause? I think you've severely miscalculated my motives and status at the University if you really think I can-"

"No. I haven't. People will be pouring in to take your classes on Consciousness and Phenomenology. Now that you have actual raw emotion that people have observed and can organize around, they believe in you; they trust you. And you can tell them whatever you want. They'll eat your version of the Truth. Don't you want to change history? Don't you want to be remembered and immortalized for eternity? Cross the Rubicon Sam, and decide what the future holds."

I took a moment to ponder his offer. My eyes wrinkled and twitched from exhaustion and my head was feeling as though it may implode from too much information or too much alcohol. I leaned over a little to stare at my reflection in the whiskey glass. A faint smile crossed my lips and I answered simply, "Non serviam..."

"Open your eyes, Sam!" O'Brien replied abruptly, an impatient rage gradually overcoming him, "Stop hating and fearing change and embrace it. Love it. Recognize that this is the next inevitable step in human endeavor. No more anxiety. No more pain. No more consciousness."

"This is all your doing! You've emotionally gouged the populace into being more anxious and destitute just for a fresh start."

"Possibly. But do you hear any complaints? The taste of the majority will always be the death of the individual. The commune always wins. You can tell your little Recusant friends that after they've finished 'playing' at revolution." O'Brien reached into his gold case to light another cigarette, "Or better yet Sam, wouldn't we say to the Recusants, and most importantly yourself, 'Victrix causa deis placuit sed victa Catoni'?"

O'Brien held up his palms and cocked an eyebrow with a certain air of confidence that suggested he knew he was right; that I should know he was right. He was fishing around in my head now. I could feel him there, preparing a riposte for every question I threw at him.

"I'm no one to decide the future of humanity." I answered, not entirely confident in myself.

449

"But it's happening with or without you. We're going to develop a new world, a new lifestyle. This has been happening for centuries. For millennia. Or would you still prefer to live in the past? Stop this madness Sam and help alter the imperiled fate of the 21st century. Remember as it was once said, the law is reason, free from passion. I need your reason now, and I need it without passion, damnit!"

I took another second to breathe, to feel the room collapsing in on me. Maybe he was right. "And yet, now that I know all of this, why should I care? Why should I join you? You've made it clear that we live in nothing more than an unnatural simulation of pure influence. What about freedom?"

"Freedom..." O'Brien muttered under his breath, letting out a quiet chuckle after the word, "You'd be amazed at the way you see the world without influence. All of your preconceived notions and stereotypes eviscerated in an instant. It's quite liberating, but also very dangerous. It could never be allowed. That's the price of civilization; your freedom." O'Brien sighed and slouched in his chair. "There is no amount of money I can offer you. There is no amount of companionship I can bring to you. I know all too well those commodities are fickle in your mind. No, instead, I can offer you agency. I can offer you a guarantee that you will have a say in this world. That you can sit at the helm of creating the narrative for America. You, like the lonely fictional author that creates the world around him, will be able to constitute what mankind is. You want your students to have a certain obeisance? It's yours. You want to see a more educated America? It's yours, within reason. Create the future Sam. You will be the best. Follow me and take hold of your fate."

The wind chill cracked against the wall behind him. One of the two torches blew out. The room became dark, its light fleeting like the souls of those above. I rubbed my head. I wanted a new life. I wanted to be respected and to be revered as a pioneer in my field. I could have it all. I could be that man I always told myself I would never be. Make a few changes and condition an entire country. A small price to pay.

"Sam?" O'Brien asked, trying to snap me back into the room.

I could feel Jerry's eyes weighing on me. His gaze was like a retroactive atonement for every sin I had the power to commit in the future. I turned to him. His visage was that of a broken man, a man ready to abandon himself in spite of the knowledge he had gained. He looked worried. He knew the temptation was far greater than any I had ever faced. Change the world for the better, but have the stigma of compromising human consciousness.

"I won't." I said finally, turning to O'Brien, "I quit. I quit UCLA and I quit this. I'll teach classes at community college. I don't care. I won't further America's decay. I'm no one to decide someone else's future."

"Then empathy will be the death of you." O'Brien hissed.

"No. I could never join you because, as confident as I am in my virtuosity, I'm certain my version of justice and virtue would eventually align itself with that of the unjust. As all those in power eventually find out, I'd become what I hate most."

"So that's it?" O'Brien lifted his chin and aggressively rubbed the stubble there, "Congratulations. You're the first to turn me down. Many have turned us down before but you're *my* first. Rejection is not something I am used to Sam. I wish I could say there was some ethical prize waiting for you on the other side, but this is it. Nothing will ever be the same for you. Whether you realized it earlier tonight or not, when you walked out the door of your house, your life was going to change drastically, one way or another. I thought I'd leave with a son, not a stranger." O'Brien snapped his neck in each direction as the poise in his eyes slowly began to wither away. He cracked his knuckles and stared at the wall behind me, hoping that a few more seconds might change my mind. When it didn't, and his eyes were closed, his face began to swell, turning a reddish hue. "You pompous, effete, ignorant dolt. Do you realize what you are throwing away? Do you?!"

"I can't live knowing an entire population is obeisant with my idea of how the world works. And I certainly can't follow a man so hellbent on making mankind into the dregs of a few."

"You think that this is some moral victory?! If anything, this... is..." O'Brien slowed to a halt. "I can see it now. It's there, in your eyes. It's all in your eyes. You hate me. Not just me but the idea of me."

"Look, the buck stops here. I can take responsibility for my life, but I-"

"You'll regret this and-"

The Call of the Void

"I won't sign the will of my life over to a bunch of quisling degenerates, and I won't be inveigled into any situation that easily!"

O'Brien rested back into his chair, his muscles relaxing in defeat. "No. I can see it in your eyes. You'd sooner see my world burn and yours thrive. I can see it, right there, in the depths of your pupil. You're imagining a world where you pick your child up off the ground and happily throw her over your shoulders, a loving wife not far behind to greet you with a kiss. The entire country turning itself on its head while rushing out to grab every CEO, every Tech tycoon, every politician and send them to the gallows. Families gather in frivolity to witness the execution of their President, their congressman, their bosses. A trite song plays distantly in the background, something uplifting, something 90s that captures the nostalgia you hold dear—something from Celine Dion no doubt. And when the executioner pulls the lever to send us off into nothingness, there you stand, smile on your face, glad to see the end of human tyranny. You recede quietly back into your classroom, the entire campus now free of litter, obdurate students and coddled nihilists alike. You make a terrible joke about the pleasure of existence while lecturing on Dasein and the class graciously laughs. You wink toward them and sip the coffee from your mug, your tweed jacket pressed ever so perfectly. But I have news for you; it will never happen. You came here tonight a pathetic man and I offered you a way out, an opportunity to be a part of something you will never again be a part of. I offered you Truth and Power, the ability to heal, the ability to mold the world. To create something, with me. But now you'll fly off back to UCLA, living as you always have, a hermit. Teaching will become gradually more difficult as the generational gap widens, and drinking will become far easier. You'll continue crying day in and day out and we will just keep whipping that horse you cling onto so dearly. Now that you possess the knowledge I have given you, life will be utterly impossible Sam."

I lifted my chin lightly to indicate to Jerry that we were leaving. A gleam in O'Brien's eye was almost begging me to stay. The only thing different about his expression from the time we walked in was his vacant smile.

"I am curious Sam," he said, grabbing my arm as I brushed past him, "in light of you refusing my offer, do you really believe that—how did you phrase it?—'The human race needs to end'? Or was that just the booze talking?"

His hidden smile returned instantly from its dormant state, his teeth now bathed in some kind of fulvous liquid. The room grew cold and the fire, cracking like a whip upon the torches, moved like a wave in constant motion. O'Brien's face began eclipsing under the waxing darkness of the room as Jerry frantically pulled me closer toward the exit and I feverishly ripped my arm from O'Brien's grip.

Darkness was all around us. I could hear Jerry fumbling for a door handle before finally breaking through the fire exit.

We were next to some dumpsters at the bottom of a long staircase that led to a street which was just out of sight. To which street, I couldn't be sure. Dawn painted the lower canvas of the sky a dark violet and orange. It was that perfect time in the early morning when night and day danced a quick jig before giving the sky to the day.

"What time is it?" I asked.

Jerry checked his phone. "6 AM. On the dot."

It had been 12 hours, but it felt like an eternity. Terrible thing to think. Jerry and I shared a weak, forlorn look before continuing.

"There are no stars," Jerry said, looking toward the sky.

"Yeah, well, you know, that usually happens when the sun comes out."

"No," he laughed, "I mean when it's this early you can sometimes see stars."

"Just not now," I answered, breathing heavily with each step.

With about thirty steps to go, a door opened on the side of the nearest building. A bartender with an imperial mustache and a pink striped apron tied tightly around his waist walked out and kicked a rock right under the door to prop it open. He gave us a congenial smile and waved a gracious hand into the bar.

"Want a drink?" Jerry asked, "I could go for one. Two even." Jerry paused and stared off vacantly. It was obvious from the expression on his face, in his empty eyes and sealed mouth, that he was avoiding the scene we had just witnessed. He caught me looking at him and snapped out of it. "It's on me."

I looked at my face in the nearby window. The bags under my eyes were so heavy they were nearly touching my cheeks. My face was completely gaunt. Far more so then when I left the previous night.

LeResche

I used to look so healthy. So, normal. So... human. A rumbling hunger pang rattled my stomach and, for the first time in my life, I had wished I finished the Boston Market from last night. I caught Jerry staring at me just as he shoved his hands into his pocket and kicked a small rock on the ground.

"Ya know, we don't have to." he said, "We should probably just-"

"No. I could use a drink too."

"Goodnight nobody." A faint voice below us whispered. We turned to face a man on the ground with his hand held out. "Paper?" He asked after snapping out of his stupor, "Paper. One dollar."

He lifted a copy of the LA Times, but it was clear he didn't work the paper route. An obvious front in Lower LA. It was common for tramps around the city to steal boxes of periodicals and sell them for a lesser fare. The front page read:

President Urges Relief Grant Amongst Talks Of Reviving Yugoslavia

We walked in to find the bartender smoking. Jerry and I shared a dazed glance.

"You okay boys?" he laughed, leaning his hip against the side of the bar.

"Yeah," Jerry answered, "Just not often we see a barkeep breaking city ordinance."

"City ordinance?" I asked, shooting Jerry an expression of disbelief.

The Call of the Void

"Normally I wouldn't," he said, flicking the ash off his cigarette, "But she won't play unless she can smoke in here."

He pointed toward the window as a white-haired woman came walking through. Her head was cast down and her eyes were closed. It struck me almost immediately that I might know her. She bumped into me; her eyes still closed as she paused. She was motionless, waiting for an apology no doubt. I thought of saying her name, to see if it really was her. She tilted her head a little, her hair falling over to one side. I couldn't see her face, but she seemed pensive, trying to soak in the environment. She walked on. The bartender shook his head a little as we sat down.

"What'll it be gentlemen?"

Jerry watched me as I watched her. I fished in my pocket for my Spirits. My lucky was all that was left. I lit it and nodded to Jerry. "Uh, two beers. And two shots of whiskey. Well is fine."

I couldn't be certain, but there was something about her. Something all too familiar about her walk, her body, the way she swung her hair. She moved like a ghost through the bar, stopping only to light a cigarette. Her hair was made of wisps of white gossamer and from her side profile I could tell her face had nearly melted away. If it was her, she had changed. Her cheeks previously so ruddy, her athletic physique just so perfect. Time in this world had starved her of life. I had met her at a Starbucks right next to the pub I worked at in college. There was a connection right away and though she loved me, and I knew in my heart of hearts I had loved her, I always sent her away because she was so incorruptible, so chaste, vestal and modest. I had no idea what I wanted. I couldn't let her get caught up with me. This felt like a nightmare I was too afraid to wake up from. Still, reality was far more heedless than this, and I needed to atone.

She took a seat on the stool in the middle of the dais. She adjusted her guitar, smoke running up through her nose as she clamped onto her cigarette, her eyes still closed. She moved the cigarette from her mouth to a hole in the guitar's headstock and strummed once, then twice, getting a feel for the notes dancing around in her head, before settling on a low, abject tune that pierced my soul when played, like a melancholic dirge. The lament was palpable from her chords alone and could be felt throughout the bar as Jerry and I became entranced in the song. Her eyes remained shut but her mouth slowly began to open.

"This is how the waves shape the stars.
Here now with me,
that beautiful voice floating hopeless for one illusion.
The supper of shadows keeping you here.
The paintings not natural do light the madness
you leaked when sense veiled its law.
But you run from my dreams each night
The only place I can find you."

"Jesus," Jerry muttered, "the voice of an angel."

We both drank from our pints as the bartender slid two shots next to each of us.

"I know," I said, uncertain still if it were her, "She's... like a siren."

"It's so melancholic but-"

Jerry's words drifted off in my mind as I continued staring at her, waiting, hoping, to see her eyes. She was much lighter, and her features were withered but if I could only see her eyes I could know. She turned to face me, her eyes still sealed shut, her mouth getting ready to open for the next lines as she slowly began to open her eyelids. I could taste the adrenaline rushing out of my mouth, now agape. It was her. She was blind. Her eyes were opaque and hoary. Even from the bar, I could see the solid white orbs filling the back of her pupils like snowballs melting in the sun. That beautiful greenish blue that had always arrested my heart was gone, but there was no doubt that it was her. She gave the song life with her voice. Each chord and each stanza raised her tone to a sweet cry before lowering it into a frightened weep.

> " *This is how the waves shape the stars.*
> *The day grows dark and dim and a vision of you slowly erodes.*
> *The moon sets ablaze only features never spoken,*
> *Softly awaiting the night's curse*
> *For me to stay far behind in the dark*
> *Wondering if you're floating in the sky"*

She belted with an almost sad yodel, fluctuating rapidly between an anodyne cry and a throaty roar. Her eyes were unyielding, bonded to mine. She couldn't see me, but I felt an unmistakable catalyst fusing our souls once more. She wasn't merely blind though. Her eyes were pocked, forcefully pierced.

Jerry and I took our shots. He made a yawp to indicate it was good whiskey. He lit a cigarette and rested his forehead on his smoke hand's thumb. I flicked the ash from my cigarette, drank from my pint, and stared back at her.

> *"This is how the waves shape the stars.*
> *Your home, your hands, your silence,*
> *an unimagined mystery the lost apparition never needed.*
> *The voice sovereign yet lost under the moonless sky.*
> *The sands of simple subtle knowledge crushing under the yoke of*
> *the wave's embrace.*
> *Love is full of deceit*
> *Where I feel most at home*
> *Wandering through a vision of life and death*
> *One of many, my love"*

"Tell you one thing," Jerry remarked casually, clearly indifferent to my obsession, "If I don't get some sleep soon, I'm gonna die."

I turned to Jerry, my eyelids heavy from exhaustion. "Why fear death, when I die in my dreams every night?"

Jerry raised his eyebrow nervously and gave me an insecure look as I turned to face her once more.

The Call of the Void

"This is how the waves shape the stars.
Praying for your call
Predator of my heart
Agony the remedy
Tenderness the curse
Casting my soul asunder
But you escape my dreams,
the only place I will ever find you
This is how the waves shape the stars."

Her plangent voice and terse lyrics bounced around the bar, hanging above our heads like the sword of Damocles, begging us not to go out and face the world once more.

"You ready to go?" Jerry asked, finishing his beer.

"Yeah," I answered, finishing mine.

She inhaled her cigarette, took a drink from her cup, and tuned her guitar once more before looking at the wall and playing a sad, slow, dejected version of 'Bullet with Butterfly Wings'. I stood up as Jerry paid the bartender and leaned my face against my left hand, staring at her somberly as she sang the verses. I turned to the bartender as Jerry waited by the front door.

"How did she ge-" I paused and pointed to my eyes, "Who did that to her?"

The bartender looked down and began to wash the glass in front of him, searching for the 'why' and 'how' he needed to answer me properly. His eyes met mine.

"She did."

"I see." I said, walking backwards toward the door, looking back momentarily to find her pale eyes staring at me once more.

As I placed my hand on the door, the phone behind the bar rang with a slow, plaintive reverberation. The bartender picked it up.

"Hello?"

He looked perplexed and lowered the phone to his waist, covering the receiver with his hand.

"Sam?" He asked.

"Yeah." I answered.

"Phone's for you."

I stared into her eyes one last time. "I'm not here."

Outside, Jerry and I moved up the rest of the steps to the street. The walkways were flooded with men and women of all kinds in business suits carrying briefcases. We looked on incredulously. I could feel my heart racing and slowing down in a deleterious rhythm.

"Life will be impossible now." Jerry remarked.

"I know," I said, taking a minute to absorb the atmosphere and the sun, "But, I guess the thing he said that resonated most with me is that I knew it all along. There's something about this world that made me believe it all along. I don't belong. I d-don't want to belong. And, honestly, I don't know whether it's my inability to keep up with the world, or that I'm living in the past, or that I'm just stuck in a way of thinking that isn't conducive with the way the world moves."

Jerry looked at me. His reluctant nod made me pity him. We moved toward the Greyhound bus stop that made stops in other states. One read 'Montana', and another read 'Arizona'. The local bus across the street read 'Figueroa'.

"It'd be so easy to leave," he said.

"Yeah," I answered, pondering the ticket booth nearby.

"Anyway, this one goes upstate. I'll email you."

"Yeah," I said, running my hand over my face, "I look forward to it."

Jerry's expression was a bit somber as he lowered his head and walked away.

"Jerry," I said, grabbing his arm, "I mean it. You're my only actual friend here. And you're a good friend. I'm sorry. I can be a bitch to deal with. Let's grab a drink soon."

"Yeah," Jerry moved onto his bus with a faint smile, "I'll write you."

Jerry's bus puttered off upstate as a billow of exhaust fumes covered the bus station. I sat and looked back and forth at the two destinations, my personal space becoming increasingly suffocated by the mob of day-walkers filling in behind me. I walked toward the Figueroa bus stop and climbed aboard, sitting in the farthest seat back and leaning my head against the window. A man with shoes fashioned from old newspapers seated himself next to me. He looked at me for a moment before snorting disdainfully and moving to the front. I cupped both of my hands over my face, the stench of my previous seatmate still penetrating my nostrils, and thought of what the future will hold. And on that bus, I left as I'd left every moment in my life; alone. I was ready to sleep. But I knew, when I woke up and went for a drink that night, the   moon   would   be   shining   in   the   sky.

LeResche

About the Author

Reece Davis LeResche is an American author born in 1989. Raised by his mother on the fringes of Tucson, AZ, LeResche developed a love for reading at a young age. Throughout High School and College, he worked several menial jobs to support himself and his family while writing in his spare time. In college, he majored in English Literature and became a High School English teacher soon after. Though his work as a teacher has been edifying, LeResche feverishly pursued his love of writing. Reece's works focus on the darker side of the human experience and are patented with an emphasis on alcoholism, guilt, existentialism, choice, depravity, and death.

Printed in Great Britain
by Amazon